MUSIC AND DESIRE

For hours Drayton had watched her, allowing the dampening effects of his laudanum dose to work its soothing touch upon his nerves. The moment she left the salon he knew it and followed.

He stood now in the hallway, listening and watching. He had heard Brahms before, but never had he heard it played like this . . . a bright flashing effervescence that showered his soul with her passion.

When she was done the final notes hung suspended in the air as he pushed the door open and entered. Tears wet her cheeks.

She watched him cautiously, but she did not wipe the tears from her face. "What is it you want?"

What did he want? He reached out and gently curled his fingers against the pulse beating quickly at the side of her throat. With a finger, he dragged open the plush of her lower lip as he leaned toward her. Her lips were soft, full and warm like fruit ripened by the sun. Innocent kisses. Then the barest ripple of her breath escaped, and as he drew that breath into his mouth, he knew he was wrong about innocent kisses. More potent than the drug he had consumed, he tasted passion.

He lifted her from the bench and into his embrace . . .

Praise for Laura Parker's
ROSE TRILOGY

"Rich with the flavor of the times . . . quite simply a treasure of reading delight."
—*Los Angeles Herald Examiner* on *Rose of the Mists*

"Parker combines history with superbly realized characters and an evocation of Ireland that can only be called magical."
—*South Bend Tribune* on *A Rose in Splendor*

"Touching . . . a delight . . . Laura Parker's latest is a winner!"
—*Affaire de Coeur* on *The Secret Rose*

Also by Laura Parker

•

Rose of the Mists
A Rose in Splendor
The Secret Rose

Published by
WARNER BOOKS

LAURA PARKER

REBELLIOUS ANGELS

WARNER BOOKS

A Warner Communications Company

WARNER BOOKS EDITION

Cover illustration by Bob McGinnis

Warner Books, Inc.
666 Fifth Avenue
New York, N.Y. 10103

 A Warner Communications Company

Printed in the United States of America

First Printing: October, 1988

10 9 8 7 6 5 4 3 2 1

"In more ways than one do men sacrifice to the rebellious angels."

—St. Augustine

※ 1890–91 ※

One

New York State, May 1890

Allegra Julia Grant sighed wistfully as the Mouton
Rothschild curled in a pale golden foam at the bottom of her
glass. The soft hiss breathed an aged sun-ripened bouquet
into the conservatory's hothouse ether. Champagne was a
wonderful invention, she decided, this being the first time
she had ever tasted it.

She had expected that her brother's graduation gift
would be unusual. Andy could always be counted upon to
do the unexpected. At twenty-five, he was clever and
witty, and enough of a bon vivant that he considered
smuggling champagne to his sister (in a wicker basket
filled with bonbons) a duty rather than the impropriety that
it was. She had not dared to open it until now. It was past
midnight at the fashionable finishing school for young
ladies in the Adirondacks. Everyone else was in bed,
dreaming of the graduation ceremonies to be held in the
morning. She felt quite safe as she reclined against the
fountain in the school's conservatory.

For weeks now, a strange agitation had been building
within her. She could not name its source but it heightened
every sense. Feelings were sharper, clearer, and yet often
inexplicable. The grass seemed greener, the flowers more

3

brilliant, their perfumes more complex and enduring. Some nights the sky brought tears to her eyes, the stars too lovely to be endured. There was a sense of great portent in every morning, a moment's regret with each dusk.

There had been April days when she faked illness in order to be left alone. In May she had rushed from bed each morning, afraid the days would begin without her. That was part of it. She feared that, if she were not ever-vigilant, life would slip away.

Just the night before she had dreamed her death. She had felt the pine walls of the coffin about her, known the mindless terror of undrawn breath, had awakened in chill fear that, in the blink of a passing night, she had spent all her years and that they were gone forever before they had ever been lived. That must not happen. She would not allow it to happen.

For years Andy had offered her glimpses of a world far different from the one in which she lived. His gifts of books and essays and stories were a secret only they shared. He would not send her a new one until she had written him a letter explaining her reaction to the last. In the beginning she had been hesitant to commit her thoughts to paper. Ladies were not expected to think for themselves or utter opinions about their elders, business, or politics. As for the more intimate feelings, a lady was not to think of them at all.

Yet she did think of them. When books in French and Latin arrived, she needed no encouragement to ferret out the meanings for herself. Balzac, Zola, and Ovid were scandalous, exciting, and thought-provoking. Soon she and Andy were corresponding on a weekly basis, the mail becoming the veins and arteries of her existence. Yet recently, Andy's letters had slowed to a trickle and she had wondered if he were growing tired of her . . . or had found more stimulating company than his eighteen-year-old sister.

She touched the letter tucked into the pocket of her dressing gown. It was an invitation from Andy to come to New York City and visit him, proof positive against her foolish imaginings.

Papa would, of course, refuse to grant his permission.

Mama would be equally opposed, saying that a young bachelor could not provide the guardianship necessary for a young lady.

Allegra smiled to herself. "I will go to New York," she whispered very low, hoisting her glass in a toast. "Nothing will stop me!"

When she had drained her glass, she set it aside and moved toward the full-skin tiger rug which lay at her feet. Most of the graduating girls had received gifts of clothing, ivory fans, silk purses, or jewelry from their parents. Justine Gilliam, whose mother was a famous explorer of the Belgian Congo, had received this rug in commemoration of her birth in the Chinese Year of the Tiger. Justine had hated it on sight so Allegra had delightedly appropriated it for her own.

Allegra stretched out on the skin and rubbed her bare leg along its length, exulting in the tickle of bristling hair. Moonlight silvered the fangs in its open mouth. There seemed to be both intelligence and a threat in the amber marble eyes. She leaned forward until the tip of her nose met the hard muzzle and stared into the glass eyes. Had the animal looked down the barrel of the huntress's rifle with the same enigmatic gaze? Had it known its fate? A cloud momentarily obscured the moon and the tiger seemed to wink.

She recoiled with a shiver. Too much imagination or too much champagne was having its effect. And yet the titillation was not wholly unpleasant. If the calico cats and gingham dogs of her childhood books could scrap, why couldn't tiger rugs wink?

Sensation, how she longed for it. Something, anything, to make her know she was alive.

"A-A-llegra!" A tentative whisper came from the conservatory doorway. "Allegra, are y-y-you in there?"

Allegra felt a rush of anger as Justine Gilliam's voice broke in on her thoughts. She had wanted to be alone. For that reason she had made certain her best friends were drowsing in their nightgowns like white poppies under the charm of the moon before she sneaked out of the dormitory. She pressed deeper into the shadows, but it was too late.

"She's here! There's the tiger!" whispered another voice

in a deep midwestern twang Allegra recognized as Reeba Braumbrucker's.

The exhilaration of the champagne ebbed and talk was all that was left. Allegra leaned forward. "Come in, but do be quiet. I've opened Andy's champagne. I intend to drink all of it!"

Reeba peeked around the corner of a tall palm and adjusted her wire-rimmed glasses on her nose. "Allegra, is that you?"

Allegra nodded, clearly outlined in the brilliant moonlight. "You may as well help me finish it."

An hour later the three girls lay sprawled on their stomachs, facing one another.

"Th-Th-That's the last," Justine exclaimed sadly as she held up the empty bottle.

"Andy sent only one," Allegra murmured in regret.

"Wish I had a clever brother." Reeba sighed. "Harold ain't clever. He's what Papa calls leather-brained, but he means well. He's coming to graduation 'cause Papa don't travel, being that he's too fleshy."

A picture of Reeba's father had caused Allegra to wonder if his expansive waistline had anything to do with his making his fortune in pork-belly futures. She raised her glass. "To our last night together!"

"G-G-Graduation means we'll no longer b-b-be together like this," Justine said softly.

"I won't mind, not if I can attend balls and wear fancy gowns and go to the theater," Reeba replied. "Then I'll find a husband and have a house of my very own."

"And live under some man's rule," Allegra warned as she licked the rim of the glass for the last drops of champagne. "Not I. I'm going to live differently." She lifted one thick shiny black tress that had hung down her back. "Perhaps I'll imitate George Sand. I may chop off my hair and go about in a pair of gentleman's trousers."

Justine clucked her tongue. "Y-Y-You just say that to shock us."

Allegra's laughter had a particularly musical sound. "Are you so easily shocked?"

"Mama says a lady's thoughts must be as pure as her linen," Reeba said reprovingly.

" 'Mama says,' " Allegra mimicked. "Jehoshaphat!"

"Your emotions rule you," Reeba pronounced censoriously. "It's your mother's southern blood. Papa says the Rebs lost the war because their passionate nature got the better of their reason. Mama says— Well, I think so, too."

"You've never had an independent thought in your life," Allegra pronounced in indignation. "Be a dear, Justine, and pass the chocolates."

Justine lifted the box of exquisite French chocolates, each wrapped in lacy gold foil, another gift from Andrew Grant. They had tasted especially good with the champagne. Now the sight of them made her stomach lurch. She passed them quickly to Allegra. "I d-d-don't feel well."

"Are you flummoxed?" Allegra questioned curiously. "I hope not for you'll toss your supper if you aren't careful."

"Toss?" Justine echoed uncertainly.

Allegra shook her head. "You'll do no such thing. You simply can't be ill. That would spoil our party."

"I'll not clean up after you," Reeba warned in horror at the thought.

Justine swallowed hard and sagged back against the rim of the fountain that stood in the center of the room. The cool granite felt good against her feverish skin and a little of her courage returned. "I—I won't be sick."

After an appropriate pause, Allegra said, "*Integros haurire fontes!* To drink from pure fountains, that'll be my motto. To truly live one must soar above the miasma of the commonplace. I wish to live life as the heroine of a great novel."

"You mean those filthy yellow-jacketed books your brother sends you," Reeba said. "If matron knew, you'd be expelled."

"You're safe from corruption," Allegra replied. "I've seen your French grades. Balzac and Zola require a deeper appreciation of the language."

"Y-Y-You are quite smug now," Justine said. "W-W-Wait until you're home again. Y-Y-You won't be allowed to drink champagne and read d-d-disgusting books there."

After a moment's reflection Allegra said, "I'm not returning home."

Surprised out of her stutter, Justine exclaimed, "You've never said that before!"

"No," Allegra agreed.

"What will you do?" the two girls chorused.

She smiled pacifically. "Go to live in New York with Andy."

"You've the strangest notions," Reeba murmured. "You pretend that you're special, but you're like the rest of us."

A chill played over Allegra's skin, for this was her secret fear. "No, I'm not. I might even consider attending college if Papa were not so opposed to higher education. He's never forgiven Harvard for turning Andy into what he calls a 'noodle-headed, no-nothing dilettante.'"

"I pity you," Reeba answered. "You want everything you can't have. You should go home. When the season begins, with its rounds of balls and dinner parties, you'll forget this foolishness."

"I've seen the life Mama lives and it bores me," Allegra answered. "Even she complains that everyone talks too much, and the men smoke too much and dance too little, and all the ladies stare at one another to determine who has the better jeweler and modiste."

"I sh-sh-should like to wear fine jewels," Justine admitted.

Allegra bit off a sharp retort, for it wasn't Justine's fault that she felt so little sympathy for Allegra's future. She turned to reach for the glass she had set on the rim of the fountain but miscalculated her aim. A pot of geraniums perched on the edge teetered and fell, shattering into a thousand fragments on the marble floor.

As the echo of the crash reverberated under the rotunda of the conservatory, Reeba scrambled to her knees. "Now you've done it! If we're sent home in disgrace, I'll die of shame!"

"Shh!" Allegra whispered, but Justine began to sob softly. She sat forward at once as she heard sounds of movement. From the end of the hall that separated the conservatory from the teachers' sleeping quarters she heard a bed creak, a scuffling of feet, and then the crack of an opening door.

She stretched out an arm into the gloom to search for the

champagne bottle. When the cold glass touched her palm, she wrapped her fingers about it, dragged it back, and stuck it into the center of the large palm behind her. It was one thing to be caught out of bed at night; quite another to be found drinking.

At the far end of the corridor footsteps now echoed. The awakened teacher was heading for the dormitory floor.

"Wait here," Allegra whispered and rose silently to her feet. For an instant she stood as still as a statue in the moonlight, her white nightgown in stark contrast to the heavy blue-black hair that flowed in waves to her waist. She could feel her heart drumming in her ears in fear and excitement. Then she stepped forward, her voice lifted in recitation.

" 'O heat, dry up my brains! Tears seven times salt burn out the sense and virtue of mine eye!' "

"Wh—What's she doing?" Justine whispered as Allegra's lovely voice rose clear and loud in the darkness.

"Ophelia's mad scene," Reeba replied. It was the part Allegra had chosen as her final recitation for elocution class, though why had she chosen this moment to reenact it?

" 'Dear maid, kind sister, sweet Ophelia,' " Allegra continued as she walked boldly toward the entrance to the conservatory. " 'O heavens, is't possible a young maid's wits should be as mortal as an old man's life?' "

"Hello? Who is there?" The familiar voice of Miss Sinclair, the music teacher, came from the hallway.

" 'There's rosemary, that's for remembrance,' " Allegra intoned sweetly, holding out an imaginary bouquet before her. " 'Pray, love, remember: and there is pansies, that's for thoughts.' "

Miss Sinclair, robed in a dark dressing gown, appeared suddenly in the archway of the conservatory, a candle in hand. Framed in the candle's glow, Allegra appeared every inch the fragile embodiment of the sad, mad, lovelorn Ophelia. "Miss Grant? Is that you?"

Allegra turned away from her teacher, hands lifted now in supplication, and began to sing.

And will he not come again?
And will he not come again?

No, no, he is dead:
Go to thy death-bed:
He never will come again.

"Miss Grant!" Miss Sinclair called sharply. "That is quite enough, Miss Grant!"

Allegra did not respond. Her hands fell to her sides and she turned without any acknowledgment and walked past Miss Sinclair out into the hall.

"What in heaven's name is this?" a voice of authority chimed and the hallway was thrown into electric brilliance.

"It's Allegra," Miss Sinclair said as she moved forward to meet Mrs. Barrie, the school's principal. "I do believe she's sleepwalking."

"She's what?" Mrs. Barrie's gaze narrowed on the back of Allegra Grant, who had reached the foyer and was heading for the stairway that led to the dormitory. As principal for the past twenty years, she had witnessed exactly two cases of genuine sleepwalking. Allegra Grant had been one of them. But that had been more than three years ago. Since then Allegra's transgressions most often had a very *sensible* motivation.

Mrs. Barrie's gaze swung about the conservatory and her brows peaked as she caught sight of a telltale ruffle. She did not need two guesses to know to whom it belonged.

"Stand up at once, Miss Braumbrucker. Miss Gilliam, is that you skulking about behind Miss Braumbrucker?"

Justine stood up behind Reeba, feeling fully as ill as she had when she had looked at the box of chocolates. "Yes, Mrs. Barrie."

"Am I to suppose you have an explanation for being here?"

Justine shuddered as Mrs. Barrie continued to regard her in disapproval. Disobedience was difficult enough for her ordinarily. Coupled with champagne, it became too much. A deep shudder shook her, a hiccup escaped, and then she groaned terribly before erupting a fountain of champagne and chocolates.

* * *

The dormitory was quiet once more. Justine remained confined for the night in the infirmary. Only Allegra and Reeba lay awake in the dark, their beds next to each other.

Reeba said softly, "Do you really expect to be allowed to live with your brother?"

"Yes."

"How do you hope to persuade your family to agree?"

"Andy gave me an idea. He explained it to me years ago. Whenever he wanted something he knew Papa would refuse, he asked first for something else, the more outrageous the better. When Andy wanted to go to Harvard, something Papa considered a useless expenditure, he asked instead that he be sent to Rome to study medieval art. Papa had an apoplectic fit. Popery, and all that. A day or two later Andy suggested that he might be satisfied to attend Harvard. Papa was so relieved he agreed without a second thought."

"That's positively diabolical!"

Allegra smiled. "Papa always says that he made his fortune by guile and tenacity. The trick is to know when to use one and when to use the other. Once I've mastered that, I shall have everything I want."

"And what is that?"

"I don't know," she answered more softly than before. How could she explain herself to Reeba when she had yet to sort out all her feelings? "I only know that something momentous awaits me. And when I find it, I will hold on to it no matter what the cost!"

"Southern blood," Reeba whispered reflectively. "I'll pray for you, Allegra. All that feeling would frighten me to death."

Allegra didn't answer. She was not afraid of the future. Her only fear was that she would lose her life before she ever experienced it. Sometimes, as now, she felt that she would simply burst like an overripe melon, spewing the pulpy juices and seeds of her youth in all directions.

She would not be trapped in an ordinary life. In the books she read she glimpsed a vivid, exciting world beyond the conventionalities of daily living. She was certain it existed for her. If only she could be free to seek it out, her future would be perfect, absolutely perfect.

London, May 1890

Lord Everett Drayton reached out until his hand met warm flesh. The girl lay face down on the black-clothed table, her wrists and ankles tethered by crimson rope to the table legs. Her buttocks quivered lightly with each breath. Half an hour earlier they had been perfect, the milk-white skin smooth and taut and unmarked by age. Now swelled ridges ran like scarlet bars across the surface of the female flesh, turgid and red but without a single drop of drawn blood. The beating had been inflicted by his hand. A ripple of shame passed through him and his hand fell away.

His gaze shifted to the tasseled end of one of the crimson bonds that held her and his shame deepened. His gaze moved upward. She was a country girl with heavy ankles and broad hips that spoke of hard work and little learning. The tangle of blond hair that hid her face was dull in the lamplight, dull as dross.

He had been told that the chloroform dose would not last long. She would be coming to consciousness at any moment. Virgin flesh to be soiled, one of the few things in life that did not sour with familiarity, the brothel's proprietress assured him. Yet he felt nothing of the desire that had brought him eagerly into this room a short while ago. Instead he felt the slow thudding of his heart as waves of disgust coursed along his veins.

He had paid her for the evening's entertainment, he reminded himself, urging his courage to return. Perhaps she had not sought this experience, did not crave it as he had thought he had. She would never understand the passions that ruled his life and pushed him to seek these extremes of experience in order to feel that he was alive, but she had not been forced. Her conduct had been governed by the coin in his pocket. Oh, she had shed a few tears over the prospect of mistreatment, though it was likely that she had been beaten harder and with less finesse by her own kin. To be well paid for one's deflowering, he had been told, was a badge of honor to one of her class.

Yet the reasoning did not calm his heart or stir his lust. As he looked back at her, the opposite occurred. There was a shrinking, softening sensation in his flesh. The need that consumed him was different. The aching was a never long-defeated cry from his soul for . . . what?

He turned away and dropped the thin resilient cane on the carpet. He remembered the luscious swish, swish sound made by the strap he had selected. He hadn't used such a thing before. From the first stroke it had beguiled him. For a short while it had taken on the only reality in the room, the fruition of a guilty dream which he had never before given form.

During his years of adolescence, many kinds of depravity had been whispered about among his friends. He thought of the essays of de Sade, purloined from his father's private cache, that had piqued his interest. In them the unimaginable had been couched in language bold, intellectual, and reasonable. Ever since he had read them, the possibility of such an experience had lurked in the shadowy recesses of his thoughts: unspoken, unspeakable, but tantalizing him still.

Since reaching his majority, he had indulged in various petty depravities, from whoring and smoking hashish to orgies and drunken revelry, in hopes that they would calm the clamoring in his blood. He assumed that the intense feeling near bursting inside him was a carnal lust for the unusual. Yet nothing long satisfied him. Every moment contained within it the seeds of future discontent.

From his Oxonian days, sculpture had fascinated him. He had learned to sculpt the semblance of flesh from marble, but the perfection of his ideal was never achieved. Each time he failed it was with a deepening sense of despair that absolute beauty was impossible to fashion. Slowly he had come to believe that if beauty existed, it wasn't in nature or artifice but in a perfect act. His despair abandoned, he had begun to envision the possibility of turning his most shameful dream into reality.

His quest for ever-new experiences had led him far. Most

recently he had fallen in with a cult of devil worshipers who defiled church altars—fornicating in the aisles, speaking blasphemies from the pulpits—all in nervous hope that there might indeed be some Almighty Father, watching and ready to cast his impudent children down into everlasting hell. To seize even for an instant the power that could force the Eternal to action, this was their quest.

His goal had been simpler. He had hoped, for a short while, to be transported beyond himself, to know a moment of ecstacy. Yet in the end, he had refrained from joining the worshipers, shut off by an awareness that theirs was a fruitless pursuit. God, if such existed, was indifferent to mankind. There were thousands of years of proof. Why did man ever believe otherwise? As his cohorts grunted and sweated and shamed themselves, he knew only the bitterness of isolation.

He had come here tonight to experience a violent fantasy which, by its very nature, was said to be a sublime ecstasy. He sought beauty, even terrible beauty, in the act. Instead, he found himself revolted by it, recognizing that such pointless cruelty was more than a little insane. Had he become so embittered by the world that the only avenue left to him was the one that led to madness? Was there nothing in the world for him?

He longed suddenly for companionship, for someone with whom he could speak of his humors and obsession. Someone like himself. There must be some living being with grace and wit and spirit, someone whose understanding of every act from joy to suffering would sanctify the torment of his own existence. He willed it. Until he found such a person, he would confine himself to some lesser nightmare of reality than this.

He reached for his greatcoat which lay upon a nearby chair and slipped into its concealing bulk. Secrecy was preferred by the clientele of this establishment, where whims even more unappealing than his own were catered to.

On the bed the girl moaned, twitching instinctively against secure bonds as she turned her head to search for him. He turned slowly, sympathy for his victim rising as the bile of self-disgust pushed at the back of his throat. He caught her eye, saw the mixture of fear and pain register there, and hesitated. Then, without reflecting upon the reasoning, he began to tear at the bonds that held her. Once she was free, he took the purse from his pocket and thrust it into her hands. "Buy your freedom," he said harshly. "I'm giving you a ticket from hell. Use it or be damned!"

Moments later he plunged into the gloom of a London back street, craving now nothing more than the freedom of the open air.

Two

Philadelphia, June

Each morning after her return from boarding school, Allegra breakfasted with her parents in the elegantly appointed dining room of the Philadelphia house that was Marabelle Grant's proudest domestic achievement. As always the table was dressed in heavy Irish linen with gold plate, silver, and crystal. Brass gaslights, unlit at midmorning, hung overhead. Brass spittoons sat on the floor at the head of the table.

"Bismarck's been dismissed by the kaiser. What do you make of that?" Angus Grant declared from behind his newspaper. "It says further that Willie's going himself to meet with Nicky at Narva. I wouldn't mind being a fly on the wall, I can tell you."

Allegra smiled indulgently as her father peeked over the paper to wink at her, his blue eyes twinkling beneath glossy black brows that grew as thickly as his beard. He always derived great delight in referring to lords, kings, and other notables by nicknames.

Angus folded his paper. "Hurley's coming in tomorrow.

Cromwell's due in next week.'' His triumphant grin bristled his silver-threaded mustache. ''They want to talk a merger. Told you I was right to sell out early, Mae.''

Marabelle Grant nodded politely. ''You're seldom wrong in matters of business, Mr. Grant.''

''Aye.'' He looked round. ''Where's me porridge?''

His wife touched the bell by her plate. To raise her voice would have refuted the cultured authority of her position. ''Porridge for Mr. Grant,'' she said when a young black man dressed in white tie and black tailcoat appeared smilingly at her side.

''Aye, and don't forget the pepper this time, lad,'' Angus added.

Allegra smiled inwardly. Each time she returned home after a long absence she was struck afresh by the differences between her father's egalitarian attitude and her mother's formality. Was she like them? She couldn't be certain. She had her father's temper and her mother's grace, but then so did Andy, and he was nothing like their parents.

''Porridge, Allegra?'' Marabelle inquired as the footman returned with a silver tureen and ladle.

''Yes, thank you.'' She was fond of her mother. At forty-nine, Marabelle still possessed the radiance of a much younger woman. Scarcely a hint of silver threaded the gold curls; hardly a line marred her rose-and-cream complexion. A legendary southern beauty from Charleston; that was Marabelle Kinloch Grant.

''We'll be putting up a few of me boys, come the middle of the week,'' Angus said, referring to men known to be some of the sharpest financial minds on Wall Street. ''We've business to settle.''

Allegra looked up. ''Isn't that terribly inconvenient? The journey from New York is exhausting, and Philadelphia is so dull this time of year. Andy says even in summer New York is never dull. Wouldn't it be nice if the three of us could go there instead?''

Angus Grant's brows gathered over his penetrating gaze. ''When it's me wish, travel inconveniences no man. As for New York, it's no place for a daughter of mine.''

Allegra lowered her gaze. ''Yes, Papa.''

"Minx!" In spite of himself Angus felt his annoyance give way under the vision of his only daughter. There was a lyrical quality in her beauty, enhanced by the careless masses of black curls which wreathed her brow. She was lovely, his daughter, quite surprisingly lovely to have sprung from his loins. He saw himself without blinders. He was short, barrel-chested, ordinary enough not to frighten horses but hardly the sort one would expect to produce the elegant pair who were his children. They were a constant astonishment to him.

Allegra's gaze shifted absently to her father's place as the footman ladled his serving of porridge. Unlike the gleaming sterling at the other settings, his flatware consisted of a battered tin knife, fork, and spoon.

"Papa! You're not still using those barbaric things?"

Angus looked up. "I'll thank you to keep your voice at a respectable level."

She blushed. "I'm sorry, Papa."

"So you should be!" He reached for his fork and jabbed the air with it. "This was good enough for your father the year he struck out for California in '49."

Allegra's gaze remained respectfully on him but her thoughts wandered. She knew the story by heart. *This was good enough for the Angus Grant who was a pauper in '49. This was good enough for the Angus Grant of today.*

Sold by the hundreds to miners arriving in California to hunt for gold forty years earlier, the cheap tin utensils had been her father's first successful business enterprise. With the money earned, and for a hefty share of the profits, he had staked miners with promising claims. Through shrewd investment he had quickly amassed a fortune. Yet he never had forgotten himself as the poor Scots immigrant tinker who arrived in San Francisco with nothing but tin knives, forks, and spoons and an outsized desire in his heart for wealth.

He carried the utensils in his breast pocket, as a reminder of his humble beginnings, and refused to eat with anything else. Allegra had even overheard her mother reprove him for offending society hostesses by pushing silverware aside and using his tin fork.

"Because of me, lass, you sit to the finest meals money

can buy, and at a reasonable price to boot!'' Angus ended, short of breath.

''Yes, Papa.'' He was not too proud to haggle over a penny a pound for beef, yet he thought nothing of the cost of bringing businessmen all the way from New York for a few days. The incongruity, she thought, explained her father well. He was a strange mixture of pride in poverty and power in wealth.

''What will you do today, Allegra?'' Marabelle asked, steering the conversation away from further antagonism.

''I must write Andy,'' she answered promptly.

''Write letters on a day so fine?'' Angus shook his head. ''That you will not. You'll go calling with your mother and chat with the ladies. Let them see that Angus Grant has reared as fine a filly as any of them.''

''Mr. Grant, how remiss of me!'' Marabelle Grant pulled a letter from her pocket and offered it to her husband. ''It's from Andrew.''

Angus regarded the letter as though it had teeth. ''What does it say?''

''I wouldn't know. It's addressed to you, sir.''

Allegra watched him reach for the letter and open it. She did not need to hear his muffled ''Hell and damnation!'' to guess the contents. The instant his face mottled in anger she knew he'd received a request for money.

Angus squashed the letter between his fists. ''Till the lad learns how to earn it, there'll be no more coins from me purse to advance his education in how to spend it!''

''It isn't as though he idles away his days,'' Marabelle ventured quietly, for talk of money always embarrassed her.

''He could earn a fortune, and he knows it,'' Angus answered. '' 'Come into business with me,' I said to him when he graduated. But not him, he's too fine for his father's tastes.''

''Andy's a genius,'' Allegra answered in defense.

''Genius, is it? And where's the fruit of his talents? A pencil-pusher, that's what he is. Writing obituaries and theater criticisms; what sort of work is that for a full-grown man?''

''Andy's very talented. He's searching for the opportunity

to prove himself," Allegra maintained. "We should believe in him. *I* believe in him! Would you rather he starved in a garret?"

"I would rather he worked for me, earning a decent wage!" Angus roared.

Allegra didn't argue, aware that it was useless. The threat of cutting off funds was her father's last hold over his adult son and one to which he was quick to resort. "May I be excused, Papa?"

"But you haven't eaten."

"I don't feel hungry. Perhaps a short walk will revive my appetite."

Angus watched his daughter until she left the dining room, then jerked his napkin from his collar and threw it on the tabletop. "I don't understand that lass!"

"She's young," Marabelle offered serenely.

"Aye, well, so you've said often enough. There's nae a thing I can do about that."

Marabelle smiled at him. She knew quite well what troubled Allegra. Her husband might not be aware that his daughter was becoming an adult, but she was confident that once she called it to his attention, he would recognize it was time they saw that Allegra was safely entrusted to a suitable husband.

When breakfast was complete she said, "Allegra has grown since the autumn. We'll be expected to include her in the social events during the coming season."

"What social events?" Angus demanded.

"We're the parents of a most eligible young lady, Mr. Grant."

"E-li-gi-ble?" Angus pronounced the word with all the difficulty of a foreign word never before heard. Then his expression cleared. "You mean she's ripe for marriage?"

Marabelle smiled serenely. "But certainly, Mr. Grant."

His frown returned. "Aye, well, I must put my mind to the matter."

"My thought exactly, Mr. Grant. A suitable match: good family, good breeding, good reputation."

"And a bank account," Angus finished unabashedly. "I won't have any Johnny-come-latelies sniffing about her skirts. A proper man, older perhaps, and with more than two coins to rub together. I'm nae a stingy man but I won't keep a laggard for a son-in-law. I've that for a son,'' he added in a mutter. "It's never stood to reason why Willy Vanderbilt married his Florry to that poor Western Union clerk, Twombly."

"It was a love match, so I've heard, and, happily, a continuing source of joy for them both."

"I wouldn't have me daughter unhappily wed," Angus admitted.

"The Twomblys met in Saratoga, I'm told. My family summered there once before the war," Marabelle said softly, the wistfulness of memory veiling her eyes. "I hear they have vastly improved accommodations. On any given day one might see the Vanderbilts, Steeles, or Fisks. Rumor came my way just this spring that the Prince of Wales may avail himself of a sojourn there this season."

Angus's ears perked up. "You don't say? Royalty frequents the Springs? Have any of them bankable sons?"

"I wouldn't know, Mr. Grant."

"Saratoga," Angus murmured as he polished his soiled tinware with his handkerchief and then placed the utensils back in his pocket.

"August," Marabelle replied, "is thought to be the most seasonable of months."

"August," Angus declared thoughtfully. "I won't have her in New York nor Andrew at the Springs."

"As you wish, Mr. Grant," his wife replied, her victory complete.

New York City, July

Andrew Grant drummed his fingers impatiently on the linen tablecloth. She was late. Very late. This would make the third time in two weeks that she had failed to keep their appointment. He should leave now, before anyone recognized him.

He turned his head, his reporter's gaze moving almost

mechanically over the rows of the well-dressed luncheoning in Henry Maillard's Confectionery. Many of them were known to him, but he had the advantage of a secluded position behind a drape, while they sat in the open. It was a fashionable spot, located at Broadway and Twenty-fourth in the heart of the shopping district. He smiled. That was not its only attraction.

The hand-painted ceiling of rococo cherubs and clouds, polished columns, and ornate chandeliers gave the shop all the respectability of an upper-class salon. The proximity of the Fifth Avenue Hotel opened less respectable and, to his mind, more pleasant opportunities . . . not the least of which was the fact that a diner of the confectionary could order bourbon in a teacup from the hotel bar.

He drained his cup and reached for his wallet, cursing softly at the thin packet that met his fingers. He could ill afford another wasted bribe for a room. Harriet could not know that, of course. She must not learn of his financial straits. She was so timid, uncertain of herself and less certain of him. No, he must continue his game of infinite patience and tender concern for her sensibilities. It was the role she expected of him.

He had long since learned to appear unconcerned about the things which mattered to him most. It was a lesson quickly absorbed in his family. Life with his father had forced him to divide himself into two people: the respectful son and the clever con man. Harvard had given him his first glimpse of his true self. The revelation had frightened as well as heartened him. He did exist as an independent, thinking individual with a will and desires. That those desires often ran counter to his father's had not been surprising. That they sometimes ran counter to his own sense of right and wrong had been fascinating.

The cynic in him jeered, *Be honest. You revel in it.*

Perhaps, he mused as he toyed with his spoon, but reveling had its price, and it was an expense that he could not indulge without his father's largess. He was a journalist for an elite literary digest. It offered him prestige but very little else. For hard currency he was forced to petition to his father. He had written three letters in six weeks, each more conciliatory and contrite than the last. Each had remained unanswered.

He felt the sterling silver spoon bending under the pressure of his hand and smiling, he tightened his grip. It felt good to exert his mastery over something. What he wanted most in life, needed if he were ever to respect himself, was success as a writer. In college he had studied the works of great minds, had felt himself as near to communion with those long-dead souls as any mortal might feel, and been moved to emulate them.

He wrote fair verse but the spark of genius had not yet lit his wick. The critic in him scorned his poetic efforts much the same as his father stood in Old Testament judgment on his life. He needed inspiration. Of late he had taken to wandering in the bohemian districts of the city, then scribbling furiously until dawn about what he'd seen and heard, seeking a flickering phrase, an ember of words that would give hope that his lamp might yet burn brightly.

Andrew smiled as he thought of Harriet. Surely he agreed with Shelley's perception that "Poets' food is love and fame." With her he possessed the first. With time he would gain the second.

"Andrew?"

He was on his feet instantly, before he fully realized that she had come. Yet here she was, fashionably gowned in cherry silk. "Mrs.—Harriet."

"Mr. Grant. What a delightful surprise." Harriet's voice, soft and high as a young girl's, sounded strained even in her own ears as she allowed him to touch her gloved hand.

"Are you alone?" Andrew continued, for he knew the game better than she. "Well then, by all means, do join me as a favor to an old friend." He pulled out a chair for her, his gaze lingering on the deep pink flush revealed by her upswept hair. Tenderness rushed over him, erasing every minute of anger of the last hour. Poor dear. She tried so hard to be artful and was so awkward. Betraying one's husband was a trying business for even the well rehearsed.

Afraid to meet his gaze directly, Harriet studied the floral pattern of his teacup, not at all pleased to see that it was a pattern she owned. Her service would have to go, as it was available for use in a public place, which meant it was therefore vulgar.

"Tea, my dear?"

"The usual," she answered and heard Andrew whisper an order for vermouth and lemon over shaved ice. Beneath her silk gown she had begun to perspire. Self-consciously she touched gloved fingertips to her brow, praying that it was not also scandalously damp.

"A charming confection," Andrew complimented, indicating her straw hat. "I am particularly fond of pink roses. The cream ribbons add a touch of élan."

He was teasing her, his smile as deep and confidential as his touch might have been, but Harriet could not smile back. He was too handsome to flirt with. Devastatingly handsome, her married friends frankly admitted to one another. As she looked across into his extraordinary green eyes, she could not help but wonder once again why he had chosen her for his particular attention. She was plain, had always been told she was, but never daring. Yet here she sat, trembling and cowardly, because of him. The July heat made damp black scallops of the hair at his brow. She yearned to touch one of his locks but she dared not. She dared not look at them, and turned her gaze away.

"You are sorry you came," Andrew said quietly, resisting the urge to move his hand across the tabletop the scant inches it would take to reach her fingertips.

"No . . . yes."

"I should not have pressed you."

"But you didn't. You've done nothing for which to reproach yourself." Her head dipped as the stain of her embarrassment spread once more across her cheeks.

Annoyance clenched Andrew's jaw and kept back an unsuitable reply. He knew she was naive. That very ignorance of life had drawn him to her when they had met months earlier at a Republican fund-raising party at the Fifth Avenue Hotel. For a married woman she had seemed curiously untouched. He had wanted to touch her, to bring out what he saw trapped behind the quiet sorrow of her gaze. Now, after a series of "accidental" meetings at dinners, theaters, and soirees, he had extended their association to the point where each knew what the next meeting must be. Yet she hesitated. Middle-class caution.

When the waiter set her refreshment before her, complete with a sprig of mint, it appeared for all the world to be a glass of iced lemonade. An expensive glass of lemonade, Andrew amended, as he paid the check. "What purchases have you made?" he asked casually, wishing he had ordered another bourbon for himself, though he could not afford it.

Harriet glanced at the packages she had placed on the chair beside her. "Shirts for Richard from Constable's. Shoes for Johnny."

"How does your son like his new nanny?"

Harriet's gray eyes clouded. "He hates her, as I do!"

The statement did not lose any of its power for being spoken softly. "Your husband's choice, I presume."

She nodded. Unforgivable that she should be close to tears when she wanted to appear calm before Andrew.

"You hate him, too." It was a statement he felt fully confident in making. If it weren't true, he had lost.

Lovers, or potential lovers, should never meet before sundown, Harriet decided as she sat staring at him. They could see too much, each learning too quickly the thoughts of the other. Indiscretion required the soft lighting, friendly shadows, and amibiguous glances that afternoon brilliance didn't allow.

"I love you."

He didn't mean to say that, but it wasn't a lie.

Harriet's tears disappeared and she straightened. There was almost—almost—a relieved look in her eyes as she said, "I suppose this is the moment when we should retire to more—congenial surroundings."

The discipline of a lifetime was still strong in him. Women he had had, a mistress never. That's what Harriet would be after this afternoon; his mistress. He couldn't afford her, couldn't hope to keep her, however discreetly one kept the wife of another man.

His hand moved that short distance to hers. "I'll never deliberately hurt you."

She shook her head slightly, a quick dismissing gesture. "I find I do that quite easily by myself."

* * *

Monte Carlo, July

Drayton's disappointment was as sharp and pungent as the black coffee at his elbow. He could not blame his host nor his erstwhile companion. No, the complete responsibility for his attitude rested upon his own shoulders. He had expected more of Monte Carlo. That was his fault.

He knocked an ash from his cigar onto the Turkish carpet and then deliberately ground the warm cinders under his heel, but the gesture lost its interest for him even before he completed it. He felt sour, bitter, useless. If he were reduced to boyish pranks he might as well be dead.

The suicide of his closest companion, Henri Saxon, six months earlier had been a poetic gesture against the injustice of life. He regretted that he hadn't shared his friend's sense of outrage against the vagaries of life. He might have followed suit: a decanter of Napoleon brandy and sliced veins.

Of course, that wouldn't do. Imitation was a trait of dull minds, and anything dull was to be detested. Besides, he had realized long ago that death didn't fascinate him. If it were anything like the crushing, grinding, isolating silence of life in his father's house, then it was something to be avoided at all cost. He attached no sentiment to life, but it seemed better than the glories and angels and harps presumed to be waiting for the unwary good, or the sharp proddings and roaring furnaces assigned to the more adventurous evildoers.

He touched a finger to his brow and found it damp with perspiration. Hell might well be the Riviera in July. It must be ninety degrees.

He rose from his chair, cursing softly as the floor creaked. He was awake at this ungodly hour of nine A.M. just to enjoy being alone. He drew comfort from solitude. It was the only time he ever felt completely whole.

He didn't understand why, but it seemed his simplest actions inevitably roused speculation among his companions. Nothing he said, no gesture, no remark ever went unnoticed. Even among those he counted as friends—though in truth they were merely familiar strangers—anything to which he attached importance immediately became a source of interest, even if they had formerly rejected it.

As for the public, he found their interest in him stemmed from the fact that he was a peer of the realm. In this new age of the affluent commoner, one of the few influences upon the minds of the bourgeoisie that the aristocrat retained was his style. If one were not born with style, one could copy it from another, and copy the masses did. One's tie was copied, one's hat and shoes advertised, one's pallor imitated, one's absences and patronage noted.

"We've become the sandwich boards for those of vulgar wealth," Henri had remarked only days before his suicide. "Tradesmen with more money than taste, milliners' wives with more cash than class look to us as arbitraters of style. Are we to be mannequins for the commoner? I won't have it!"

Drayton frowned as he stood in the doorway, looking out upon the glorious beauty of the seaside town. Isolation, obscurity, absence from feeling; those were his weapons against prying eyes and boredom. If one chose carefully, unemotionally, one could live a life of diversion and delicious sin without ever disturbing the center of one's being. It was an art to live as he did. If gratified only occasionally, even one's most despicable yearnings could be managed.

Turning away from the morning, he drew the curtains closed on the blue intensity of sea and sky. He had come to Monte Carlo to be amused. A woman waited for him in the next room. He had paid well for her, and she was quite accomplished. His slightest whim met her instant attention. It was really quite amazing—and ultimately boring. She offered him forbidden pleasures, her eyes gleaming with lust as she described what they might do.

It was a frequent experience. The death knell to his interest had tolled so loudly in his head he hadn't been able to silence it until he had put her out of his bed. She lacked what all such women lacked: delicacy, subtlety, light and dark shadings; intensity born of one's soul rather than one's glands.

He would send her away when she awoke, and the thought of the tragicomedy that would ensue didn't appeal to him. Women were first, last, and always actresses. Was there no creature whose nature matched his own?

He stared at her bedroom door for a long moment before he crossed the salon to open an ormolu cabinet and withdraw a Persian water pipe.

A quarter of an hour later, heavy lids half shut, he sat wrapped in a blue-white haze of smoke. A notion had come to him without anxiousness or delight, and so he felt free to indulge it. America. He had never been there. He had traveled the continent and found nothing of lasting interest. Colonials and savages might offer the diversion he sought. America. Why not? A smile transformed his face, but the corners of his lips didn't turn up.

Three

Saratoga Springs, August

"How perfectly awful the summer has become!"

Allegra dangled her straw boater by its ribbons over the edge of the upstairs banister of the ten-room cottage her father had rented on Saratoga Lake. In the distance the setting sun was a bright orange ellipse on the horizon. Silhouetted ospreys made slow rolls in the sky overhead. The soft *slush, slush* of the lake came to her ears as it had every day for the past month.

She openly detested the clear blue summer skies and allowed herself to be drawn as little as possible to the gorgeous lake. She refused to admire the red tiger lilies in the garden, or the silver poplars and blue larkspur that shaded the restful landscape, or even the cool breezes of evening; all because they were reminders that Andy was in New York City and she was not.

Nothing had gone as she planned. Every mention of Andy had only intensified the thunderstorm of her father's temper. Her assertion that she wished to attend college in the fall had been met with her father's amusement. He hadn't even considered the possibility that she was serious, and so that ploy had failed.

Now there was another, devastating result of her return to her parents. Andy no longer sent her books, explaining that if their parents discovered the kinds of things he had supplied her with he wouldn't be allowed to write to her. The only mystery and adventure in her life, the nearly indescribable pleasure that reading gave her, was gone.

This was the final blow and one which had set her thoughts this afternoon upon a new course of action. Soft pleadings and good behavior had won her nothing. A new tactic was required. Something extraordinary, something—

Below, in the dining room, the gong was struck to announce supper.

"Hell and damnation!" she whispered defiantly, using her father's favorite remark. She didn't mean to cry; that was quite childish and melodramatic, but the sobs came anyway, drowning out the sounds of approaching footsteps.

"Allegra, whatever is the matter?"

Allegra found it surprisingly comforting to be enfolded in her mother's arms and the fragrance of lilac cologne. "Mama, you must make Papa see that Andy and I must be together, or I'll die!"

"Oh, dear." Marabelle patted Allegra's cheek. She longed to reassure her daughter that the joy she thought to find in her brother's company would be surpassed by that she'd find in marriage. But Allegra was not often comforted by sensible words. Often she cleverly turned those words inside out and made them appear to say the opposite of what was meant. Retreating from that delicate subject, Marabelle offered instead, "Your father's a busy man, but I'll speak with him about Andrew when he returns."

Feeling a little foolish, Allegra wiped away the last of her tears with a handkerchief and said crisply, "I suppose Papa's been too busy to notice that while he spends most of the month in New York, we're left to sit like wilted lilies in the shade."

"A young lady never allows a disparaging remark to pass her lips," Marabelle reminded her.

She looked at her mother quizzingly. "Why shouldn't we offend others when they trample upon our sensibilities? Men don't turn their backs on insults and injustice."

Marabelle smoothed a wisp of hair back from Allegra's cheek. "There's never an occasion where a lady may give offense."

Stung by the reply, which was not so much answer as a motherly reflex, she said, "Then I wish I weren't a lady."

Marabelle restrained a smile. "You're too old to resort to tantrums. After supper I'll send Mary up to help you dress for the Grand Union ball."

"I danced last evening."

The petulant tone wounded Marabelle. Nothing distressed her more than dissension in the family. "Your father is expected back any day. He'd be pleased to hear that you're carrying out your social duties."

Allegra heard the plea for reconciliation in her mother's tone, and it hurt her to realize that her mother was more interested in harmony than in her feelings. So her father would be back any day. Then she had only a short while to think of a new tactic. Still, that was no reason to distress her mother. Besides, she couldn't bring herself to spurn the company of other young people. They were tedious and frivolous, but at least they provided a diversion. Once her father returned she wouldn't have time for such things.

She shrugged. "Oh, very well, I'll go to the dance. I only hope there're new people there tonight. My head still aches from last night's silly chatter."

As the early afternoon sun streamed in through the windows, Allegra considered the possibilities. She could be sent back to Philadelphia summarily. That didn't seem so bad. She would be no more miserable at home than she was in Saratoga. Papa might refuse to allow Andy to return home before Christmas, but certainly he would welcome his son home for the holidays. No, there didn't seem to be anything worse that could happen to her than being denied the chance to be with Andy. Whether that occurred here or at home, the effect was the same.

Still, she scooped up a pale pink voile dancing dress she hadn't yet worn from among the pile of dancing dresses, walking dresses, and summer wear heaped upon her bed. There were pink satin bows on each shoulder and a bouquet of pink rosebuds at the waist. She would keep this one.

After stowing the dress and a few articles of lingerie away, she picked up her silver-backed hand mirror and stared at herself. She didn't look any different. Her cheeks were flushed, but nothing else betrayed her excitement. No one would guess that she was about to embark on a crusade.

The idea had come to her as she reread a childhood book of Celtic fairy tales. In one story a poor man, unable to gain justice at the hands of his master, had begun a hunger strike outside the lord's door. Day after day, the people of the village watched the poor man's sufferings and the unjust lord's embarrassment until, in their rage, the villagers forced the lord to compensate the poor man far beyond his claim.

In her case, she was the poor man and her father the powerful but unjust lord, and so some public display of her plight was in order. She had yet to view the results of her outrageous act, but before nightfall the "dye" would be cast.

What a terrible pun! Her laughter was self-indulgent. No, she wouldn't think about what she was about to do. According to her mother, scandal was something to be avoided at all costs. Yet there must be ways to bend public opinion to her advantage. By morning she would know whether her actions would succeed or be hopelessly doomed.

She put the mirror down and tucked her shirtwaist into her blue linen skirt before slipping on the matching jacket. She was expected to make the fourth for couples lawn tennis, an engagement her mother had made for her at breakfast.

Two hours later, reclining in a chair under the shade of a tree, Allegra swung her racket with the negligent air of a victor with a clear conscience.

"You really should practice more, Sarah," Ruth Cameron remarked to her partner. "We might have beaten them if your backhand were stronger."

"You would not," Lettie Beal interjected, her pale complexion mottled by her exertions. "Allegra and I are simply better players, isn't that right?"

Allegra shrugged. "If I have expertise in the sport, it is because of Andy's instruction. Dear, dear Andy. How I do miss him."

Lettie and Ruth exchanged looks. Until two hours ago, they hadn't been aware that Allegra had an older brother. Now every other word out of her mouth was coupled to his name in praise or in die-away sighs of sadness.

"Well," continued Ruth, "at least Sarah's a better whist player than— Oh! Look! It's Monsieur Girard. Who's that with him?"

"That's Marguerite Fatherall," Lettie replied in a shocked voice.

"You mean the divorcée?" Sarah whispered.

Ruth nodded, the power of speech banished by the proximity of the notorious woman.

Curious, Allegra turned her head toward the pair strolling past the tennis lawn. She did not know what she expected, but certainly something more dramatic than the sight before her. What she saw was two attractive people: the tall gentleman's darkness a foil for the petite lady's golden prettiness, which was half hidden by an enormous hat with ostrich feathers. Thanks to gossip, she knew that the woman was at the Springs to recover from a well-publicized divorce, while the gentleman accompanying her was suspected to be more interested in her settlement than herself. The sight of them walking along as though unaware of the stares and whispers following in their wake evoked within Allegra the fervent hope that they might find happiness together, if only to spite the gossips of Saratoga.

"How disappointing," she said in a bored voice as she looked away. "I'd rather hoped they'd be displaying pitchforks and cloven hooves."

"You're one to talk. But then I suppose you've judged for yourself. Allegra waltzed with Monsieur Girard two nights ago," Lettie said in glee as she turned to Sarah and Ruth. "Mama was quite shocked to hear it."

"She never! She did? Truly?"

Sarah leaned forward in her chair to question Allegra. "Tell me, is he positively wicked?"

Allegra looked into the girl's avid gaze and wondered why she was spending her afternoon in such disagreeable company. They had cut to ribbons the reputations and characters of every person they knew or claimed to have knowledge of. No doubt she would suffer the same verbal assassination when she left them. She had made one improper turn about the dance floor, and apparently not a single eye had missed it. She was conscious of a new emotion stirring within her, something which until this moment she had never before experienced. The feeling was contempt. "Wicked? What would you describe as wicked, Sarah?"

The girl blushed. "I'm certain I couldn't say."

"Well, I will admit that Monsieur Girard did try to make love to me on the dance floor. But, of course, there was such a crush that we couldn't proceed in a manner a lesser crowd might have permitted."

Allegra couldn't contain her amusement when they accepted her story at face value, and she laughed aloud. "How gullible you are! We're the merest acquaintances."

"He kissed your hand. I saw it!" Lettie persisted.

Allegra smiled, but she felt suddenly depressed. After she left them, they would talk about her waltz with Monsieur Girard, picking and pecking at the incident until they had worried every scrap of titillating emotion from the vicarious experience.

With relief she glimpsed her parents strolling across the

grass toward her. Her father had returned the evening before but had absented himself from the breakfast table in favor of an early start at the racetrack. "Did you enjoy the steeple races?"

"Indeed we did," Marabelle answered. "The spectacle was invigorating, though your father didn't choose to remain for the conclusion."

"There was sport of another sort at the Grand Union," Angus said. "Some of the lads were discussing railroads."

"You look well, Papa," Allegra said, an inexplicable impulse of affection for him rising suddenly to the surface. "Did Andy look well, too?"

Angus's half-formed smile died. "I didn't see the lad."

"Didn't see him? But, Papa, you promised you'd make time for him this last trip."

The sheepish look that crossed her father's face was quickly followed by a scowl. "You've no cause to raise your voice. He wasn't home the evening I called nor did he leave his card at my hotel. It seems Andrew Grant's got better fish to fry than entertaining his papa."

"Excuse me, did I hear you mention the name Andrew Grant?"

The Grants turned to the tall man in straw boater and flannel coat with white trousers who had addressed them.

"Who's asking?" Angus questioned testily of the man.

Allegra rose and smiled serenely at the newcomer. "We did, indeed, mention Andrew Grant. He's my brother."

"Brother?" The man's look of pleasurable surprise pleased Allegra. "Is Andrew here in Saratoga?"

"Unfortunately, no."

"Do you know this lad?" Angus demanded.

Flushed with pleasure at discovering someone who knew her brother, Allegra was not about to let her father frighten him away. "He's Andy's friend, Papa. He can't be a stranger." She extended her hand to the man. "I am Allegra Grant."

The man lifted his hat from his head before taking her hand in a gentlemanly handshake. "Forgive my rude introduction. I am Dr. John Boyd of New York City."

"There, you see, Papa? This is Dr. Boyd."

"Doctor? Andrew ain't ailing?"

"Not that I'm aware of," Dr. Boyd replied, his gaze moving back with renewed interest to Allegra.

Allegra studied him quickly, noting that the chestnut highlights in his hair matched his mustache. There were lines on his brow and about his eyes, signs that he was perhaps a dozen years older than she. Andy had never mentioned a Dr. Boyd as one of his acquaintances. She would have remembered. "How do you know Andy?"

"We were at Harvard together."

"Hrumph! Should have guessed as much!" Annoyance soured Angus's features as he turned to his wife. "Come along, Marabelle. I've better things to do than stand about. And you, me girl," he added with a penetrating look at his daughter, "you're to be at the carriage in five minutes." Without a word to the doctor, he offered his wife his arm and walked away.

Allegra turned to the doctor with an apologetic smile. "Do forgive Papa. He didn't— But, of course, Papa *did* mean to be rude to you. Your mention of Harvard is the cause. He detests the very name. Andy isn't in Papa's good graces just at the moment either."

"If memory serves, that isn't unusual," Dr. Boyd replied with a rueful smile.

"You do know Andy well! How positively wonderful. You must sit and tell me everything. When did you see him last? Which subject most occupied his mind? Was he happy? Oh—" Her own laughter interrupted her. "What an idiot you must think me. It's only that if Papa has his way I won't see Andy again until we're both gray."

"I very much doubt that, Miss Grant. You seem to me a young lady of remarkable persuasion and persistence. Why, I can't imagine doing anything other than answering the questions you've put to me."

He was flirting with her and she knew it. The glint of interest in his blue eyes was not quite hidden. "Perhaps Mrs. Boyd would like to join us," Allegra suggested. "There's room for another, isn't there, Lettie?"

"I'm afraid that will not be necessary, owing to the fact there is no Mrs. Boyd . . . as yet."

"How prettily you say that," Allegra commented. "Wasn't that prettily said, Lettie?"

Lettie, who had been watching them with rapt interest, nodded.

It was Sarah Cunningham who spoke up suddenly. "That's who he is! Don't you recognize the name? It's on those odious posters." She turned a wide-eyed stare on the doctor. "You're—notorious!"

"Notorious?" Allegra repeated, her full attention now on the doctor. The very word conjured up possibilities that made him instantly more attractive. "In what way are you notorious, Dr. Boyd?"

He smiled slightly, but there was a definite heightening of the color in his cheeks as he said, "The young lady must refer to the handbills for lectures littering the Springs. I do, on occasion, lend my small service to various forums."

"You lecture? How positively thrilling," Allegra exclaimed, not quite able nor wholly willing to keep the disappointment from her tone. So much for attractive possibilities. It was her experience that lecturers were notoriously boring.

"Women's rights," Sarah offered smugly. "Mama says that men who advocate women's rights truly hate our gender."

Dr. Boyd's amusement was obvious as his gaze moved from Allegra to Sarah and back. When he smiled, Allegra experienced the unexpected sensation that his amusement was at their expense. "I beg your pardon for disturbing you, Miss Grant. Do convey my felicitations to your brother when next you see him. Good afternoon, ladies." He replaced his boater with casual ease and turned away.

"Doesn't that beat all?" Lettie said in a great sigh.

"Curious," Allegra remarked as she turned her back on the man strolling away. "He seems, well, too correct to indulge in anything truly radical."

"I wouldn't know about that," Sarah answered. "Did you see the way he smiled? It positively chilled my blood."

"It's the breeze," Allegra offered, but she, too, was remembering the doctor's secret smile. "The breeze has cooled. I must go in before Papa sends a maid to fetch me."

"See you in church," Lettie called after her.

Church! Allegra's heart missed a beat. She had completely forgotten that the next day was Sunday. Well, it was too late to alter her course now.

Allegra awakened to the rustic freshness of a Saratoga morning. Everything in the room, from the heavy solid bulk of the gleaming mahogany furniture to the lengths of Brussels lace curtains undulating in the morning breeze to the thick moss-green carpeting, was designed to engender in the beholder feelings of luxury and ease.

She rose from her bed and for a moment stood curling her toes into the tiger-skin rug sprawled beside her bed. She smiled as she remembered how Mary, the maid who had done the unpacking, had been frightened into full hysterics when the tiger's head, fangs bared, emerged suddenly from between the jungle of petticoats packed in her trunk.

The scent of violets combined with the toasty aroma of crisp waffles and the pungent brew of coffee drew Allegra to her breakfast tray. Remarkably she did not feel as though it were her final meal before facing some mortal judgment. There was no predicting what her father would say, but she could not turn back now.

The knock at her door brought her instantly to her feet. "Who is it?"

"Mary."

"Come in."

Mary appeared unusually subdued. "Well, where are they?" Allegra asked.

"In there," the maid answered, pointing to the armoire.

"All of them?"

"Yes, miss. Only . . ."

"Yes?"

Mary bit her lip. She was new at being a lady's maid, having risen to that position only when Miss Grant returned home from school for good. But she had been a part of the Grant household nearly five years and knew her employer's temper well. "Miss Allegra, it's Sunday. Maybe you'd like to wait a day before wearing one of those dyed gowns."

Allegra crossed to the armoire and swung open the doors. "What would you suggest?" she asked pointedly. Revealed to the morning's light was a sea of billowing black skirts. Every item in the closet had been dyed the deepest shade of mourning.

Mary gazed at the results of the lady's temper and yielded to common sense. "Guess you don't have a choice."

"No, I don't." Allegra reached into the sea of dresses and pulled out one. "Please take an iron to the hem. Oh, no, you'd better not. Mama might see you, and that would never do. My chemise and corset, Mary."

"Yes, miss."

Allegra turned away toward the window and took a deep breath. It was such a lovely morning, quiet and still, not at all like the other busy mornings at the Springs. Only the pious and guilty crept early from bed to attend services. She hoped the congregation would be receptive to a desperate daughter's plight.

Suddenly a woman appeared on the balcony of the adjoining cottage. Though she was too far away to see distinctly, Allegra knew who it was. Her likeness had been plastered about the Springs on billboards advertising the new play at the Grand Union Theater. The actress wore a tea gown. The shawl collar trimmed in ruffles embraced her naked shoulders. Tiers of lace formed the skirt and short train of her gown. As she moved across the balcony the gown flowed back and away from her to reveal a scandalous length of lace stocking and beribboned garter.

Allegra drew back from the window, embarrassed to have been spying, but even as she turned away she heard the woman's voice floating softly but distinctly across the lawn, saying, "Darling, do come and see the morning."

Looking back at her bed, Allegra faced the results of her own temper. Like a blot on the landscape, rather than the flag of rebellion it was meant to be, lay her pitch-black gown.

* · * · *

Allegra had the distinct feeling that she had made the monumental mistake of her life when she met her parents at church. She had contrived to do so by arriving with Lettie and her family. Lettie's shocked expression when Allegra appeared had heartened her hope that her campaign of protest would be effective, but that feeling soon abated. The drive from hotel to church had been accomplished in silence while Lettie stared at her in a combination of horror and awe and Mrs. Beal fussed unnecessarily with her lace bertha. Nor was Allegra unaware that the Beals had purposely left her and walked off in the opposite direction once the hansom set them down before the church steps.

Allegra glanced at her father's profile and was astonished again by his composure. He had said nothing. After her mother's initial intake of breath when she recognized the figure in black, her father had cut short any attempt at conversation by saying, "We're late for worship, Marabelle. Step along now."

Now he sat as if carved of stone. Or perhaps his mind was at work, for she had never seen him give such attention to a cleric's sermon. No, if he seemed in awe of the lackluster sermon droning on, it was because his mind was elsewhere, and she knew by what he was absorbed.

She and her parents were the source of ceaseless glances. The gown was serving its purpose of drawing attention. Yet she could feel one gaze in particular and lifted her chin to give the starer the best angle of her profile.

As a rule, Dr. Boyd never attended church. At an early age he surmised that the vast group of humanity who trooped to Sunday morning places of worship were, in fact, the same people who regularly beat their children, stole from the weak and helpless, and generally brought hell into being for the six other days of the week. He was here for one reason only. She sat three pews away, her profile turned so sweetly toward him that he felt a physical jolt of esthetic pleasure at every glimpse of it. He supposed it was a hazard of his profession that it had stripped from him all romantic allusions about the anatomy of femininity. Yet Allegra Grant made him feel things he had nearly forgotten. He had never seen a lady look more radiant.

It struck him that he used the word "lady" when thinking of her because the designation had long ceased to be a compliment in his mind. He knew women of all stations and classes, and could say without hesitation that those in high society were the most spoiled and useless creatures in existence. It required no character or goodness to be rich. They were provided for on all sides, every whim catered to, every drudgery relieved by the toil of servants he knew to be far superior in character and spirit.

He preferred the poor. How much more sympathetic was the plight of a consumptive young mother with three young children who worked a twelve-hour shift in order to provide for the bare necessities. He admired the courage, strength, and tenacity of her life. When a rich lady cried on his shoulder, he felt no sympathy for her. Yet he could not say that he was any more attracted to a poor woman than a rich one. He treated all who came to him, forgoing payment in the first instance and charging double in the second.

John smiled to himself. In his own way, he had become like a latter-day Robin Hood. It had begun by accident, but now the pattern was established. On the rare occasion when "a small error in calculation" resulted in an unwanted pregnancy for one of the Upper Ten Thousand, he knew how to suggest the delicate necessity of medical intervention, a service seldom offered by a college-trained physician. Of course, as his reputation for "discretion" grew in certain quarters, so did the danger of discovery. Yet he enjoyed the irony. Through his exorbitant fees, the rich provided services they would otherwise deny the deserving poor. That was why he supported women's suffrage—because it posed the threat of reducing the luxury of idle rich women.

He turned toward Allegra once again, hoping to discover what it was about her that continued to draw his interest. She was swathed in the deepest of mourning, yet her mother's gown was pale blue and her father wore no black armband. He didn't give a fig for the reason for her mourning. It mattered to him only so far as it might prevent him from engaging her attention again, for his curiosity was aroused.

He had noticed her at Saratoga before overhearing the

conversation between her and her parents, but recognizing her brother's name had been the purest chance. He might not even recognize Andrew Grant on the street now, but he remembered Grant as one of the rich undergraduates while he was in medical school at Harvard. Spoiled and indifferent scholars, they had walked about campus demanding admiration they hadn't earned. Perhaps it was the fact that Grant was more handsome and more talented than the others that made him memorable. Yet none of this explained his own continued fascination with Allegra Grant. Pretty women weren't rare in Saratoga, nor in New York City. Why then this irresistible urge to seek her out?

As he rose with the congregation and turned to the final hymn, he glanced at her once more. Before he could decide whether or not to approach the Grants, the decision was taken away from him. At the conclusion of the service they left their pew quickly and strode out the flung-open doors. They didn't pause for a chat with the parson, and by the time Boyd gained the front of the church their carriage was rolling away.

"Three thousand dollars in clothing ruined by temper! It comes from a lack of discipline, that's what!" Angus Grant glowered down at his guiltless wife. "I'm nae a stingy man nor a hard one, but my patience is at an end!"

"What will you do, Mr. Grant?" Marabelle asked.

"Do? Why, she must be sent away. Immediately. She's not to appear on the streets of Saratoga again. We'll put about the word that she's taken ill. The heat; yes, that's it. The heat has turned her brain and she requires complete rest."

"Mr. Grant! Really!"

"Do you have a better solution, Mae?"

"I don't—" Marabelle rose from her chair, feeling as weary as if it were past midnight when in reality it was just past noon. Her temples throbbed and her throat burned with unshed tears. The greatest test of a wife and mother, she decided, was to be caught between her husband and her children. Her gaze strayed to the closed door behind which Allegra had been locked a short time earlier. She had become hysterical when her father turned the key. Now there was only silence. "A nervous complaint, perhaps?"

Angus shook his head. "I've no fondness for sickly females. Nervous complaints are unreliable. No, it must be specific and curable."

"If you're worried about what people might think—"

"What do I care what people think? I could buy half the families at the Springs, and don't suppose they don't know it. But what would become of me business clout were me enemies to see me bested by me own flesh and blood? I'd not be worth this copper button, that's what!" He jerked the button on his coat so hard it came off in his hand. In disgust he tossed it away.

"I suppose that Caroline might be persuaded to have Allegra visit her, though Charleston is dreadfully warm just now."

There was no affection between Angus and his sister-in-law. They seldom agreed on the time of day, but this once Angus held his tongue. "If Caroline will take Allegra, then I give me consent. But your sister must maintain the story of Allegra's illness. I won't have her flaunted about Charleston like a filly on the market."

Marabelle did not reply, for there was nothing Caroline liked more than an excuse to entertain. Having a pretty young niece under her roof for a few weeks was certain to spark her matchmaking tendencies. "I'll telegraph her immediately."

"Be sure to put in the part about brain fever owing to the heat," Angus directed.

Marabelle shuddered. "Is that really necessary?"

"Half of Saratoga will know the contents of the wire in an hour. The other half will be apprised of it before dark. Gives them something to gossip about. Keep the message short. Words are money."

* * *

Allegra stood leaning her weight against the edge of the vanity, but she didn't even glance at the mirror. There was pain, a new never-before-felt aching deep inside her.

Her father thought she had behaved childishly. That was because he thought of her as a child. He indulged her when it pleased him, but when her desires went against his she was called difficult, spoiled, recalcitrant. He hadn't seen her protest as the cry from her heart that it was. He saw it as a tantrum, a whim.

"I will be taken seriously!" she whispered.

Suddenly she was crying again, hard, deep, shuddering sobs that left her gasping for breath. There was only one thought in her mind. She had to get away to see Andy!

When the hysteria passed, she picked up her powder puff and dried her tears. She went to the cabinet and chose the first hat within her reach, mechanically smoothing back her hair before she placed it on her head. She found her purse, counted the scant change in it, and pulled on a fresh pair of white gloves.

She went to the tall windows and, opening them, stepped out onto the small balcony beyond. The undergrowth along the lake provided a hedge between her and the Sunday afternoon holidayers, but she could hear their voices and laughter. Between the heavy boughs of the trees she could just make out banners of blue and gold and black. On the lake in the distance, the sculls looked like long-legged water bugs skimming the mirrored surface. Life went on without her. The realization was the greatest insult of all. She was of no consequence in the world about her.

She had half turned away before she saw in the distance the man and woman on the balcony of the house next door. The actress wore a bathing costume, a bloomered suit banded in red at knees, elbows, and waist. The man was in shirt-sleeves and braces. What caught and held Allegra's fascinated gaze was the fact that they were locked in an embrace. They must have thought themselves secluded by the branches of the nearby trees. She knew she should turn away before they realized she was watching them, but her curiosity was stronger. She had never before witnessed a lovers' kiss.

* * *

Everett Drayton wasn't enjoying himself. Cecilia Fletcher had persuaded him to come to Saratoga Springs with her because American men seldom brought their mistresses to this family holiday spot. New York was stifling in August, and, besides, the opportunity to outrage the colonial rustics was too good to pass up, or so she had said. Unfortunately, she had changed her mind once they arrived. Rather, the bourgeois in her had surfaced amid the provincial middle-class morality of their surroundings. Just this morning when she thought he couldn't hear, she had told an overdressed matron that they were wed, but secretly, because his family, being English aristocracy, objected. He was leaving. Today. At once.

When Cecilia came up to him, he didn't speak. Nor did he close his eyes when her arms snaked about his neck. Her lips spread wetly under his but he kept his firmly shut. As he reached up to break her embrace he glimpsed a figure from the adjoining house staring down at them through the foliage.

Surprise jolted him. Who was it? He could discern nothing of feature or gender. The spy on the balcony was too well hidden. He scotched the impulse simply to call out in challenge. Instead, he watched steadily, oblivious to the kisses he was exchanging, as curiosity pumped through him.

Finally the peeker moved and he glimpsed a straw bonnet with roses behind the foliage. He smiled, his lips parting. A woman. A young woman, to judge by her hat.

The hot tongue insinuating itself into his mouth gave him another jolt, this time one of pleasure, and he suddenly knew why the watcher was staring and why he wouldn't chase her away.

He had never given any thought to exhibitionism. It ran counter to his inclinations as a very private man. But this was different. He had come to America partly to astonish and partly to be amused. The watcher was astonished no doubt, and he was amused by it. *She* had paused to witness a kiss. *He* would show her that curiosity is a dangerous snare. The curious never knew what she might discover.

His hands moved to Cecilia's waist and he pulled her closer, forcing her to ride the knee he thrust between her thighs. She was hot there, the contact with his trouser leg drawing an embarrassed gasp from her.

"Darling! Someone might see us."

"Shut up!"

He undid each button of her bathing dress slowly, allowing his gaze to wander between the shadowed cleft he exposed and the balcony next door. He paused to squeeze a buttock. Did *she* see that, he wondered. Did *she* know that he acted not for Cecilia's pleasure but to shock *her*? Was *she* a female of some imagination or did *she* feel revulsion and fascinated abhorrence at what *she* witnessed?

The thought aroused him and what had begun as a deliberate effort to frighten away a spy became lust. No longer was it Cecilia he held in a passionate embrace, but the young woman hiding in the bush. In his mind these buttons were *her* buttons, the flesh he exposed was *her* flesh.

Cecilia's breasts were snow-white in the sunlight, each capped with a bright pink nipple half an inch long. He bent his head, his eyes fastened on the balcony—did he only imagine that *she* trembled now—and engulfed one strawberry bud with his mouth. *My tongue to your flesh.*

He bent his partner back against his arm. He was ruthless in his manipulation of her, plying her with kisses and thrusting his hips against hers until she began to whimper. There were no protests. She wanted him. It was a vanity of his not to allow any woman, even a whore, to fake her desire for him. While he, this time, wanted the spy.

He released her abruptly, slipped his suspenders from his shoulders, and began to unbutton his shirt himself. He did it automatically, without any thought of asking for Cecilia's help. He always insisted he not be touched until he was ready. Mastery of women was so easy, if one assumed it naturally.

He peeled back his shirt with the quick economical movements of everyday life but then slowed as he drew off his undershirt, aware of the effect it might have on the lurker. He thought fleetingly of an act he had seen in a Parisian brothel. The whore had peeled off each article of clothing as though counting the biblical seven veils. He had stood hard and erect in his trousers long before she was embraced by her lover. Expectation, it was a divine aphrodisiac. He flexed his shoulders, unself-consciously proud of his physique. Women praised him often. He had a rower's chest and arms and a flat belly. He smiled as he reached for his trouser band.

He heard Cecilia's indrawn breath of approval as a substitute for *hers*, his lonely voyeur. As she entwined her body about his, he held back from her questing mouth, his gaze hard on the face in the shadows. *She* must know he knew she was there. And yet *she* remained.

Suddenly he jerked his partner toward him and without a word tore her bathing suit in two, from collar to waist. Her cry of surprise pleased him. He meant to frighten the Peeping Thomasina away. He pushed his partner back against the wall of the house, lifted one of her legs until her knee was waist high, and then thrust into her without warning.

A cry of discomfort quickly turned into pleasured moans as he thrust again and again into Cecilia's wet warmth. It was not Cecilia he rode; it was the spy. The quick angry thrusts slowed, deepened, became a deliberate deep rutting that inched Cecilia higher up the wall with each plunge. She clung to him, wetting his chest with tears of joy and shuddering, shuddering.

Your pleasure, he thought. *Your pleasure, my sweet bold spy. Deep and hard, for you and you alone. Do you feel it? Does your belly fill with my thrust? Do you tremble with my heat? Deep inside you, little watcher. Only . . . for . . . you!*

A shudder began in him, built until he trembled, and then burst free with a thrust of his pelvis.

He remained a moment embedded within Cecilia's flesh as in his mind he pictured a different face, veiled, indistinct. In all his life he had never felt his pleasure more. And yet his partner had had little or no part of it. He had behaved shamelessly, as brazenly and immorally as a whore. No. Not a whore. He had earned nothing but his own pleasure and . . .

The figure was gone and with her the roses of her hat.

Allegra hurried along the dusky road. Once she had skirted the back of the house she found her path unimpeded. She was amazed at how easily one could leave a locked room without being seen. One simply crossed the balcony to another room and reentered the house, descended the stairs, opened the front door, and walked out. Transportation was even simpler. Strangers stopped their carriage fifty yards from her door.

She didn't count the time that passed before she heard in the distance the familiar signal of the station bell which announced the arrival of every train into Saratoga Springs. That was her destination.

She didn't allow herself to think about what she had seen, what she had shamelessly witnessed from her balcony. Conflicting feelings of fright and exhilaration made her dizzy. She had no vocabulary for what she had seen, no reference beyond the vague words in books that attempted to explain the inexplicable. No, the moment when she put her thoughts and feelings in order must wait until she reached Andy.

Four

New York City, August

The arrival of the Hudson River train from Saratoga caused no undue interest among the crowd of holiday travelers thronging the immense, glass-roofed cavern of Grand Central Depot. It was the final weekend in August. For those who clocked daily hours, and had therefore spent the warmest weeks of the summer in the city, this was a last chance to imitate the carefree existence of their wealthier counterparts by spending a little time breathing the rural air, watching gently flowing rivers or sparkling breakers.

The appearance on the platform of a young woman in black was not unusual. Pretty women were not uncommon in the railway station nor were signs of mourning a rarity in this city of a million. But the sight of Allegra Grant in deep mourning yet wearing a frivolous, wide-brimmed straw hat with cream ribbon and pink roses was enough to arrest the interest of the most hardened of city dwellers. More than one male traveler paused to watch as she strode in elegant, purposeful steps through the station.

Dr. Boyd paused among the lingerers on the platform, watching her with more interest than the others. He knew that, if he chose, she would never know that he had followed her. They had occupied the same train car for the half day's journey from Saratoga and still she was in ignorance of his presence. He was not certain why he had followed her nor what he should do next.

Chance had set him strolling past the Saratoga railroad station just as she boarded a train. Impulse had made him step on behind her without knowing where she was bound or why. There had been something deceptive about her calm. Once aboard, he divined the reason for her furtive manner. She traveled alone, without even a maid. She was running away.

Earlier in the afternoon, he had learned the reason for her mourning attire. Gossip said that Miss Grant was furious about her brother's exclusion from the family's summer holiday and that, in retaliation, she had chosen this most unorthodox method of advertising her feelings. The later news that the girl suffered from heatstroke was discounted. Several of the gossipers sympathized with the parents of so willful a daughter. After all, who could be expected to marry such a female?

John allowed himself a small superior smile as he strolled

after her. She had no luggage, a thing the porter had noted with lifted eyebrows. It was he who had smoothed over the moment by hinting, in the most tactful of phrases, that he was the young lady's fiancé and that, owing to a spat between them, she had peremptorily departed Saratoga without him. Being a man of some presence of mind, he had followed her, realizing that once she was over her fit of pique she would be lost.

The porter had pocketed the bills discreetly pressed into his hand, and smiled his assurance that Allegra would receive the best attention the coach's accommodations could provide.

Boyd had watched her being served tea and cakes which she accepted as her perfect right to have, though no one else in the car received similar service. A pillow, a fan, a lowered blind; each of these small considerations she allowed without ever once resorting to her purse. He noted in disappointment that she didn't think to tip the porter. She was like all other cosseted girls who never traveled without a maid or parent to see to those things for her.

When John passed through the doors of the station to the outside, he found her standing irresolutely near the curb. He didn't slow his pace but walked past her, knowing that if she so chose, she could acknowledge him.

"Dr. Boyd? Why, it is!"

In relief John turned to her. "Miss Grant?" He looked past her as if expecting to speak next to her parents.

She smiled and blushed. "Oh, I'm quite alone." She paused, her eyes suddenly serious and fathomless. "Dr. Boyd, in your profession I'm certain you're frequently called upon to use your utmost tact and discretion."

"But, of course, Miss Grant," he agreed expansively, beginning to see the direction their conversation would take. "Confidentiality is part of the Hippocratic oath."

She leaned toward him, laying a gloved hand lightly on his sleeve. "Oh, Doctor, I scarcely can believe it. I've run away! Well, not precisely *away*. I've run *to* Andy."

"I see," he answered in what he hoped was the appropriate blend of gravity and sympathy.

"No, you don't, and I can't blame you. I left because I

was bored to distraction. All those overdressed ladies gossiping about everyone and each other when they might be doing something constructive; it was too much! Of course, Mama must be half prostrate and Papa—'' Her imagination began to construct a scene that had been curiously absent from her mind's eye when she escaped. "Oh, bother!"

She looked up in a gesture that made John wonder why such inconspicuous items as lashes should cause a faint quaking movement in his chest. Yet he realized that she expected more of him than a masculine appreciation. She needed reassurance. "I admit you've been thoughtless, Miss Grant, but I believe you must have been sorely provoked to resort to this action."

Her faltering smile regained its confidence. "If only you knew!" She glanced about, aware that they were in public view. "Dr. Boyd, might I further impose upon you?"

"I consider it my duty that you should," he answered.

"I've been more precipitate than you can imagine, for you see, I'm flat."

The slang phrase was so out of place in a young lady's vocabulary that, for a moment, he was at a loss to understand her. "Oh, I see." Ordinarily he wasn't a man given to impulse, yet for the second time this day he was compelled by her presence to extraordinary action. "Would you do me the honor of allowing me to accompany you to your brother's residence?"

"Yes, please," she replied in a soft voice and readily took the arm he offered.

A wave of his hand brought a hansom cab to a halt before them, and he helped her up into it before climbing in beside her.

"Andy has rooms at the Dakota," she answered when he looked questioningly at her.

After ordering the cabby to that address he turned to her again. "Now, how may I further serve you?"

She allowed this to pass unanswered. "Why didn't you speak to me on the train?"

The question startled John. Had she known he was there all along? "You saw me?"

Allegra shook her head. "I was much too preoccupied to notice anything beyond the tip of my nose."

"I confess the same preoccupation," John answered in relief. "I've surgery to perform in the morning, a delicate case that required a great deal of thought. Had you been waltzing in the aisle I might not have noticed. Not that you would," he added, realizing that it sounded as though she might have deliberately sought his attention.

"Oh, but I might've been tempted, had I realized rescue was so close at hand."

As her husky laughter filled the air, he found himself looking at her in a new way. There was strength and a surprising amount of character in her small, strong-featured face. Her extraordinary confession, too, had surprised him. It was the dream of most wealthy young ladies to spend a month in Saratoga. Yet she rejected the idea as boring. What did she find stimulating? He hadn't yet discovered the answer and the mystery intrigued him. She wasn't what he expected and that was enough for now.

"I'll repay you," she said, breaking the silence that stretched to uncivil length between them. "Andy will be furious with me but he'll be glad to see you."

He didn't answer her. Instead he looked down and pulled his watch from his vest. When he pressed the button the gold cover lifted and music tinkled sweetly from it.

"Why, it's a nursery tune!" she said in surprise.

"Alas, yes," he answered as he snapped it shut. He had forgotten about the silly tune. If the piece weren't solid gold, he wouldn't carry it. "It was a gift from a patient."

"I think it's quite nice," she answered and rephrased her question. "Are you and Andy frequent companions?"

He looked up. "Why, no. I haven't seen him in four or five years."

"I see." If Dr. Boyd had been a close friend, less explanation would be needed.

John knew what went through her mind for he had the same thoughts. Running away was scandal provoking. Allowing herself to be accompanied by a near stranger was as bad. It suddenly occurred to him that, because of his reputation, were she to be recognized in his company after her disappearance from Saratoga, events might be tragically misconstrued. It was a slight risk but one he didn't wish to take. As a genuine lady, she deserved his protection.

He replaced his watch, murmuring, "One advantage of being a physician is that one is never late for an appointment, no matter at what time he appears."

It was the opening Allegra hoped for. "Oh, but you mustn't allow me to detain you when you have patients waiting. I'm in no hurry. You must direct the cabby to drop you first at the hospital."

And thereby save you the awkwardness and embarrassment of explaining my presence to your dear brother, John finished in his thoughts. "The hospital is quite out of your way and the neighborhood isn't all it should be. I'd be loath to leave you there. No, I couldn't allow it."

He paused thoughtfully. It was so pleasant to sit here beside her and listen to her quiet husky voice. Yet he knew that it would be a mistake to remain. Somehow he would manage to see her again. "Perhaps the best solution is for me to step down at the next corner and hail another cab. Fifth Avenue is quite safe."

"Perhaps it would be best," she agreed slowly.

He was flattered by her reluctance. That was all the more reason to spare her the gossip that might ensue if he remained. He rapped on the hansom roof to get the cabby's attention and ordered him to the curb.

When the cab drew to a halt at a busy intersection, he took her hand lightly in his. "I'm certain you'll sort things out with your family. You may give my regards to your brother. Tell him that he missed a lovely August in Saratoga."

Grateful for his discretion, Allegra briefly squeezed his hand. "Thank you, Dr. Boyd. I'll never forget your kindness."

He returned gallantly, "Never before have I so enjoyed a hansom ride. *Au revoir!*"

"Au revoir," Allegra called after him, aware that the French phrase was more than a simple good-bye. It held a promise of a future meeting.

Though the doctor had proved to be her angel of mercy, as soon as the cabby snapped the reins, Allegra thought no

more of him but flashed instantly back to the reason for her
journey.

For the first time doubts began to assail her. There had
been no time to warn Andy of her plan. She hadn't thought
of sending a telegram until just this moment. He might not
be glad to see her. He might be horrified and scandalized by
her actions. Openly defying her parents and running away
like a common brat might be too much for him to accept.
She had been precipitate, reckless, and careless, unforgivably
inviting scandal upon them all.

New doubts grew and expanded upon the first. Dr. Boyd
had given every sign of regarding her peccadillo as an event
he would treat with the utmost confidentiality, but he hadn't
been the only passenger on the train from Saratoga. Someone else might have recognized her, might have seen them
meet in the station and then climb into a hansom together. If
word of her actions became common knowledge, they
would appear much more lurid than they were.

"I don't care," she said aloud, aware for the first time
that unconventional actions required a surprising amount of
courage.

The hansom turned off the busy expanse of Fifth Avenue
into a shaded lane of Central Park, and the noisy, lurching
lanes of traffic suddenly disappeared. The horse kept a
steady clip-clopping pace through the narrow avenue between the trees, past a bandstand where uniformed players
offered the small crowd a piece by Strauss, past a pair of
tandem bicyclists and, shortly thereafter, a smart set of riders
on horseback. "Andy, please be at home," she whispered as
the cabby drove them farther into the deep green shaded
seclusion of the park.

Finally, through a break in the trees, she recognized, from
magazine pictures she'd seen, the pale yellow brick building
standing majestically on a rise above the park: the Dakota
Apartments. The nickname had stuck because the luxury
apartment building was so far from the hub of city life that
early skeptics had claimed that it might as well have been
built in the Dakota Territory.

Andy had inherited his apartment two years earlier, when
one of their mother's relatives died and willed him the

paid-up lease. He would not have been able to live there otherwise, for it was common knowledge that some of the accommodations rented for as much as $60,000 per year, a staggering price even for the wealthy. Andy's was one of the smallest apartments, four rooms on the seventh floor.

Knowing the Dakota's reputation for elegance and wealth, Allegra was shocked as the hansom climbed out of the park and she glimpsed the city blocks surrounding its grand facade. Squatters' shanties lined the park side facing the Dakota, complete with chicken coops and pigsties and clutches of barefoot, ragged children. The lots on either side were empty.

Before she could frame a question for the cabby, the hansom rolled across Central Park West onto Seventy-second and made the broad turn into the arched entrance of the apartment building that brought them into a long *H*-shaped courtyard. She had only a moment to draw a quick, bracing breath before the door of the cab was opened by a doorman in brass buttons and braid.

"Afternoon, miss," he said in a smart but indifferent tone.

She alit into the courtyard with as much dignity as she could muster. "Is Mr. Grant at home?" she inquired.

"I wouldn't know, miss," the man answered, his gaze directed somewhere above her head.

"I am Mr. Grant's sister," she said crisply. "Please inform him of my arrival."

The man's gaze lowered, traveling quickly over her outlandish costume before he said, "Are you expected, miss?"

Allegra could not miss the implied insult, but she was too eager to see Andy to be bullied. "I am."

The doorman tipped his hat, mumbling, "Very well, miss," before turning to do as she bid.

Allegra schooled herself to remain perfectly calm as she waited for Andy. There was little activity in the courtyard, and for that she was grateful because she didn't wish to be remembered by the residents in her present state. Yet the seconds ticked by so slowly she felt the mounting desire to flee as she paced the distance between the two stone fountains sprouting dozens of iron calla lilies. Finally, with clanking and whining and straining, an elevator came to rest on the ground floor and the ironwork door was opened by a matronly figure in black bombazine.

When Andy stepped from the elevator, he looked as she remembered, but disorderly, for he had bolted from his rooms without taking time to straighten his tie and comb his hair.

She stepped forward and said, "Hello, Andy," her deep, modulated voice betraying nothing of the turmoil roiling within her.

"Allegra!" Andrew Grant took in in a single glance his sister's black gown and his heart contracted. "What's happened? Good God! Is it Papa, or—it is Mama? Allegra, has something happened to Mama?"

"Oh, Andy! It's all so horrid!" She didn't wait for him to reach her but ran to him, cast herself into his arms, and burst into tears.

Allegra sipped the cup of tea Andy had hastily prepared once he had whisked her upstairs and ensconced her in a chair in his spacious drawing room. Now he was below, using the apartment's public phone to apprise their parents of her arrival. He had wanted her to make the call, but she couldn't, not until she knew exactly whose side he would take. Not that it mattered. Now that she was here, she meant to stay. Andy would just have to be brought round.

She had embarrassed them both, dissolving into tears at the sight of him. She hadn't expected to be so moved. Sometimes she was a complete stranger to herself.

Curiously, she circled her brother's abode. One glance told that he couldn't have made many changes in the decor since the days a maiden lady lived here. A scattering of old Turkish carpets in shades of red and blue matched the heavy swags which hung above summer muslin curtains. The mahogany-paneled walls were hung with old prints and small oils. She disapproved of the furnishings. They were dark and heavy, upholstered in wine velvet and gold tasseled. They must definitely go to the ashman. She liked better the imposing desk in one corner of the adjoining library. It was littered with papers and books. Behind it, two walls of shelves crammed with books attracted her eye. These she would savor at her leisure. The chimneypiece was passable, but the shabby leather chairs that flanked it reeked of mildew and she wondered how Andy could abide them.

In the hall she saw an entry table piled with unopened mail, newspapers, and assorted magazines. In fact, the entire apartment stood in careless disorder, as though it hadn't been favored with dusting, sweeping, and picking up in some weeks. Had Andy been away?

"Well, that's that!" Andrew announced as he entered the apartment a few minutes later. "They'll be down on tomorrow's train." He sat down across from his sister and casually crossed his legs. "Now you may tell me your side of the story."

Allegra smiled warmly at him. "I ran away."

"How artlessly you say that. To hear Papa tell it, you've ruined Mama's health and scandalized the summer residents of Saratoga. I suppose you know that you can't go back; not this season, at any rate."

"I haven't any intention of that. I'm staying here."

"In New York?"

"Here." She pointed to the floor.

"You can't be serious!"

"You did invite me."

"Yes, well, that was before."

"Before what?"

"The summer became quite busy. I've been away these last weeks. Newport."

"Rotter!" she flung at him. "You could have come to Saratoga."

"God forbid!" he exclaimed. "Too many mamas hawking their insipid daughters with more expense than taste. I always feel that I've failed to do my duty when I return unmarried season after season."

"Newport is different?"

"Newport is . . . Newport."

"That says exactly nothing."

"You're changing the subject."

Allegra looked away from him, not wanting to discuss

their parents just yet, and noticed the frayed edge of the nearby carpet. "Must you live in such frightful surroundings?"

His laughter made her feel more at home than anything else he had done so far. When it subsided into a deep smile he said, "God, but you've become a beauty."

"Nearly as pretty as you," she rejoined and they both laughed. It had always been a joke between them, begun by their nurse, as to which of the Grant children would grow up to be the more handsome. "We could truly pass for twins now that we're grown."

Andrew nodded. Looking at his sister was like seeing his reflection in a magician's trick mirror. Her profile was softer, more delicate, but a feminine replica of his. The eyes were an identical hue. Friends still marveled to see them together and strangers often turned to stare.

"Father's furious," Andrew said after a moment.

Allegra nodded contritely. "I shouldn't have run away, but honestly, Andy, it was like prison, the deepest of tortures to be kept from you. It's been more than a year since I've seen you."

Andrew shrugged. He had not gone home for Christmas because of Harriet. They had just met and he had remained in town in hope of crossing her path again during the holiday rounds of parties and dinners and galas. "I'm sorry about that. You can't imagine how complex life becomes once a man harnesses himself to a job."

"Do you mind that?"

"Sometimes." He reached into his pocket and withdrew a gold cigarette case. "I'd rather do newspaper work. One meets the most interesting people."

"At least your writing appears in print," she added encouragingly.

He winced, then struck a match to light his cigarette. "My writing—if you can call it that—consists of obituaries and a smattering of theater reviews. I've even been reduced to contributing to the society page on occasion. God, if you reveal that to a soul I'll wring your pretty neck!"

"But you have prospects, opportunities to do better. Your novel, for instance," she insisted.

"Prospects." He exhaled a huge cloud of smoke and

studied it a moment. "I'm thinking of going to Paris and becoming a bohemian."

"Truly?" Allegra paused in reaching for her teacup. "Oh, you're not serious. They live such tawdry lives, starving and mooning about. Their habits and clothing are quite disreputable, I hear."

Andrew regarded his sister in amused tolerance. "You can't begin to realize how utterly provincial and ignorant you are." Before she could voice her resentment of this assessment, he continued, "When I was in London a few years ago, I met men whose minds are filled with untainted knowledge, who have so true an understanding of human nature and ideals that they espouse the supremacy of good and beauty and perfection above every other aim. Once you've heard them it's damn—demmed difficult to live with the crippling conventionality of one's former life."

Allegra leaned forward expectantly. This is what she had come to New York to hear. "Show me this new life. It's why I came to you. Oh, please, Andy!"

"Father would revile me as the worst of sons and a thorough villain were he to guess the extent to which I've already corrupted you. The books, goose!" he added at her mystified look. "You've had too much of radical notions. What else would explain your present actions?"

"Boredom," she answered. "I was reduced to cutting the pages of one of those dreadful novels Mama packed along. If I'd had to listen to one more word of Lettie's gossip, I believe I would have strangled her."

He did not ask who Lettie was. Allegra had written daily missives on everything that occurred in Saratoga. It was as though he had been there. "That doesn't excuse your behavior. You've been unforgivably reckless. Father's right; you're incorrigible."

"Thank you very much for your confidence." She rose from her chair and reached for her hat.

"What do you think you're doing?"

"Leaving. I wouldn't dream of causing you further embarrassment. Despite your talk to the contrary you've become a most conventional sort of fellow: a bachelor with lodgings." She gave the room a peremptory glance. "Grubby lodgings, but I suppose one must rub on as best one can."

"Where will you go? I shouldn't think a return to Saratoga would be possible at this hour, or advisable."

"I'm perfectly capable of caring for myself. As you can see, I arrived without a scratch."

"But with more than a few wrinkles," he observed. "Gad, what a rig. I thought you had more style."

"The mourning drapery was for you, brother dear, but since you're not appreciative I'll reserve my demonstrations in future for a more deserving cause."

"Really?"

His snide expression was more than she could bear. "I may join Dr. Boyd in the crusade for women's rights, for instance." As soon as she had said it, she knew she shouldn't have brought up the doctor's name so soon.

Andrew's interest quickened. "Who's Dr. Boyd?"

"Someone you should have kept in touch with," she answered, covering her discomfiture by removing her hat. "He was in Saratoga. We met one afternoon when your name was mentioned."

"My name? Why?"

"As an example of vice," she remarked sweetly. "Dr. Boyd introduced himself to Papa and inquired whether or not you were the same Andrew Grant who had attended Harvard."

"Boyd? Boyd—John Boyd, of course." Andrew whistled. "Haven't seen the fellow in years. You never mentioned him in your letters."

"I don't tell you everything."

"My little sister was smitten, was she?"

"Don't be vulgar," Allegra replied and sank back into her chair with a sigh of annoyance. "I simply found him stimulating company. At least his collars were clean and his suits impeccably cut."

Andrew heard this assessment of a man by his sister in faint surprise. Her presence was a forceful reminder that she was no longer a child, but he hadn't gotten beyond that realization to think of the consequences. "It's odd that Boyd should remember me after all these years. He was in medical school during my undergraduate years. He didn't collect many friends. No scandal, but if I recall, some indefinable air of distance clung to him."

"Perhaps he found the posturing of school-age literarians hopelessly gauche."

Andrew fixed his sister with a jaundiced eye. "Don't you have a train to catch?"

"Oh, that. It's quite late. I should arrive after supper and I'm famished."

"Good lord!" Andrew rose to his feet and reached for his watch. "I'm late for an engagement. I didn't expect you," he added unnecessarily. "I suppose I could send my regrets, family emergency and all that."

Allegra felt ill at ease for the first time. She had not asked if she was welcome; she had assumed it. "I've made a pudding of things, haven't I? Please don't keep your companions waiting. I imagine there's something to eat." She looked about hopefully. "Somewhere."

"I'm afraid not. I don't eat at home as a rule. When not dining out, I eat at the club."

"I see. Well, then, I shall console myself with food for the mind." She gestured toward the bookshelves in the next room. "There must be one or two here I haven't read."

Andrew put a hand to his brow. "I'll go and make my excuses. Then I'll escort you to the dining room on the ground floor."

"Shall I go with you dressed like this?"

Andrew faked a shudder of horror as he looked her over. "Mama says you dyed the lot."

"Nearly," she said contritely. "It was all for you, Andy, truly it was."

"I should remain in those weeds were I you. When Father's done with us you may have need of them."

"Us? You've done nothing to make Papa angry."

"I haven't yet attempted to persuade him to allow you to remain in town."

"You want me to stay?"

"I invited you, didn't I?"

"Yes, but—"

"But not as you came," he agreed. "I'm not sure you

should be allowed to prevail, after what you've done, frightening Mama half to death. I'll think about it.''

"When will you have a decision?" she asked impatiently, knowing that this was his method of punishing her.

His expression was bland. "Even if I am persuaded that you may remain, how do you hope to persuade Father?"

"You could tell him that a taste of city life will cure me of my romantic notions," she suggested.

"So that when you return home you'll be content to settle down?"

She smiled at him, part imp and part the fetching woman she was fast becoming. "I won't, you know. I'll never return home to live. I may not even wed."

His black brows winged upward again. "Not even the redoubtable Dr. Boyd?"

Allegra's smile didn't falter, but she was surprised by the tingling along her limbs at the mention of the doctor's name. It was just as well that she didn't know whether they would actually meet again.

"A sister?" Harriet looked blankly at him.

"I do have family. Why should the mention of a sister surprise you?" Andrew questioned in amusement. "Did you think I'd sprung full-grown from the head of Zeus? Of course, I'd have been named Athena in that case."

"What?"

"Never mind, dearest." He reached for her hand to counter the irritation he felt at her ignorance of his reference to Greek mythology. Harriet was appallingly ignorant of so much. Though, to give her credit, she had struggled through the few books he had given her to read. It wasn't her fault that she couldn't discuss them intelligently and that their one attempt had ended with her in tears and him chagrined by her distress. Though it subsequently turned into the most passionate hour they had yet spent together, he had firmly resolved not to instruct her further.

"Atlantic City was wonderful," she said softly.

"I hoped you'd think so once we returned." He had half

expected guilt to keep her from admitting that their tryst had been absolutely perfect. He squeezed her fingers tightly before slipping his hand free. They sat at the back table of a small crowded cafe in the French Quarter off Washington Square, surrounded by strangers, but even strangers expected a certain amount of decorum in public.

"Will your sister be in town long?"

"I can't say. I don't think so." He drummed his fingers on the tabletop, impatient with the small civilities expected of him at times like this. "In any case it doesn't affect us."

"How can you say that? We mustn't see each other while a member of your family is in town."

Andrew reached for his cigarettes, his annoyance mounting. "In that case, we might as well part. My father is in the city on the average of one day a month. He's been here half a dozen times since the spring."

"Oh." Harriet looked away.

"Why do you turn away from me?" he demanded testily.

She shook her head. "Because I—I can never think properly when looking at you."

His exasperation melted as it always did under the simplicity of her honesty. No actress could affect a natural innocence such as hers. He had seen many try, and written reviews on the degrees of their various failures. Yet there were times when he wished there were a little more artifice in Harriet. It would make him less anxious for her feelings, less afraid that he would do her some mortal harm before their affair was done.

"I would marry you if I could."

She looked up at him then, and the wretched misery in her gaze made him wish he had kept silent.

"That was unforgivable, unforgivable!" he said hoarsely, adding an oath under his breath.

"No." She reached for his hand as he moved to stub out the cigarette he had not even lit. "No! Don't say that. Don't you know that those words are all that I live to hear? I love you, too. It's intolerable that we should've met now, when it's too late. Sometimes I've thought it would be better if we hadn't met at all."

It should not have crossed his mind that this declaration

from her sounded ominously like one of the more emotional passages from popular melodrama. Perhaps he had underestimated the reality of the sentiment expressed in them. Indeed, he too felt the unfairness of their situation. That he was prepared to live with it was perhaps a measure of his familiarity with the gulf between desire and actuality.

"Dearest Harriet. Your sweetness charms me beyond enduring." God! Was he, too, reduced to mouthing stageisms? Yes. He wanted to take her away from prying eyes and sly glances. He wanted to take her where they could always be together, shutting out the minor and major annoyances of life and its authority. But he couldn't. There was no time to dream and less money to dream with. He released her hand. "I can't stay. I'm sorry. But I must see you again. Tomorrow, perhaps? The Fifth Avenue confectionery?"

"No. We're giving a dinner tomorrow. It's a political affair with aldermen and wardmen. I detest them! Their cigars stink, their boots are dirty, and their table manners are enough to set tongues wagging belowstairs."

"But they turned out the vote, and your husband owes his latest victory to them," he reminded her.

"I hoped he would lose."

"No! He must win, again and again. With him away in the state legislature in Albany, we're free."

"Your meal, monsieur."

Andrew looked up as the waiter set a tray of covered pottery before him. "You've included the eclairs?"

"*Oui*, monsieur."

"I'll have my doorman return the dishes in the morning."

"As monsieur wishes," the waiter replied, pleased by the number of coins Andrew placed in his palm.

"You're bringing your sister a meal from this place?" Harriet asked in astonishment.

"I promised to fetch her supper. Her baggage was misplaced by the railroad and she refused to be seen on the street without the proper garments," he lied smoothly.

"I do hope she has a partiality for bohemian fare," she said, eyeing her own untouched plate with misgivings.

"She'll love it," he answered with absolute assurance, for Harriet had unknowingly given him the perfect phrase with which to give his cheap meal the aura of an adventure. Bohemian fare; Allegra would be thrilled.

An hour later he watched in bemusement as his sister finished the last of the goulash. Five short minutes ago he had been bracing himself for his parents' arrival in the morning. Now, with the delivery of a telegram, everything had changed.

Some things didn't lend themselves to the wishes of a tycoon. Illness was one of them. Certainly Allegra could not be expected to go to Charleston now that Mama had been called there to nurse Aunt Caroline and her children through a putrid fever. Fate had outmaneuvered Angus Grant this time, and that fact gave his son a gleeful satisfaction.

"Bohemian food is quite nice," Allegra remarked as she buttered a final piece of bread.

"But murder on the figure, my girl. If you plan to live here you'd better curb your appetite or I won't be able to afford you."

"Stay here? Does that telegram concern me?" At his nod she leaped from her chair to hug him. "You're the sweetest, dearest, most wonderful brother a girl could have!"

"Wait until you've read this."

Allegra snatched the telegram and scanned it quickly. "Poor Aunt Caroline. Still, it means you can keep me."

"I've yet to confront Father. He'll be furious with me for suggesting that he shouldn't look after you himself while Mama is away."

"But, like Perseus, you shall free me from the chains of Papa's rule, and in return I'll make domestic your humble domicile," she vowed.

Andrew smiled as she hugged him once more, and the faint perfume of her cologne reminded him of earlier years. "Yes, it's time we broke our chains, Andromeda." He was glad his sister had come. Unlike his failure with Harriet, his tutoring had not been lost on Allegra. "Did I tell you about the new volumes I've just received from Munich?"

* * *

New York City, September 1

A light summer rain slicked the windows of the New York hotel room and cast deep gray shadows over the interior, but Drayton scarcely heeded his surroundings. His mind was focused on possibility; a possibility that had been absent from his life until a short while ago.

He didn't attempt to speculate on her appearance. He refused any image. Something more primitive preferred the vague symmetry of abstraction. It had been easy enough to learn the name of a neighbor, a simple matter of conjecture to identify his voyeur. Pink rosebuds on a straw boater could only belong to a young lady, the daughter. But pursuit was another matter. That is why he had taken the first train back to New York.

Yet he shied from the thought of pursuit. The possibility of disappointment haunted him. If she were the person he sought, she should come to him somehow, in some manner that did not entail the social conformities of meeting and courting. If she were the soul mate he sought, he dared not force the moment which made his heart beat thickly within his chest. Oh, God, but there must be some sign!

The door opened behind him but he didn't move from the deep seclusion of his wing chair. She entered shoeless, as he had demanded. When she appeared beside him he shut his eyes, breathing in the fragrance of life that stood so close. This was not the woman he sought and ached for, but she would do for now. When the heat of a naked breast brushed his cheek, he sighed in satisfaction. After a long interval of detached usage, his lust had been stirred to its deepest recess. All because of his faceless spy.

He reached for the buttons of his trousers, slowly opened them, and took the familiar weight of his flesh in his hand. Tantalizing possibilities were all that kept him alive. That possibility made him quiver and his manhood swell.

"Kneel," he whispered softly. His eyes closed as she bent over him.

Five

"Andy! You're early!"

Andrew stepped cautiously into what that morning had been his drawing room. Now he scarcely recognized it. Every surface was covered with lengths of cloth and rolls of wallpaper. Scarlet and turquoise, bold strips of kumquat and puce and bitter lemon, yards of navy and cream, ribbons of gold and silver, florals, arabesques, and stripes; everywhere he looked the jumble of color and patterns offended his gaze.

"We need a new arrangement now that I live here, too," Allegra began in explanation. "The bedroom furniture Papa ordered for me arrived today. Rather than displace yours, I put it in the dining room, which works quite well. The drawing room easily accommodates the dining table, which you never use. I sent that vile velvet settee and side chairs to the basement. You'll never miss them. New furniture requires new drapes and wallpaper. What do you think?"

"Am I to have a say in the matter? I thought perhaps the lease had been changed into your name. Where did you get this?" He lifted a tag on a bolt of cloth. "How typical!" he said bitterly. "I must beg for the wherewithal to live decently while Father thinks nothing of squandering a king's fortune on . . ."

Though his voice died away, Allegra could finish the thought for herself. Papa was often generous but seldom fair in his treatment of his children. "It wasn't Papa's idea. It

65

was Mama's. She believes that redecorating will keep me occupied until it's time for me to go home.''

"Will it?" he questioned in surprise.

Allegra shook her head. "I won't leave New York until I've seen my fill. Not that you've let me set foot out of the building since I arrived. With my meals up from the dining room, I see no one but waiters and the charwomen. Papa couldn't have punished me better!"

Her outburst elicited only silence. She cast a calculated gaze at her brother as he attempted to extricate his favorite chair from beneath her tiger-skin rug, where she'd spread it to air the moment it arrived with her baggage. "You're thoroughly put out with me, aren't you?"

"No, of course not," he answered unconvincingly as he gingerly set the rug aside. He sank into his chair and pulled out a cigarette, only to sit staring at it for a long moment. Finally he shook his head slightly and turned to her with the smile of welcome that had been missing when he first entered. "Poor sis, imprisoned like a felon."

"Oh, I know I'm being willful and cross, but I'll put it all behind me now that you're home. I ordered enough supper for two."

"I've plans for dinner."

"Oh." He had been absent during the evening hours for the past few days.

"I'm sorry that I must go out again, but you gave me no notice of your coming. Many of my engagements were made before you arrived."

"I don't suppose I might be allowed to accompany you?" Allegra ventured hopefully.

Andrew shook his head. "It's at my club. Tomorrow, I promise, we'll do whatever you wish."

Her disappointment was sharp, but Allegra only said, "I'll hold you to your promise."

He gave her his best smile. "You're a wonder! Now I must go or I'll be very late." He paused as he headed for his bedroom. "I'm sorry to be leaving you. Truly."

Allegra nodded, but her chin wobbled as she said, "Don't worry about me. I'll find something to fill the lonely hours."

The appeal was calculated, and Andrew knew it, but he had left her alone too often not to feel a twinge of guilt. He poked his head back into the room. "I rather like your tiger rug. It gives the place a smart look."

She was surprised by how quickly he changed his collar and cuffs and then departed. He had been preoccupied ever since her arrival, but she hadn't yet been able to learn the reason why.

The arrival of her dinner just after Andy's departure was the only thing that distracted her from a thorough sulk. Even so, when she had finished a small portion of the meal, she could not scotch the feeling that she was no better off than she had been in Saratoga. Things were not proceeding as she had hoped. Reaching for the pen and paper she had set beside her plate, she began to describe in exact detail just how miserable she was.

It had occurred to her after the first few days that now that she was in Andy's company, she had no one to whom to write her long, expansive letters. Yet the need to put her thoughts into writing had not abated. Contrary to her expectations, Andy had little time for conversation; thus many of her opinions and feelings were left unspoken at the end of each day.

She had begun her first letter to him as a lark. Pride hadn't allowed her to tuck it under his pillow as she had first thought to do. Instead she had tucked it into her lap desk, embarrassed to have given in to so strange an impulse. Yet, daily afterward, she had added another missive to her collection of unposted letters.

Tonight she included a note about the arrival of her new wardrobe and the fact that the gowns failed to lift her spirits.

They look exactly like the ones I dyed—Mama just repeated the original order. One glimpse of them was enough to set in motion all my feelings of exasperation, defiance, and distaste for those weeks in Saratoga. I can't bear these reminders of my former life! Perhaps I'll wear my black gowns until autumn.

The charwoman Kate says that Mrs. Haden on the third

floor does much of her shopping herself. She purchases furnishings at W & J Sloane, confectionaries at Maillard's, and her jewels at Tiffany's.

Allegra tapped the end of her pen against her lower lip and then wrote in a great flurry:

Just once, I'd like to shop in a real store. Mama rejects the idea, saying that ladies don't purchase clothing off the rack like shop girls. "It simply isn't done." I'm very put out with the world of 'mustn't" and "simply not done." What I'd very much like to do is something quite exceptional and daring!

The knock at the door surprised her until she remembered that it must be the waiter sent to pick up her supper dishes. Any distraction was better than none, she decided as she set her letter on the table. Perhaps the waiter could be persuaded to stay and talk for a short while. It was from waiters and charwomen that she had learned what little she knew of life at the Dakota. With a wide smile of welcome she opened the door, unprepared for the three young men lounging on her threshold.

In one amazed glance she took in their appearance. Hair too long from lack of a barber's care spilled over their high collars, frayed cuffs peeked out from beneath their stylishly slim coats, and elaborate soft ties drooped below their chins. Without a word she pushed the door to close it, but an insistent foot intervened and then a hand shot out to open it again.

"What have we here?" said the redheaded man whose hand held the door. Taller and broader than his two companions, he had a flattened nose that gave him a pugnacious look.

"Grant's muse?" suggested the blond as he regarded her in frank appraisal.

"Perhaps we should leave," suggested the third. Slight and grave with a scraggly brown beard, he spoke with an accent she couldn't place. "We'll visit Grant another evening."

"Nonsense. Grant isn't the sort to turn off his friends, is he, darlin'?" the redhead asked.

For a moment Allegra was too stunned to speak. They were obviously her brother's friends, yet she resented the familiarity with which they addressed her. The redhead in particular was offensive. His companion with the curly blond hair and side-whiskers was more to her liking. Still, it wouldn't do to allow him to know that. "Whom do you seek?" she inquired in her most formal voice.

"A lady!" the blond declared in surprise.

"You expected someone else?" she questioned tartly.

"Not a bit of it, darlin'," the redhead replied. "Grant never told us about you!"

"Do you wonder?" said the blond, "I, too, would squirrel away so delightful a creature, were I fortunate enough to possess her."

"I'm not a possession," she answered with faint irritation.

"An expensive hobby, perhaps?" the redhead suggested as his gaze swept her again.

Allegra's eyes widened, for he had quite obviously reached the conclusion that she was something less than a lady. "You, sir, are no gentleman."

"That sets the cap on your character, Rhys," said the blond.

Allegra turned her disapproving expression on him. "And you, why do you stand there cluttering up my doorway? Have you no home of your own?"

Throwing his hands up in defeat, the blond took a step back. However, the one named Rhys was not so readily defeated. "Fact is, darlin', we're after looking for your—er, Andrew Grant."

"He isn't here."

"And when would you be expecting him?"

"I don't *expect* him," she answered frigidly as she struggled not to smile, for she was quite enjoying herself. Just wait until Andy found out that his friends assumed she was his paramour.

"In that case, you won't be minding if we make ourselves comfortable while we wait," Rhys replied, forcing his way inside. "Faith, would you look at this?" he said as he strolled into the drawing room. "There's a fortune in fabric piled about. What's this?" He picked up the unopened bottle of wine from the supper tray. "Look here, Seton!" He held the bottle up for the blond's inspection. "Wine, and a good vintage, too."

Allegra hurried into the drawing room to snatch the bottle from him. "You're not welcome here. Go away!"

"There're places set for two," Seton observed as he picked up the lid of one of the dishes. "Fricasseed fowl and new potatoes, enough for a party."

"It would seem we've stumbled upon a lovers' tryst," Rhys said as he stared anew at Allegra. She wore housekeeper black, but the stuff of her gown was not at all like the serviceable serge most servants wore. There was something puzzling about her that he couldn't quite name. "You weren't after giving us your name."

"Neither, sir, were you," she returned.

"You've fine airs for a housekeeper."

Allegra turned away without a reply. There was nothing she could do to prevent them from remaining and she had the presence of mind to realize that there could be trouble if any of the other tenants should note the fact. Once she secured the door she checked her watch pinned in the lace on her bodice. It was nearly ten P.M. Andrew would be back shortly. She would let him handle the situation.

With a resolve to see the matter through, she walked back into the drawing room. In the short time they had been there, two of the young men had made themselves at home. Seton occupied the sofa while Rhys had seated himself at the table and helped himself to a chicken leg. Only the quiet one, whose name she had not yet heard mentioned, stood a little apart in obvious discomfort.

"Fine chicken," Rhys pronounced. "Me own mum wouldn't be ashamed to be claiming it as hers."

"Most assuredly the same wouldn't be presumed about claiming her son," she retorted and set the wine bottle back on the table with a thump.

"Don't mind if I do." Rhys reached for it.

She reached for it, too, but he beat her. "I won't tolerate

drunkenness in my presence," she said flatly, for there was already the distinct odor of wine on his breath.

He leaned toward her, grinning, and it altered his plain pudding face into interesting angles and crags. "There's nothing to fear, darlin'. Were I to consume the entire bottle, you'd never be knowing it, were you not to witness it. A hard head, I have. I'm Irish, you see."

"You have my sincerest sympathy," she answered but resisted the urge to try to snatch the bottle from him.

Seton chuckled. "I'd give ground before the formidable lady, Rhys."

Rhys extracted the cork with a pop. "There! Shall we drink to your health, darlin'?"

"Better you should drink to your own." Allegra reached for her letter which lay beside Rhys's plate and folded it in quarters before sticking it up her sleeve.

Rhys watched her a moment over the rim of his glass, his eyes full of mischief.

From the corner of her eye Allegra saw that the quiet man had picked up a bolt of fabric and was examining it closely. When he realized she was watching him, he quickly put it down.

"Who's in charge of Grant's redecoration?" Seton asked between bites of chicken. "Grant should consult Edssene." He indicated the third member of his party. "He's clever with color."

Allegra turned to the man standing irresolutely near the windows. "You're an artist?"

A faint blush darkened his gaunt cheeks. "I aspire to be worthy of the title."

In challenge she held up the bolt of cloth he had been examining. "What wallpaper would you choose to match this fabric?"

"A Morris is the only possible choice," Rhys answered quickly. "Morris's symmetry is never at fault. Even his most detestable patterns can be admired for their adherence to an accepted order."

The artist's thin cheeks grew painfully red. "I disagree! A man of sensibility and . . . and . . ."

"Don't talk nonsense!" Rhys retorted, his voice loud and belligerent.

"Just a moment—" Seton began, only to be roared down by a Gaelic oath from Rhys.

"I would not hang the Morris paper!" the artist cried, clearly insulted that his opinion should be impugned. "No painting can properly exist in a room draped with vines and fruits!"

"No painting of yours, perhaps!" Rhys scoffed.

The raised voices blotted out the sound of a key in the lock, but all started guiltily as Andrew Grant appeared in the entryway. "Allegra, I— What the devil?"

Allegra turned to him in relief. "Andy, you're back! You've guests. They were most insistent about waiting for you."

Rhys rose from his chair. "I wouldn't say insistent. The lady wasn't averse to our company."

"That's entirely untrue," Allegra answered indignantly. "They forced their way in."

Rhys shrugged. "*Musha*, so she wasn't after inviting us in, but you've no cause for complaint. She's been as stiff and proper as a Fifth Avenue matron."

Andrew turned to him. "In the past I haven't objected that you appear at my door unannounced, but when you take liberties with my sister you go too far!"

" 'Liberties with my sister'? Andy, you sound just like Papa!" Allegra chided as she brushed an errant curl behind her ear. "I haven't been molested."

"Sister?" Seton echoed at the back of Allegra's speech. "She's your sister?"

"Of course," Andrew answered testily. "Who else would she be?"

"They believed, brother dear, that I was your housekeeper." Allegra smiled. "Isn't that so, gentlemen?"

"That's enough, Allegra," Andrew replied impatiently. He turned to the Irishman. "This is your doing, Rhys. My sister's new in town, no more than a child, really. She doesn't understand the consequence of what might have occurred. I demand your silence on this matter, as a friend and a gentleman. A wrong word and . . ."

Rhys waved away the end of this speech. "Naught to fear. I'm known as a man who can hold his tongue as well as his liquor. Let's go, lads."

Rhys's companions sketched hurried bows for Allegra and headed for the door behind him.

"Do come again," she called after them.

"What exactly has been going on?" Andrew demanded when they were gone.

"The most fun I've had in ages," Allegra answered, seeing humor in the situation now that it was past. After a brief recalling of the events, she finished with, "So, you see, nothing untoward occurred."

"I see that I've been careless in leaving you alone. I thought you'd be safe enough, but I'd forgotten about those fellows."

"Who are they?"

He frowned. "Three starvelings of wild ways whose acquaintance I made to further an article I'm writing."

"The funny little man called Edssene is a painter. What do the others do?"

"Seton's a gentleman, if one can say that of a Princeton man. He paints, writes poetry, and generally plays the dilettante. It's his coin that goes to pay the rent on the wretched place they call a studio."

"And Rhys?"

"Rhys is a writer. A rather good one from what little I've seen."

"He doesn't seem the type who needs to be coaxed into revealing himself," she observed.

"Not at all. It's simply that the last time I saw him his manuscripts were being held in hock by his typist. He hadn't paid his bills."

"But that's horrid. How can he be expected to earn a living if the source of his income is held hostage?"

Andrew smiled indulgently. "I lent him the money to retrieve his work. He spent it on wine and food for the inhabitants of his favorite saloon. A *beau geste*, that."

"But entirely impractical. He might have sold his work for more money than you lent him. Then his friends could have eaten and drunk even more."

"There's seldom any income from their work. What they do earn is spent on paint and canvas or paper and ink. They exist on sardines, potatoes, and buns."

"Yet you sound as though you admire them."

He nodded. "Perhaps. I'd like to be free to do as I wish without the constraints of mortal considerations."

"Like money and shelter and food?" she suggested.

"Admit it, you've just met them and you're fascinated."

"They're your friends. I wouldn't presume to pronounce judgment on them after so slight an acquaintance."

"Spoken like Mama at her most diplomatic."

"And you emulated Papa precisely when you came in. Do you suppose that in the end we'll grow to be just like them?"

He gave her a startled look. "Not if I can help it!"

"May I read the article you've written about your visitors?"

"It isn't finished. I'd show you the preliminary sketches if I were able to find them." He looked over at the heap of fabric and paper rolls on his desk. "Really, you must do something about this clutter."

"Tomorrow." Her gaze lit upon the scraps of her meal. "Do they truly starve, Andy?"

"Don't pity them. They choose to starve and consider people of wealth, moneylenders and tycoons, the lowest creatures upon the earth."

"Yet they hope to sell their artistic endeavors to those same low creatures," she observed. "How did you gain their confidence when Papa reeks of business and gainful enterprise?"

"How repugnantly you phrase it."

"You are avoiding the question."

He shrugged. "I omitted the details of my personal life."

"Didn't they wonder how you can afford to live here?"

He gave her an annoyed look. "I told them the truth, that the rooms were an inheritance."

"Oh." She was quiet for a moment. "No wonder they thought you could afford a mistress!"

"Gad! You *will* speak the unspeakable."

"Only with you," she answered. "Andy, do you have a mistress? What I mean is, I wouldn't be shocked. Well, perhaps just a bit, but it's quite the thing for a young man to have one, isn't it?''

"Unlike a new opera coat, mistresses hardly qualify as the 'thing to have.' Now, I refuse to converse further with you on the subject."

"You can be positively gothic at times. How will I ever learn about these things if you won't tell me?" A mischievous smile lit up her face. "Andy, you did say that tomorrow would be my day to do anything I wish? I want to visit a real bohemian saloon."

Andrew pretended not to hear her as he fished his watch from his vest pocket. "It's nearly eleven o'clock. That means bedtime for you while an hour of work lies ahead for me. If I don't finish tonight, I'll be forced to work tomorrow."

"Very well, brother dear." Allegra rose and went to drop a kiss on his cheek. "Tomorrow is my day and you won't be allowed to spoil it with work."

New York, September 28

"You mustn't speak, do you understand?"

Allegra glanced at her brother through her thick veiling. "Not speak? How absurd, Andy. People will think I am a mute or wandering in my wits."

"Better that than they learn who you are," he answered, gazing critically at the black bonnet and veil he had brought to match the gown she wore. It was a passable disguise. No one would suspect her to be a wealthy young lady. "Keep your veil lowered. You mustn't be able to be recognized at a later date."

"But I shan't be able to see as well as I'd like."

"You'll see enough," he answered. *Too much*, he mused, wondering yet again how he had been persuaded to undertake this escapade. "Here we are. Now remember, I shall speak for us." When the cab pulled to the curb on Third Street near MacDougal Street, he stepped down and helped her out.

The noise of the street startled Allegra. As the din and

stench rolled over her, she hung back. Never before in her life had she seen the slums.

Though it was nearly dark, a boisterous crowd milled beneath the dim yellow glow of the street lamps. The odors of the city rode the warmth of the late-September night breeze, stifling combinations of manure, onions, garlic, urine, and noisome humanity. Yet, there was an almost carnival atmosphere to the street life. Men and women lounged in doorways, their voices accented by foreign inflection but their laughter universally voluptuous. Children, ragged and barefooted, chased one another across the street in careless disregard for their own safety while older boys crouched in self-absorbed knots on the curbside.

"Changing your mind?" Andrew suggested.

"Not at all," she answered but tightened her clutch on his arm as he moved onto the sidewalk. She wanted to experience this, had spent the better part of the day in argument with Andy over the opportunity. She would not forsake it because of her momentary revulsion. Yet she balked again when she saw where he was leading her.

"Down there?" she asked in alarm as he took the first of a flight of narrow steps leading down into a bright cellar from which flowed music and laughter.

"You wanted to dine in bohemia. Marie's is one of the most famous spots in town. If you'd rather not . . . ?"

As he spoke, Allegra realized that the cellar was the source of the pungent aromas of garlic and onion that floated into the street. Her stomach gurgled uneasily, but she lifted her chin. "I'm positively starving. Don't keep me standing on the street."

The doorway was open but for an instant her impression was that there were no people present, only light and noise, laughter and smoke. Tears filled her eyes as Andrew led her inside, but she blinked them back with determination and her vision cleared a little. Figures appeared, swimming in and out of focus amid the dense smoke of cigars and cigarettes. Shoulder to shoulder, the mostly male clientele formed jacket-clad walls around the long tables that filled the interior. Their voices were loud, cheerful, and pugnacious, several foreign tongues vying with English for predominance. Waitresses dressed in shirtwaists and aprons and bearing trays of food and wine threaded their way among the crowded tables.

"Shall we sit here?" Andrew suggested in a loud voice as he urged her toward a corner table not too far from the entrance. The chair he pulled out for her creaked ominously but held as she perched on its seat. The table was not much stronger, wobbling as he placed his hat on it. The white tablecloth, littered with used cutlery, was freckled with wine and dusted with cheese gratings.

Allegra found her handkerchief and dabbed her cheeks, for the sweltering heat of the September evening seemed concentrated here.

"Well? What do you say?" Andrew fairly shouted over the din. "Are you ready to go home?"

She saw his smug expression and knew that if she retreated now he could never again be persuaded to bring her to such a place. "Before I've eaten? I should say not!"

"Very well." He pounded the table with his fist, a maneuver Allegra found startling, for the cutlery jumped as the table bucked under the punishment. "Waiter!"

A short, plump man swirled about, his white shirt and apron a startling contrast to his swarthy complexion. Black oiled mustaches curled up like fishhooks to frame his cheeks. "Signore Grant! *Buona sera.*" His dark eyes moved immediately to Allegra and he smiled. "Ah, the signor has company this evening." He nodded approvingly. "*Bellissima.* A ballerina, perhaps?"

"Spaghetti, Giuseppe, and Chianti," Andrew answered.

The man's smile widened, unoffended by Andrew's curtness. "We have this evening ravioli." He kissed his fingertips. "Perfection, signore. I made them myself."

Although Allegra was not at all certain this should be a recommendation for the dish, Andrew nodded his consent.

The waiter fixed Allegra with an arch look. "Signorina, if the signore does not treat you properly, you have only to ask for Giuseppe," and he turned away murmuring in his native tongue.

Curiously Allegra scanned the room. Several men at a nearby table stared at her and there was nothing reserved about their glances. They smiled at her, one raising his wineglass in salute. Embarrassed, she looked away.

A moment later Giuseppe reappeared with a heaped tray. "A specialty for the signorina," he said as he placed a large plate before Allegra. "Osso buco! For to help the signorina dance like the angels, if angels could be so womanly."

Allegra eyed the plate of oxtails suspiciously, wishing instead for the bowl of ravioli he placed before Andrew.

After pouring the wine, the waiter reluctantly left the table, but not before giving her another adoring glance.

When he was gone she picked up her fork, only to pause. "How do you suggest that I eat without revealing my face?"

"This was your idea. You work it out," Andrew answered as he tucked into his meal.

Determined not to be bested, she lifted her veil and slipped a forkful beneath. "Why, this is delicious!"

In spite of his reluctance to bring her here, Andrew was pleased that she was enjoying herself. They ate in companionable silence for there was little need to speak once a piano, unseen but heard, began to play. Many of the other patrons seemed to agree and for a short while a soft hum of voices replaced the boisterous din. A popular song gave way to a Gilbert and Sullivan tune, followed by yet another lively song that many of the patrons joined in singing.

Between bites Allegra surreptitiously watched the other diners. Like the artists who had come to her door the night before, they wore ill-assorted clothing and sported bushy mustaches or beards. Though many consumed piles of spaghetti, others confined their consumption to the bright red wine which flowed continuously. In spite of the aura of geniality and good spirits, she detected an undertone of melancholia. Or, she thought, perhaps it was only that the idea of brave faces appealed to her romantic sense.

"Grant! Is it Andrew Grant!"

The Grants looked up together at the loud greeting to find a fair-haired man in seersucker approaching them.

"Jack Achland!" Andrew was on his feet in an instant with his hand extended while Allegra lowered her veil to chin level. "What brings you to these depths?" he asked as he pumped Achland's hand. "I didn't think you were fond of dyspepsia."

"Soaking up atmosphere," Achland returned. His gaze shifted to Allegra. "Miss," he greeted with a nod before he leaned toward Andrew. "Where'd you find the stunner?"

Andrew grinned. "A journalist never reveals his sources, especially not to the competition."

Achland's laughter was straightforward and Allegra found herself liking it immediately. "May I sit?" he asked, seating himself before Andrew could reply. He turned to Allegra and held out a hand which she didn't move to take. "My name's Achland, James Achland. Reporter for the *New York Tribune*. I may not be as handsome as Grant, but I make a great deal more money and have more influence. How would you like to see your picture in the society pages?"

Allegra eyed with distaste the huge blue polka-dotted handkerchief in his breast pocket. "I should like it about as well as you'd like having yours in the *Police Gazette*."

"Ouch! She bites, Grant."

"Sometimes severely," Andrew answered. "What's that under your arm? The new *Revue des Deux Mondes*!"

Achland handed over the paper and turned once more to Allegra. "Amuse yourself, dear boy. I've better things to do."

Andrew set the paper aside. "You've heard the latest? Astor's decamped."

Achland's gaze never left Allegra. "Old news. Packed his family and boarded a ship for England, vowing never to come back. Heard him myself. I suppose losing the election was the last straw."

"It was having his own party reject him," Andrew said.

"I say the old fellow had it coming. Gave himself too many airs. Held himself too high against the common man. The rank and file don't mind success. Look at Morgan. He's made a good bit of money but kept the common touch. Astor's candidacy for Congress was never taken seriously by the machine. He filled his purpose by lining the party coffers. Of course we're not allowed to print that."

"Do they have that much power?" Allegra asked, her

curiosity piqued by the conversation despite her promise to remain silent.

"If by *they* you mean the political machine that runs the state Republican Party, the answer's yes and yes again," Achland answered. "But let's not concern ourselves over political matters. I'd rather talk to you of other things." His gaze narrowed as he tried to penetrate her veil. "You've been holding out on me, Grant. Is she by chance a well-bred debutante out on the town in the guise of shop girl?"

"You wouldn't expect me to answer in the affirmative, if that were the case," Andrew replied. "Ah! A reading. Do let's listen."

One of the restaurant's habitués had climbed upon his tabletop with a sheaf of papers clutched in one hand and a wine bottle in the other. Allegra smiled, amused that the audacious fellow looked exactly like a cartoon she had seen recently in *Puck*. His hair was parted in the center and oiled to sealskin sleekness against the sides of his head while his mustaches were waxed to cat-whisker resilience. He wore striped pants but his coat was not formal and his tie was askew.

"He looks like an animated puppet," she whispered to her brother.

He began speaking low, so low, in fact, that they did not catch the first phrases of his oratory, but gradually his voice rose, blotting out the ever-present kitchen clatter. Finally they understood that he recited poetry. Though his voice was thickened and slurred by wine, the words were vivid, energetic, the imagery evoked stunning in its power to subdue those who listened.

Like the Grants, the other patrons of the restaurant were soon drawn into the spell of his words. Within minutes a receptive silence had fallen over the crowd. The poet redoubled his efforts to push his words forth. He spoke of simple things, of long-ago places that lingered in his mind more sharply than his present existence, of love discovered in a shanty, of betrayal and deep sorrows too long borne.

Allegra leaned forward expectantly, drawn toward the awkward figure by the eloquence of his words. Never before in her life had she heard poetry expressed in the powerful voice of its creator.

Tears came to her eyes as she listened to his ballad for a dead child. She shivered with cold as he spoke of Januarys without heat or light or food. The anguish of his loss seared the back of her throat and made her tears burn.

He nearly lost his balance more than once, but the physical danger only added to the immediacy of the moment. He went quickly from one poem to the next, scarcely glancing at his pages, driven by the need to communicate his art to his audience, as though doubtful of its reception and therefore afraid to pause for response. With the end of each poem he dropped a sheet of paper from his hand.

Minutes passed, half an hour, and then an hour. Only when his fistful of papers had dwindled to a few sheets did he begin to sip from the bottle he held.

When at last he wound down to a dry-throated rasp, a sob escaped him. He upended his bottle, drained it, and tossed it away. For an instant he stood still and then a shudder racked him.

For a moment the room was silent. Allegra glanced at Andrew, expecting him to do something, but he merely shook his head slightly and reached for her wrist when she moved as if to rise. "Don't," he said softly.

Heart pounding in the aftershock of the poet's mesmerizing words, Allegra heard in mingled surprise and relief the first crack of applause that quickly rose to a thunderous ovation.

The man seemed not to hear it. His eyes were lifted heavenward, his hands slack at his sides. Then, suddenly, he reached into his pocket and withdrew a metal object.

Allegra had no time to see what it was, for with a shout of warning Andrew grabbed her and turned her face into his chest. There were other shouts, then a single sharp explosion, and finally the crash of crockery and furniture.

Struggling free of her brother's grasp Allegra cried, "What's happened?"

Several men rushed forth to the place where the fallen poet still lay. They hoisted him up as others cleared their table of plates and glasses and carried him there to lay him down.

A woman bent over him and then reared back. Crying out in Italian, she flung her apron over her head and backed away. Her cry was taken up by other patrons, repeated over and over until the exclamations filled the room.

Andrew stood and gripped Allegra by the arm to lift her to her feet. "Let's go before the authorities arrive!"

"Yes, best get her out of here," Achland agreed as he took Allegra's other arm. "Can't have a lady's name attached to the evening's doings."

Caught between their gentle but unyielding control, Allegra was propelled out of the restaurant and up the stairs. As they reached sidewalk level a crowd was already gathering. The shrill of a policeman's whistle carried up the block and she heard Andrew muffle a curse as they set off in the opposite direction.

"Hurry!" both men urged her as they sped along the sidewalk. Quickly they turned the corner and then came to a halt. "Wait here," Andrew demanded and stepped into the street to hail a cab with a broad wave of his hat.

The driver halted immediately, recognizing his luck at picking up a well-dressed fare in this neighborhood.

Achland hurried Allegra to the curb, where Andrew held the door for her and lifted her up into the cab.

"Aren't you coming?" Andrew asked as Achland stepped back.

"And miss an opportunity for a story?" he answered. "The man committed suicide. Goddamn!" he cried, forgetting that Allegra was within earshot. "That's about the most fascinating thing I've ever seen. Good night!"

Andrew stepped in without a reply and tapped on the ceiling. "Drive on!"

Allegra huddled in the corner, the natural human aversion to death warring with a strange sense of elation. "Was he really dead, Andy?"

"Probably," he answered shortly.

"Why?"

He turned to her, his face half lit by the street lamp they passed. "What difference does it make?"

Allegra shook her head. "I don't know."

Andrew reached for his cigarettes, noticing that his hands shook.

"It doesn't make sense, not really," she murmured. "Why would he kill himself after so fine a performance?"

"You ask hard questions," he replied. "Perhaps it was his art that killed him."

"Can one die for one's art? Did he put all his soul and spirit into his writing, leaving nothing for himself? Is that possible?"

Andrew was silent a long time. "A poet died tonight. A drunkard plagued by debts and doubts and bad habits. He tasted daily of life's bitterness. Tonight he chose the taste of death."

"That's almost poetry, Andy," she said softly. "I think he would find that a fitting eulogy."

"You're a queer girl," he answered but reached out to hug her close. "I'm sorry you witnessed that. I wanted you to have fun, and perhaps I hoped you'd be shocked just a little. I'd no idea you'd be subjected to tragedy."

She lifted her head from his shoulder. "You mean tonight wasn't an everyday occurrence in Bohemia?"

He gazed down into her face and saw with relief that she was smiling. "You're a bloodthirsty little savage, you are! Just for that you'll go straight to bed."

"He was grand and tragic, Andy. In his voice I heard that world you spoke of when you talked of Rhys. For an hour we were there with him. Didn't you feel it? It was bitter and sweet and mysterious and—and—"

"And mad," he finished.

"A grand madness, then. His talent burned through him. What would you sacrifice to possess so fine a talent?"

Andrew didn't reply.

Six

The boozy ambience of the hall was by far the best diversion America had offered him, Drayton decided. Here, at last, he had found something truly and uniquely American. No gilded den of vice such as he had frequented in London, this Bowery establishment offered unapologetically the lowest forms of iniquity to its blowsy, unregenerate denizens. This was McGlory's, nestled in the cankerous heart of the city slums.

There was no pretense at elegance. The barroom was dim and cheap. In the concert hall no velvet draperies covered the tar-papered windows. No Turkish carpets disguised the heavily scarred floors. Only the dance floor gleamed with wax, the better to entice the clientele to embrace the scores of whores and wantons gowned in silk and satin who plied their trade on the premises. The music was loud and lively. Plain wooden chairs and tables served the customers. Balconies ran along either side of the hall. Compartmented into tiny curtained rooms called French boxes, they provided privacy for entertaining women. From one of these boxes Drayton surveyed the company below.

The crowd was young, mixing freely the tawdry glitter of ill-gained wealth and the innocence of virgin poverty. Though drunk and boisterous, they wore the kind of hard faces that came from lives that lost innocence too early and joy too soon.

"We won't be alone much longer," promised Gerald Coleman, who sat by Drayton's side.

"I did wonder," Drayton murmured as his companion winked at him. They had met by chance in a Thirty-first

Street saloon where Drayton had paused in his midnight stroll along the most notorious section of Sixth Avenue. He had been in search of adventure, of a novel experience, and had found the key to it in the person of Coleman.

Drayton was not fooled by Coleman's soberly attired bulk and hearty chatter. He caught the gleam that brightened the American's eyes when he noticed Drayton's diamond studs and solid-gold pocket watch. Coleman was so interested in the watch that Drayton was certain he had not even noted the pearl-handled pistol tucked in his waistcoat.

The question of whether or not the man was a simple pickpocket was settled when Coleman offered to buy the first three rounds. Drayton assumed that he had been selected as a pigeon in some scam. The possibility of danger stimulated him. Curious to know what the man had in mind, he accepted Coleman's offer to show him a bit of "local color."

So, for the past hour he had watched with a certain amused disdain a series of entertainments unique in their tawdriness. There had been the Human Pincushion, who allowed members of the audience to stick needles and pins in him without apparent harm. Then had come a woman unicyclist who rode a wire stretched across the stage as she dropped various articles of clothing in a striptease. Following her in quick order were the Human Anvil, the Tattooed Woman, and a boozy rendition of the French cancan, with a chorus of harlots lacking style and bloomers.

"Look there!" Coleman pointed. "The fellow's forgotten to close his curtain."

In a box across the hall a young man in evening dress sat in his chair while a woman straddled him, the spread of her white thighs visible as she held her skirts aloft while she vigorously rode him.

Drayton turned an amused glance on his companion. "Are you so anxious for your turn, Coleman? Or have you discovered a new position for pleasure?"

Coleman laughed heartily. "Would take more than a young tart to teach this old dog a new trick. Still, I don't mind telling you, there ain't much a dollar won't buy here. Not much. Ah, this is more like it!" he added as the curtain behind them parted and two young women dressed as ballerinas entered with a rush of skirts and laughter. They were as different as possible: one dark, plump, and pleased with herself; the other blond, angular, and shy.

"You look in need of company," the brunette said as she came forward and sat down beside Coleman. "Oh, ain't you smart," she added as she ran her hand lightly along the length of Coleman's sleeve. "Very nice material for a very nice gentleman."

The blonde neared Drayton reluctantly, her young face heavily painted to make her look older. "You look lonely, too. Don't he look lonely, Jewel?"

"Lonely as a dog without a bone," Jewel answered, but her roguish smile was for Coleman. "Buy us a drink, birdie, and we'll sit with you a while."

The blonde tentatively reached out and stroked the expensive cloth of Drayton's evening coat. "Ooh, that's lovely you're wearing. Ain't this lovely, Jewel?"

Drayton reached up and very deliberately removed her hand from his shoulder. "Don't do that."

Jewel's eyes narrowed slightly at Drayton's tone but she said nothing. It was none of her business. He was Flora's bird. Still, she was glad she had chosen the older man. Young and handsome gentlemen were usually less generous. They seldom needed to purchase a woman and resented the cost when they did. She had chosen easier fish to fry. She leaned nearer Coleman. "If you're going to treat us to a bottle of champagne, you'd best be quick. We go on in the next act."

"But of course. Our treat. Right, sir?"

Drayton merely nodded. If Coleman thought three scotches and a bottle of champagne would render him senseless, the American very much underestimated his constitution. More interested in the fact that the entertainment was about to begin than in a flirtation, Drayton nonetheless kept the blonde at his elbow within sight. He had no desire to lose his pocket watch.

The footlights had been lit and from behind the curtain a man emerged into the limelight. "Evenin', ladies and gents," he began. "Welcome to McGlory's. Tonight's musical entertainment will commence with Miss Evelyn Connery to sing for you 'My Innocent Eyes.' "

"There ain't nothing innocent about Miss Evelyn Connery!" came a shout from the crowded floor.

The announcer looked up over the footlights, his funereal features unaltered. "Nevertheless, Miss Evelyn Connery will—"

"Ride any man here for half a dollar!" came the second rejoinder.

Laughter crackled through the hall but the announcer didn't give up. With a hand lifted high for silence, he waited until the laughter faded, then said in his lugubrious style, "Miss Evelyn Connery will sing 'My Innocent Eyes.' And at the conclusion of the song, she'll ride any dick here for half a dollar!"

Behind Drayton the curtain parted and a waiter appeared.

"What will you have, ladies? I'm a generous sort," Coleman said expansively.

"Brandy mash," the blonde said at once.

Jewel leaned forward again and Drayton saw the front of her bodice gape wide for Coleman's benefit. "I'll take a quarter instead," she said in a whispery voice.

With an indulgent chuckle Coleman produced a quarter and tucked it into her bodice, his hand lingering. "What else would you like?" he asked with an arched brow.

"Champagne!" she said in answer. "Flora and I do so like champagne. It goes straight down to tickle me right here." She pressed his hand inside her bodice against her breasts.

Coleman turned to Drayton. "What'll you have?"

"A change of scenery," Drayton replied dryly.

Coleman sighed and reluctantly removed his hand from Jewel's bodice. "You want something more interesting? I can produce it," Coleman reassured him. "There are French and German girls about. Even Spanish and Russian. Maybe you're partial to something more exotic? They cost more, of course, but I judge you're a connoisseur. I know just where to get little China dolls or black Nubians from Arabee. Virgins, every one of them. Anything to your taste, my English friend."

"What's wrong with us?" Jewel demanded.

"I prefer to observe . . . for the present," Drayton answered and turned back to the stage where a young woman stood singing.

"Well, ain't that a pity," Jewel said. As she rose she pressed both hands down the front of her gown to mold the fabric tightly over her curves. "Come on, Flora. We're wasting our time. I've told you about this sort. They carry all their flash in their purses!"

Drayton's laughter startled Jewel, but she didn't stop to discover its cause. He frightened her.

"Creepy, that's what he is," she said to Flora once they were in the hall.

"He was handsome!" Flora answered.

"Handsome as Lucifer and just as dangerous!" Jewel answered. "I've seen eyes like his before, so cold, and a smile you could cut yourself on. Knew a gentleman like him once." She unconsciously rubbed her wrists as she added, "Like to killed me, he did.'

The curtains shielding the box they'd just left parted and Drayton emerged. Jewel smiled. "Change your mind, did you?"

Drayton shook his head but reached into his pocket, then tossed the younger one a coin. "For your trouble."

Flora gaped at it. "It's a fifty-dollar gold piece!"

"Come on! That's our cue!" Jewel cried and jerked Flora after her down the corridor before the man changed his mind.

"Hey! Where're you going?" Coleman demanded as he stepped into the hall and saw Drayton leaving.

Drayton turned gracefully on his heel, his face expressionless. "I've remembered a previous engagement. Thank you, Mr. Coleman, for a most—interesting evening."

"But, you can't—!" Before the last word was fully formed, Coleman jerked back the hand he was about to lay on the Englishman's arm. "There's no need for that!" he cried as he stared at the muzzle of the pistol the man had whipped from beneath his coat.

"Good. Then, for a second time, I bid you good night, Mr. Coleman." Drayton turned away.

He did, indeed, have another appointment, one that he had debated keeping all week. His visit to the Sodom and bedlam of the Bowery had been a failed attempt to divert himself from the real purpose of his trip to New York City—as empty as the declaration he had made to himself that his "spy" must come to him. The truth was that he was afraid. He had come to New York to find her, and he had discovered where she lived. Now he must summon up his courage and take the next step. It was time.

As he strolled in a leisurely pace down the hall, he casually repocketed the pistol he had drawn on Coleman, then lightly brushed away a speck from his untouched sleeve.

Harriet gasped out her pleasure in short expulsions of ecstasy. Always afterward, she was a little ashamed of herself. But now, at the peak of her pleasure, she could no more control her responses than she could still her heart.

From behind her closed lids she saw the flickering of the bedside lamp and smiled. Andrew always liked to make love with the light on. How mortified she had been the first time. She never before looked at herself when undressed. From an early age she had always thought of herself as plain. It was the reason her mother gave for always dressing her more elaborately and expensively than her friends. Her mother always said she needed the aid of a few baubles to set her apart from the wallpaper. To have a man, a man as handsome as Andrew Grant peel away her protective layers of silk and lace and velvet had been nearly too much to bear.

That he found her beautiful was nothing short of miraculous. Hadn't he said the words? *You're beautiful*. She believed him, against all reason and knowledge and history of the past twenty-five years of her life. For Andrew she was beautiful; she allowed herself to be what he saw, not what she knew to be true.

Only at times like these, with dear adored Andrew straining over her, the muscles of his back rigid with desire, his sex buried deep within her own, his breath harsh and slow in counterpoint to his thundering heartbeat, only then was she completely free of the nightmare dread of her daily life.

A drop of his sweat struck her cheek, hesitated a moment on the crest of the bone, and then slipped down and around the side of her neck. His mouth found hers, his tongue imitating the motion of his hips. She grasped him shamelessly by the buttocks, straining with him to encourage the swelling, the feeling rising from deep within where the two of them were one.

Yes. Hurry, hurry, my love. The time is so short for us. Too short. Never will we have enough. But hurry, and when it is done, we may remember and think ourselves blessed.

Andrew lay on his back, staring at the shadows cast on the ceiling by the early dawn light. They had made love through the night, a rarity for them. It was seldom possible for them to spend even an hour together. Often he felt constrained not to push for a physical union between them for fear that she might begin to think that this was all he wanted of her.

If not this, then what else? his conscience jeered.

She was a married woman. He could have more companionship from a single lady. He could have more freedom in courting a single lady. He could have the pleasure of publicly claiming his love with a single lady. He could have marriage with a single lady. He could—not have Harriet.

Even now he was thinking of how they might next contrive to be together. There was a house party coming up, a weekend in the Connecticut countryside, with discreet and private lodgings for each guest. Could she be persuaded to join him? And then there was Allegra, dear sweet sister. How was he to explain his absence to her? She must not suspect his motives. If he were wise he would send Allegra back to his father and replace Harriet with a mistress of a different sort.

She stirred beside him, exposing the alabaster slope of a ruby-crowned breast, and he swore under his breath as his wisdom evaporated under the heat of desire. Once more, before dawn.

* * *

Dawn streaked the night sky with pale ribbons of light as the hansom stood in the shadows at the edge of Central Park. Beyond, the bulk of the Dakota took shape against the lightening sky. Gables and pyramids, peaks and towers, turrets and chimneys, dormers, finials, and flagpoles; the roof line emerged from the deep blue of night like a Gothic city perched on the crest of a solid square pedestal. Here, somewhere inside this fortress, she lay sleeping.

Drayton smiled and felt the taut pull of muscles unfamiliar with the task. The fanciful architecture appealed to his sense of the absurd. The cool night air had whisked away the lingering effects of the liquor he had earlier consumed. Still, he felt as light-headed as if he had spent the last hours in the company of a brandy decanter. He was one step closer to her, and yet a strange caution continued to hold him back. Once his quarry was run to ground, the game would end. That realization kept him from pushing the conclusion. He much preferred the dizzying intoxication of the chase which filled him now.

People of wealth thought themselves safe from prying eyes, safe from intrusion, safe from discovery. How wrong they were! By the very nature of their wealth, they made themselves conspicuous. He had found her easily. People, tradesmen in particular, were ready to boast of their transactions with the Upper Ten Thousand.

Now it is I who am the spy, lovely voyeur. Do you feel my presence? I feel yours, in my thoughts, in my blood, in my flesh.

"The opera, how droll," Allegra exclaimed as she held out the invitation to Andrew. "Shall we go?"

"If you like," he answered without looking up from his writing.

"What does one wear? Pink tulle? I think that would be perfect, don't you? Andy! You're not listening."

"Yes, I am. I'll wear pink tulle if you think I should."

Allegra sighed and turned away. There was no point in continuing their conversation, if one could term "conversation" her monologues punctuated by occasional brotherly sarcasms. Never mind, she wouldn't allow anything to spoil her excitement at being invited to one of the highlights of the New York social season now beginning in October very slowly to get under way. It was just what Andy needed to take his mind off his work and what she needed to dislodge her mind from its morbid fancies.

She glanced at Andrew, but his head was bent over his work. He was working on an article about life in MacDougal Street, but he wouldn't share it with her. Perhaps it was just as well. By silent agreement neither of them had mentioned the poet's death at Marie's nearly a month before, yet she couldn't stop thinking about it. In an effort to exorcise the memory, she had written her own essay.

It was entitled, "The Sleepless Soul." Wordsworth's description of the young poet Chatterton who had taken his life in despair of his art mirrored the scene she had witnessed. At the exquisite moment of achievement, death claimed the poet. Had he courted death or had it lain in wait for him, preying upon the vulnerable pride of a life driven to despondency?

The notion worried her even in the brightest hours of the day. Yet she felt no deep empathy for the poor soul, only a detached inquisitive desire to understand. It was ghoulish, she supposed, but she could not help it. She had witnessed a supreme moment in the human journey: a death.

The night before, just before dawn, a second thread of memory had entwined with that of the poet's death as uneasy dreams overtook her. She thought she had forgotten her last impression of Saratoga until it came back.

The dream was sharp, its clarity as blinding as sunlight splintered by crystal. Once more she was witness to a man and woman in the carnal act. When the scene had actually taken place, she had felt nothing but shock, embarrassment, and the irresistible, guilty urge to remain and watch. But the dream brought a new sensation, a quickening through her body. The hammering, clamoring anticipation gathered strength even as her mind withdrew from the reality of the event. It was a memory to which her nature responded, and in an instant came the disturbing realization that her response was not unlike what she had felt during the poet's recitation.

"Will you dawdle all evening?"

Allegra started at hearing her brother's voice so close. Her face suffused with color when she saw that he had moved from his desk to stand over her. "I was thinking. 'Fears and fancies thick upon me came.'"

"Wordsworth? Your thoughts are surely deep." He glanced at the invitation to the opera that lay in her lap. "Is the opera so very important to you?"

"Absolutely," she responded to divert him from divining her true thoughts. "Every lady wants to attend the opera. Of course, it's short notice. The pink tulle will need a thorough pressing and, oh, who can be found to do my hair?"

Andrew shook his head. "I suppose a woman would absent herself from death were she consulted beforehand and had nothing suitable to the occasion in her wardrobe."

"I should think so!" Allegra responded, but the mention of death made her uncomfortable.

"If I petrify before the evening is done, do stand me in the northwest corner of the drawing room. I'll keep better away from the sun's fading light."

Andrew accepted this whispered comment from his sister with barely a smile. He, too, was weary of the evening. Italian opera was not his forte, and their hosts, the Coreys, would never be companions of choice.

Allegra was amazed at the lack of attention paid by much of the audience to the production. A continuous hum of voices underscored the first act while sudden outbursts from the gallery crowd repeatedly interrupted the second. It seemed that for most people the real entertainment lay in observing those who occupied the boxes and orchestra seats. Every person who entered the theater was subjected to scrutiny through Mrs. Corey's opera glass, discussed, and given judgment.

As the houselights came up, signaling an intermission, Mrs. Corey turned to Allegra and said for the dozenth time that evening, "How lucky you are to be attending your first opera, Miss Grant. You must be favorably impressed."

Allegra gave her hostess a slightly faded smile. "Thanks to you, Mrs. Corey, the moment is etched irrevocably upon my mind."

Andrew heard in her voice the edge of sarcasm he hoped Mrs. Corey missed. "I, too, would like to once again add my thanks for the evening's entertainment. You were quite courageous, taking us on sight unseen."

"It was nothing, my dears," Mrs. Corey answered, thrusting forth her bosom in a manner that reminded Allegra of a courting fowl. "I find matters of social etiquette most edifying. New York society can be so awkward for the uninitiated and quite, quite unforgiving. When Mr. Corey related to me the unfortunate circumstance of your sister's situation, I was bound to respond. Why, a young person improperly launched might never recover. Your mother would have arranged matters very well for you, I'm sure, but illness knows no master, as Mr. Corey said. 'It is our duty, Mr. Corey,' is what I said. 'Our duty is to set the Grant girl off on a proper footing.'"

"Mama certainly said that, I heard her myself," offered Amy Corey, whose only function that evening had been to echo her mother's words.

The Grants merely nodded for they knew Mrs. Corey's sentiments were colored by the fact that Angus Grant was a major stockholder in Mr. Corey's company.

Mrs. Corey rose from her chair, forcing the rest of her party to follow suit. "Shall we retire for refreshment? The emotion of high drama drains me so."

"Not as much as her chatter fatigues me," Allegra murmured for Andrew's ears alone. "Is she never silent?"

The corridors of the Metropolitan Opera House were filled to capacity, but Allegra found herself breathing more easily than she had within the close confines of the box. She also found that Mrs. Corey's considerable bulk and blunt-edged voice were wonderful social battering rams as the crowd opened to make way for them.

"Oh, look, Mama! There's a footman in maroon livery!" Amy said suddenly.

"Why, yes, you're right!" Mrs. Corey turned to Allegra. "You're indeed fortunate this night. It's a wonderful portent for your first venture into society." She leaned close as though to impart the most personal of revelations. "The Vanderbilts are here!" she whispered.

"You recognize the members of their staff?" Allegra questioned in surprise.

"Dear child, all Vanderbilt servants wear the maroon livery. I've heard the Astors have followed suit with footmen in powdered wigs, though I've yet to spy one. I knew someone of consequence was in attendance. There was movement in the Vanderbilt box at the end of the first act. It isn't one of *the* Vanderbilts, for it's the wrong night. But a Vanderbilt, even a nephew or cousin, is singular enough to write up in your diary."

"Then do tell me if you spy an Astor or a Morgan," Allegra answered. "I prefer writing couplets."

Andrew murmured under his breath and reached out to catch Allegra's free arm. "One Vanderbilt is all any young lady deserves on her first evening in society. Isn't that so, Mrs. Corey? Ah!" he hurried on. "I believe I see a familiar face. Why, yes! You will allow me to borrow my sister, Mrs. Corey? We must say our hellos. Hurry along, Allegra."

"Such a burden for Miss Grant, that vivid coloring," Amy offered unenthusiastically as the Grants stole away. "Ebony is a man's coloring, don't you think? How she must abhor the attention it draws to her. It's nearly theatrical. Yes, theatrical is the only word for it."

The drama of the Grants was having its effect on the rest of the opera patrons as well. As they strolled through the crowd, they turned the heads of the sophisticated as well as the gauche.

"Is opera always so dreadful?" Allegra questioned as she walked beside Andrew.

"You're easily bored."

"Aren't you?"

He nodded. "I'm sorry. We might have declined."

"I never thought opera would be so—so dismal."

"I rather think it's the Coreys who are dismal."

"Thank goodness you recognized someone. Where is this acquaintance you'd have me meet?"

Andrew smiled blandly. "There wasn't one. I sought to save Mrs. Corey from your sharp tongue. Are you sorry?"

"Can you save me from the remainder of the evening?"

He shrugged. "We could beg off by saying you're ill."

"I do so hate ordinary excuses," she murmured.

"Miss Grant!"

Even before she turned, Allegra recognized his voice. "Dr. Boyd, what a delightful surprise."

"My dear young lady, the delight is mine, all mine."

The look of appreciation on his face gave his commonplace flattery a special meaning.

"Andrew Grant, this is a pleasure," John Boyd continued and put out his hand. "Five years, isn't it? Imagine my surprise to hear your name spoken in Saratoga just this summer. Once I met Miss Grant, I knew you must be the same Grant who once pickled my beer. Your father didn't care to hear Harvard mentioned, but your sister was kind enough to have a good word for me."

Boyd felt he was talking too much, explaining too much, but the sudden sight of the Grants had quite wiped away any thoughts he had entertained of a civil but restrained first meeting between them.

"Evening, Dr. Boyd," Andrew greeted, prompted by Allegra's nails curling into his coat sleeve when he failed to speak up at once. "I didn't recognize you, the mustache and all."

"Here's someone I know! Mr. Grant!" a young lady greeted as she came up to Andrew. She was a tiny blonde with a row of crimped curls hugging her wide brow.

This time Andrew didn't hesitate to answer. "Good evening, Miss Simpson."

She looked at him with huge blue eyes at once tender and intense. "What brings you to the opera? I'd heard you'd forsaken the civilized world for a decadent existence." Her glance moved unmistakably to Allegra.

"Allegra, this is Miss Eugenia Simpson," Andrew interposed smoothly. "Miss Simpson, my sister, Allegra."

"Sister? How sweet," Eugenia said in a thawing voice.

"Not really. I'm quite filled with pepper when the need arises," Allegra answered with an arched black brow of challenge.

"Why, isn't that clever." Eugenia colored prettily, an event, Allegra noted, that interested her brother far more than she thought it should. Blondes had an unfair advantage when it came to things like blushes. Was Andy's admiration so easily snared? Was Dr. Boyd responding to Eugenia too? As she turned to look for confirmation, she discovered in surprise that Dr. Boyd had disappeared.

"Say, Eugenia, what's a fellow need to do to get an introduction?" The deep southern drawl belonged to a tall fellow with a huge mustache who extended his hand across Miss Simpson's shoulder toward Andrew. "Silas Kenton. Grant, isn't it?"

"Mind your manners, Silas," Eugenia admonished. "This is Miss Grant, Mr. Grant's sister."

Silas Kenton bowed exaggeratedly. "Proud to make your acquaintance, Miss Grant. Your presence in the Corey box created quite a stir in the orchestra seats."

"Don't be vulgar," Eugenia chided. "Nothing that occurs in the orchestra seats could be of the slightest interest to Miss Grant, I'm sure."

Before Allegra could respond, two more young gentlemen and their ladies joined their circle, seeking introductions. Soon she found herself in the midst of a group of young amicable faces much different from the mother-dominated sons and daughters who had inhabited Saratoga. There was a self-assuredness among the group, a feeling of certainty of one's ability to dazzle. As the crowd strolling past stared, they feigned an indifference to the curious.

A few minutes later Allegra was surprised to find Dr. Boyd once again at her side, offering her a glass of lemon ice. They didn't exchange even a single word, but his concern for her comfort was flattery enough. When he faded back into the crowd again, she was left with the feeling that he would seek her out at another time.

"I'm having a few friends in for a late supper," Silas Kenton said to Andrew as the bell rang to announce the beginning of the next act. "Informal. A moment's notice, really. You and your sister will have made other plans, of course, but I hope that you'll consider altering them.''

"Why, we'd be delighted, Mr. Kenton," Allegra answered before Andrew could speak. "How wonderfully kind of you to include us."

"Yes, kind of you to invite us, Kenton," Andrew answered less enthusiastically than she. "But I'm afraid Allegra isn't feeling well."

"Oh, that," Allegra responded. "It was the heat." She smiled brightly at Dr. Boyd's thoughtfulness. "The lemon ice has completely refreshed me."

"Do say you'll come, Mr. Grant," Eugenia pleaded sweetly. "I'd consider it a special favor if you would."

"In that case, we'd be delighted to accept," Andrew replied, though he was mystified by Allegra's sudden interest in people whom she scarcely knew.

"Delightful! You'll ride with us," Eugenia said. "Tommy, be a dear and tell Brooks to bring the carriage round. We're ready to leave." She turned back to Allegra. "One meets the most interesting people at Kenton's place. Never the ordinary sort at all."

"Is he fond of artists?" Allegra asked.

"Whatever do you mean?"

"Writers, painters, literary people."

"Oh, my, no! Don't give it another thought," Kenton answered. "Wouldn't think of filling my drawing room with rabble-rousers."

"Even musicians and lawyers must be handled sparingly," Eugenia agreed. "One or two, perhaps, but never more. They might disturb or, worse, bore the other guests."

"Ideas are all very fine within the walls of academia," Kenton added with a grin, "but never on a social occasion."

"I see," Allegra replied.

"You do play whist, Miss Grant?"

"Cards? Hardly ever."

"Well, you have a treat in store," Eugenia said. "We don't usually encourage new people to join us, but you must sit at my table. No, I insist. We play for the merest pittance. Never more than a hundred exchanges hands."

A hundred dollars! Allegra glanced at Andrew but he was

looking over her head with an intent expression. Luckily, Eugenia did not seem to expect a definite reply for she had turned to chat with another of the group.

Her interest piqued, Allegra followed the direction of Andy's gaze and saw a young woman standing a little apart from an animated group of gentlemen. Her robin's-egg blue gown, beaded and trimmed with rows of Venetian lace, was an extravagant item, just the sort of thing that would be written up in *Harper's*. The gown demanded a personality to equal it, but the fragile blonde seemed weighed down by her finery. She stood with head slightly bowed and her hands folded tightly together before her. Suddenly the lady lifted her chin and looked directly at them. Allegra saw her give a fractional shake of her head and then resume her neglected pose.

"Who is she?" Allegra asked as she touched Andrew's sleeve.

Andrew looked down at his sister in surprise. "Who's who?"

"The lady in blue. She acknowledged you."

"You must be mistaken," he answered blandly. "I caught no lady's eye. Besides, Eugenia wouldn't like it."

Eugenia turned, hearing Andrew speak her name. "Wouldn't like what?"

"Wouldn't like it if I spurned the invitation of a beautiful lady," he returned. "Therefore, we'll go round to Kenton's for an hour. But first, we must give our regrets to the Coreys. Please excuse us," he said as he drew Allegra away.

"We shouldn't have accepted that invitation," he said firmly once they were out of earshot.

"Why ever not? Eugenia Simpson couldn't possibly be worse company than the Coreys."

"Eugenia's set has a reputation as a fast crowd."

"Really? They seem so ordinary."

Andrew eyed her sideways. "Eugenia is in what you might call a unique position. She's been engaged these last three years."

"Three years? Why so long?"

"Her fiancé is an Austrian aristocrat with political connections. They're to be married at Christmas."

"It all sounds very unexceptional to me," Allegra declared. "What's unique about being engaged?"

"It's not the engagement, it's the fact that Eugenia lives on her own. She's an orphan who came into an extraordinarily large inheritance upon her eighteenth birthday. A maiden aunt lives with her but can't control her. Eugenia's an independent woman."

"How I envy her that," Allegra responded, ready to amend her first impression of the lady.

"Even if she gambles at cards for entertainment?"

"I suppose an affianced lady with an absent suitor must amuse herself as best she can."

"Then I hope you've brought enough currency for the whist table."

"Oh!" Allegra had thought he had not heard that part of her conversation. "Must I play?"

"Not if I can help it!"

"Then do let's go, if only for a short while. They're the first interesting people I've met. Please, just a little while?"

Andrew sighed. Harriet's denial of his request to see her had ruined his plans for the latter part of the evening. "How can I resist you?"

"Don't try!" she answered pertly.

Seven

"Satan take your luck, Sarah! I'm done for!"

"Don't be a poor loser, Edith. You know how Eugenia hates a poor loser."

"Sarah's right," Eugenia agreed as she gathered the

cards strewn upon the felt tabletop. "We mustn't frighten away our newest player."

"Miss Grant has nothing to complain of," Edith answered with a pointed look at the paper money scattered at Allegra's elbow.

"Beginner's luck," Eugenia pronounced. "You believe in beginner's luck, don't you, Miss Grant?"

Glancing down, she saw that the cash pile at her place was by far the largest. She had scarcely heeded the amounts of money changing places at the close of each hand. "I suppose I must," Allegra answered.

During the past two weeks, she and Andy had been invited to dinner at Eugenia Simpson's on three occasions. She enjoyed the outings but dreaded the high-stakes card games which the ladies played after dinner. After each evening's game, she promised herself that she would find an escape from the card table, but that wasn't so easily accomplished. She had agreed to come tonight, though Andy had declined Eugenia's invitation to dinner, because not to do so would have meant spending the evening alone.

"I suggest we break for a champagne refill." Eugenia laid a perfectly manicured hand over the card stack, and the ruby engagement ring on her third finger seemed to wink with a proprietary gleam. Several times Allegra had been tempted to inquire about Eugenia's aristocratic fiancé, but the subject never came up. She found it extraordinary when Andy said that the wedding was to take place right after Christmas.

"Don't leave your winnings scattered about for the draft to catch," Eugenia admonished. "It creates disorder and I abhor disorder." She scooped up the paper money and presented the leafy green bouquet, which Allegra accepted with a blush. "Thank you."

"Mr. Grant, you appear at last!" Eugenia said happily as Andrew strolled into the library. She possessively threaded her arm through his. "Your sister's luck has quite depleted my enthusiasm for this game. Now that you've escaped whatever dreary business kept you away, it's your responsibility to find other entertainment for me. Something in which skill, daring, and chance play a part."

"Miss Simpson, the possibilities stagger me."

Allegra's lifted brows brought no discernible response from her brother. His full attention was upon his flirtatious partner. Only when she moved to walk past him with her "bouquet" of bills did she catch his eye. "Sister dear, it's *de trop* to display your winnings in that manner."

"I considered making a corsage of it," she replied, "but the color clashes with my gown." On impulse, she pushed the money into the front of his evening coat. "You decide how best to arrange it."

She turned away quickly and left the table, wondering where Andy had been. He had become secretive of late and she meant to find out why. But at this moment she was more determined to escape the card room before Andy glanced at his pocket watch and declared that it was time for them to say good night.

Each evening after dinner the number of Eugenia's guests swelled. The original dinner party of twelve had now increased threefold. Eugenia's comment on the first evening had been, "Oh, they're the merest acquaintances. One must have acquaintances, you know."

Allegra had wished that Dr. Boyd had been among Eugenia's acquaintances. She had not seen him since the night of the opera and then only for a few moments.

"Do you find the company of the socially insatiable more palatable in New York than in Saratoga?"

Allegra turned with a startled smile. It was Dr. Boyd! He had come upon her silently, as, she decided, appeared to be his habit. He was dressed in a tweed suit, much too informal for the occasion, and she wondered fleetingly if he had come directly from the hospital. "Why, Dr. Boyd, I had no idea you were among the company."

The little secret smile she had first noticed in Saratoga appeared. "I'm often present but not seen. It's an affliction of possessing a middle-class heritage."

"I detect disapproval in your tone. What have I said to displease you?"

His enigmatic smile remained. Each time he spied her he felt a slipping away of the social boundaries that he had striven to erect most of his life. A month ago he would never have sought to waste an evening among the Ten Thousand. Yet a chance conversation with a member of Eugenia's set made him aware that Allegra would be here tonight, and so he had crashed. But he couldn't tell her that. She would think him drunk or a little mad. "Why should you think I hold you in anything less than esteem, Miss Grant?"

"Then why did you slight your middle-class heritage? I'm no snob. I'd consider you an equal in any case."

"How do you come to that conclusion?"

"You're Andy's friend," she answered evasively.

"That's enough for you? My goodness, Miss Grant, you're easily accommodated. Your brother's a fine fellow, I grant you, but are all his associations of the first class?"

"You must mean his bohemian friends. I've met a few of them and they strike me as both more interesting and greater snobs than even present company." She was satisfied to see surprise replace his smug expression. "Does my frankness disturb you, Doctor?"

She had astonished him, reminding him once again that her unpredictability was charming. "I admire your frankness," he said softly, "but there are others who might misunderstand your admission."

"I couldn't care less about such pettiness. At least Andy's rascally friends have ideas to occupy their minds, which is more than can be said for those present. Shall I demonstrate?"

Turning to face the room, she singled out a young woman in yellow dimity whom she approached. "Do come to my aid. Dr. Boyd and I are having a most interesting discussion. I say Chopin was a far superior composer to Liszt. Wouldn't you agree?"

The young woman looked taken aback. "Chopin? Didn't he have that scribbling Frenchwoman as his—well." She blushed.

"His mistress," Allegra supplied in annoyance, "though what that has to do with his music I can't imagine."

"Inspiration, perhaps?" offered the young woman's male companion.

"Then Liszt should win!" rejoined another man who

stood nearby. "Liszt collected mistresses as some men collect butterflies."

"That must have been most uncomfortable for those who suffered his attentions," Allegra answered, adding after a moment's pause, "To be pinned to a velvet cloth would ruin one's gown."

The answering masculine laughter was quite satisfying to her ego, though she did notice that several of the ladies exchanged disapproving looks.

"Speaking your mind again, sis?" Andrew asked as he walked over with Eugenia still on his arm.

"A bit," she replied. "Dr. Boyd doesn't wholly approve."

Andrew turned to Boyd. "Evening, Doc. What brings you to this end of town?"

"The search for pleasant company," John answered with a nod in Allegra's direction.

As Andrew's brows rose, Allegra said in vexation, "He doesn't mean it. He prefers middle-class virtues. Isn't that true, Doctor?"

"If it pleases you to think so, then I'll bow to your perception of me," he answered lightly.

Andrew missed none of the subtle flirtation between his sister and the doctor. The question was, why should Allegra give the fellow a moment's notice when there were a dozen men present who were more witty and better dressed?

"Dr. Boyd was telling me how he detests the idle wiles of the socially elite," Allegra said, unable to resist an opportunity to continue the controversy.

" 'Detest' is hardly a fair description," he answered. "I believe that the cream of society has a responsibility to be more than mere ornaments. They have a responsibility to see to the needs of the less fortunate; to provide laws to protect women and children from the trauma and degradation of sweatshop labor, poverty, and disease. I wouldn't visit upon you any of the harsh realities that are a part of the daily lives of this city's poor, but that doesn't mean that you shouldn't be aware of them. If that makes me something of a crusader, then I see little harm in it."

"A pretty speech, Dr. Boyd," Eugenia said genially, but she glanced about the room to gauge the reaction of her other guests. "I had no idea that physicians were as prone to sermonizing as parsons."

"I hope my presence doesn't disturb you, Miss Simpson."

"Not at all, Doctor!" Eugenia answered a little too warmly to seem genuine. "You're welcome anytime, though you're likely to find the company a bit frivolous for your tastes."

"Not all of us find conversation about serious subjects disturbing," Allegra volunteered.

"I'm a man of action myself," another of the gentlemen remarked. "I prefer to do rather than preach."

Eugenia brightened. "Do you, like Dr. Boyd, venture into the slums, Mr. Kirby?"

The young man blushed deeply. "I have, a time or two. It's not the sort, uh, I couldn't . . ."

"Andy, why don't you tell them about your adventures in the artistic colonies of the city?" Allegra suggested, impatient with Mr. Kirby's timidity.

"This isn't the time or place for that."

"Oh, please, Mr. Grant," Eugenia encouraged.

Andrew smiled deprecatingly. "It's difficult to know where to begin."

"The food is quite good . . . so I hear," Allegra remarked with enough of a pause to receive an alarmed look from Andrew. "I've been reading extensively on the subject. Let me see. Ah, yes. I quote: 'Cafe society of the freest sort is best fortified by wine and words. Here the dreams of the artist and the poet, the hopes of the émigré starveling, and grand designs of society's young scion, are woven into the harmonic pattern envisioned by the architects of our nation's finest tapestry, the Constitution.'"

"What a magnificent sentiment!" Eugenia enthused. "Wherever did you read that?"

"In Andy's essay on bohemian life," she replied with a sideways glance at her brother that dared him to contradict her. "It's quite good and should be published."

"Is that so?" A new man joined the conversation, a tall slender man who, the instant she saw him, made Allegra wonder how she could have missed noticing him before. His hair was outrageously long, flowing in abandon over his collar and sticking out wildly above his ears. His goatee was sharply pointed and his eyes were of a startling penetration.

"Allow me to introduce myself," he said with a flourish of his hand. "I am Sidney Luska, a journalist of some small note and sharer of the torch that illuminates the plight of our immigrant brothers."

Allegra felt Dr. Boyd slip away from her side, but before she could wonder at his action, Andrew spoke.

"Luska!" he greeted heartily and offered his hand. "I've heard of you, read your work. It's an honor, sir!"

Eugenia's greeting was less enthusiastic for he had a suspiciously Semitic-sounding name. "Mr. Luska. Have we met?"

The writer turned his extravagant gaze on her and took her small hand in his. "Dear lady, if we have not, the loss is mine. A mere mortal stands mute before your beauty."

She wasn't a fancier of journalists nor particularly broad-minded, but she was female and his elaborate praise assuaged her misgivings concerning his ethnic origin. "Welcome to my home, Mr. Luska."

He saluted her hand in the French fashion and then turned to Andrew. "I should like to read your work. If I'm as impressed with the rest of it as I was with your sister's quotation, I've contacts which you may find useful."

Andrew looked abashed. "I didn't expect to have my work bandied about when I allowed my sister a glimpse." He glanced sideways at Allegra. "She may have misquoted me for I can scarce recall writing those words. In any case, it's not finished."

Allegra said sweetly, "Mr. Luska wouldn't mind if you sent your rough draft round, would you, sir?"

"But, of course not," Luska replied.

"Thank you, I'll remember that." Andrew withdrew his watch in an agitated motion. "Hm. It's nearly midnight. Time for us to bid our hostess adieu. Allegra?"

"I'll fetch my wrap," she said and turned toward the library where she had left her coat. Just inside the archway stood John Boyd. "Why did you forsake us?"

John held up his cigarette. "Miss Simpson doesn't allow smoking in the drawing room. In any case I didn't think you'd miss me. You were quite engrossed in the conversation. Doesn't your brother object when you embarrass him as you did me?''

"The green silk jacket," Allegra directed the maid before turning to Boyd. "Why is a woman considered the most willful of creatures when she dares speak her mind as men do daily?"

"You didn't speak your mind. You sought to provoke the company, which you did. That smacks of tantrum."

"Ah, yes. It was remiss of me to forget that when women aren't fools they're children. How utterly fatiguing it must be for gentlemen to be constantly consorting with the simple and the ungovernable."

John looked into her eyes, which were shadowed by anger and some unexpressed emotion that moved him. She didn't simper or seek his favor, but neither did she dismiss him as an inferior whose opinion was of no consequence. She met him as an equal, something he couldn't remember any woman ever having done. "May I call on you, Miss Grant?"

Allegra felt a quickening of her pulse, an emotional response new to her experience but welcome just the same.

"Am I refused, Miss Grant?"

"I would be delighted to receive you, Dr. Boyd," she answered. "Say, Sunday at three o'clock?"

He bowed slightly. "If my schedule permits, I'd be honored. I'll notify you."

His acceptance wasn't exactly a wholehearted reply, but she supposed she deserved it after the way she had treated him earlier in the evening.

He glanced up at the sound of voices and frowned. "If you will excuse me, I must go," he said and turned away as Andy entered the room with Eugenia.

"Ready, Allegra?"

"Yes, Andy."

At the door Eugenia addressed Allegra, her eyes bright with some secret knowledge. "May I call on you tomorrow?"

Allegra nodded. "Certainly."

"I can't face Luska again," Andrew said once he and Allegra entered a cab. "You know very well I didn't write the lines you quoted tonight. No doubt he recognized them as written by someone else but was too polite to call me a plagiarist before my sister. Whom did you quote in my name?''

She smiled, thinking of her essay. ''You needn't worry. Mr. Luska hasn't read the lines. They aren't in print.''

''That's not an answer.''

Allegra shrugged, her thoughts running ahead to Dr. Boyd's impending visit. ''Do you suppose the new draperies will be hung before the weekend? We should give a party now that we've friends to invite.''

Andrew groaned. As a bachelor he wasn't expected to entertain in his rooms, though some gentlemen did bring off a simple supper now and again. But, he supposed, now that his sister was in town, he should make some effort in that direction. ''I might be persuaded to consider a party were you to tell me whose work you quoted tonight.''

''A poor obscure scribbler whose work will never see print. Now about our party . . .''

''So you see, it was too, too wicked of you to mention the bohemian quarter and then leave us. It was all so exciting. Why, I couldn't sleep a wink for hours after you'd gone. Aunt Flora wanted to send for a doctor but I resisted.''

''You might have asked Dr. Boyd,'' Allegra suggested.

Eugenia flushed. ''Yes, well, I don't know that it's proper for a lady to be tended by an unmarried gentleman. Even if he were married, it would be awkward. Which, Aunt Flora says, is the reason why doctoring isn't a suitable occupation for a gentleman in the first place.'' She paused to take a sip of her tea.

''Another macaroon?'' Allegra offered the plate of cookies in hopes that the morsel would keep her guest occupied while she thought of a way to get rid of her.

She accepted one. ''Couldn't eat a thing before noon. I must appear haggard. Afternoon light is so unkind.''

Allegra smiled. Dressed in primrose yellow with a matching hat set at a tilt on her golden head, Eugenia Simpson looked remarkably well for someone who claimed not to have slept a wink. "I admire your courage in setting forth after so trying an evening. We might have had tea another day."

Eugenia cocked her head to one side, the gesture too graceful to be unfashionable. "You think me a silly woman," she declared in a voice quite different from the breathless speech she most often adopted. "You needn't respond. I think so myself often enough." She set her cup aside, her face grown quite serious. "I don't know why I should appeal to you. Perhaps it's your contempt for what I am that makes me seek you out."

"My contempt?" Allegra repeated in acute embarrassment. "Dearest Eugenia, if by any gesture or word I have given you the slightest offense, allow me—"

"No apology's necessary, I assure you. I phrase myself badly. It isn't often that I express opinions on anything of importance. You've heard that I'm to be married?"

"It's been mentioned," Allegra answered, glad that the subject that had so enticed her was at last being introduced into conversation.

"His name is Baron Josef von Wallenstein, an Austrian aristocrat of impeccable breeding and the bluest of bloodlines. Any American girl should think herself lucky—no, blessed—to be honored by a proposal of marriage from such a man."

"So it seems," Allegra replied diplomatically.

"You agree? Of course you do. Everybody agrees. That's why I am so—so—so—" To Allegra's astonishment, Eugenia burst into tears.

Years in a girls' boarding school had accustomed Allegra to inexplicable tears. Offering first a linen napkin and then her own shoulder, she soothed her guest with equanimity.

"Such a fool! Such a fool!" Eugenia murmured between sobs.

"You're unhappy and the reason for it is quite obvious. You don't wish to marry Baron von Wallenstein."

"Oh, but I do!" Eugenia took a deep breath. "It's just that I don't know what he's like or what he thinks of me. I don't even know if I'll like Vienna."

"Don't know—?" Allegra swallowed her amazement. "How did you come to be engaged?"

"Through a photograph." Eugenia blushed. "Aunt Flora carries a photograph of me opposite the clock face of the jet locket she wears. Aunt Flora has lived with me ever since Mama died. She was on the Continent three years ago and met the baron. I've never understood why she showed him the picture of me, but she says he declared that he fell in love on the spot. He wrote a request for my hand to my father which Aunt Flora carried back to New York with her. Papa accepted on my behalf, for I was away in school."

"That's medieval!" Allegra pronounced, her voice full of unloosed laughter. The betrothal sounded like the plot of a penny dreadful.

"Not really," Eugenia answered seriously. "I've always fancied myself worthy of royalty." She paused and blushed again. "That sounds conceited, but it isn't. Mama always said a lady should know her worth. If she doesn't, no one else can be expected to."

"But surely you can't be held to an engagement with a man you've never met."

"I don't suppose I could, but I do wish to marry the baron. Just before the influenza claimed Papa, I promised him that I would, to ease his mind over his final hours."

"Then why are you crying?"

Eugenia smiled. "You'll think me a little mad. The baron's been very patient. He has written me once a month for nearly three years and often sends me presents. He's very important at court, you see, and can't come to see me. Yet he wanted me to debut in New York. That's why we didn't marry when I finished school. Then Papa died, and I was in mourning for a year. Last fall I made my debut, and it was everything I'd hoped for. Well, nearly. I didn't fall in love."

"Fall in love?" Allegra repeated in bafflement.

Eugenia sighed. "All my friends had several love affairs before they accepted marriage proposals. It's expected. Fanny Frasier claims to have fallen in love at least once a week during her season."

Allegra's fertile imagination couldn't picture New York

debutantes behaving like wantons. "How does one conduct such an affair?"

"Oh, accidental meetings in the park when one is out with friends. Visits to a lady's box at the opera. A basket of flowers from a secret admirer. I confess I did receive rather more than my share of flowers from secret admirers, but what's a lady to think when none of her suitors will admit their tendre for her?"

"That she's already engaged?" Allegra suggested pertly.

"Oh, that shouldn't matter. Fanny Frasier was engaged for three months when one suitor threatened to murder himself if she didn't break it off and marry him instead. Of course she didn't, and of course he didn't. At one time, I tried to snare your brother's interest, but he keeps his heart closely guarded."

"Andy's always been impossible," Allegra replied with a chuckle, for she didn't wish to discuss Andy's private life or admit that she was as ignorant about it as everyone else.

"The baron and I are to be married in a small ceremony in New York and then sail to the Continent where his family wishes us to wed a second time in the style befitting a baron and baroness. So, you see, there's very little time."

"Very little time for what?"

"Why, for me to fall in love."

"If it's Andrew—"

"No, no, I'm thinking of a more untraditional connection. A random moment, a meeting of strangers."

Allegra stared at her. "What has this to do with me?"

"When last night you mentioned poets and artists, I knew instantly that's who it must be, a man so sensitive to his own emotions that he can recognize at once tender feelings in the mute heart of a fellow creature."

"Rubbish, Eugenia," Allegra said acerbically. "You're too sensible to give speech to such thoughts."

Eugenia looked crushed. "I thought you'd understand."

"What I understand is that you're wishing that you weren't engaged to wed a man you've never met. Once you're wed, you'll remember this as just a violent case of nerves." *Goodness*, Allegra thought, *I sound just like Mama*.

"Have you never longed to do something wonderful and wild and thoroughly beyond sanctioning?"

What lady of spirit wouldn't like to see more of the world than the clamshell existence that she is allowed? Allegra thought of how she'd felt the day she ran away and then how she'd felt when she realized how much she had hurt her parents. If she related her experience it might serve to dampen Eugenia's enthusiasm.

Eugenia's eyes were shining when she finished. "I think you're terribly brave."

"I'm not," Allegra maintained. "I came to New York because I knew Andy was here. My parents were hurt terribly, and later I realized that I needlessly exposed them to possible scandal."

"But, if you can do as your heart commands, so can I."

"Who would introduce you to these artists? You—you can't think that I—?" Allegra protested as Eugenia's smile became roguish.

"Why not? You've read your brother's essay and must know where they're to be found."

"You can't truly expect me to assist you in this enterprise? If Andy found out . . ."

"He need never know," she countered. "He has his club nights and his bachelor dinner parties. One such evening we could slip away and return without anyone being the wiser. Why, you could say you're spending the night with me. But that's a splendid idea! Aunt Flora's going on a short trip next week and she's asked me to find a companion to keep me company during her absence. No one would suspect a thing. It's perfect."

"It's madness. It's folly! It's—it's—unthinkable. Absolutely not!"

After a futile attempt to swirl the long thin strands of spaghetti onto her fork as she had seen the other patrons do, Allegra abandoned her exercise and cut the pasta into segments she could manage.

The delicious aroma and raucous din of Marie's was as

she remembered it. She and Eugenia had taken a table near the door, the hurried exit required during her first visit uppermost in Allegra's mind, and so the rambunctious cafe life continually flowed past them with the stream of patrons. In one corner a man with an accordion sat on a stool playing an Italian air. The conversation nearby was appreciatively low, though never entirely abandoned.

"Aren't you hungry?" she asked when she noticed Eugenia's untouched plate. "Isn't it everything you expected?"

"It's, well, different," Eugenia replied with a decided lack of enthusiasm as she eyed with distaste the tattered cuffs and untrimmed hair of a new arrival. "What is that horrid odor? Oh! Did you ever!"

Allegra turned to see a smartly dressed young woman who had hiked her skirts halfway up her calf so that a small black boy could apply polish to her shoe.

"Doesn't she see the way those gentlemen are staring?" Eugenia remarked.

"I believe," Allegra answered, "that's the point."

"You don't mean . . . ?" Eugenia's voice fell to a whisper. "She's a harlot?"

Allegra blushed but refused to reveal her own innocence in the matter. "I shouldn't wonder, though appearances can be deceiving."

Eugenia's eyes grew enormous. "I shouldn't like to be mistaken for *that* sort."

"You're perfectly safe," Allegra answered. "Think of this as a play. Just look there."

At a nearby table a rowdy group of men and women were engaged in a heated debate. The subject of the conversation was lost in the confusion of voices as both sides seemed convinced that emotional verbosity would carry the day. With a scraping of chairs, a woman and man on opposite sides of the table came to their feet, their faces within inches as they shouted at one another. Suddenly the man grabbed the woman by the shoulders and pulled her to him for a quick, hard kiss. The woman, when released, playfully boxed his ear and then caught his face in her hands and kissed him back. The resulting laughter seemed to end the discussion, for when the couple sat down, voices subsided into more natural tones.

"She should've slapped his face!" Eugenia said indignantly.

Allegra glanced at her with sympathy. It really was too bad that Eugenia's courage hadn't followed her into the cafe, for she had seen the effect of Eugenia's resourcefulness when she schemed to make her wishes come true.

The clothes they wore were borrowed from two of Eugenia's maids. What reason she gave the girls Allegra couldn't imagine. With their white shirts tucked into navy serge skirts, grosgrain ties, and straw boaters, they looked just like shop girls out on the town for the evening. Even Andrew, who had his own opinion of Miss Simpson, had been persuaded by Eugenia to agree to the visit.

She suspected that his readiness to agree was spurred in part by the invitation he had received to spend the weekend in the wilds of Connecticut before autumn's chill took a firm grip on the season. He said the invitation could be altered to include Allegra, but he didn't argue when she insisted upon staying with Eugenia.

"I thought there'd be at least one or two romantic figures present," Eugenia murmured, "but I don't see a one, do you?"

Allegra didn't answer, for the thing she least expected had come to pass. Among the throng entering Marie's was a man she recognized. It was the writer Rhys.

They saw one another at the same moment so there was nothing she could do but watch dumbfounded as he made his way straight toward her with a cocky grin of recognition.

"Faith! What have we here?" he boomed as he reached them. "Well, if it isn't Grant's housekeeper."

"Mr. Rhys," Allegra acknowledged. To deny knowing him would doubtless only make him more determined to embarrass her. Also, she wasn't too rattled to realize that he hadn't announced for all to hear who she really was.

"I don't recall your name, darlin'," he said.

"Miss Stone," she lied promptly.

He nodded. "Happy to make the acquaintance. Don't mind if I do." He reached for the empty chair at their table and sat down. He wore a clean brown jacket with a velvet collar, but his tie was loose and his red hair fell carelessly across his freckled brow. "Does your employer know what his housekeeper does on her night off?"

"No," Allegra answered frankly, her gaze holding his.

"Ah, well, he'll not be hearing from the likes of me," he answered with a wink.

Allegra wished she trusted him, but she suspected that his good spirits were fueled by liquor, and that made him unreliable.

"Aren't you going to introduce me to your gentleman friend?" Eugenia prompted in faint annoyance.

"This is Miss Sampler," Allegra said, improvising on the spot.

"Oh, don't be silly," Eugenia interrupted. "I'm Miss Simpson."

"Mr. O'Conner, Rhys O'Conner, not to put too fine a point on it." Rhys held out his hand. "It's grand to meet you, Miss Simpson."

"And you," Eugenia murmured, amazed to find her slim hand engulfed in a workman's rough grasp.

"I've an artist friend who'd be willing to pay you three dollars a day to pose for him. It's your hair, you see. Like ripened wheat." Rhys touched the curl dipping down into Eugenia's brow. "I might make a sonnet to it myself, given the proper inspiration."

Eugenia sighed, "I've always wanted my portrait done. Only three dollars a sitting, did you say?"

"It depends. He might give you four." He eyed her slowly from head to toe. "He's doing a portrait of Psyche for a gentleman with a high regard for feminine beauty."

"And he'd pay me?" Eugenia smiled her best smile. "Now that's a singular offer. Mama's always said portrait painters charged far too much for their efforts."

Suddenly the import of Rhys's offer became clear to Allegra. She rose. "Come, Eugenia! We're leaving."

"But why?" Eugenia asked as she came irresolutely to her feet. "I'd rather like to have my portrait done."

"It's not a portrait he speaks of. He asked you to pose!" Her voice dropped to a whisper. "In the nude!"

"In the nude!" Eugenia exclaimed in horror and, blanching, sank back into her chair in a half swoon.

"I hope you're satisfied," Allegra said as she glared at Rhys. "You make a fine bully, Mr. O'Conner."

"*Mushla!* I didn't know she'd carry on so. 'Twas only a jest." Pulling a ragged handkerchief from his pocket, he bent over Eugenia. "Poor colleen. Strike me dead if ever I frighten another woman me livelong life!" Crooning Gaelic endearments, he patted her cheek while Allegra stood by in embarrassment and frustration.

After a moment Eugenia's eyes opened and she drew back from his solicitations with a sob. "What a fool I am!"

The wail of contrition sounded vaguely familiar to Allegra, but Rhys heard in it the trumpet call for masculine defense against her self-abuse.

"Never say that, lass. A man'd think himself set right atop the glories to be worthy of the likes of you."

Unimpressed, Allegra said, "I hope your considered pen shows your poetic efforts to better effect. That was perfectly awful."

"Allegra!" Eugenia admonished in an injured voice. "I think Mr. O'Conner's words were rather sweet. They were original, weren't they? I do so hate it when people quote those who're long dead. What could they know about the present?" She looked up through her lashes at the man who both frightened and intrigued her. "Besides, it's all so morbid, don't you think? Rather like robbing a crypt."

"For you, colleen, I'd make words ring in peals of homage. Only tell me you'll not be turning me away from the inspiration of your lovely presence."

Eugenia twisted his handkerchief between her fingers. He had embarrassed her moments before, a practice she couldn't abide, yet she sensed with female intuition that there'd been admiration in his lewd suggestion.

Allegra scowled at her friend, unable to believe that she would even consider the matter. "It's getting late."

"You wouldn't be thinking of leaving?"

Allegra glared at him. If he chose, he could create a great deal of mischief. "What do you suggest, Mr. O'Conner?"

"Why, nothing but a straight-as-you-go invitation to call on the lady."

"You know that's quite impossible."

But Rhys was no longer looking at Allegra. He smiled at Eugenia. "I'm thinking there's ways and then there's ways.

There's parks where any man can walk free as you please. Isn't that so, Miss Simpson?''

Meeting young men in secluded spots caused Eugenia no undue embarrassment. After all, it was part of the adventure she'd planned for herself. He wasn't handsome, but he was a poet and he'd already paid her many compliments. He was the perfect young man to fall in love with her. If she passed an indiscreet hour or two in his company, she'd have memories to take the chill from long Viennese evenings when the newness of marriage had worn through, as all her married friends assured her it would. Still, a lady never acquiesed without a struggle. "I'll not be pressed on the matter," she said softly.

"A man wouldn't press a flower, Miss Simpson, for fear of crushing it. I'd be happy to escort you home. Marie's isn't a place for ladies, that it isn't!''

Eight

"You wrote this?''

"Well, yes I did," Allegra answered, vexed to have returned home from her weekend with Eugenia only to discover that Andy was there before her. How he had come upon her unposted letters she was too agitated to ask.

"You wrote this," Andrew repeated. The astonishment of it wouldn't leave him. He had come upon Allegra's cache of letters quite innocently and wouldn't have read them had he not seen that they were all addressed to him. Beginning to read them in chronological order, he had spent the first hour in amused appreciation of her rueful wit in describing their first weeks together. He even smiled when he read the words she had quoted to Luska that night at Eugenia's. They were hers, the minx! Then he had come to the letter written after their tragic night at Marie's.

The breadth and passion of her haunting tribute to a man she had never actually met stunned him. The power of her words captured in intensity and lyric quality the doomed poet's own words. He read it twice before he could begin to assesss it critically. And as he did, the latent talent of the writer kept deflecting his best efforts to discredit it as the whim of a facile amateur.

"Is it that bad?" Allegra ventured as he continued to stare at the paper in his hand. "Oh, give it to me!" She snatched the letter from his hand and crumpled it. "I'll throw them all away!"

"No!" Andrew pried her fingers loose from the paper and began smoothing it out. "This is good, quite good." Why, he wondered, did his voice sound unconvincing? The writing was better than good. It was wonderful. Why couldn't he tell her so?

"What are you doing here?" he asked, remembering suddenly that he was to have collected her from Eugenia's after the dinner hour.

"I might ask the same of you." She looked at the disarray in the drawing room. "You've been home for hours."

"I didn't go away," he answered distractedly.

"You didn't— Why not?"

"My plans changed, that's all."

"Why didn't you inform me?" she pressed, feeling that she had been in some way betrayed by his presence in the city when she thought him in another state.

He shrugged. "Why spoil your weekend?" He looked at her, scrutinizing her from head to foot. "You did enjoy yourself?"

"Yes, of course. How could I keep from doing so?" she replied lightly, strolling about the room to avoid his intent gaze. "Eugenia's diverting company, if fatiguing."

"I did try to warn you."

"Yes, you did. Well, I've learned my lesson." She deliberately turned her back to him. "If you didn't leave town, how did you occupy your time?"

"In the usual pursuits."

"Does that mean that you visited your unsavory artist friends?"

"Actually, I spent the weekend at my club. There seemed no point in knocking about the apartment alone."

She turned back to him. "You missed me?"

He smiled ruefully. "I suppose I did."

She launched herself into his arms. "Oh, Andy, I missed you, too! Let's not ever be apart again. I was wrong to go to Eugenia's. She's spoiled and selfish and knows nothing about anything really important. Do you know she asked me who Euterpe was? Imagine not knowing the muse of lyric poetry?"

"Not everyone has had the benefit of your classic education, sis," he answered indulgently.

"I don't care. I'm home now and I won't stray again."

"Mother wrote. The letter's on your bed."

"How is Aunt Caroline?"

"Better, but still very weak. It seems that each member of the staff has come down with the fever in turn. Mother fears she'll be away at least another month, unless we need her."

"I miss her, I do. But truthfully, I hope she'll stay in South Carolina another month."

"Father wired. He'll be in town on Wednesday."

Allegra sighed. "He won't be staying here, will he?"

"He's taking his usual rooms at the Plaza and he expects you to stay with him."

"Then we must think of a good reason why I can't." She gave her brother a speculative glance. "Now that the decorating of our apartment is complete, we should have a party. Nothing elaborate, just a few people. I was thinking of inviting that Mr. Luska we met at Eugenia's. He said he might be able to help you place your work. He could be just the boost you need."

Andrew brushed a curl back from her brow with an affectionate touch. "You do care about my writing, don't you? Then I'll share a secret with you. I've already seen Luska. I went by his rooms on Saturday. He took me round to the Tile Club and then to Lüchow's where I met James Huneker. I have an assignment!''

"Andy, that's wonderful! Who's going to publish it? What's it about?''

"It's my piece on the bohemian scene, and, no, I won't show it to you. Call it superstition or whatever you like.'' His face was flushed with excitement. "I think this could be it. If it's well received, my career will be launched.''

"I knew it! I knew it! You'll be famous soon, Andy. I'm certain of it.''

Her enthusiasm for his good fortune should have made him happy, but Andrew wasn't wholly comfortable with it.

"If you'll hurry, I'll take you out to dinner.''

"Wonderful, I'm starved.''

When she was gone, he took out her letter and read it again. Allegra was ignorant of its value and would have tossed it in the ash can without a backward look if he had agreed. Why did he feel so guilty about saving it from that fate? Perhaps for the same reason he felt guilty and undeserving before her praise.

"It's only the fact that she wrote this damned piece that so impresses me,'' he muttered and stuck it back into his pocket. From a professional's pen it would seem run-of-the-mill. Yes, ordinary.

The muses were fickle creatures. Why should they not light, for a brief instant, on the shoulders of a clever sister? After all, his pursuit of them was a serious courtship, and ladies liked to pique the jealousy of their suitors before accepting them. Yet, accept him they would.

Allegra was jealous. Now that she was home, she could admit it to herself. Not that she wanted Rhys O'Conner's attention for herself. He was arrogant, something of a bully, a drinking man, and a terrible poet. He was not to be trusted. She had said as much to Eugenia. For all the good it would have done, she might as well have saved her breath. They had quarreled. Eugenia felt she'd had a momentous meeting with a stranger, a sensitive soul. She wouldn't abandon her image for the reality of the man.

"So much for romance,'' Allegra scoffed as she dressed her hair.

Visiting Eugenia had had its advantages. For instance, she had forgotten how much she missed the attentions of a maid. Since her arrival in New York, Andy had been pressed into service to snap the snaps and fasten the buttons she couldn't reach. Luckily she had convinced her mother of the practicality of front-buttoning corsets. Only once had she had to resort to Andy's help in lacing up. Eugenia had two personal maids, one to dress her and a second to dress her hair. During the weekend they had shared the maids' services.

Allegra paused in brushing her hair as a memory struck her. Her lips began to twitch. She shouldn't have been shocked. It was really too silly. After all, they were sold openly in advertisements in ladies' magazines and even newspapers. But the fact that Eugenia Simpson resorted to such subterfuge struck her now as impossibly funny.

"What's up?" Andrew questioned, drawn to Allegra's door by her laughter.

"Oh, Andy, the funniest thing!" she gasped between gusts of amusement. "Eugenia wears bust improvers!"

"Really, Allegra!" he admonished, but his lips twitched in spite of himself. "Gentlemen should be denied access to some secrets."

"Do you think Papa will be very angry if I don't move into the Plaza?" Allegra asked in a sudden change of mood.

"When was Father unable to forgive you anything?"

Allegra bit her lip. She hadn't seen her father since she'd run away. "If he asks, I'll go. I wouldn't want him to think badly of you because of my misconduct."

He nodded. She was right. Their father might spare his daughter parental indignation, but he wouldn't stint to find an excuse to vent it upon his son.

"You never did say why you didn't go to Connecticut," she said, watching him thoughtfully.

"No, I didn't, did I?" he answered enigmatically and moved away from the doorway.

* * *

Angus Grant eyed his children from beneath lowered brows as they finished their dinner in the Plaza Hotel dining room. "For a pair of society swells, you're unusually quiet."

"We're eating," Allegra said, scooping up the last bit of *fruits crèmes de glacé* from her dish.

"Doesn't Andrew see to your proper feeding?" Angus grumbled with a jaundiced look at his son. "She looks a bit peaked to me, as I said when I first saw her."

"Trim figures are all the fashion," Andrew returned with a slight smile.

"Yes, Papa," Allegra quickly added before he turned his full attention on Andrew. "A lady likes a gentleman, even her father, to say that she looks in the pink."

"When I think it, I'll say it!" Angus muttered. "Now what will you have? More dessert or another chop?"

"Neither, thank you, Papa. I couldn't consume another spoonful."

"Maybe it's your lacing that's got you white-faced." He cocked a suspicious eye toward her bodice. "Told your mother many a time she'll ruin her health one day for the sake of a waist span a man doesn't count as natural."

"Papa, please!"

"Oh, that's right. I forgot that you're a pair of fine-feathered fowl, easily flustered by the brusque ways and plain talk of your common father."

Allegra cast a quick look at the tin fork which lay by his plate but didn't say anything.

"How's Philadelphia?" Andrew asked.

"No change that would interest you," Angus answered.

"And that puts me in my place," Andrew said with a sarcastic edge to his voice. He wondered how long he would be able to keep his bitterness in abeyance.

"How's the pencil-pushing business?" Angus returned with a raised brow.

"Andy's soon to have his first by-line piece published," Allegra said proudly. "He's going to be famous."

"Is that so?"

"The enthusiasm of your response, Father, is all that I had hoped for," Andrew said bitingly.

"Will this expected fame pay well?" Angus questioned.

"Would that make it more significant in your eyes?" Andrew challenged.

"Aye, that it would. Anything that fills your pockets and keeps your hands out of mine is significant to me."

"It's a beginning," Allegra explained, her gaze moving worriedly between the two men she loved most in the world. "He's going to make you proud, Papa, you just wait."

"If you say so," Angus temporized, reading in his daughter's eyes the distress that often darkened his wife's when he and Andrew shared the same room. Allegra loved her brother, that was plain enough for a blind man to see. "You grow to be more like your mother every day," he said in a low voice.

"You must miss her greatly," Allegra said sympathetically.

"Aye, that I do. Until now, we'd never been parted for more than a fortnight in twenty-seven years of marriage. The house is too big for one man."

Pretending not to hear the subtle plea in his words, Allegra said, "Then you must come into town more often to visit us. Andy and I are getting on famously. We've been to the opera. Oh, yes, I said that before. And my friend Eugenia Simpson is the kind of girl of which Mama would approve. Did I say that she's to wed a baron?"

"Twice," Angus grumbled, unimpressed. "What of you, daughter? Have you met any eligible young men?"

As Allegra pinkened, Andrew said, "Tell him about your suitor."

"Suitor? What's this about a suitor?"

"Nothing so dramatic as that, Papa." Allegra glared at Andrew. "You remember meeting Dr. Boyd in Saratoga? We've seen him here in the city. He's one of Miss Simpson's acquaintances."

"What's that to do with you?" Angus pressed.

"It's only that that's how we happened to meet him again. He's come to visit us once, on Sunday afternoon. We had tea."

Angus grunted noncommittally. "It's natural for a man to wish to be in pleasant company, but I won't have him wasting your time." He turned to Andrew. "I want a full report from now on, on the comings and goings of men visiting your sister. Any man seen in your parlor three times within a month had better be prepared to answer to me.''

"Papa, you wouldn't!" Allegra protested.

"Certainly! You're of marrying age; your mother says so and she should know. I'll give you your head in the choice of a husband, as long as he meets my standards.''

"Thank you very much," she replied tartly, "but you may put all thoughts of marriage from your mind. I doubt I'll even consider marriage before I'm twenty-five."

"Twenty-five? You'll be called an old maid long before then," Andrew teased.

"The title holds no horrors for me," she answered.

Looking at her, radiant in pink tulle and with the candlelight picking blue highlights from the inky waves of her pompadour, Angus could well understand her imperturbation over age. She wasn't yet at the height of her beauty and was confident of its duration as only youth can be. "We'll say no more on the subject now. Andrew has his orders."

"As always," Andrew murmured, too low for his father to hear.

"Will you have your brandy now, Papa?" she asked, assuming her mother's place as hostess.

"I'd prefer a cigar," he answered bluntly but smiled at her with great affection. "As you've no lady to keep you company while Andrew and I retire to the smoking room, I'll have my brandy."

Allegra smiled back at him. He was difficult and sometimes unfair, but he was her father and she loved him. She turned to share her smile of contentment with Andrew when, at a distance, she noticed a seated stranger.

For one crystallizing instant she stared at him. He sat in shadow, making her perception of him unclear. He wore evening dress. Above the pristine whiteness of his collar, his face was composed of strong angles. To her amazement, he nodded and smiled, as though they shared some secret joke. She looked away, her skin prickling with the palpable intensity of his gaze.

"What is it, sis?" Andrew asked when he saw her face. "You're white as a sheet."

Allegra turned quickly toward him as embarrassment

flooded her cheeks with color. "Nothing. I need to powder my nose, that's all."

"In that case," her father said, rising to his feet out of courtesy, "Andrew and I may as well take a stroll through the billiards room." He unconsciously patted his breast pocket where he kept his cigar case. "We'll meet in the lobby."

"Fine." She was surprised at how disconcerted she had become over so slight a matter as a stranger's stare. Men had looked at her before. Determined not to give the matter, or the man, another thought, she marched purposefully from the room.

As Drayton watched her cross the dining room, his heart pounded so thickly in his chest that he couldn't think, couldn't act, couldn't move. Was it a trick, a great celestial jest? Even in the deepest of hashish dreams he had never imagined that the "spy" who had so intrigued him would be so beautiful.

The night before he had overheard the concierge at the Plaza giving instructions about the accommodations of Angus Grant. He wasn't surprised to learn that Grant was checking into the Plaza. It was the reason he was here. The old Scotsman wouldn't remember their brief conversation in Saratoga when Grant had recommended the Plaza to him. He had quite enjoyed rubbing shoulders with the father of his quarry. Sooner or later he had known Grant would arrive, and with luck, his daughter.

For the past two hours she had sat before his riveted gaze, composed and remote as some Eastern princess. When she looked up at him he had feared the look would smite him. It had. He felt shattered, fragile, and afraid.

He waited until the Grants left the room before very deliberately rising from his chair. He wasn't prepared to deal with the sudden attraction he felt. Until tonight the lady had been an abstraction, a possibility. Now she was real.

Half an hour later, Allegra emerged from the ladies' room, her composure restored by an application of lavender water to her wrists and temples as she reclined on a chaise. As she entered the busy lobby, she heard her name called.

"Allegra!"

"Eugenia!" Allegra greeted when she spied her friend.

"Imagine seeing you here," Eugenia said. "What have you been doing? You haven't been round since your visit."

"Papa's in town. I've been busy getting ready," she lied. "What have I missed?"

Eugenia linked arms with her and pulled her away from the crowded lobby concourse. "You'll never guess. I'm having my portrait done!"

"By whom?"

"Oh, you wouldn't know him. He came recommended. His name's Edssene."

"Edssene? But he's a friend of— Eugenia! You've seen Mr. O'Conner again."

Eugenia blushed. "How vulgar you make it all sound. He called last Sunday, looking quite the gentleman, I might add. He came to apologize. He'd written the most lovely poem, all about my grace and beauty. He compared me to a Greek goddess!"

"How original."

"Oh, do you think so, too? He says I misunderstood his comments about becoming an artist's model. An artist must be above fleshly consideration when he chooses his subject. To him a beautiful figure is the representation of Truth. It's a question of color, texture, and contrast; not unlike a flower arrangement. The true artist can't allow himself to be seduced by his subject, no matter how compelling. It's a point of honor."

Allegra was amazed that Eugenia remembered so much of Rhys's speech. Certainly those thoughts were not her own. Could it be that she had heard them repeated on more than one occasion? "Don't you think you should choose a society portrait painter? You don't want to find yourself burdened with unsuitable results."

"How kind of you to be concerned," she answered with a little less warmth than before. "Aunt Flora has already approved Edssene. She saw his work when he came to the house. My first sitting was yesterday."

"Was Mr. O'Conner satisfied with the day's efforts?"

"He said—" Eugenia checked herself. "I really must go. They're waiting for me."

Allegra caught her up in a quick hug. "Do be careful, Eugenia," she whispered.

Eugenia's laughter was joyous. "I'm happy, Allegra. You must be happy for me, too."

"I'll try." As she watched Eugenia hurry away, Allegra felt more than a little guilt in the matter of her friend's happiness. Still, she could understand Eugenia's infatuation with artists. There was a freedom in their style of living that she would never know. It made them exotic and mysterious, and just a little dangerous.

She turned away from the alcove and met a new crowd pouring into the lobby. At the last moment she sidestepped to avoid a portly woman in purple satin and bumped shoulders with a tall man in evening dress.

Instinctively, she glanced up with a bright smile and words of apology. "Pardon me! I fear I've left my grace in my other purse." Further words failed. It was the man from the dining room. He was the most striking man she'd ever seen. Black hair and heavily marked brows contrasted with his silver-blue eyes, but there was nothing remotely congenial about his expression, or his mood.

"Graceless colonial!" he muttered in a bitingly precise English accent and swung past her without another glance. The crowd gave way before his advance toward the elevators.

"Who the devil was that?" Angus Grant demanded as he came up.

"We saw that," Andrew said. "The fellow nearly ran you down."

"Did he?" Allegra murmured, at a loss to understand the degree of anger that scored deep lines in the man's cheeks and broad brow. It was only an awkward moment. They had scarcely touched.

"I'll ask the doorman about him. If he's a guest, I'll have a word with him before bed."

"No, Papa. It was I who bumped into him. I feel a headache coming on. It must be the wine."

"You should be in bed," Angus declared as he signaled the doorman for a cab. "You should be staying here with me, come to that."

"Oh, Papa, don't let's quarrel," she begged. "It's been a perfect evening."

"Very well, but I'll be round first thing in the morning to look in on you. If you're not better, I'm taking you home to Philadelphia," he said with a glance at Andrew.

"Yes, Papa." She replied automatically for other thoughts occupied her. Arrogant, austere, remarkable; she remembered the Englishman's expression with its mixture of anger, resentment, and the faintest hint of amusement.

She had been embarrassed by his stare in the dining room. It occurred to her now that he might have deliberately stepped into her path. But why? He hadn't taken the opportunity to speak to her. Perhaps it was a jest.

From the shadows of a nearby portico, Drayton watched as the Grants emerged from the Plaza. An unexpected surge of desire had moved through him when he brushed against her and she looked up at him. When she had spoken to him he had been further surprised. He hadn't hoped for character, intelligence, and wit that had nothing to do with artificial poses and languid tableaux meant to draw the eye.

As he watched her brother take her arm to help her into the cab, he again experienced conflicting emotions. Suspended between desire and fear, he fought the inclination to cross the sidewalk, thrust the brother aside, and climb in after her to steal her away. Trembling, stricken with the fever of a passion he hadn't known existed, he watched the hansom leave the curb.

Even before he had learned her name, long before he had seen her face, heard her voice, he had wanted her. Now he knew he must have her. Must possess—what? What was she? A challenge? A relief from his boredom? The unattainable? Perhaps all that and more. What, then, if he were disappointed? He shivered with an exquisite dread of that moment.

"Then this fever called living will be conquered at last," he murmured, smiling at the aptness of paraphrasing an American poet he'd always admired: Poe.

Nine

Bourbon had a few very fine virtues, Andrew decided as he poured himself another glass from the half-empty decanter. It was tasty, it went down with a minimum of fuss, it warmed the cold places in the heart, and it wasn't outrageously expensive. His father wouldn't approve, of course. According to him, scotch was the only drink for a man. There were many things of which his father disapproved. Adultery was, doubtless, one of them.

Harriet had refused to see him again. When she canceled their trip to Connecticut, he told her it was over. But it wasn't. He didn't want it to be. That was the thing that amazed and fascinated him, even now when it seemed as though whiskey and blood flowed in equal parts in his veins. Theirs was an untenable relationship. He had other plans for his life, and other worries. In just a few weeks his first important work would be in print.

He reached for the sheaf of papers lying on the desk before him. He had been writing and revising for nearly a week, and still he was dissatisfied. Now his inky scrawl wouldn't resolve itself into words. He bent his head lower but it was useless. He was drunk beyond redemption on this night.

"Damn!" He flung the papers away. Where was his imagination, nourished so long upon the lives and works of the best and brightest men? He could quote by heart passages of Plato and Aristotle, felt an echoing of his soul in the words of Byron and Keats, had an instinctive need to feed his intellect on the beauty, truth, and imagination of the world's art. Why, then, when he was called upon to reveal the truth of his experience, was he so incapable?

"What sacrifices must I make?" he muttered and drained his glass.

He needed Allegra. Yes, that was it. He missed her quiet presence tonight. If she were home, sitting in her usual place by him, he would feel the silent encouragement that was missing tonight. Why had she chosen this night to accept Dr. Boyd's invitation to dinner? No, that wasn't right. He'd encouraged her to go because he had hoped to have an assignation with Harriet. No matter. When Allegra came home he would ask her to sit awhile with him. He might allow her to read what he had written. She believed in him more than he believed in himself just now, and he needed her utter confidence in his ability.

He rested his head on the desk, the cool feel of the embossed-leather blotter comforting to his sweaty cheek. It was foolish of him to pickle his brain when he needed to work. Regardless of what many writers claimed, he found drunkenness a singularly ill-fitting state in which to compose.

"Yes, a wonderful evening, Dr. Boyd. Thank you so much. Good night."

Andrew lifted his head from his desk as Allegra's voice sounded in the hall. She was home. He sat up, struggled with his tie, and then gave up as she entered the drawing room.

She was caught in silhouette by the fire's glow in the darkened room. For a moment she stood still, lost in thoughts too deep to disturb with movement. Her head was lowered, her hands clutching her evening bag against her breasts. It was an attitude of sadness or even grief. Then with a slight shake of her head, she straightened and looked around.

"Andy? Andy, are you home?"

He lowered his head quickly to his desk to keep her from realizing that he had watched her private reflection. "In here," he murmured in a sleepy voice.

Allegra was surprised to find him stretched over his desk in the dark. "Did I wake you? I'm sorry."

"No, no, need to be awake," he answered and reached for the lamp to turn it up. "Been polishing my essay."

She looked at the papers scattered on the floor and shook her head. "I'd say you've been having a tantrum." She bent and began retrieving the papers. "Andy, really! You mustn't mistreat your work this way."

With her scolding Andrew realized that the pleasant hum of his drunkenness was beginning to turn into the headachy nausea of a hangover. Too soon for that, he decided, and reached to pour himself another shot.

When Allegra had gathered and stacked the last of the papers, she brought them to him. "You don't look well. What's wrong?"

"Everything," he muttered. "Confounded work's a disaster. Due tomorrow and not a sentence in it I care to have attributed to me."

"It's nerves," she answered confidently. "You're bound to be nervous, but that's no reason to disown your efforts. In a few weeks you'll be the literary toast of New York and I'll be forced to sit on you to keep you from floating away with your swelled head."

His laughter was dry. "You can't begin to understand."

Allegra's gaze shifted from his face to the decanter and back. His cheeks were flushed and the lines of his well-shaped face seemed blurred. "You're flummoxed!"

"Yes, and what of it?" He leaned back with his eyes half closed. "I've had a beastly sort of day and a worse evening."

Sympathy and love swelled up together in Allegra as she looked at him. It was so unlike Andy to be unhappy. Something must be seriously wrong, but what? She glanced at his work. Was his writing as bad as he thought? He hadn't asked her to read for him and she perfectly understood his reluctance. She hadn't written another word after he discovered her cache of letters. Even though he had complimented her, she'd been left with an abiding sense of vulnerability.

"You need a cup of tea. Did you eat any supper?" He shook his head and winced. "No wonder you can't think properly. You must have regular meals and sleep to be at your best. Shall I call down to the dining room for a tray?"

"Couldn't eat a thing." Andrew rose none too steadily to his feet, gripping the desk for support.

She rounded the desk to slip a shoulder under his arm. "You need rest, Andy."

When they reached his room, she eased him down on the bed. "Must finish," he muttered, but already his eyes had fallen shut. "Due tomorrow."

She stood a moment in indecision. She knew nothing about drunken stupors, and what little she had overheard through the years didn't seem of much value. She remembered how ill Justine Gilliam had been after drinking her graduation champagne and decided to forgo the tea. The sonorous sounds coming from Andrew's open mouth convinced her that he would sleep for a long time.

After covering him with a candlewick spread she wandered back into the drawing room where she removed her jacket and hat. Dinner with Dr. Boyd had been pleasant but uneventful. He was an attentive and solicitous host, but there was nothing in his manner to inspire the slightest excitement or anticipation.

"You want too much, Allegra Grant," she admonished herself softly. Throughout the evening she had compared the doctor with the rude Irish poet Eugenia was so taken with and found the better man wanting in imagination and interest. If not for a single incident, when they were leaving Delmonico's, she wouldn't have given the dinner another thought.

The impact of their first encounter was too fresh in her mind for her not to start at the Englishman's sudden appearance in her path. He must have seen trepidation reflected in her face because he actually paused in his stride, looked directly at her, and then without a word passed on.

She couldn't shake the suspicion that he had been watching her throughout dinner, present but unnoticed in the vast dining room. The very idea made her shiver. Who was he? Why did he look at her as though gazing upon an apparition? Was he following her?

"Stuff and nonsense!" she said aloud as she marched over to turn up the lamps and scatter the gloom.

It was only natural that they should encounter one another again. Vast though the city was, Delmonico's and the Plaza Hotel were two of the best-known establishments and likely to draw the wealthier class of tourist. No doubt the Englishman had also been to the Metropolitan Opera House, the National Academy, and Madison Square Garden. Possibly she would glimpse him again if he remained in town. If so, she would cut him just as he had cut her tonight.

She rubbed her temples as she strolled into the library. It was late. She was tired. She should be in bed. Even so, the papers lying on the desk drew her. At first she merely sorted them into chronological order. She promised herself that she wouldn't read them, but her eyes fell naturally upon the opening lines, swept on to pick up the entire paragraph, and moved lower. Without quite deciding to do so, she sat down and began reading in earnest.

She was at the top of the third page before she reached for an ink pen and flipped back to the opening words. At first she edited the spelling and punctuation, smiling at Andy's characteristic misuse of commas. After a few paragraphs, she opened a drawer and withdrew clean sheets of paper to copy in a neat hand what he had written.

It wasn't until she reached the second page that she began to write in the margins, adding more appropriate phrases and deleting his repetitions. It became a game to re-sort his words, glean from contorted sentences a cleaner, sharper image. When she came to his description of their night at Marie's, she couldn't still the insistent urge to add her own thoughts to his. Words flowed from her pen onto the pristine sheets, quick, clever sentences that cavorted about his longer more majestic phrasing. Her light touch, she thought, offered leavening to his lofty tone.

It was nearly three A.M. when she sat back and replaced the cap on the pen. On the desk before her was the achievement of four hours' work.

The excitement of the effort filled her as she restacked the papers and placed her draft beside Andrew's. She had added only suggestions, she reasoned. Andrew could pick and choose from among them when he awoke. It struck her then that she might have found something with which to occupy her days. If Andrew were amenable, she could become his secretary. Much of the drudgery of his writing time would be removed if she copied each morning his efforts of the night before. As she turned out the lights, she knew a moment's hesitation. Suppose Andy didn't like what she had done? Suppose he was furious when he found out that she had not only read his work but tried her hand at reworking it?

"Then he may destroy it," she murmured and turned out the light.

Andrew awoke at dawn, the insistent tapping in his head echoed by the rumbling in his stomach. A belch drove up through him and made him groan. After a long moment in which he fought for mastery of his stomach, he eased himself off the bed and onto his feet.

There were only a few hours left before his essay was due at the office of *Harper's Weekly*. That had been his last thought as he drifted into unconsciousness. It was the source of the insistent tapping that awakened him just now.

He made his way with great care through the apartment, mindful that any noise would awaken Allegra. He entered the library on stiff legs and flung open the drapes in a defiant gesture. The pale autumn morning sunlight struck his eyes painfully and he turned away. When he opened his eyes he looked at his desk. There beside his rough draft was a clean copy of his essay which he didn't remember writing.

He picked up a page and began reading it. Between surprise and disbelief, he recognized the words as his and the handwriting as Allegra's. After no more than a few lines, he replaced the paper and turned away.

He dimly remembered Allegra's offer to help him but not the fact that she had. It seemed impossible that he could have revised the work in his condition, but there was the proof. He smiled. Perhaps he had underrated the influence of bourbon after all. But was the work any good?

His hand trembled as he reached toward the pages again. He shouldn't read it. It would only reinforce his fear that it wasn't worthy of print. He scooped the pages into an envelope and sealed it. In bold strokes he addressed the package and then pushed the buzzer to ring for a messenger.

It was early but he wanted it out of the apartment before he began second-guessing himself again.

He opened the door the moment he heard the elevator stop at his floor. "Deliver this to the address marked on the envelope immediately," he directed the young man who came toward him.

"Yes, sir," the bellboy replied sleepily. It wasn't his business to wonder why the delivery couldn't wait until a decent hour.

"What's the matter with you?" Andrew questioned testily as he watched his sister pace the drawing room floor. "You'd think it was you, not I, about to be eaten alive by the critics."

"I—I know," Allegra answered, avoiding his eye. Little did he suspect how close to the truth he was. "It's just that I copied it for you. I hope I spelled everything correctly."

"That's an editor's job," he said. "However, I do wish I'd read the final draft before I sent it off."

"So do I!" Allegra murmured. She'd been appalled to discover that he had sent her version of his work to his publisher without reading it first.

"You should've told me you made the copy without my permission."

"You were asleep."

"You might have left a note."

"Yes, you're right." She twisted her hands tightly together. "I hope you won't be angry when you see the final copy."

"Why should I be?"

She took a deep breath. "I changed one or two things."

Andrew sat up. "Changed things! What kind of things?"

"Oh, nothing important. Only one or two things," she finished lamely.

"God, Allegra! I can't believe you'd touch a word of a professional's work. It's like adding brush strokes to a painter's canvas."

"I suppose so," she said faintly. She would have told him exactly what she had done that first morning if only he had been home, but both he and the draft were gone when she awakened. For a short time she had been thrilled, thinking that he had thought enough of her revisions to take them to work. It wasn't until dinnertime that she learned the full implications of the missing papers. By then she found it impossible to tell him the truth.

"If you're going to be my secretary, there'll have to be rules about such things. The first is never change my work without my express permission."

"You can be certain I'll never so much as cross a *T*, Andy, I swear it!"

The note of hysteria made Andrew rise from his chair and approach her. "Allegra, what's this? Why, there're tears in your eyes. Are you so certain that the critics will hate me?"

"Oh, no, Andy, I think you're a wonderful writer. I do! It's only that if the critics don't like it, I'm afraid that you're going to hate me for destroying your chance, and I'll hate myself and then everything will be ruined forever."

Andrew smiled at her. "All this distress over one or two changes? I admit that I reacted strongly to your confession. Permit me my artistic temper, but I'm no ogre. I'll not throw you out over a mischosen word or two."

"No, you wouldn't," she agreed and looked at him. This was Andy, the brother she loved more than anyone else on earth. Why couldn't she tell him? She wanted it over with, but the words were glued to the back of her throat. He would know soon enough. To tell him now, as the edition of *Harper's Weekly* was being put on the stands, seemed too cruel. Soon enough he would see for himself how she had betrayed him.

"What we both need is a change of scenery," Andrew said. "Go fetch your coat and I'll take you out for lunch. I've not yet spent a penny of my advance. It's only fitting that we use a portion of it in celebration."

"Wouldn't you prefer to wait for—for something to celebrate?" She wasn't certain she wanted to be in public when he learned of her duplicity.

Andrew cocked his head to one side. "I believe that you've taken this matter so much to heart that you've begun to think of it as your own."

"How foolish of me," she said as she turned away. "I'll get my coat."

Andrew watched in rapt fascination as Allegra repeatedly dipped her spoon into the double-scoop ice cream sundae oozing rivers of hot fudge and capped by whipped cream and slivers of toasted almonds. "You're certain you wouldn't prefer lunch first?"

"No, this is wonderful," she replied between spoonfuls.

Henry Maillard's Confectionery and Ladies' Luncheon Establishment wasn't exactly what he had had in mind when he asked her to choose a place to dine. He supposed he must have mentioned the place in casual conversation, for he didn't know she knew of it. He and Harriet had met here on several occasions but always at a less conspicuous table.

He smiled politely at the numerous ladies who passed their table, finding amusement in their sharp, secretive glances at his pretty companion. Luckily Allegra couldn't suspect what they were thinking.

Finally a familiar face appeared among the luncheon patrons. The moment he noticed Andrew, the man came hurrying over.

Without preamble he said, "Hang it all, Grant! Should've guessed what you were up to by the way you left Marie's in such haste that night."

"Hello, Achland. Whatever are you talking about?"

"Your piece." Achland pulled a magazine out from under his arm and dropped it on the table. Aghast, Allegra stared at the copy of *Harper's Weekly*.

"I'm not too proud to say you did a fine job of it. To give you credit, I didn't think of it as contrived until after I'd read it a second time."

"Your praise overwhelms me," Andrew replied with a grin. "Do forgive me, Allegra. This is Jack Achland. Achland, my sister, Miss Grant."

"Miss Grant," Achland greeted, only to stare at her. For an instant Allegra thought he recognized her from the night at Marie's but his words dispelled that fear. "By Jove! The resemblance between you is remarkable."

"Yes. You were saying?" Andrew prompted.

Achland reluctantly turned from Allegra. "I—um, congratulate you. Still, you can't call your observations completely original. There were traces of de Kay's *The Bohemian* in that satire on Expressionist poseurs. You were right, in my estimation, to make an exception of the suicide's case. I especially liked the reference to Chatterton there."

"Chatterton?" Andrew repeated.

"Don't be patronizing, Grant. 'I thought of Chatterton, the marvelous boy, / The sleepless soul that perished in his pride.' Wordsworth. *Resolution and Independence*. Just because I'm not a Harvard man it doesn't follow that I'm an illiterate, you know. I might've used it myself had I not considered it a tad too maudlin."

The clanging of Allegra's spoon on the marble tabletop distracted Andrew from what he was about to say. As he looked across at her stricken expression, Achland continued speaking.

"The thing I'd like to know is how'd you get in with *Harper's*? That's nearly as good as getting in at the *Atlantic Monthly*. I've been trying for months to get a reading there. Don't suppose, now that you're in, you could put in a word for me?"

"I rather think we should wait until the verdict is in on the piece before you elect me as your sponsor," Andrew hedged, his attention fully on his sister. "I say, you wouldn't mind lending me your copy, would you?"

"Didn't you get one?" Achland asked.

"No, I didn't. I don't usually read my work once it's in print, but this time I think I'll make an exception."

Pinned by his gaze, Allegra could only stare back dumbly at him.

"I make you a present of it," Achland said expansively. "Just remember to mention me at *Harper's*. Good day, Miss Grant." With a tip of his hat he was off.

"You'll excuse my rudeness," Andrew said to Allegra as he opened the magazine.

"Andy I—"

"Please, Allegra. Ah, here we are."

Allegra swallowed carefully and lowered her gaze as he bent his head over the pages. She quickly sorted out the possibilities and concluded that no matter how angry he became, he wouldn't make a public display of it. She considered just getting up and walking out but scotched that idea as cowardly. She owed him the courtesy of her presence at her condemnation.

He seemed to take forever to read the piece. After a few minutes she glanced over at him. His face was expressionless. He might have been reading facts and figures instead of her revision of his work. Once his right eyebrow lifted questioningly, and her heart skipped a beat. Finally he turned back to the beginning and began to read again.

The ice cream in her stomach had become an indigestible curd by the time he folded the magazine shut and laid it aside.

She wanted to be the first to speak, to say something that would defuse the moment, but from the instant he looked across at her, his green eyes shaded by some held-in-check emotion, all she could murmur was, "I'm sorry."

The pitiful tone didn't seem to reach him as he sat staring at her. Nothing moved in his face; no emotion regulated his gaze. There was neither anger nor hurt nor reproach, no disgust, no sense of betrayal or indignation, nothing to which she could respond.

"Why did you come to New York, Allegra?"

The question was so unexpected that she stared at him in incomprehension.

"Let me rephrase myself." His voice was curiously void of emotion. "What did you hope to gain by coming here?"

Allegra wet her lips, feeling the constriction in her throat tighten. "I wanted to see and hear for myself many of the things you wrote to me about."

"And, perhaps, write about them yourself?" he urged.

"No, not the way you mean." She looked away. "I wanted to tell you what I'd done, but you'd sent it off and it was too late, and I didn't know what to do." She glanced back with an appeal for understanding. "I only meant to rewrite your draft, but I was so carried away by your words that I found myself adding the thoughts you inspired in me.

I never imagined that you'd send it in without reading it.''

"No, you wouldn't," he answered mildly.

"I didn't think anyone but you would see my work."

"Then you should be quite vexed, for a better part of the literary constituency of the city will have perused your words by nightfall."

Allegra made a sound that was very like a squeak. "Is it so awful?"

He picked up the magazine. "Perhaps you should read it for yourself."

She shook her head. "I couldn't! Andy, have I—will this—is your career ruined?"

A slow smile began at the corners of his mouth. "It's early yet, but you heard Achland's praise with your own ears. In a day or two we'll have a better idea of its general reception."

She looked at him, still uncertain of his mood. "Aren't you angry, even a little? You should be furious. If you like, I'll go back to Philadelphia this very afternoon."

"That won't be necessary. Now finish your ice cream. Oh, it's quite melted. Would you like another?"

She shook her head.

"Very well, then, let's go home. We've been invited out for dinner. I rather think it'll be an interesting evening." He picked up the magazine.

"Oh, leave it for the ashman!" Allegra said feelingly.

Andrew cocked his head to one side. "Consign your first published work to the trash? I think not."

In the cab on the way home Andrew suddenly said, "How would you like to go into partnership with me?"

Allegra roused herself from her sulk with difficulty. "I don't understand."

"No, I don't suppose you would." He patted the magazine. "This is good work. No, better than good. It's excellent! You were able to weave into my work the threads that eluded me. That's made me think that we might continue to profit from a collaboration."

She stared at him. "Are you serious? Truly, Andy?"

"Truly. You need guidance. To be honest, you wouldn't have fared as well if you hadn't followed my construction.

In time, under my tutelage, you'll learn that structure. There's just one thing and it's no idle or arbitrary rule, so think it over very carefully before you speak. If you agree to a collaboration, it must remain a strict secret between us. All work will be published in my name or a pseudonym. No one else is ever to know. No one."

"But I don't understand why I shouldn't—"

"We won't be writing sermons or morality plays. The world of satire and controversy will be our milieu. Women who venture into these areas are often scorned, slandered, and deemed unsuitable for genteel society. Father will be furious if I ruin your chance to make a good marriage."

"Enough, enough! I agree," she said readily.

"Think it over awhile," he cautioned.

"I don't need to. It's perfect for us, Andy. That's why you thought of it." She glanced at the magazine in his hand and then back at him with a mischievous smile. "If it's really that good, maybe I should read my first published work, after all."

With a chuckle he handed it over.

Ten

New York, November

"Here it is, Andy! Shall I read it aloud?"

THE CITY CIPHER

Overheard on a recent evening's outing:
  I'm having my portrait painted.
  Are you? How marvelous! Who's the artist? Not that dreadful P—?

He's been mentioned. Who is he?

I'm certainly not one to soil innocent ears with tales of depravity, yet I'm persuaded that ignorance is not always a sufficient guard against the machinations of scoundrels. It's said that while in Chicago he took *ad-van-tage* of a certain young lady's passion for Artistic Ideals.

It was a good likeness, I'm told, so good in fact the parents paid an enormous sum to purchase it. They packed the girl off to England in hopes that a match could be made before the scandal crossed the Atlantic.

A word to the wise, dear reader: He who would be immortalized in paint must demur from "the altogether" frankness with which some artists would view their subjects.

J.A.N.U.S. Writwell

"We should've suggested that such portraits be auctioned off along with the subjects at Sotheby's. That way the groom would know exactly what he was getting." Allegra finished with a laugh as she refolded the paper.

"If that's an example of your mood, I'd better write the City Cipher column myself this morning," Andrew answered as he reached for a second serving of breakfast.

"Not after you've persuaded me to accept nearly every invitation that has come our way this past week." She picked up and waved a handful that had come in the morning mail. Andrew's first literary success had precipitated a stream of invitations from people who wished to be able to say they knew Andrew Grant socially. "I haven't stuffed myself full of horrid heavy dinners and tepid conversation only to leave the results to you."

"You do possess a knack for ridicule," he admitted.

"Ridicule?" Allegra paused in spreading pear jam on a scone. "We only repeat what we hear. If our subjects appear ridiculous, it's because of what they do and say."

"Just remember that we've more than one career to manage. If Writwell becomes too clever for his own good, he'll be axed."

Allegra shrugged, then dissolved into giggles. "Oh, Andy,

it doesn't seem real, does it? A month ago you were anonymous. Now you're famous!''

Andy chuckled. ''I don't know that I'd call myself famous just yet. Three essays published in the past two months makes me of popular interest. We've yet to see whether or not I can endure beyond the season.''

''You're too pessimistic. What of the talk that you'll soon be given your own column?''

''As you well know, it's only talk.''

She patted the newspaper beside her plate. ''Well, there's the City Cipher. We're a weekly event.''

Andrew nodded, then finished his tea. The social satire column had begun one morning a few weeks ago as they sat at breakfast exchanging stories about the previous evening's entertainment: hers at the opera and his at the theater. Both had mercilessly satirized their companions, inventing ironic pseudonyms for some of the leading society figures of the city.

It was Allegra's ear for dialogue, her ability to capture the essential foolishness of a subject, that led Andrew to consider turning their chats into profit. He jotted down notes about the Dickensian assemblage they invented, and soon the satiric notes became part of the breakfast ritual.

He had collected six sketches and taken them to a weekly paper where the thinly disguised gossip was instantly snapped up. Complete anonymity was guaranteed by the publisher, who believed that Andrew was a conduit for a loose collection of society gossips who wished to remain behind the scenes of their social tattling.

Andrew gazed fondly at Allegra. The gossip's pen name, J.A.N.U.S. Writwell, was her idea, a witty reference to their dual authorship. At first he balked at the notion. The suggestion of dual authorship emblazoned so boldly on their work was a sharp reminder that Allegra had had a large part in his first success as an essayist. Then the irony of it began to appeal to him. He controlled the content and final draft of everything they wrote. Allegra's talent was raw, undisciplined. He reminded himself that she would never have been published if not for his professional credential, his experience, his knowledge of popular tastes. She was a clever assistant. For that he bore her no ill will.

Then, too, the Grant coffers were beginning to fill. He had sold two more essays to *Harper's Weekly*. *Atlantic Monthly* was the next mountain to be scaled. Then there was the novel that had been circulating in his head for more than a year. When it was done, it would go to Scribners. No, he begrudged Allegra nothing. She was making possible his dreams.

"Whom shall we skewer this week?" Allegra asked as he reached for pen and paper.

"Let's see. Writwell attended a political rally last week, a confectionery the week before. How about the opera this time?"

She shook her head. "I didn't hear a thing that would be of interest. It seems that the more I mingle in society the less interesting it becomes. Then when I do hear something useful, there are too few people about for it to be repeated."

Andrew nodded. They had agreed that in order for Writwell's identity to remain a secret, they would use only those incidents that were witnessed by a number of people. Parlor gossip, often the best, was out of bounds. "I know the rules impose certain strictures, but sometimes they can be overcome by clever phrases. For instance, did I tell you what occurred in the cloakroom of my club yesterday?"

"Moving, that's the only adjective that will suffice," Eugenia Simpson enthused.

"Sentimental is, perhaps, as good a word," replied her dinner partner, himself a writer of note.

"Mr. Marchier, you're jealous," she answered.

"Mademoiselle, I am never jealous," he answered. His gaze lingered boldly on her décolletage before he added, "Envious, on the rare occasion, but I'm seldom deprived of that which is mine."

The implication of his remark struck her as much too familiar, and Eugenia turned from him to gaze down the candelabra-lit table set for twenty-four to where Andrew Grant sat at the right hand of their hostess, Mrs. Throckmorton. This celebration dinner in Andrew's honor was being given by one of the foremost hostesses of the Upper Ten Thousand. Andrew had just received a post with *Century* magazine.

At that moment Mrs. Throckmorton addressed Andrew. "Mr. Grant, do tell us more about how you came to write your latest piece. I understand from your sister that you've made yourself a familiar figure about the more colorful districts of the city in order to study artists in their habitat."

"In her enthusiasm, Allegra will overdramatize," Andrew returned politely with a nod at his new boss, poet-editor of *Century* magazine, Richard Watson Gilder. It was well-known that Gilder disapproved of what he called the tragedy of bohemianism. "I've made friends among the artists of the area, that's true. However, I don't consider myself an expert or an exotic. I'm a humble scribbler of some talent and discrimination."

"The *Herald* disagrees with you, Mr. Grant," Alfred Throckmorton called from the head of the table. "Just today it declared you show promise of becoming one of the few genuine American voices of the decade."

"High praise, indeed, Mr. Grant," agreed Mrs. Ehlin, the lady on Andrew's right.

"Oh, I don't know that I agree with the *Herald*," Allegra remarked in a voice that drew the company attention. "I think I might give the tip of my hat to that new fellow who's recently made his appearance in the pages of the *Harper's Weekly*. Now what's his name? Oh, yes! Who could forget so ambitious a pen name? J.A.N.U.S. Writwell."

"That pompous puppy!" Mr. Throckmorton replied. "I read his drivel. Spying on his betters. No doubt he's some disgruntled night clerk at the Fifth Avenue Hotel."

"Why so?" Allegra questioned with a puzzled frown.

"How else could he claim to know the goings-on of his betters?"

"I found his comments on the Ten Thousand amusing," Allegra persisted.

"That, my dear, is because you weren't mentioned," returned Mrs. Ehlin.

"Were you?" asked Eugenia.

"We both were," answered Mr. Ehlin, who sat at Allegra's right. "City Cipher is a disgrace. I've written the editor to say so and protest any further publication by this fellow Riddled."

"Writwell," Allegra corrected. "What, in particular, did you find disobliging?"

Mr. Ehlin's ruddy cheeks darkened a shade. "I won't stint on laying the matter plainly before you. Last week at my club there was some discussion of that ridiculous business of giving women the vote in Wyoming. Made them a state too soon, in my opinion. Stirring up trouble before they're capable of understanding one iota of politics."

"Was it you who compared the citizens of our newest state to a herd of cattle?" Allegra asked in her most innocent voice.

Ehlin chuckled. "Won't say I didn't, for I did. Giving women the vote! Uncivilized! They wouldn't know better than to give the cow the vote if they could."

"I believe Mr. Writwell's reply was, 'And why not, when in New York many an old goat votes already!'"

Ehlin's complexion burned brighter as awkward laughter ringed the table. "It's all very well for you to smile, Miss Grant, but who can trust himself not to be overheard in more delicate matters?" He gazed purposefully around the table as he said, "If a man isn't protected in his club, who's to say what lady will be safe in her own drawing room?"

His eyes came to rest on Allegra, making her feel obliged to speak again. "Well, I for one won't cringe to come under his sharp observation. After all, no names were used. Combing the column for clues to identify oneself and one's acquaintances caught in foibles adds piquancy to dull news. There's nothing malicious in his observations. You admit you said those things. Why, think of it. We may all become famous!"

"Why, yes," Eugenia murmured. "It could be the best fun, like a game to figure out who is who."

"The man shouldn't make fun of his betters," Ehlin maintained. "And if he dares, then he should be man enough to identify himself."

"Perhaps he isn't a servant. Perhaps he's one of our friends," Mrs. Throckmorton suggested. Her eyes gleamed with satisfaction, for this was the kind of stimulating talk she treasured at her dinner table. Let other Fifth Avenue hostesses smooth and soothe their guests. She invited controversy, the decorous sort. "What if he's one of us?"

"I admit it. I'm Writwell," Andrew said readily.

For an instant there was an embarrassed hush, and then Allegra's clear laughter shattered the moment. "Don't let's brag, Andy. You've cornered enough praise for one evening with your mention in the *Herald*."

Her admonishment broke the suspicious silence, and afterward a sprinkling of relieved laughter and conversation resumed round the table once more.

Allegra glanced frequently at Andrew as the meal continued, but he refused to catch her eye. Perhaps it was just as well, she decided, for his teasing confession had nearly been believed and that would have been disastrous. There were many pitfalls in this new enterprise.

For the remainder of the meal she suffered in near silence Mr. Ehlin's vitriolic discourse on the character of the City Cipher. These dinners offered them the perfect opportunity to observe their peers, but there were times like tonight when she would gladly have traded the brilliant but decorous Throckmorton salon for the smelly, polyglot ambience of Marie's.

When at long last Mrs. Throckmorton rose from the table, indicating that it was time for the ladies to retire to the drawing room while the men remained to drink brandy and smoke, she heaved an audible sigh of relief. At least there would be a short break before Mr. Gilder was persuaded to read from his latest poetic effort.

Eugenia fell into step beside her as they crossed the hall. "We're so proud of Andrew. His name is appearing everywhere. Why, he's mentioned in Town Talk regularly. And to think that you're his only companion."

Allegra smiled, refusing to acknowledge Eugenia's continued interest in Andy's choice of lady companion. "Andy's always been good to me, though the pace can be fatiguing. I haven't seen you about lately. You were missed at the opera last night. Mr. Kirby in particular remarked on your absence."

"Did he?" Eugenia murmured as her cheeks pinkened. "I can't think why he should. Opera's never interested me. All that warbling in foreign tongues bores me."

"You've found other things more to your liking?"

"Well, yes, I have." She paused, her lips parted as though to say something more, but then she shook her head. "Did I tell you I've begun painting lessons?"

"I wonder what prompted that?" Allegra responded.

"Prompted what?" asked Mrs. Throckmorton as the ladies entered the drawing room.

Eugenia turned to her hostess. "I've begun painting. I may even keep a studio."

"Never, my dear, but never consider that!" Mrs. Gilder admonished. "I've heard that such things are occurring among the daughters of the middle class, but it wouldn't do for a lady to consider it."

Her interest piqued, Allegra rejoined, "Do you mean, Mrs. Gilder, that a lady may not keep a studio to support her artistic sense and still maintain her reputation?"

Her social prominence as a hostess called into account, Mrs. Gilder replied in a haughty tone, "It's a matter of style. Mr. Gilder and I maintained a quite fashionable literary salon just off Union Square for several years. Of course, we never condoned the ill-mannered nor the ill-bred."

Something began to perk in Allegra's thoughts. "Isn't it agreed that the creative spark often resides in a turbulent soul?"

"Perhaps, my dear, but a hostess needn't subject her guests to the 'eccentricities of genius.'"

Sensing that this controversy was about to take an indelicate turn, Mrs. Throckmorton intervened with, "Speaking of genius, has anyone read the new work of Henry James?"

"Oh, do you like him, too?" Mrs. Ehlin replied. "I do think he's the most elegant of writers, quite continental in tone. We made his acquaintance in Paris last spring."

Unabashed that the conversation had been diverted from her, Allegra tactfully withdrew from further comment. Thoughts sparked by Eugenia's announcement occupied her for the remainder of the evening. Later, not even Richard Gilder's droning recitation intruded upon her reverie.

She said nothing to Andrew of her idea on their ride home nor while they shared a final cup of cocoa before bed.

But the next morning she was up early, waiting impatiently for him to appear. Finally she heard a sketchy melody floating out through his door, recognized the tune as "The Yeoman of the Guard," and knew that he was up.

When he appeared a few moments later, she could wait no longer and sprang up from her chair. "Andy, I've had the most marvelous idea!"

He held up his hand. "Absolutely not."

Her face fell. "But you haven't even heard it."

"I've seen that look before. It can mean only one thing: trouble."

"You always like to squash my ideas, yet when have they been anything but wonderful?"

Andrew took his place opposite her at the breakfast table. "Well, let's see. There was the time you ran away from Saratoga. Then there was the night we went to Marie's and were nearly caught up in the police raid that followed the suicide. Then there was—"

"Oh, very well." She sank down onto her chair and folded her arms. "If you won't help me, then I'll just have to find someone else." She looked across at him from under the sweep of her lashes. "Eugenia will be glad to help me."

Andrew paused in buttering his toast. "Eugenia Simpson is a goose, a pretty goose, but thoroughly silly."

"That doesn't prevent her from being useful on occasion."

"Spoken like Father," he replied before biting into his toast.

"I want to open a salon," she said baldly. "Not just a salon for the stiff and proper, but an artistic salon that welcomes the unknown as well as the established poets and painters, novelists and singers. There's never been anything like it before!"

"With good reason. For example, can you imagine the result of Mrs. Gilder in conversation with Rhys O'Conner?"

"Well, perhaps not the Gilders, but their sons and daughters might come. Think of it, a true egalitarian society composed of the best of genius and the most prominent of benefactors."

"I am imagining it . . . and it's a disaster."

"The Gilders once held forth with a salon."

"It was for the mutual benefit of those they considered socially acceptable."

"There are those who're more adventurous and would take their cue from us."

"Those who take their cues from others allow the Gilders, the Lays, the Huttons and their like to set the standard."

"We'll set our own standard."

"Dear sister, remove the thought from your mind. I'm trying to break into the established *literati*, not break out of the present order."

"You're afraid!" she said in amazement. "You're afraid that they'll be offended."

"I fear we should be looked upon as presumptuous upstarts. Be reasonable, Allegra. I've just begun to find myself confronted by more open doors than closed ones. That river of invitations you constantly refer to could dry up on a day's notice. We've only one foot in the door."

"And you don't want to get your toes mashed," she finished disdainfully. "Andrew Douglas Grant, I'm ashamed of you!"

Retreating behind his coffee cup, Andrew reconsidered his first impression of her idea. It remained unchanged.

"It wouldn't do to turn our apartment into a salon. You'd never again be able to work in peace," Allegra mused aloud. "A separate studio would give us greater freedom with our guest list. We could rent a town house here in the West End. We would devote one room to a gallery where artists might show their work. Another room would be for music, and a third for recitation. Let's see, with the receiving hall and kitchen we'd need five rooms."

"Five rooms don't come cheaply, not on Tenth Avenue," he answered.

"Rent," she murmured. From where were they to find the rent? "I don't suppose we could charge admission? No, that would spoil the effect. I know! We'll levy a commission on works sold through our salon. A small charge that wouldn't discourage the seller or the buyer."

"Mercantile enterprise, what will you think of next?" he asked in frank amazement at this turn of her thoughts.

"And a piano," she continued, pretending not to hear

him. "We'll need a piano. I'll tell Papa that I've decided to keep up with my music and need a piano."

"You'd lie to Father?"

"Andy! I never lie. I'll play, unless, of course, we have more proficient musicians as our guests. It would be rude to deny them access to the instrument because I'm at the keyboard. Furnishings! Now that will take some thought."

"No doubt," he murmured. "While you're at it, you'd better give some thought to Mama. She's due back from Charleston any day."

"Mama! I'd forgotten about that. I can't possibly go home now. What shall I say?" She tapped her forefinger against her lips. "I know! You'll tell Mama that now that you're famous you can't possibly do without me. I'm the steadying influence in your life, your secretary and moral support. I'm indispensable." She gave him a radiant smile. "You see how easy it is?"

"I see that it's impossible. Absolutely impossible!"

As she paused on the first step to gaze the length of the block, the concrete and masonry construction of the row of town houses recently erected on Eighty-first Street between Columbus and Amsterdam struck Allegra as the perfect combination of respectability and modern, forward-thinking enterprise. Here at number 107 she and Andrew would open a salon the likes of which New York had never before seen.

When she had toured the three floors for the third and final time, she turned to the real estate agent with a cat-in-the-cream smile. "I suppose we must make do," she murmured in her best imitation of an English accent. "My employer hoped for something a little more spacious, but I understand that these little bachelor quarters are all the rage here in America."

"Yes, indeed!" answered the nattily dressed gentleman in brown tweed. "You will find there ain't much a Yankee can't do, once he puts his mind to it."

"Indeed?" Allegra gazed across at the mahogany doors which opened onto the dining room. "Could these doors be removed and the companion ones which lead to the drawing room? I do detest closed rooms. Once one has become accustomed to the proportions of a castle, the least constriction makes breathing difficult.''

"Of course, miss—my lady," he stammered. Never before in the five years he had been selling real estate on the upper West Side had he had the opportunity of speaking with a genuine English lady. "Whatever you'd like, Levy and Associates can provide."

"Then you'll change the color of the rooms? Excellent. I'd so like to see Pompeian-red in the drawing room with the appropriate border. Something moorish, perhaps. Now in there"—she indicated the dining rooms—"we must have moire silk walls in a soft green. No border. Paint the molding a darker shade of green. As for the carpets, take them with you. I won't deduct them from my rent, since you've been kind enough to agree to my small changes without cost.''

"Without cost? But, my lady, I didn't agree to—to—" He faltered, stung to the quick by her stare.

"Are you saying that you expect *me* to pay for embellishments which will add to the value of a property on which you hold the mortgage? I've never heard of such a thing.''

Blushing, the agent checked the figures in his head, measuring them against his employer's instruction that he close this deal. Having a member of the British aristocracy in residence on the street was bound to make up in prestige the loss of revenue that her changes would require. "We'll make the changes as soon as you've paid the first month's rent.''

"I should think not!" Allegra replied. "What if I disapprove of the color or the border? No, I shall call upon you for a final inspection of the house once the alterations are complete in, say, a week's time. Good day, Mr. Cohen, and do hurry things along. I particularly wish to be situated before that quaint holiday you Americans invented. Thanksgiving, isn't it?''

* * *

"You rented this place without conferring with me first?"

"Andy, it's a lovely little town house. Did you notice the bay window here on the front and cornucopias decorating the balustrade of the front steps? There're trees with little iron fences about them and gas lamps along the sidewalk. We'll have a perfectly wonderful time here."

Andrew made a turn around the drawing room, pausing by the ornate oversized marble mantel. "Where will you get the money to pay the rent?"

"Remember the evenings I spent playing bridge at Eugenia's?" She pinkened. "I won rather more than I admitted."

"How much 'rather more'?"

"Nearly nine hundred dollars."

"I see."

"I can easily afford the rent at one hundred and twenty-five per month. You'll like it better when the furnishings arrive."

"From what source will they spring?"

"You're being peevish, and I did so much want you to like the place."

"I like it very well, Allegra. I just don't see how you expect me to maintain two dwellings."

"I don't expect you to maintain this. It will maintain itself."

"Really, how?"

She was prepared and pulled an invitation from her purse and handed it to him. "I had two dozen of them printed. I've been very selective about our first guests. Once word gets about, we'll be inundated with requests." Andrew crossed the room to take the heavily embossed paper from her hand, unable to keep himself from calculating the cost. The vellum envelopes were beautiful. "All I see is more expense in entertaining guests . . . if they come."

"Oh, I think they'll come," she replied with an arch look. "The list includes all those whom Writwell has satirized in his column."

He sighed. "What good will that do?"

"You didn't ask how I was able to rent an apartment without your knowledge. It's because it's not in your name. It's in the name of Lord J.A.N.U.S. Writwell."

"Allegra! You didn't!"

"Well, yes, I did, but if you're going to take that attitude I don't know how we're going to succeed."

"Succeed?" He threw the invitation away with a muffled curse. "See here, sister dear. You seem to have forgotten that ladies don't succeed in business or any other kind of enterprise that smacks of the mercantile class. As for me, you might as well have given my career to the ashman. Do you think for one moment that men like Gilder or Miss Booth of *Harper's Bazaar* will associate themselves with a social snoop like Writwell? Why, when they learn he and I are one and the same— God, my career's over!"

"Such drama, Andy. You really must learn to control your temper. Besides, you and Writwell are not one and the same. You're merely his representative. What is surprising in that? Your publisher knows as much. We need a drawing card for our salon. Writwell was the logical choice."

Admiration and anger vied for control of his feelings as Andrew looked at her. Her powers of persuasion were quite frightening. Nerves of steel, that's what she had while he trembled in anxiety. Or maybe it was that while she didn't perceive what he stood to lose in her reckless gambling with his career, he knew only too well.

Allegra bent and picked up her invitation, feeling that belated sense of hindsight over what she had done. "Perhaps I've been precipitate, but what's done is done. We may begin moving in tomorrow. Our opening will be a week later. Do you think people like Rhys and Edssene might be persuaded to come?"

"Oh, Rhys will be here if there's wine," Andrew said casually as he consulted his watch, all protest run to ground for the present.

"Good, I've had this maddening urge for weeks to meld the 'eccentricities of genius' with the purses of society."

Andrew looked up sharply, at a loss to understand her reference but certain of one thing. "There'll be no selling of merchandise under this roof. Is that clearly, perfectly, unalterably understood?"

"Yes, Andy," she answered contritely for she heard capitulation in that command.

"I suppose the worst that can occur is that we'll be snubbed," Andrew mumbled as he watched Allegra pace the drawing room. "Careful, that carpet's not ours."

Allegra turned sharply on her heel to face him. "If you won't be helpful, then do be quiet."

"You look wonderful, a real stunner."

She made a moue, but secretly she was pleased. She had given a great deal of thought to what to wear, certain that her example would set the mood for future evenings ... if there were future evenings. She had chosen a romantic French design in keeping with the continental atmosphere she wished to cultivate. The form-fitting gown of maroon stamped velvet was a style considered unsuitable for a young unmarried lady but perfect, she felt, for establishing her role as a hostess of a literary salon. To soften the severity of the style, she had added a high collar of white lace and matching deep cuffs.

"We should've waited," Andrew said as he gazed about. "There aren't enough chairs for a dozen people, let alone the fifty we invited."

"They weren't invited to sit," she replied, but she, too, wondered at her temerity in inviting some of the best-known social figures to a home that, by the standards of the day, was empty. The red-lacquered picture frame walls were devoid of art above the wainscoting of yellow top-cream. Black floral Turkish carpets covered the floors, and matching antique portieres, which Andrew despised, hung at the windows. Allegra smiled at her tiger rug lying before the fireplace. Something from home for good luck. Smaller Turkish rugs, run up as pillows, had been stacked together with silk cushions of every shape and color in the corners. Bare, but not for long. "Our salon is to be very much like a gallery, not an evening at home," she mused aloud. "Circulation is everything."

"There's plenty of room for that," Andrew muttered as

he consulted his watch for the fifth time in thirty minutes. "It's past nine o'clock. They're not coming."

Allegra turned her back on her brother to keep him from seeing her flush of anger. "Is that—? A carriage has paused outside. Oh, Andy, someone's come!"

"Damned odd, I say. Where're the furnishings? Looks as though no one lives here. Think we've had one put over on us, if you want my opinion."

"I would have accepted an invitation to a paddock, to have the satisfaction of telling this Writwell fellow what I think of him!"

"Is that color suitable for a young lady?"

"I didn't know the Grants knew Writwell. They've been very closemouthed about the whole affair."

"He's an English lord, did you say?"

"I received half a dozen inquiries about my invitation today alone. I wasn't going to come until I realized how exclusive the guest list was."

"Do you think he'll write about us in his next column?"

"I hope he lives up to his name. Do you suppose he'll be dark and Byronic or a pale blond prince?"

"The wine ain't bad for an Englishman's choice. I prefer Astor's cellar myself."

"Did you see the dining room? There're several ragged young men standing about in there and," the whisperer finished, "I swear, they *smell*!"

For more than an hour Allegra had circulated about the room, greeting her guests and eavesdropping as subtly as possible on the comments of the arrivals. One thing worried her more than the dissecting comments about Writwell and the salon. That was the fact that neither Rhys nor Edssene had arrived. The few young bearded scions of bohemianism who had dared show their faces had retreated like a frightened clutch of quail into the one corner of the opposite room, their only animation the consumption of glasses of wine.

She caught Andy's arm as he made to pass her. "Where're Rhys and the others?"

He shrugged. "He said he'd come if there was wine, but he may have found a genial bottle nearer Twentieth Street."

"You did tell them to bring examples of their work?"

Andrew gave her hand a quick squeeze. "Don't lose heart now, my girl. I thought no one would come and here are the Gilders, the Throckmortons, and even Huneker. They're positively avid for the chance to meet Writwell."

"The realtor did a rather good job of spreading that rumor about," she agreed pleasantly. "I must keep that in mind. Merchants can be useful in so many ways."

"Can they produce Writwell?" Andrew asked with a wink.

"Yes, that's the question of the hour," said Mr. Ehlin, who had chanced to overhear Andrew. "Where is Writwell, or is this a little joke he's having over on us?"

"It's no joke, Mr. Ehlin." Allegra smiled warmly at the man, who was not an inch above her height but twice her girth. "I can't say when or if Lord Writwell will appear. He's most unpredictable, though a gracious host, wouldn't you agree?"

"Da—darned inconsiderate of him not to show. Think he's turned tail and left the city." He turned to Andrew. "Come to that, what's he to you?"

"You might say that I am acting as his representative in the States."

"Representative? Just what do you represent?"

"His writing. I act as go-between with his publisher."

"Is that so?" inquired Charles de Kay, the brother of Mrs. Gilder and bon vivant of the otherwise staid family. "Then you know Writwell personally?"

Andrew greeted the man who joined them with a handshake. "Evening, de Kay."

"Do join us, Mr. de Kay," Allegra agreed. "Mrs. Gilder has told me so much about you. I hope you're finding our small effort as social arbitrators to your taste."

He leaned near her. "Miss Grant, your salon boasts charms which even Miss Booth could never provide."

Unable to miss the interested sweep of his gaze over her form-fitted gown, she said sweetly, "Why, Mr. de Kay, I had no idea you took such an interest in fabric design."

Blushing at her rebuff, he backed away and turned to Andrew. "Tell us more about Writwell."

Andrew took de Kay's measure with an amused glance. "What would you have me do, describe him?"

"That'd be a start!" Mr. Throckmorton said forcefully, one of the many guests who had gathered about Andrew and Allegra at the mention of Writwell. "If I pass him on the street, I'd like to know it. I most particularly wish to introduce the tip of that Englishman's nose to the end of my fist!"

"Is that threat made to someone in particular or does it apply to any Englishman?" inquired an authoritative British baritone at the edge of the group.

The group broke apart like an egg struck against the side of a bowl, the crack beginning at the edge near the speaker and splitting to the center to expose a startled Andrew and Allegra.

Allegra recognized him immediately. Once met, his oddly bright stare was impossible to forget or ignore. The man from the Plaza Hotel and Delmonico's. Who was he and why was he here?

Eleven

"It's him!"
"It's Writwell?"
"Writwell?"
"Writwell!"

Complete silence followed the tidal wave of whispers.

"Are you the scribbler Writwell?" Throckmorton demanded when it appeared no one would confirm the matter. The Englishman didn't reply, and Throckmorton took steps toward him. A ripple of very uncivilized excitement ran through the guests. Clearly the heavier set of the two, Throckmorton was at a disadvantage next to the taller, leaner, younger man, who didn't move to defend himself. "Are you or aren't you Writwell?"

The stranger's gaze never left Allegra as he said, "I'm Lord Everett Drayton, Seventh Earl of Dundare."

At the announcement a little of the starch seemed to go out of Throckmorton, for his shoulders drooped. "Drayton?" he repeated in disappointment. "Do you know Writwell?"

Drayton's gaze moved to Andrew's flushed face and Allegra's heart skipped a beat. An English lord! He must know that there was no such person as Lord Writwell. Was he going to expose them as frauds?

"No," Drayton replied, his attention refocusing on Allegra.

At that moment there was a scuffle at the front door, followed by a rush of curses with a distinctly Gaelic tinge.

"That will be our artist friends," Andrew said smoothly. "Please excuse me while I welcome them properly."

With an easy grace, he made his way past his startled guests, pausing long enough to offer the Englishman his hand. "Welcome, Lord Drayton, I'm pleased to make your acquaintance."

After a fractional hesitation, Drayton accepted the extended hand and Andrew was surprised to find the Englishman's grip not only firm but roughened, like a workman's grasp. Before he could stop himself, his gaze lowered to their joined hands.

"Marble isn't usually a gentleman's medium," Drayton remarked, quickly releasing his hand.

Andrew had the impression that Drayton meant to smile, but the expression was trapped between the vertical furrows bracketing his mouth. "An artist! Do feel free to come and display your work. It'll be perfectly safe, I assure you."

"No," Drayton answered tersely, his interest drawn once more to Allegra. She was staring back, and he wondered what thoughts ran like deep currents behind those loch-green eyes. "You will introduce me to the young lady?"

"Of course," Andrew began, only to have his attention drawn once more to the door, where sounds distinctly like the beginnings of a fight had started up. "Excuse me a moment."

Allegra turned away from the entrance the moment Andrew left the Englishman's side. "Excuse me, Mrs. Throckmorton. Do you know Lord Drayton?"

Mrs. Throckmorton shook her head. "Never heard of him. He's most extraordinary-looking, though, isn't he?"

"Quite unusual," she answered.

"You will introduce us?" Mrs. Throckmorton encouraged. "It's so seldom that we have a real aristocrat in our midst. And, as it seems Lord Writwell won't appear . . ."

She let the thought trail, but Allegra understood the implied disappointment at Writwell's absence. If she didn't act promptly, the momentary triumph of the evening could turn into disaster. Perhaps the stranger's unexpected presence could be used to her advantage.

It was her duty as hostess to welcome him, but resentment reared up in her as soon as she turned toward Lord Drayton. He was watching her, his light eyes burning like twin fires beneath his black brows.

As she moved toward him, Drayton felt no unease for he had fortified himself with the rare indulgence of two drops of laudanum in his dinner wine. His spirits were high but with the sharp edge of expectancy blunted by the aura of an opium haze. She wouldn't disappoint him, could not disappoint him, in his present state of peaceful bliss.

She looked like a dream. Gaslighting sallowed complexions, but hers appeared luminous in the golden glow. It touched the dark halo of her pompadour, gleaming like moonlight on curling midnight breakers, accented her patrician nose and high cheekbones and the curve of her bottom lip. She looked radiant, composed, and competent. She would light up not only a salon but even the dank depths of Dundare Castle.

The thought unnerved him, and he wished suddenly that he had added a third drop to his glass.

Allegra felt every muscle in her body tauten as she neared him. He was tall, his savagely handsome features more daunting close up than she remembered. Her heart hung heavy in her chest, but she wouldn't give him the satisfaction of knowing that his presence caused her a moment's disquiet. She stopped before him. She smiled. She spoke.

"Welcome, Lord Drayton. I believe my brother has already introduced himself. I'm Allegra Grant."

He gave the slightest nod of his head in deference to the introduction but said nothing.

"Did you come with friends?" she persisted, commanding herself to keep the strict code of civility in her tone, though his stare was unnerving her.

Again the faint movement with his head. This time in the negative.

Stung by his supercilious manner, she said, "I don't recall your name among those on the guest list, my lord."

"That's because, as you very well know, it isn't there."

His voice was deep and harsh, as though the act of speaking shifted stone upon stone. She remembered it well.

For a desperate, terrible second she feared she would blurt out in public the question uppermost in her mind: *Who are you and why have you been following me?* She sensed that he deliberately provoked her agitation. "Do you often crash private parties?"

"Seldom," he said, his gaze wandering away as though he was growing restless in her company.

This display of rudeness checked her curiosity, and she simply turned her back on him and moved away.

Drayton watched her go with his breath suspended. The opium had failed its purpose. His pleasant calm had vanished completely. Yet he couldn't remember a word of the last seconds. What had she said? What had he answered?

God! The feeling congesting his heart and lungs was different from anything he had ever experienced. He wondered fleetingly if the laudanum was numbing his heart, if at any second he would fall over dead. What did it matter? She had, at last, spoken with him.

"Arrogant snob," Allegra murmured as she entered the hallway. "Why—? What on earth is that?"

A huge canvas-covered rectangle, tightly wedged at an angle through the front door, was balanced by Andrew and Edssene on one side and Rhys and Seton on the other.

"The first artwork to grace the Writwell salon," Rhys pronounced from the far side of the parcel.

"Allegra!" Eugenia greeted as she appeared from the opposite end of the hall. "I was just looking for you. They've brought my portrait to be unveiled!"

Swathed from toe to neck in a coat of gray cloth trimmed in chenille and oxidized silver cord, and closed with a boa of black ostrich feathers, Eugenia appeared more lovely and ethereal than ever.

"Eugenia, how nice of you to come." Allegra squeezed the hands thrust into hers. "Why, you're freezing! Come in by the fire."

"Poo on the cold! I've something really important to tell you." She leaned very close. "You're the first to know. I've broken off my engagement! I'm not going to be a baroness after all."

"Eugenia! Why?"

"I couldn't bear the thought of leaving the city," she said evasively, but her eyes betrayed her as she looked at Rhys.

Following her gaze, Allegra said in disbelief, "You haven't thrown away a perfectly good arrangement for that Irishman?"

"Allegra dearest, don't scold me. I'm too happy. I never guessed what love could be."

"But he's so—so unsuitable."

Eugenia's expression changed to one of resentment. "Are you going to lecture me on the necessity of making a proper match? I assure you, you needn't bother. As an heiress, there's no compelling need for me to find a husband to support me."

A gust of misgiving sailed through her thoughts, but Allegra didn't give it voice. "You're to wed Mr. O'Conner?"

Eugenia pinkened. "He hasn't asked me yet, but I know he will. For the moment he must keep his head clear of the mundane matters of life in order to create. Once he's famous he'll have time for other matters. Oh, here it comes," she cried as the portrait slid free and into the hallway. "Wait until you see it. Rhys says Edssene has captured my soul on canvas. It's all been quite exciting."

Having been freed of his corner of the canvas, Andrew approached the ladies. "This is what I call luck. An unveiling on our very first evening. Eugenia, you're a dear. You might have made a production of it at your annual Christmas Eve party. Ah, but that's right, you won't be here on that occasion this year."

"Perhaps not," Eugenia answered vaguely. "I'd better see where they're putting it. Edssene was most insistent that I be present for the unveiling so that a comparison can be made to life."

As she slipped away, Allegra took Andrew's arm. "You'll never guess what Eugenia just told me!"

Andrew patted her hand. "Can't it wait? We've an unveiling to attend to. Be a dear and announce it to the guests in the drawing room while I go into the kitchen to order up the champagne. We must toast the evening."

Allegra returned reluctantly to the drawing room to find that Lord Drayton had become the center of a discussion. She overheard him saying, "I doubt very much that Writwell is English," as she neared the group.

"Why do you say that?" Mrs. Ehlin asked.

"Isn't it obvious? What Englishman could conceive of the atrocities permitted by the American class system? Here society consists of anyone who can buy, bluster, or blackmail his way into the vaunted circles. Breeding is nonexistent. Scum as well as cream rises to the top."

The collective gasp of the assembly further provoked his humor. "You did ask my opinion. I see I should've been less than honest in my response."

"Not at all, Lord Drayton," Allegra inserted coldly, her cheeks burning with indignation. "Like you, I believe that civilized breeding is a thing of the past. Your demonstration of the new breed is most appreciated."

He had met a few French women renowned for their intellect, but their very foreignness made it acceptable. However, this was different. He stepped toward her, a frown on his face.

Allegra held her ground. What could happen here, surrounded by her friends and guests?

"Never again wear jet," he said. To her astonishment he plucked the black-bead earrings from her lobes and pocketed them. "A lady of your beauty and character should wear only pearls. So unnecessary, this American insistence on gaudy display and frightful dress."

Had he doused her with a bucketful of ice water, Allegra couldn't have been more taken aback. She hadn't indulged in physical violence since the age of twelve, but the urge to slap him was so great that she curled her fingers into the skirt of her gown to keep from acting on the emotion.

"You are familiar with Beaumarchais, Lord Drayton? There comes to mind a suitable phrase. 'Parce que vous êtes un grand seigneur, vous vous croyez un grand génie.' "

She saw the barb strike, part of her pleased that he understood the quote and the other bracing for his reply. She was too self-possessed to strike him but curious enough to provoke whatever strength of character ruled the wild look in his eyes.

Drayton stared at her, but too many emotions were careening through him to allow his sight to bring her face into clear focus. He could feel beads of perspiration gathering on his brow. Each breath was a labor. But through the confusion, he found his voice. "Miss Grant, I answer you with a countryman's words. 'There is little friendship in the world, and least of all between equals.' Until next time."

He turned slowly, encountered the gaze of the man nearest him, who hastily backed out of his path, and strode out of the room.

The inhabitants of the salon seemed to draw a collective breath of relief when the front door had opened and shut behind him.

"Well, I never in all my life saw the like! The arrogance of the man. Whatever did you say to make him leave?" Mrs. Throckmorton demanded.

"Only that because he is a great lord he believes that he is also a great genius. Oh, he took my jewelry with him!" Allegra took no more than a step toward the door when reason checked her. A pair of earrings was little enough to lose if they rid her of the odious man. Still, she would speak to Andy about him, tell him how and where she had seen Lord Drayton before. He must not be admitted to the salon again.

"The unveiling is ready!"

Within minutes the guests, still rattled by the aristocrat's eccentric behavior, had assembled in the gallery room before a huge draped canvas. Eugenia had shed her coat to reveal a ball gown of pink and ivory satin. She stood to one side of the easel, frequently licking her lips. The nervous gesture surprised Allegra, for even at the worst of moments Eugenia had always displayed an admirable amount of self-possession.

Andrew stepped before the painting, his champagne glass lifted in salutation. "First, allow me to welcome each and every one of you on behalf of our host Lord J.A.N.U.S. Writwell, who regrets his inability to join us tonight. As your hosts, my sister and I hope that you will continue to favor us with your presence from time to time. Welcome." After a sip of champagne, he turned to Eugenia with a broad smile. "All of you know our guest of honor, Miss Eugenia Simpson. Thanks to her we'll be unveiling a work by a new artist this evening. Before the moment of triumph, allow me to offer a toast to her generosity and graciousness."

A congenial tinkling of glasses accompanied murmurs of delight and felicity directed at the blushing Eugenia.

"Will the artist come forth now for the unveiling."

Edssene stepped cautiously from the dark shadow cast by the canvas and bobbed his head in acknowledgement of the polite applause. Rhys stepped forward boldly and gave Eugenia a wink as he reached up to help Edssene lift up the drape.

A unanimous "Ah!" rose from the audience when the portrait was revealed. At first glance it seemed to be a conventional portrait. A lovely young lady dressed in pink and ivory satin dominated the center of the canvas. The play of light and shadow upon her beautiful skin and sumptuous finery was skillfully executed. The lines of carriage and chin provided an elegant example of the very best of New York society womanhood.

However, there was nothing the least bit conventional about her expression. The Eugenia Simpson who sat gazing out from the picture was not the Eugenia Simpson her acquaintances had ever before glimpsed. There was an emotional intensity in her gaze, a frank welcome in the slightly parted lips, a feeling that she had spied someone behind the viewer who was special, cherished, loved.

Allegra looked at her friend and then back at the portrait. The flesh and bone reality of Eugenia was the less compelling of the two visions. The lady in the portrait was vivid, alive with intensity, caught in the full rapture of primitive, sensuous love. It was an intimate moment, a moment not to be viewed by any other than the person at whom she stared.

The comments came softly at first, whispered with a turned head or behind a raised hand, but quickly gathered volume.

"It's quite, quite dreadful!"

"How unfortunate."

"Completely unsuitable for a drawing room."

"One can never be too careful in one's choice of artist!"

"The man's made a caricature of her. What else can explain that pained expression?"

One glance at Eugenia's faltering smile made Andrew speak up. "Miss Simpson, you've never looked more radiant."

"Radiant, did you say?" Mrs. Ehlin challenged. "She looks positively theatrical! Lord, what an expression! It's like she's bitten into a poisoned apple."

"I think it's quite romantic," Allegra said firmly as she made her way toward the front of the crowd. "You're to be commended for your courage, Eugenia."

Eugenia smiled as her cheeks flared with color. "I didn't want a simple assessment of my features. I hoped the work would reveal the soul."

"You received less than you hoped for," Mrs. Ehlin responded coldly. "I hope you haven't paid him. I'd sue, instead."

Edssene, who until this moment had hung back in mute shyness, stepped forward to answer the lady. "You, what do you know of art?" he shouted, his accent heightened by indignation. "You speak of money. That is because you are a merchant with a merchant's mind!"

"Oh, dear!" Allegra murmured, caught between amusement at Mrs. Ehlin's suddenly livid face and Edssene's defense of his work and the horror that the evening was about to take yet another nasty turn.

"See here, you'll not address my wife in that manner, you heathen!" Mr. Ehlin called in challenge.

Ignoring him, Edssene rounded on Eugenia. "For you I present my work to these philistines. What do they do? They spit on it! It is too much. Rather I should destroy it with loving hands than allow them to revile it!" He whirled on the painting, withdrew a knife from his breast pocket, and before anyone understood his intent, struck the canvas, cutting a long jagged tear down the center of the satin skirts.

As Edssene swung away from the painting, Eugenia screamed, and many thought she had been attacked as well. The room erupted in masculine oaths, feminine shrieks and fainting spells. In the pandemonium, Edssene slipped from the room and escaped through the front door.

Drayton affixed his family seal to the envelope. preferring the impression in hot wax to the new glue available for such purposes. When he was done, he reached for the velvet-lined case that lay by his hand and opened it. Inside, nestled against the black, lay a pair of earrings and a collar of pearls with a diamond-pavé clasp. She would be furious when she opened it. It pleased him to think of her anger. It was the last emotion he had seen her display.

She had very nearly slapped his face, and he had hoped in that instant that she would. But she was very much a creature of habit and manners and couldn't bring herself to behave in a manner unfitted for the salon. It disappointed him to recognize that niggling bit of bourgeoisie in her character. But perhaps she was capable of change. He would console himself with that thought. For now he must remove himself from the game. London and responsibilities too long neglected beckoned him home.

His aim in going to the Writwell salon had been to begin his seduction of her, yet something held him back. From the moment he entered the salon, he had felt like a wolf among the flock, a predator with his choice of victims. Yet she had crossed the room toward him like a countess greeting her consort: his equal. He remembered the precise intensity of the lilac scent rising from her skin. Her voice still whispered through his thoughts at odd moments, the husky notes colored by emotions as dark and lovely as her beauty. The taste of her . . . Ah, it didn't serve to think of that. Yet he could not keep himself from conjecture and the shiver of aroused passion which accompanied it. She would be like black cherries: bitter and sweet; ripe and brimming with the warm juices of her youth and femininity. He ran his hand strongly down his lower belly and part of his left thigh, feeling the tumescence. He had longed to fill his mouth with her taste, drink her in like a thirsty man. A pity he must leave.

She was not only beautiful and desirable but something more. Her knowledge of Beaumarchais' quote had displayed in a single instance both her wit and the extent of her education, a rare thing in a lady. Her power of attraction had not diminished with reality. All in all, his sojourn in America had been quite a pleasant diversion.

The Grants made an astonishing couple, the kind that seldom came in pairs: beauty and genius. A man of a nature different from his might consider seducing them both. He knew men of such tastes, finding equal allure in the embraces of men and women. Such a man would desire them both with pleasure. Alas, he wasn't of that disposition. He preferred to match wits and passions with Allegra Grant.

He had connected J.A.N.U.S. Writwell to Grant from the first column. How could Americans be so easily misled by a pen name? There was a sharper wit given rein in the Writwell works, but the style was recognizably similar to Grant's acknowledged work. In fact, in writing Writwell's satire he had developed a new piquancy that improved his other work.

Drayton closed the jewel case and laid the letter on top, then reached for a second sheet of stationery and picked up his pen. A slow smile spread across his face as he penned the salutation, "My Dear Mister J.A.N.U.S. Writwell."

When the letter was finished and sealed, he sat back and pulled his watch from his pocket, pausing to tease lightly the jet earrings attached to the chain; his talisman against the future until they met again.

"Send them back!"

"Back where?" Andrew questioned. "There's no return address or jeweler's mark. Good lord, but they're beauties. Persian, is my guess. The soft blue-gray shade would look smashing with your coloring."

"You don't seriously believe I would wear them?" Allegra replied.

"No, I don't guess that would do, a gift from a strange man and all. Though, to be fair, they were sent to replace your earrings."

"Those earrings were mere baubles. There's a king's fortune in that case."

"An earl's fortune." Andrew straightened up. "You don't suppose they're family heirlooms?"

Allegra gasped, "No, of course not! The earl's eccentric, but he wouldn't squander family jewels on strange foreign ladies."

Andrew cocked his head to one side. "Strange foreign lady. I rather like that phrase. Writwell must make note of it."

"You wouldn't!"

"Now, now, we agreed that Writwell must write about the Grants or people will become suspicious. As to that, you haven't read the final draft of the column devoted to the opening of Writwell's salon. It was easy enough to write. No exaggeration needed."

"No, indeed. We were a three-ring circus, a Bowery show hall, and Bellevue all rolled into one. I thought Eugenia's hysteria would never subside. As for the Ehlins, they'll never speak to us again. My salon is ruined."

"*Our* salon isn't exactly ruined. Haven't you read the mail?"

"I haven't had the nerve. Are we to be sued?"

Andrew laughed. "Our popularity is mixed. Half of the mail contains curt thank-yous for the 'stimulating evening.' The other half is filled with thinly veiled requests for invitations to the next Writwell evening."

"Are you serious?"

He lifted a handful of mail. "Read them for yourself. I've work to do. Ah, yes, what should I do with this?"

Allegra held up a restraining hand. "I don't want them. Send them back. Oh, very well. We don't know where to send them now, but someone must know where to find Lord Drayton."

"As a matter of fact, I do." Andrew reached for another envelope and passed it to her. "It's an apology of sorts from Lord Drayton to Writwell. He admits receiving no invitation 'beyond that that draws like minds together.' It also says he's sailing for England on the next tide. So you can enjoy the pearls in good conscience, knowing that you would have returned them if possible."

Allegra shook her head. "I won't touch them and I don't ever again want to hear that man's name mentioned."

Andrew didn't comment on her outburst, though it puzzled him. No man, however wealthy, sent a lady an extravagant gift unless he was greatly taken with her. Under ordinary circumstances, the gift would have required that Drayton make his intentions clear. Yet the fact that he had left the country relieved Andrew, as Allegra's nearest male kin, of the obligation of calling upon him. There the matter could rest for now. He stood up. "We've work to do. Are you ready?"

"In a moment." When Andrew had moved into the library, Allegra pulled the letter that accompanied the pearls from her pocket and reread it.

Miss Allegra Grant:
Her lament: *Perverseness is one of the primitive impulses of the human heart.*

His answer: *Change in a trice/The lilies and languors of virtue/For the raptures and roses of vice.*
        Be brave.

Drayton

Poe and Swinburne. She thrust the letter back into her pocket. Now that the incident was past, she could see a certain humor in it. Lord Drayton's peculiar wit revealed a well-educated mind—surprisingly, from what she had heard of English aristocrats. Even so, she was not about to be soothed by poetry and extravagant gifts. "Good riddance!"

January 1891

"Happy New Year to you too, sir!" Allegra returned with a clink of her wassail cup against Harry Chatham's. "I can scarcely believe that a new year is upon us."

"And yet there isn't a happier day the entire year," he replied. "It's the time of fresh beginnings, new hopes, a time for planning and resolutions to do better."

"I can't think how we'll do better than last year," Allegra said. "Andrew's writing is coming along so well. As for the salon, I think Writwell can be justly proud."

Harry nodded even as he was jostled by the press of people filling the Writwell salon. "Speaking of our host, will he not show himself, even on this prestigious occasion?"

Allegra pretended to look about. "I do believe that he was here earlier. In fact, I'm certain someone remarked on it. The guests began arriving at noon, but I didn't arrive until nearly half past one. I had the good fortune to be last on my hairdresser's list. Tsk, I don't see him about. The earlier crowd must have fatigued him."

As she spoke, Harry Chatham leaned nearer on the pretense of listening but really to give himself a better view of the décolletage of her snow-white velvet gown trimmed in red satin *choux*. "A natural stunner," is how he would describe her to his bachelor brother who had refused his invitation to spend a part of New Year's Day at Writwell's.

"This is my first New Year's in the city," Allegra said, hoping to draw the gentleman's attention away from her bodice. "Is it always such a crush?"

"At popular places, always. Why, a man can scarcely creep up and down Fifth Avenue today. Clever of the ladies to take the part of receiving while the gentlemen are put to the trouble of traveling the city to pay calls to them. Why, my Abigail put her head together with Mrs. Rush and Mrs. Covington and decided to sit up in our parlor, cozy as you please, while the world comes to them. Saves wear and tear on the gowns."

"I see. Oh, look, there's someone I haven't seen in ages. Do excuse me, Mr. Chatham. Keep an eye out for Writwell. He's certain to appear again before the doors close."

"I'll do that!" Harry called over the buzz of the crowd.

"Gracious!" she murmured as she sought a moment to herself behind one of the dozens of hothouse orange trees rented as decoration for the occasion. Even though there was snow on the streets, the press of people had heated the town house to an uncomfortable degree. Still, she couldn't complain. A few short weeks ago, Writwell's salon had been on the verge of failure.

After an opening night when the resulting pandemonium had caused a scandal that made every gossip column in the city, she and Andrew were ready to abandon the salon. Even Writwell felt obliged to give the evening a scathing critique. She and Andrew had learned their lesson. Never again would they mix proper New York society with the wilder elements of the artistic community. While most of the older members of society refused invitations to Writwell's, their places were quickly filled by their younger, more adventurous peers.

The New Year's Day reception was necessary to Writwell's continued prestige. Every room was lavishly adorned with boughs of fresh flowers and garlands of greens, handsome tables filled with delicacies and French wines and fancy punches. She had no earthly idea of how they would pay the debts incurred, but she refused to worry about that just yet.

It was the beginning of a new year. Nothing could be wrong with a year that started as well as this one.

Andrew peered around the shrubbery. "I thought that was you." Looking especially handsome in his formal attire, he stepped behind the orange tree, two glasses of champagne in hand. "A toast to a successful year?"

Allegra took a glass. "And successful collaboration?"

"But, of course," he answered.

"Now, we must toast our resolutions," she said after a sip.

"Very well, what do you wish for most in the coming year?" Andrew questioned.

"A unique and exotic salon!" she answered readily and smiled at him over the rim of her glass. "It's going to work, Andy. It really is."

He smiled back. "To Writwell, bless him!"

Allegra met his glass. "To Writwell!"

* 1892 *

Twelve

New York City, March 1892

Allegra turned the key in the latch, her spirits high with expectation. Caught by a gust of March wind, the door dragged her in so quickly she nearly fell over the slight aproned figure polishing the floor.

"Miss Grant! I dinna hear yer knock," the flustered maid answered as she scrambled to her feet and bobbed a curtsy.

"That's because I didn't, Annie," Allegra answered with a laugh. "I received a note saying a parcel's been delivered. Where is it?"

Annie pointed toward the main drawing room. "'Twas put in the Araby room."

"It's called a Turkish salon," Allegra said.

"Turkish, Araby, 'tis all the same to the likes o' me, beggin' yer pardon, Miss Grant."

Without replying, Allegra moved across the entrance hall toward an inlaid lacquer screen standing in the corner. "This is new. It's lovely, isn't it?"

"Ifin ye say so, miss. Don't know as how I'd have it in me house. A pagan thing, it is."

"Much of what we're accumulating is pagan," Allegra mused ruefully, remembering the bronze satyr and nymph an artist guest had unveiled last evening. He called it "Dissolution of Youth." Youth was slender, graceful, and innocent in her nakedness. The lascivious satyr who embraced her was disease, poverty, and death. It had been snatched up quickly by one of the more prosperous of their many guests, though the man was admittedly no connoisseur of art. "We've very little call for the religious."

"I do so like them paintings hanging in the gallery."

"Thank you, Annie. You may take your tea now."

Annie bobbed a curtsy, leaving her task unfinished. After five months on staff at the Writwell House, she had learned not to try to understand the eccentricities of the household. For instance, the way that lovely Miss Grant and her handsome brother came and went without so much as a rap was most peculiar. Then there was the fact that never once had any of the staff seen Lord Writwell, their employer. Away on the Continent, she had been told when she first applied for the job. She soon discovered that there were no personal effects of Writwell's in the house. No shirts or linens, no suits, not even a boot button could be found. If not for the generous wages and relative freedom offered by an absent employer, she might have quit. There was something decidedly un-pious about some of the guests who frequented the house. Why, she'd even seen women smoking!

"Good!" Allegra said when Annie had turned into the servant stairwell behind the hall stairs and disappeared. She didn't want a single soul to watch as she unwrapped this particular parcel.

She turned and walked into the drawing room slowly, her eyes appraising every item. Her New Year's Day resolution of 1891 had been met by the enthusiastic response of the many guests of Writwell's salon. The once bare room was now an opulent salon. Like a pasha's tent, its bounty spilled forth jewel tones in silks and carpets and fabric. Electric lights set in Moorish-design antique silver globes hung from the ceiling. Even sunlight was drenched in color as it filtered through the stained-glass fanlights above the windows, a gift from Tiffany's. Two bohemian artists had painted the ceiling pale blue and inset it with vermeiled aluminum stars. The red walls were hidden by sketches and paintings of nearly every description and size, works of guest artists or gifts from patrons of the salon. Poems, stories, antique books, rugs, japanned furnishings, glassworks, bronzes, marbles, statues, and paintings of every kind and description had accumulated so quickly that she began to refer to the drawing room as a Turkish bazaar.

She smiled in self-satisfaction. The salon was open one evening a week. Some nights were reserved strictly as highbrow affairs with guest performances by opera singers and musicians of renown. Other nights invitations went out to the bolder community of artists. Then gypsy music replaced the strains of Wagner and Brahms as wine replaced punch and spaghetti replaced mousses and pâté. Artists brought their works for display or read aloud or played compositions.

Gossip kept each element guessing about the identity of the other. No one bothered to deny the rumors that a carriage marked with the Astor crest had paused before 107 West Eighty-first Street on more than one occasion. Nor did they deny the rumor that Tchaikovsky had performed one evening. After all, the famous Russian composer had been the guest of a Dakota resident and neighbor of the Grants, the Schirmers, while conducting the opening concerts at the new Music Hall the previous spring. Edwin Booth, appearing at the Brooklyn Academy of Music in *Hamlet*, had often dropped by. Rumors that Andrew was Writwell were rampant, almost an open secret, but the truth was never admitted by either Grant.

From month to month she and Andrew walked the delicate balance between the two worlds in which they mixed. They were equally at home at the opera and an elegant dinner in the Fifties or in the Writwell salon on evenings when bearded poets traded professional insults or mired themselves in heated political or philosophical debate. Their parents knew of their social activities among the Ten Thousand but had no idea that their children were hosts at the latter functions.

The cost of the salon was a continuing strain on Grant finances. Allegra had accidentally found a partial solution one evening when several society guests were admiring a particular painting and she jokingly offered it to the highest bidder. To her surprise they responded and the piece was sold for a hefty price. Treating the impromptu auction as a game, other guests begged her to offer items. Intuition made her refrain. The Writwell salon wasn't to be an auction house. But, after that night, she would occasionally offer an object chosen at random for sale. It astonished her that the expenditure of money pleased the wealthy more than any other activity. For the guests, her auctions offered an added fillip, the covetous pleasure of finding oneself the owner of a piece which under normal circumstances one could never have purchased from a friend.

"Thank goodness for gifts," she murmured as she reached for the package on the table. This was what she had come to see. She turned and crossed the room. In one corner a Damascus saber, its sickle gleaming like a slice of moon, hung above a divan piled with cushions and sheltered by a *gobbah* of paisley print. Here she sat down, kicked off her shoes, nestled her toes in the tiger skin that lay at her feet, and pulled the string which bound the package.

Brown butcher paper had been wrapped several times around the item. Just before the final turn a slip of paper fell out and she paused to read it. *"For Beauty, the Truth,"* it said.

She smiled. She knew what the gift was. It was a portrait of herself. She had received a letter apprising her of its delivery but not the name of the sender. No one had ever painted her before, nor had she sat for this picture. Flattered that someone had captured her in moments unaware, she was eager and excited to see the results—in private. Through the paper she could feel the heavy ornamental frame. It was small, no more than ten by twelve inches. With an inhaled breath of excitement she tore away the last of the paper and held it up.

The likeness staring back at her was an exact replica of herself. The black fringe of curls framing her forehead, the straight black brows above enormous green eyes, the trace of mauve beneath, telltale signs of long evenings spent writing with Andy, the line of the nose and sudden flare of nostril, the soft mouth and determined chin; she recognized every feature, yet it wasn't a portrait. It was a reflection of herself in a mirror set in a solid silver frame into which sunflowers had been hammered with extraordinary detail.

Allegra stared at it. What had the sender meant by the gift of a mirror? Was it a joke? Whose joke? Curious, she turned it over and found another note attached to the back.

Youth is fleeting. Disease and age wither mere flesh. What will be left of Beauty? Dare to be more!

The whack made by the impact of mail falling onto the hall floor from the door slot made her jump. A moment later she heard a familiar voice and then a key in the lock. Andy had arrived. Without reasoning out her reactions, she picked up the mirror, quickly rewrapped it, then stuck it behind a cushion on the divan.

"Andy, at last!" she greeted as she hurried out into the hall. "I've been waiting for you."

Andrew looked up. "To what do I owe this enthusiastic greeting? As I recall, your last words to me this morning were something on the order of 'antiquated, puffed-up, vainglorious scribbler!' "

"Did I say that? Well, you were being stubborn about phrasing. Still, it must've been the coffee that made me so cross. I must be careful not to drink coffee before noon."

Andy tucked the package he carried under his arm. "Let's eliminate coffee from your diet altogether. What have we here?" He bent and picked up the scattered mail. "The usual: bills and thank-yous and bills and invitations and bills and magazines and bills— Really, for a man of simple appetites, Writwell does run up a steep liquor tab." He looked at Allegra with a mischievous smile. "Ah! A fan."

He held out the missive to Allegra and she opened it. For more than a year, Writwell had received frequent, volatile letters from admirers and detractors. "Listen to this. 'Dearest' so forth um, ah, here: '. . . am indebted to you for exposing the latest philistine vulgarisms that pass for style among the vultures.' To what do you suppose he's referring? Could it be the piece about the silver and crystal service birthday parties for pets making the rounds of Fifth Avenue?"

Andrew shook his head. "No, that hasn't run yet."

"Ah," Allegra said when she'd scanned the letter. "He refers to the article addressing society's attitude toward the works of painters, writers, and sculptors."

"I've had complaints from other sources on that one. We shouldn't have compared the Four Hundred's list of famous artists to an obituary notice from the Louvre."

"It's the truth," Allegra maintained. "Don't you remember the conversation that prompted Writwell's article? We were in the National Academy last fall. I thought I'd burst with laughter when that old gentleman complained of the rising interest in the French school of painters. 'Just when I'd learned to roll those I-talian names off my tongue, now they've gone and changed countries and pronunciations. Damned inconsiderate, I say!'"

"Very well, you answer him."

"Oh, no. It's your turn. I couldn't fit another thing into my schedule. Mama and Papa are coming to town before the end of the month. I must appear fresh and unrended, as Papa so indelicately phrases it. He's again talked Mama into concern about my lack of suitors."

"There's not so much a lack of suitors as there is a lack of interest on your part. You frighten them away."

"*I* frighten them? Well, thank you very much for the compliment. Very well, I'll wed when you've led the way, brother dear."

"God!" Andrew made a face that puckered his moustache, a new sartorial addition of which Allegra wasn't quite certain she approved.

"It still reminds me of a caterpillar," she remarked.

"Perhaps I'll let it grow into a handlebar," he said, stroking his upper lip.

"You do and I'll yank it out myself."

"Ouch! A lady of my acquaintance says my whiskers are quite the thing."

"Which lady would that be? There've been so many about of late, I can't keep count."

"Speaking of suitors, aren't we expecting Dr. Boyd for dinner?"

"I believe so." Allegra sighed. "Andy, do I really appear

so indifferent to the gentlemen? What I mean is, why do none of them attempt to make violent love to me?''

Andrew burst into laughter. "My God, Allegra, you can still amaze me!"

"Entertaining you wasn't my purpose. I just don't understand why men don't find me attractive."

"Don't find you . . . ? Dear girl, look about you on any evening. Men scarcely can take their eyes off you. You hear the sonnets that are read on salon evenings. You figure in fully ninety percent of them."

"It's flattering," Allegra admitted, "but they're guests, after all."

"And the society toffs, don't they vie with one another to occupy your time? You were surrounded in our box at the opera last Thursday."

"Oh, those boys! I hardly think they care who they're chasing as long as they prevent the other fellow from claiming the lady. As for the older men, they wheeze and ogle me until I wish for my cloak. I want something more than that."

He smiled knowingly. "Love?"

"Yes. Love."

He put an arm around her shoulders. "I thought you were quite content with Dr. Boyd's attentions."

"He's hardly a suitor. He's more interested in discussing Writwell. Sometimes I think I'm merely the excuse he uses to come and talk with you. He won't admit that I have a mind. He wouldn't even allow me an opinion on Nietzsche the last time he dined. God is dead, indeed! Do you know, he's never even tried to kiss me."

"Kiss you? Would you let him?"

"I don't know. I've never been given the chance. It's most vexing."

"If you fell in love and married, I'd miss you greatly. Who'd help with my columns?"

He said it lightly, but suddenly the full implication of what Allegra's marriage would mean was borne in on him by his own words. He could get along without her. Of course he could. He just didn't want to . . . yet.

"What's that under your arm?"

Andrew glanced down at the package in his possession. "This? It's a manuscript I've agreed to read for one of the fellows from Washington Square."

"Oh, how delicious! Let me see it."

"No." He hugged the package tighter. "He's most particular about who reads it. He made me promise not to show it to Writwell."

"But you are Writwell."

"To be precise, half of Writwell, so half a promise is better than none. Have you made out the list for our final Writwell evening? With the season coming to an end in another month, people will soon be planning for their summer vacations. Last minute invitations are often overlooked."

"I wish we had plans for summer," Allegra said wistfully. "I've never seen Newport."

"You're a working girl. Working girls don't visit Newport. If it's idle leisure you desire, marry." He held up the mail. "What shall we do about these bills?"

"Give them to me. I'll manage them somehow." She slipped the mail into her purse. "Now I must dash. There's much to be done before dinner. See you about seven."

When she was gone, Andrew drifted into the drawing room, his mind still very much on their conversation. His parents were pressing Allegra to marry. It came up each time they called or wrote or visited. His success as a writer and the attendant need for a hostess had convinced them to allow her to live with him for a time. After all, what better place was there for her to make a proper match than in New York? But they considered it a temporary arrangement. If they knew Allegra attended those evenings when Writwell's salon became a bohemian oasis, she would have been back in Philadelphia long before this. He needed her, now more than ever.

Allegra was indefatigable. It was she who goaded him to stay up and work on articles when he would have gone to bed. Deadlines made her glow while they leadened his mind. She believed in positive thought. Or was it ignorance that buoyed her above life's realities? He couldn't decide which, but it worked.

He admired the way she so often smoothed over the banes of his life and disposed of them with her "I'll manage it" attitude. He supposed that she had inherited their father's head for financial matters. There were times when he was tempted to hand over all his money matters to her, but pride stopped him. It was better that she remained unaware of how often he veered across the fine line between solvency and financial ruin.

He was just on the verge of establishing himself. How could a man who cultivated an air of success be expected to pinch pennies? When among others of his class, he was obliged to show a careless disregard for finances and schedules in order to overcome the social prejudice against having a job. Dinners were expensive. Clothing, theater tickets, opera boxes, even his cigars were expensive. He would have been thought a miser if he didn't regularly stand for several rounds of drinks at his favorite saloon, dine at his club, and gamble at the races.

The package slipped from under his arm and struck the floor. He stood a moment staring at it, thinking about his pursuit of membership at the prestigious Century Club, whose members were the artistic and intellectual giants of the city. One of the membership had recently suggested to Andrew that he should have a major work published in order to insure his acceptance. Writwell was a regional phenomenon. He needed national stature as a writer. He nudged the package with his foot. This was to be his crowning effort, the work to catapult him to national recognition. His novel.

Half a dozen publishers had rejected it. Those who received it as the work of Andrew Grant were polite, calling it an estimable first effort but lacking in substance, clarity, and breadth of design. Amusing, yes, but missing the true wit of social satire. When his name wasn't attached to it, they called it "a slight, amateurish effort in the style of Writwell."

Andrew's laughter caught in his throat. It must be something of a feat to be castigated as a plagiarizer of one's own work. Allegra would laugh herself silly if she knew. But he couldn't bring himself to tell her about the novel's existence. This was to be something entirely of his own.

"Damnation!" he cried and kicked the package. The blows burst the string binding it and scattered papers in all directions. He needed time and peace and quiet and inspiration. Allegra must not be taken from him now.

Allegra smiled at Dr. Boyd and felt her face strain with the effort of a long evening. Andy hadn't returned at seven, nor at half past, nor even at eight, and so she and the doctor had eaten their catered dinner without him. It was improper for her to dine alone in her apartment with a man. This bit of daring gave the evening its only sparkle.

A pierced silver epergne served as a centerpiece, holding a bunch of May roses and tiny baskets of sugared almonds, striped peppermints, and honeyed fruits. As she reached for an almond she said, "Do tell me where you'll be lecturing next. I've never yet heard you speak."

"You'd be disappointed," John answered as he set his dessert spoon down. "And I wouldn't want to tarnish your perception of me."

"Why would your lecture do that?"

"You've been spared much in your life. Therefore, you can't imagine the sort of people for whom I speak."

"You'd be surprised by the sort of person I've met at Writwell's. But, of course, you don't approve of Writwell." She smiled, keeping up the charade that John hadn't guessed that Andrew was Writwell. "Is that why you never accept his invitations?"

John demurred. "As I have no artistic talents and I cannot afford to assume the role of patron, I am caught neatly betwixt and between."

"Dr. Boyd, you are equivocating."

"Very well." He lightly dabbed his mouth with his napkin before continuing, and she was struck by the fact that she quite liked his brown mustache, though she disapproved of Andrew's black one. "I don't like charlatans who masquerade as geniuses. Which is not to say that I disapprove of you or your brother. To the contrary, I'm delighted with Writwell's accomplishments. I'm among his most faithful readers." His expression grew serious. "Yet there are dangers in his genius. Andrew's very popular with the fast set. He accepts invitations to events that you aren't permitted to attend."

"I'm aware of that."

"Then perhaps you'll heed my warning. The creative nature in man seeks the forbidden. You mustn't allow yourself to be drawn too deeply into your brother's life."

"If you're about to lecture me on Andy's character, then you may save your breath," she said curtly.

"Your attachment to your brother is quite noble. I'll say no more. You may never need know what I would tell you. I hope you don't!"

"Such passion, Dr. Boyd, and here I've always thought of you as a man of reason, sense, and above all else, self-possession."

"You mock me as usual."

"You disapprove of Andrew's character, yet you come here again and again," she ventured daringly. "I wonder why."

"You know why," he answered.

"Do I?" she said, holding his gaze. "Can it be because the Dakota serves the best fare in the West End? No? Then it must be because you've so little time to keep up with acquaintances that you've settled upon a pleasant, undemanding situation with the Grants."

"You make me sound like a sponger."

"Not at all. You're merely a man of habit who finds comfort in regularity and even tempers. I'm neither, but you wouldn't know that."

"Why do you provoke me?"

"Perhaps because Andy isn't here, and so we are left to converse about things that aren't of interest to either of us while we wish we were doing something, anything else!"

The outburst shocked Allegra more than her victim. She caught her napkin against her lips, her eyes enormous. "Oh, Dr. Boyd, forgive me! I can't think why I said that."

John gazed at her, his heart swelling with emotion he had

tried for weeks to deny. Yet it was true. In Allegra Grant he had at last found the perfection of his ideal: beauty, refinement, compassion, and purity. He was falling in love. "A lady like yourself deserves a more worthy suitor than I. Forgive me. I haven't known how to begin."

Allegra felt a fluttering of excitement at his words. "I didn't mean to startle a confession from you, John. Don't say what you'll later regret."

As he rose from his chair and slowly rounded the table, she nearly ordered him back, but she didn't. The spiteful gift of the mirror had brought back to her the almost forgotten fear of living her life without ever experiencing all that living had to offer. She would be twenty in May. She had never had a beau, never been kissed, never been in love. The improbable stituations in romantic novels made desire seem a silly occupation for two reasonable people, but there were other sources at work within her. *"One impulse from a vernal wood / May teach you more of man, / Of moral evil and of good, / than all the sages can."* Was Wordsworth right? She rose to her feet.

John paused just short of touching her, his gaze on her face. Nearness didn't diminish her loveliness. A finer air than mere breath seemed to come and go in his lungs. He felt it as a sweet burning inside him. There was a question and wariness in her returned gaze, but he saw also the great hope that he would embrace her.

As he reached out, Allegra inclined her body toward him and lifted her hands to his shoulders. His hands found her waist but didn't draw her closer. He held her steady. And then he bent his head and she raised hers as she had waited to do all her life.

It lasted only a moment. The touch of his mouth was warm and dry, the pressure light and unsatisfying to the vague stirrings she felt rise on the contact. She pushed her lips against his and his mustache brushed her nostrils. Abruptly she recoiled, afraid that she would sneeze.

He released her immediately. "I'm sorry."

Allegra brushed the tip of her nose with the back of a finger and then began to laugh. A kiss was nothing, nothing at all to fret about. How absolutely foolish she had been to bait him so brazenly for want of the experience.

John watched her in concern. Hysteria was a common female response to an emotional upset, but she genuinely seemed to find the moment amusing.

"Forgive me, John. It's just that, well, I didn't know what to expect."

"You look especially lovely tonight," he said warmly, resisting the impulse to touch her blushed cheek. "I've not seen that necklace before. I can't imagine a finer jewel for you than pearls."

"Thank you." She touched the pearls encircling her throat. Why had she chosen this night to wear the one gift she had vowed never to touch? Because it represented the only forbidding impulse she had ever had? Lord Drayton had hinted that her beauty would be enhanced by pearls. Tonight she had wanted to prove to herself that she was desirable and so had worn the pearls as part of her design to seduce a kiss from the doctor. As a vision of the tall, dark, light-eyed aristocrat came to mind, she murmured, "Dreadful!"

"Was it?"

She looked up, startled. "No, not the kiss. My manners. I'm being quite dreadful to you." She put a hand on his arm. "Oh, do kiss me again, John. Please."

This time his embrace was more direct. He pulled her close, stepping into her inclined body as his mouth again met hers. A tremor of surprise went through her. His lips were moist now, their pressure more demanding against hers. It was different from before, and faintly repulsive.

They jumped apart as the front door swung open, but the guilty color that mantled their faces left Andrew in no doubt of what had been occurring only a moment before. An ugly look instantly replaced his look of amazement as he started across the floor. "What's going on here?"

"Nothing that should disturb you, Andy," Allegra answered. "Dr. Boyd was giving me a demonstration."

"Looks damn peculiar to me," Andy answered, squinting against the light. "His hand is on your waist."

"People usually touch when they're dancing," Allegra invented smoothly as she slipped out of Boyd's embrace.

"Dancing, huh? Where's the music?"

"Oh, the band's in the closet. Would you care to greet them? Really, Andy! You're embarrassing Dr. Boyd. And me as well, I might add."

"You shouldn't be here alone with him."

"Whose fault is that?"

"I was detained." Andrew glared at Boyd. "I thought you'd have the decency to behave."

"We've done nothing that would reflect poorly on Miss Grant's reputation," John said formally.

"No? Well, good." Andrew started across the room and stumbled slightly.

Allegra hurried over to him, but he had righted himself. "Are you ill?" No, not ill, she realized as she looked at him. "There's whiskey on your breath."

"Yes." Andrew grinned ingenuously. "I've been hoisting a few with the boys at the Harvard Club. Seems I'm something of a celebrity among the alumni. Know what they call me? Writwell!"

"How imaginative," Allegra murmured.

"I've never had occasion to attend the Harvard Club," John said.

"Your loss," Andrew answered in a surly tone. He looked at Allegra. "Isn't it time he went home?"

"Andy, you're drunk!" Allegra said in an embarrassed whisper.

"That's right, accuse me of misconduct. Why not? What's another kick to a man who's down?"

John came forward and roughly took Andrew by the shoulder. "You'll cease insulting your sister."

Angered by the touch, Andrew knocked the hand away and swung round at the doctor. "Who the hell do you think you are? Allegra's in my care. You'll not have her! Do you hear me? I won't give my permission."

"Thank you very much for that unnecessary threat," Allegra said as she caught her brother's face between her hands. "Andrew Douglas Grant, unless you wish to deal with my temper in the morning, you'll go straight to bed and stay there until morning.''

For an instant the Grants stood nearly nose to nose in profile, and John experienced the disconcerting feeling that he was looking in a trick mirror where one image was made female and the other male.

"Puss, puss," Andrew chided, resorting to a nickname Allegra hadn't heard him use in years. "You know I'd only do what's best for you. You know that."

"I know that you're going to have a sore head in the morning and you'll deserve every bitter moment," she replied but slipped a comforting arm about his waist. "You need to rest. I'll only be a moment, Dr. Boyd."

When she had steered him to bed she began unlacing his shoes as he lay staring up at her. "It's my novel," he mumbled after a moment. "It's no good."

"What novel?" she asked as she dropped the first boot. "You've written a novel?"

Andrew rolled his aching head against the pillow. He hadn't meant to tell her, but someone had to know. "Needs work. It's all this rubbish we churn out that robs me of my creative urges. Writwell to hell, that's what I say!"

"Sh!" she warned as she pulled the second shoe free, then moved to close his bedroom door. She came back and sat gingerly on the edge of the bed. "What's this about a novel, Andy?"

"You really are beautiful," Andrew said, looking up at her. "Boyd wants your beauty. What man wouldn't? You mustn't accept him, Allegra. There're rumors. . . ."

"What sort of rumors?"

He looked away. "Just rumors. That should be enough."

"Oh, that's a nice thing to do, tell a lady her only suitor is a man with rumor attached to his name. It makes him sound very mysterious, and I do like mysteries."

He caught her by the wrist. "Won't you understand?"

"I understand that you're full of brandy," she replied calmly though he disquieted her. "We'll talk tomorrow."

He released her. "You're right as usual. Don't you ever resent your sensible nature?"

The barb struck a sensitive spot. "You've grown weary of my company."

Andrew reached up and cupped her cheek in his hand. "What would I do without my sensible little helper? You're the most reasonable woman I've ever known. If you weren't my sister, I'd marry you."

"I wouldn't have you," she answered with a laugh. "I finished the Writwell column before dinner. The clean copy of the Grant piece is on your desk. I think your spelling grows worse with each day. Would you like me to look at your novel?"

"No!" He knew he answered too harshly and tried to soften it with, "It's something I must do myself."

She stood up. "Very well. Good night." As she drew the spread up over him she spied a piece of paper that had fallen out of his shoe and picked it up.

"Give me that!" he said sharply.

She handed it over at once, but she'd already seen the single line of writing. *"Until tomorrow night, my love."* Andrew had a lady friend!

John rose the instant the bedroom door opened. "Is he all right? I could prescribe something."

"It isn't necessary," she answered with a polite smile. "Allow me to apologize for Andy's rude manner. He received a disappointment and is reacting badly."

"Nothing serious, I hope."

"No. Call it artistic temperament."

John bit his lip. "As a friend I shouldn't speak, but as a physician I am compelled to ask whether Andrew's conduct this evening is a regular event."

"Andy drunk? I should say not! It's happened only once before and that was more than a year ago. A brother's entitled to a cup too many on the odd occasion, I suppose."

"If you say so."

As silence fell between them, Allegra remembered that she had been in John Boyd's arms when Andrew returned, and that she had no idea where she would be at this very moment if Andrew hadn't arrived at all.

John read her thoughts in the falling away of her gaze and damned the ill luck that had brought the brother home too soon. But she mustn't know that. "I should leave. It's late. The evening was delightful, and eventful." He paused until her eyes rose again to meet his. "I won't forget this night, nor the great honor you've done me."

When he held out his hand, she had to repress the urge to laugh as she took it. How formal things were again. "Good night, Dr. Boyd."

"Don't you think you should continue calling me John, in private, anyway?"

"Yes, John, of course. Good night, John."

After a final squeeze of her hand, he left her.

Later, when she was ready for bed, she took out the black case in which the pearls were kept. She pushed the button and the lid flew open, releasing a piece of paper. She picked it up and the lettering caught her eye. There was something quite familiar about the bold script.

"Now where did I put that bag?" she murmured, looking round for the purse she had carried earlier in the day. She spied it by the bedside. In it she found the piece of paper she sought and compared them under the bedside lamp.

"The devil himself!" she whispered in recognition of the identical script. Lord Drayton had sent the mirror. It was mere coincidence that his gift reflected so accurately her feelings about her life and that she had chosen his pearls to wear this night, but the coincidence vexed her.

She sat down on the edge of her bed, weary all of a sudden. It had been a most trying day, beginning with the mirror, continuing through dinner, the kiss, and then Andrew's horrid behavior.

She touched her lips. The kiss. Her first. It had felt odd to be kissed by John. Odder still the second time he did it. She didn't think she wanted the exercise repeated again in the near future but she was happy to have the memory of it.

Thirteen

New York City, June

With a sigh of frustration Allegra laid her pen aside and
pressed her aching eyes with her fingers. For more than an
hour she had been searching for the perfect phrases to
describe a recent society tea.

"Writwell, where's your usual wit!" she murmured with
another heavy sigh. It was summer, and the sting of perspiration fueled her irritation. A vague discontent overlay her
mood like the first heat of the season settling in over the
Hudson.

"Andy, where are you when I need you?" she murmured,
though she knew the answer. He was spending all his time
and efforts on his novel. She understood when he moved his
work and notes from their apartment to a rented room at his
club. She even encouraged him to sleep there if he was
working really well.

When she had offered to take over the responsibility of
writing Writwell, she didn't mind the extra work. Yet
without Andy to share her amusement, her enthusiasm had
waned until her wit had honed itself into rapier-fine contempt. Her last piece had been a scathing attack on a society
matron whose only crime was her stupidity. The *Herald* had
deemed the piece "unworthy of space."

Perhaps it was time to murder Writwell.

That thought had come and gone often in the last weeks,
but now it stuck in her mind.

Nearly two years had passed since she had vowed that she
would live an exceptional life. By every measure she could

think of she had achieved that goal. She should be proud that she was contributing to the creation of Andy's great work, yet all she felt at the moment was resentment. The novel took up all his time and attention.

She gazed discontentedly about the apartment. She should have accepted John's invitation to dinner. The column wasn't due for a few days. Now, because Andy hadn't returned, she was constrained by a lack of an escort to remain at home.

"No play for you, my girl. It's work, work, work!" she muttered as she picked up her pen.

The doorman's whistle sounded a welcome respite from Writwell. Half an hour had produced exactly three lines, two scratched through and a third with two large ink blots acting as punctuation.

"There's a Miss Simpson to see Miss Grant," the doorman's hollow voice announced.

Eugenia was back in town! "Send her up at once!"

It had been nearly a year since she'd waved bon voyage to the heiress bound for a lengthy continental tour with her aunt. At the time, she had hoped Eugenia had finally come to her senses and was going to Europe to scotch the vicious rumors that had surfaced after the breakup of her engagement to Baron von Wallenstein. For months she had scanned the newspapers, hoping to read of a reconciliation between the baron and Eugenia. Then, just after Christmas, she had received a letter from Eugenia, who was in Florence. It had been full of praise for Italian scenery and art, and Rhys O'Conner. She had been so shocked, she burned the letter to keep Andrew from discovering it.

She opened her door and stepped into the hall to wait for the elevator. The dark deep corridor with its tall ceiling and mahogany paneling had always reminded her of an elegant dungeon. It was eerily cool out here, though the day had been so warm. She shivered in her linen frock. Finally, with a clanking of chains and wheezing of the steam-driven engine, the black iron grill work elevator rose into view.

She smiled as the cage slid open and Eugenia's small familiar figure emerged, wearing a glossy traveling coat of copper satin merveilleux, the cut unmistakably French. Had

Eugenia come straight from the dock to see her? She must be bursting with news of some great triumph. It was only when Eugenia stepped into the light from the open door and Allegra saw her face that her opinion changed.

"Eugenia! You look awful!" The words burst from her before she could stop them.

"And here I thought I was only fashionably pale," Eugenia returned in a whispery husk of her normal voice. "Lend me your arm, Allegra. I think I may faint."

Scarcely were the words said when her eyes rolled back and her knees gave way.

"Saints preserve us!" the Irish elevator matron cried as Eugenia slid to the floor in a whisper of satin.

"She's going to be fine. Please help me carry her inside," Allegra called even as the woman came forward to help.

"A child?" Allegra repeated.

"Born dead," Eugenia answered woodenly as she set aside a second cup of tea. "May God forgive his poor tiny soul."

"And Rhys?" Allegra ventured softly.

Eugenia shivered. "Gone! Gone before the birth. He promised to marry me! It was why we went abroad, why I agreed to go. We arranged it so that his friends thought he had received a grant to study abroad. I paid for everything!" She closed her eyes, her complexion lead-white against the sofa's maroon velvet cushions.

"If he didn't marry you, then how could you—?

Eugenia opened her eyes, her gaze a combination of defiance and hurt. "Shall I tell you that there's fire and ice and glory and shame all rolled together in a man's embrace? Oh, I can't explain what you've never known!"

"Perhaps I haven't your experience," Allegra said, "but I've found little in a man's kiss to make me throw over my good sense for— oh! I'm sorry, Eugenia. You didn't come here for a sermon. You've been through so much. How can I help you?"

Her expression changed, sadness revealing tiny lines drawn upon her face by months of despair. "You can't. I simply needed to tell someone all about it. And so I will. Those first weeks were wonderful. His writing went well; he was more creative than ever. I didn't mind his drinking. It seemed to stimulate him. But then I discovered that I was expecting, and he began drinking instead of writing. I tried everything but I could no longer please him." She shook her head. "He left me as soon as my condition prevented me from going about in public. She was a titian-haired Florentine. A singer, I believe."

"There was another woman?" The shock was plain in Allegra's voice. "He knew about the child and still he left you? How could he?"

The faint sound of Eugenia's laughter was more unsettling than her tears had been. "I've been a mistress, Allegra. Don't you know what that means? I've been a diversion, a delightful plaything that he grew tired of."

The melodramatic sentiment seemed appropriate and yet there was an underlying chill in her words. "Did your aunt know? I mean, did she remain with you?"

"Aunt Flora? Yes, one might say she's had more reason than most to keep her own counsel!" A flash of anger raised blood in Eugenia's cheeks. "We rented a villa in the hills those last months while I pleaded a Mediterranean illness that kept away visitors. No one suspected a thing."

"Then you're safely beyond the breath of scandal," Allegra mused aloud, trying to subdue her own scandalized sensibility with practicality. "What will you do?"

"Do? Why, go on with my life. What else is there?"

"Very well. We'll announce your return. Perhaps a small party? Unfortunately, many people have already abandoned the city for the summer."

"That's why I returned from Paris. The city was filling with the incessant chatter of American voices. I couldn't bear it!" Tears again rolled down her cheeks.

Allegra touched her friend's hand. It was cold. "You're too ill to think of anything now. You should be seen by a physician. Shall I send a note to Dr. Boyd on your behalf?"

Eugenia sat up, alarmed. "No! You must never breathe a word of this to him, do you understand me?"

"But Dr. Boyd is very discreet."

"Oh, yes, he's very discreet," Eugenia mimicked. She looked at Allegra. "Does he still come and sit at your table? Why do you allow it?"

"Andy doesn't like him either, yet he won't say why," Allegra replied. "Why do you dislike him?"

Eugenia shook her head, then hurriedly reached for her cloak. "I must go." She stood up quickly but then turned back. "You've been my only true friend, Allegra. You tried to warn me about Rhys and I didn't listen. I hope you're more clever. Stay away from Dr. Boyd. And marry, marry quickly."

When she had accompanied Eugenia down to her carriage and waved her good-bye, Allegra returned to her apartment in a much subdued mood. There was no thought of working now. After turning the key in the lock, she strolled from room to room shutting off lights and thinking.

Rage and pity and just a shade of envy colored her feelings toward Eugenia. Certainly she wouldn't wish to trade places with her. Yet the way Eugenia had spoken of passion, as something as incandescent and consuming as flame, fueled the discontent lingering in her thoughts.

"Change in a trice! The lilies and languors of virtue! For the raptures and roses of vice."

"Impossible," she whispered even as something of wondrous strangeness strained to become free inside her.

Entering her bedroom she went over to the vanity, opened the box of pearls, and lifted them out. When she had attached them to her ears and neck, she lay down on her bed and fell into a deep but troubled sleep.

"He found it?" Andrew was incredulous. All concern over Harriet Wharton's unprecedented appearance at his club was forgotten as he stared at her.

Harriet nodded and the heavy veil which had covered her face upon entering rippled on her shoulders like a nun's wimple. "It was incautious of me, but Richard had never before searched my room. He rarely enters it except—seldom."

Andrew glanced at the closed door of the private parlor he'd borrowed before speaking in a lowered voice. "When did you say he found the apparatus?"

"Yesterday, while I was out shopping. It seems he's been suspicious for some time."

"What could you have done to gain his mistrust?"

She looked up at him and her frank gaze made him blush. "I always tried to do my wifely duty and not to arouse his suspicions. I truly tried but he knows nothing of tenderness and gentleness."

"What reason did you give him for choosing to prevent conception?"

Harriet's expression became one he'd never seen before. "Why, that I didn't wish to bear any more children at present."

"How did he respond?"

"He said that it was not my decision to make. He said that what I've done goes against the laws of man and God. Man and God, indeed! I asked him what laws of man and God he upheld in his dealings in Albany." She looked at Andrew with an odd smile. "I asked for a divorce."

"Divorce?" Andrew exclaimed. "A year ago you said that that was impossible."

Her voice wavered. "Don't condemn me for past weakness, Andrew. I've asked and shall obtain my divorce."

"On what grounds?"

"Adultery. You don't imagine that I remain in New York while he's in Albany because *I* wish it? If he found having a wife convenient, you can be certain I'd be there."

"He'll fight it. Divorce is unthinkable for a politician, and your husband hopes to go far."

Her alert, birdlike attention was fully on him. "How broad-minded you are, to be able to think sympathetically of his career when he seeks only the ruin of yours."

Andrew started like a match had been struck under his nose. "What do you mean?"

"Richard is convinced that there is a man in my life. He

says he'll ferret him out and find a method to ruin him.''

Andrew rose abruptly and walked over to the mantel where a fan of peacock feathers had replaced the fire screen for the summer months. "Did you admit that such a man exists?''

"No.''

He swung round to face her. "Then he can't prove what his guilty conscience goads him to suspect. You mustn't admit anything, no matter how wild or provoking his accusations. Take my word for it, a man hears only as much of the truth against himself as he is forced to do. He may suspect till his dying day, but he'd rather you lie to his last breath than admit that he is right.''

She rose and went to him, laying a gloved hand on his sleeve. "I won't remain with him. I want a divorce.''

Andrew clenched his free hand. He hadn't expected this matter to come to a crisis just as he was enmeshed in other concerns. Now it was too late. He was expected to do the gentlemanly thing. "If you mean to go forward with this business, you must maintain the utmost discretion. Take Johnny and go to your parents.''

She tightened her grip on his arm. "Let's leave New York! We can go west, to a state where the divorce laws are more liberal.''

Andrew stiffened, feeling as though every word was designed to further unnerve him. "That's impossible. The scandal would ruin my career!'' A sudden uncomfortable feeling struck that he had betrayed more about himself in that remark than he intended. "I'm not thinking of myself. Without a career I couldn't afford to keep you in the manner which you deserve. As it is my father will cut me off without a cent if I—''

"Marry a divorcée,'' Harriet finished and released him.

Andrew blushed. "We must be practical. Neither of us is fit for poverty, and there's Johnny to think of. No, it's imperative that throughout this ordeal we maintain our standing in the city, for both our sakes.''

He embraced her shoulders. "One thing is certain. You mustn't come here again. Think things through again before you decide about a divorce. I can't ask that sacrifice of you.

Only you can make the decision. In the meantime we mustn't give your husband any grounds to suspect you of infidelity.''

She kissed him, holding him in a desperate embrace. "Please, let's leave the city! I don't care about poverty or scandal!''

Andrew cradled her head against his shoulder so that she wouldn't see the look in his eyes. "You've been very brave, my dear. You must be brave a little longer.''

When she pulled away from him, a full smile brightened her face. "I only wish I'd had the courage before. Just think, in a year I'll be free to marry you!''

"Yes, my feelings exactly,'' he murmured and bent to kiss her cheek. Marriage. Why did people always talk of marriage as though it were the panacea for the ills of life? Marriage was the last distraction he needed. Lately he'd been thinking of taking a trip abroad. Such a trip had helped clear his head and inspire him the summer after he graduated from Harvard. That was what he needed now.

"I may leave the city for a short time. It would be best for us both to put temptation out of the way, so to speak. Do be careful.''

The rhythm of the waltz enfolded her, her pulse joining time to the music.

Here and now. Flame and ice. Strong and faint. Virtue and vice.

The melody carried her round and round, swept up in a tidal tow of unceasing power, an ever-increasing emotion too sweet, too full, too near cresting, and yet ever curling onward, outward, over the edge of time.

She could not see her partner's face. Arms held her, strong and protective, impelling her to match a rhythm to which she had never before danced.

Impatient. Dizzy. Alert. Restless. Watchful. Incautious. In alternating beats she gave herself up to the spiraling need to be.

Tenderness and sorrow. Flame and ice. Heaven in hell. Virtue and vice.

There was a hand at her throat, touching, caressing, encircling, holding, then pressing, very gently at first, then with more intent. Her breath could not enter, no word escape. The music moved closer, came inside her. Confusion replaced pleasure as she lifted her eyes.

Lord Drayton appeared before her. His eyes were as she remembered: jewel-light gems penetrating even his own barriers. In them she saw reflected her own hopes and fears, the desire to experience at her peril the joys and sorrows of ecstasy.

Wildness and vertigo. Flame and ice. Heaven in hell. Virtue and vice.

Allegra woke suddenly to the dawn graying her curtained room. Blood roared in her temples and all at once she knew why. She was choking, straining against a binding pressure at her throat.

She tore at the strangling hold with both hands and was suddenly released from the choker of blue-gray pearls when the clasp broke. She sat up and burst into tears.

Drayton stood in the morning-bleached shadow of a tree and stared across at the Dakota. Nineteen months, three days. He had come back . . . for her.

Allegra paused in putting the finishing touch to her pompadour. Guests were due at any minute. "Europe? When?"

"I don't know," Andrew replied as he leaned against the mantel in the Turkish salon. "Next week, perhaps."

"Next—?" Allegra turned from the mirror. "Andy, you can't be serious. What am I to do in the city alone?"

"I thought you might go and visit Mother and Father. They've been wanting you to go down to Cape May."

"You know how much I would hate that. Besides, there's Writwell's column to be written." She turned back to the mirror and patted down a loose hair. "By the way, how do you expect me to do that in your absence?"

Andrew left the mantel and began to pace. "Actually, I've already worked it out. My publisher has agreed to fund Writwell for a continental tour. That sort of thing's been done for years: writer sends home essays from abroad to entertain the local folk. The trip will cost me very little."

"I see," she said calmly, though her peace of mind evaporated with his words. "My usefulness is at an end."

"Now, Allegra, I wouldn't say that."

"No, you wouldn't. You're too kind." She turned toward him and gave her China silk skirts a gentle shake to dislodge a wrinkle. "But I see no other conclusion."

He shrugged. "You can't be entirely surprised."

"Can't I?"

"You must have realized that Writwell couldn't go on forever. He's grown stale of late."

"My fault, I fear."

"No, no, I didn't say that. What I'm saying is that the idea of a self-important society gossip has run its course. Writwell needs a fresh direction or to be retired gracefully. A European adventure would give him new worlds to conquer."

Allegra flushed with resentment. Nowhere in his plans had he suggested that she might have a part. "Have you already made arrangements for your voyage?"

"No, I wanted to tell you about my idea first."

"Yet you met with our publisher without telling me."

Andrew didn't mistake her tone. "*Our* publisher. How possessive you've become about it all. Remember, it was just a lark, a game we invented which allowed you to see your words in print. It wasn't a truly literary effort."

"Oh." His words were depressing her more with every moment. "This will mean an end to the salon."

"It's served its purpose," he agreed with a slight laugh and sat down on the sofa. "Tonight will be our final performance, so to speak."

"I'd like to keep the town house a little longer." She

gazed possessively about the room that she had furnished with such wit and charm. "We've paid the rent through the summer. Perhaps I'll stay here while you're away."

"You can't live here alone."

"Why not? Eugenia Simpson does as she pleases."

Andrew's attention quickened. "Eugenia? What made you speak of her?"

She hesitated only a moment. "She's back in town."

"Yes, I know."

She turned to him. "You knew? Why didn't you tell me? She came to see me last evening."

"She came to the apartment? And you let her in?"

"What is the matter with you, Andy? Of course I let her in."

He didn't meet her gaze. "In future, you must make some excuse, any excuse, for you can't be seen in her company again."

She made an effort not to reveal too much surprise. Andy had heard something, but how much? "Why shouldn't I see an old friend?"

"I don't wish to discuss it. It's enough that I say she shouldn't be allowed in my apartment again."

"Very well. When I've moved into the town house, I'll entertain whom I please."

Andrew stood up. "Listen to me. Rumor has followed Eugenia's return. Your name mustn't be joined with hers on any account."

"That's the most ridiculous thing I've ever heard. I don't care what people are saying. People will gossip about nothing when that's all there is."

"It's more than nothing."

"I don't question your friendships," she rejoined in anger. "Allow me the freedom to manage my own."

He had hoped Allegra would not have to be told. "Very well. If you must hear the worst, I know for a fact that Rhys O'Conner was present at every sitting for Eugenia's portrait and that he often visited her after it was done."

"How do you know that?"

"Rhys told me."

"Rhys told you? Now, that is heady gossip!" she said scornfully.

"If you must have it plainly, Eugenia broke her engagement because of Rhys."

Allegra's jaw dropped. "He told you that, too?"

"No, not directly, but he let slip on occasion that he had just come from her home or was on his way."

"That shouldn't be enough to ruin a lady's reputation. After all, he might have said the same about me. Would you have believed him then?"

"It's not the same, and you know it. I'm not saying I entirely believed the stories circulating about them. I didn't want to believe them. I've always thought of Eugenia as a rather nice girl."

Allegra flushed to her temples. "She's a lady whose reputation has been impugned by a braggart. Why do you say *did*? What has changed your mind?"

"They were seen together in Naples."

"Perhaps they met by chance. Eugenia went abroad long before Rhys."

He waved away her words with a hand. "What difference does it make how and when they met? They were seen walking arm in arm like lovers."

Allegra took the insult as personally as if the rumors were about herself. "Charged, judged, and convicted in a flash; this is a pretty society in which we live. I don't suppose it has occurred to anyone that she might have simply enjoyed the company of an American friend for an afternoon and then gone about her merry way."

"The talk about town is rampant. Just today three different people told me the story I've just told you."

"But that is outrageous!"

"Now do you understand?"

"Yes, and I'm ashamed of you!" Allegra retorted.

"Allegra!"

"What a feeble thing is a lady's reputation when it can be ripped to shreds by hearsay and conjecture."

"She was Rhys's mistress."

"Was she? Do you have his word on it?"

Andrew had the grace to blush and turn away. "Very

well, I can't swear to what is true. I only know that you can't stop gossip by ignoring it. It's like warm tar. If you brush against it, it'll leave its mark upon you."

"You've composed better verse on less inspiration," Allegra tossed back.

He turned angrily on her. "You're impossible!"

"And you—you're— 'Thou art but a dunce/ And dost not know the garment from the man; / Every harlot was a virgin once.' "

"My God—!"

"Don't use that—"

"I think I am early."

The voice stopped the Grants in midsentence.

"The maid let me in," Lord Drayton continued amicably as he strolled into the salon.

"Lord Drayton," Andrew said, recovering first as he moved to extend his hand in greeting. "This is an honor. Why didn't you inform us of your presence in the city?"

"I did." Drayton looked skeptically at Allegra. "I dropped my calling card by a few days ago but received no reply."

Allegra felt her face burn with embarrassment, for she had torn it up. "It must have been misplaced."

"Perhaps." He looked at Allegra. "I couldn't miss overhearing your quote. I'm reminded of another. You're familiar with Blake? 'A truth that's told with bad intent/ Beats all the lies you can invent.' "

Obviously he had overheard more than was proper. "I would have chosen another of Blake's observations. 'This life's five windows of the soul/ Distort the heavens from pole to pole/ And lead you to believe a lie/ When you see with, not thro' the eye.' "

Drayton nodded slightly. "I bow to your judgment of the situation."

"Of which you can know nothing," she snapped.

Amusement glinted in Drayton's eyes, but Andrew was aghast. "Allegra, I know you don't mean to give offense, but Lord Drayton is unfamiliar with your stinging wit."

"Do forgive me, Lord Drayton. I sometimes regret that people in our position must respect appearances. You'll excuse me? I hear voices on the doorstep." She turned quickly away. After the exchange with Andy, she was in no mood to be pleasant. Lord Drayton's sudden appearance was unwelcome as well. If he thought, after nearly two years' absence, that she would welcome his arrival, he was mistaken.

"A splendid evening. Writwell does himself proud, as always," Cecil Bankston pronounced to his hostess. "Couldn't be here himself, as usual, but I see he sent along one of his countrymen." He nodded toward the tall figure with his back to them. Strange fellow, this Drayton, but I do admire the cut of his suit. He's got himself a first-rate tailor."

"Oh, indeed," Allegra observed with feigned politeness. "Everything about Lord Drayton is of the very best quality, so I hear, but his reputation."

As if he had heard her across the distance of the crowded room, Drayton turned at that moment and she met his glance. As she had the very first time he looked at her, she felt consumed. Nothing of his handsomeness, his perfection of build, his aloof European manner affected her. It was his gaze: that open avid hunger, that deep-searching, startling clarity with which he observed the world. Yet she sensed also the weary watchfulness in his manner, which was borne of repeated disappointment.

She turned away. Fanciful notions, that's what her thoughts were. He was only a spoiled bored nobleman with nothing better to do with his time than crash parties and insult his hosts. She should pity him. She did pity him.

"You're not smiling," Andrew observed critically as he passed her by with glasses of chilled champagne in hand.

She didn't bother to reply. She didn't feel cheerful. It was Writwell's final party and she hadn't been given more than fifteen minutes' warning. Their guests laughed and chatted and ate and crowded in upon one another in complete faith that there would be other nights in the autumn when they would return, but they were wrong. There was nothing to celebrate, nothing to mourn. It was simply over.

Feeling her isolation increase even as the front door

opened to admit new people, she melted into the shadows of the back hall and turned into the servants' stairwell to climb to the second floor. Once she reached the top, she crossed the hall, opened the door to the music room, and in the darkness sat down at the piano.

The notes flowed from her fingertips, effortless and yet all-consuming. She leaned into the music, hands stretching toward the keys, sending notes cascading ever forward, ever reaching. Lush beauty, sweet longing, passion for the moment; this is what she sought.

For hours Drayton had watched her, allowing the dampening effect of his laudanum dose to work its soothing touch upon his nerves so that he might remain in her company. The moment she left the salon he knew it and followed.

He stood now in the hallway listening and watching. He had heard the Brahms before, played with more skill on a finer instrument, but never had he heard it played like this.

He closed his eyes, the better to absorb the sound, and a peculiar and rare effect of the opium took hold. Every sound was heightened, altered by the excitement of emotion. Each note seemed flung out with assuredness, in defiance that it should connect with another. Yet the tripping, rushing, melodic fall of notes did hold together in a sweet torrent, a brilliant gurgle of sound, a bright flashing effervescence that showered his soul with her passion.

When she was done, the final notes hung suspended in the air as he pushed the door open and entered. She sat ramrod straight, as though she hadn't given in to those exquisite minutes of spending passion. It was only when he reached her and she turned so that the light from the hall lit her profile that he saw that he was mistaken. Tears wet her cheeks.

He leaned forward, the strain of great emotion on his face. "Why do you weep?"

"Brahms."

She said it so softly, only the trembling of her chin confirmed the breath of sound. Brahms. He might have guessed.

She watched him cautiously but did not wipe the tears from her face. "What is it you want?"

What did he want? Anticipation surged through him. She had given more to her music than any woman had ever given him. He had heard the sensuous notes, the passionate stroking of the keys, the latent desire, the voluptuous lull of the quieter passages.

He reached out and gently curled his fingers against the pulse beating quickly at the side of her throat. With a finger, he dragged open the plush of her lower lip as he leaned toward her.

Her lips were soft, full and warm like fruit ripened by the sun. Innocent kisses. How long had it been since he had shared an innocent kiss?

At first there seemed no emotion, only satin smoothness. Then the barest ripple of her breath escaped; and as he drew that breath into his mouth, that rarest of fires, the pure flame of desire, ignited deep within him. He was wrong about innocent kisses. More potent than the drug he had consumed, he tasted passion.

The terrible need, the desire of two years' accumulation tore free of its opiate mooring. He lifted her from the stool and into his embrace as his tongue found passage between her lips. His hands moved down her back to her hips, pulling her tightly against his legs.

From the moment he touched her, Allegra felt as if she split into two beings: one an observer, the other a recorder. The suddenness of his kiss surprised one. The violence of his embrace astonished the other. She was aware of a hand kneading her buttocks through the layers of her skirt, of the hot plunge of his tongue, of the cool velvet of his collar under her hand, the warmth of his cheek against hers, and overriding all, the hard length of his body surging against her.

His hand rose from her waist in a slow deep caress that seemed to erase the barrier of her clothing as it moved. He found the shape of her breast and enclosed it. She felt the moist heat of his mouth on her skin through the bodice of her gown and, an instant later, the shock of his teeth nipping her breast. She cried out at the brief pain and was released.

Feeling more vulnerable than she had in his embrace, she gazed at him. A feverish blush stung her skin. The imprint of his teeth was like a brand encircling her breast. The guilty desire to step back into his embrace made her shudder. Guilt and shame. Sorrow and pain. And pleasure, such bursting pleasure, as though she had caught fire with the bright burning of a falling star.

Drayton reached out, his palm brushing a deep caress over her assaulted breast. Frightened, she struck his hand aside. "Don't do that!"

He nodded. "You're afraid. That won't last. You're as curious as I to solve the mystery."

She seized on his thought. "Men have a passion for enigma. Yet once they know the answer—or believe they do—they leave, having discovered that the mystery was not quite unique enough. I won't be your victim."

His smile surprised him as much as his desire to touch her again—not in passion but in the human need to comfort. But he didn't believe in compassion, only passion. The conquest of his equal, that was what she represented.

"There's never been anything civil in our manner towards one another. It means there will be no victims." He stepped away from her. "Remember that. It will give you courage next time."

Fourteen

. . . the doctor he brought here tonight. He says my agitated manner of late, my furtive actions, and the gross impropriety of seeking to avert the natural womanly condition of motherhood, all point to a hysterical condition of the mind. Richard means to have me shut away, Andrew! You must come at once!

* * *

Andrew laid the letter on his desk with a curse and rubbed his aching head, as the heat of midmorning poured through the windows at his back. Three days had passed since he had arrived home and found the note slipped under his door. Tired and filled with spirits, he had taken it to bed unread. The next morning, fear had kept him from answering. Now, given a few days' thought, he struggled for a suitable reply.

It was like Harriet to panic at the first of her husband's threats. Wharton wasn't a fool. No doubt, he had deliberately sought to frighten her. Did he hope that she would contact her lover?

He loosened his cravat with unsteady hands as he marshaled his headachy thoughts. He must think clearly. His reputation was at stake. He was aware that her husband might have had someone follow the person who delivered Harriet's message to the Dakota. The doormen of the Dakota were well paid to be discreet. They didn't allow strangers into the building but would, for a small fee, slip a letter under a door. The most damning thing Wharton might have learned from a spy was that Harriet's lover lived at the Dakota. Little enough of a threat in that. The Dakota housed hundreds of residents. At least he had kept his head and not gone off like some Don Quixote to save her.

His eyes fell once more on the letter where a tear had smeared Harriet's salutation. Reason told him that Richard Wharton wouldn't subject himself to the scandal of a wife in an insane asylum. Why didn't Harriet realize that herself?

"Damnation!" he muttered, rising from his chair. Where was her courage, her new resolution, her good sense?

He supposed having a physician sprung upon her without warning and his diagnosis that she was hysterical were justly frightening. He only hoped that she hadn't said anything foolish or indiscreet.

The note was three days old and there had been no others. Perhaps Wharton had used the threat of commitment to extract a promise from his wife that she wouldn't bring a divorce suit against him.

Andrew picked up the letter and tore it into tiny pieces. Absolutely the worst thing he could have done was to answer her. Anything he did now was likely to come into her husband's hand. Wharton knew his address, if not his name and apartment number. He couldn't risk anything more.

In a few days he would ask a mutual friend to drop by Wharton's home and see what could be discovered about Harriet's health. Harriet would know then that he was concerned and be calmed by it. Discretion and subtlety—he hoped she would be wise enough to understand it.

He heard Allegra answer the bell that announced their breakfast and swept the scraps of the letter into the waste-basket. He would go ahead with the plans for his trip. An absence from town was more important now than before. If Harriet persisted in seeking a divorce, she would have to learn to manage these minor crises herself, for there were certain to be others. Maybe she would reconsider altogether. He wasn't the prize she thought him to be. Why didn't she see that?

"Breakfast," Allegra announced in a cheery voice as the waiter pushed the breakfast cart into the library. "It's been much too long since we've shared a meal, so I insist that you stop whatever you are doing and allow me to eat with you."

"Yes, come in," Andrew returned. He lifted the first cover and made a face. "Kidneys? You know I hate kidneys."

"You must grow accustomed to them if you're going to live in England. I ordered grilled tomatoes and kippers as well." She came forward as the waiter left. "What time did you return? You were out much later than usual."

"Three-thirty," he answered, reaching for the newspaper folded by his plate. "Lord Drayton and I met for a late supper." He paused before unfolding the paper. "He's an amazing fellow. Did you know he dabbles in the arts?"

"I never inquired," she answered with an air of indifference as she mentally recorded every word. "What sort of art?"

"He sculpts. You don't like him, do you?"

"I find him arrogant, ill-mannered, and rude."

"Handsome, though. Calls you a ravisher."

Her brows rose. "Does he? Perhaps he might pass for

handsome on a gray day at dusk, with the light behind him.''

Instead of the laughter she expected, Andrew suddenly gasped. ''Oh, God!''

''Andy, what's wrong? You've gone white!''

Andrew stood up. ''I—I— There's something I must do. Immediately!'' He turned and hurried from the room.

Allegra bent and picked up the paper he had dropped. It was a copy of the *Police Gazette*, a lurid yellow journal that he found amusing but she detested. In funereal black the bold letters of the headline read, SENATOR'S WIFE A SUICIDE?

Allegra swung the door open the instant the bell sounded. ''Dr. Boyd! I'm so glad you've come.''

''I received your message only an hour ago. You say there's an emergency concerning Andrew. He is ill?''

''No. Oh, I don't know.'' She raised a self-conscious hand to her hair as she crossed into the drawing room by his side. Now that he was here, she was embarrassed. He might think her a silly woman worrying needlessly. ''I must apologize for my appearance. I've been preoccupied of late.''

''I was going to lie and say that you look wonderful, but the truth is, Allegra, you look awful.''

''Thank you,'' she answered with the barest hint of a smile that dissolved into a tremble of apprehension. ''Oh, John. It's Andy. He has simply disappeared!''

With a nod of sympathy, John patted her shoulder. ''Scoundrel spent the night abroad, did he? Though you shouldn't be subjected to the needless worry, I doubt it's serious. Most likely he's been detained by friends or a billiard table.''

Allegra met his sympathetic gaze. ''For three days?''

He stared at her, appalled. ''You've been alone three days? Good lord! Why didn't you send for me sooner?''

With a dismissing gesture Allegra looked away. ''Like you, I've thought he was with—someone. I've sent repeated messages to his club but they've gone unanswered. He must be in terrible trouble not to have contacted me. Perhaps he's been injured." A spasm of pain contracted her brow. "That's why I thought of you. You know the hospitals. Andy may be so badly injured that he cannot give his name. I can't bear to think of him hurt and alone and with no one to care for him."

"I'm certain it's not as serious as you imagine," John answered, determined to spare her his growing misgivings. "Come and sit. When did you eat last? Have you slept at all?"

"Don't coddle me, John," she said impatiently as she sat. "I'm perfectly fine. It's Andy I'm worried about. What shall we do?"

"Contacting the police would be in order."

"No! If something is wrong they'll wire our parents, and Papa is the last person Andy will want to contend with when he's home again. We must do this ourselves."

"But where am I to begin?"

"I've thought of that." She reached for a sheet of paper on a nearby table and handed it to him. "This is a list of the places that Andy frequents. As you will see, many of them are establishments that a lady may not enter. Will you go there for me?"

"Of course," he answered, scanning the list with lifted brows. "How do you know of these places? Some of them are in the worst areas of the city."

"As Andy's secretary, I'm privy to many of his resources." She touched his arm. "You'll do this for me?"

"Of course. I'll need time, several hours, perhaps a day. In the meanwhile, if Andrew should reappear, you may contact me through the hospital, as before. I'll be in touch with them by phone so that your message will reach me."

"That won't be necessary for I'm going with you!"

"That's impossible," he answered even as she reached for her hat and gloves.

"It can't be impossible. If Andrew is ill or injured, I must be there to look after him."

"What if he's simply, well, indisposed?"

Allegra halted in drawing on her second glove. "If Andy were merely occupied with a woman, he'd have sent word." She hesitated. "Something sent him suddenly bolting from the breakfast table three mornings ago. This."

John took the newspaper clipping she offered. "Ah, yes,

the Wharton death. A sordid and scandalous business, by all accounts.''

"In what way?''

"The wife committed suicide. Her husband is distraught, of course, particularly since she had just been diagnosed as hysteric and was to be committed to an asylum.''

"How horrid for her!'' Allegra exclaimed. "But I don't see why her death should affect Andrew.''

"Neither do I,'' John said thoughtfully. "Perhaps you misunderstood his reaction. It might have been to another article or something else entirely.''

"Yes, I thought of that. It doesn't matter. We must find him.''

"I'd rather you waited for me to return with him.'' Before her determined expression, he retreated a little. "But I'm afraid that you'd take a second list and go out yourself.''

"You know me very well, Dr. Boyd.''

He looked at her. Even with the shadows left by sleepless nights encircling her green eyes, she was still the most beautiful woman he had ever seen. And the most determined. "Very well, but you must promise to remain in the cab at every address. Your reputation demands it.''

Reputation, Allegra thought, it's always a matter of respectability.

"You've found him?'' Allegra leaned eagerly out of the hansom window into the mist of the late evening's rain.

John nodded and opened the door to climb in beside her. "I think I've found him. I've been given an address by the barkeeper.'' He leaned forward and ordered the driver, "Seventy-second and Park West!''

Allegra grabbed his arm. "You're not taking me home! Not until Andy's with us.''

He swung round on her in the narrow confines of the cab. "For God's sake, Allegra! You can't go where I'm headed now. It's late. You're blue with fatigue and chilled from the damp. Let me bring Andrew to you.''

She stared stonily at him. "If you insist on putting me out, I'll hire another cab and follow you."

John muttered under his breath. For nearly twelve hours they had scoured the city, driving from hotel to club to saloon to restaurant, each destination taking them farther and farther from polite and fashionable places until now, at half past ten in the evening, they were deep in the Bowery. "You don't understand the danger. Besides, there's nothing you can do that I can't. Think of how Andrew will feel to have you find him there."

"Where?"

John shook his head. "If you were my sister, I'd horse-whip the man who dared to take you where we're going." He leaned forward again and issued new orders to the cabby.

Allegra did not speak again as the cabby made his way into an even more desperate area than she had yet seen.

When they turned onto Water Street, within the shadow of the magnificent East River Bridge, she kept her growing fears to herself. Rows of rum shops lined the street filled with the boisterous revelry of whiskey-sodden sailors. Having read Andrew's account of the area, she realized that these shanties and dilapidated tenements must house the places he had characterized as "rat-pits and gambling dens and thieves' dives."

Here and there along the street a brilliantly lit house revealed couples dancing to the strains of raucous music. Along the sidewalks men and women stood chatting, the women's voices soaring like brawling cats' above hard male laughter and roaring profanity.

Finally the cab paused before one of the few substantial brick buildings along the street. Over the door hung a lantern bearing the inscription, "Jerry McAuley's Prayer Meetings."

She leaned forward in surprise. "Prayer meetings? Why would Andrew be in there?"

"Not there. There," John replied and pointed to the building next door.

Allegra gasped in spite of herself. The tenement had bars on the windows and an iron grate across the door which gave it the appearance of keeping its inhabitants inside as well as intruders out.

John sat staring grimly at the building without speaking. Finally he opened the cab door and stepped out, shutting it firmly behind him. To the cabby he said, "If I'm not back within five minutes, you're to drive the lady to the address I gave you previously. And God help you if you don't get her safely home!"

"Wait! I'm coming, too," Allegra said, reaching for the door.

Thinking it best to ignore her, John turned abruptly away and climbed the steps to pound impatiently on the door with the handle of his umbrella.

She gained the street with some difficulty, splashing mud over her skirts as the cabby called to her to stop. She saw the door open a crack as she reached the sidewalk, revealing an interior little brighter than the gloom of the night. As she reached the steps, she heard John speak a few terse words to the shadowy figure inside and then with both hands give the door a hard shove, forcing his entry. Lifting her skirts, she took the final steps in a rush and threw herself against the closing door. "Wait!"

The door gave under the force of her body and she slipped through the narrow opening. With a gasp of horror, she clapped a hand over her nose and mouth to prevent the stench from overwhelming her.

Clearly startled, John turned on her in fury. "Are you mad! Get out of here!"

But she was already looking past him, down the hall to where the shadowy doorman was moving out of sight. Without a word to John, she hurried after him. If Andrew were somewhere inside this cesspool, that man would know. Given no alternative, John followed her.

The man who had opened the door halted at the end of the hall and pointed to a flight of steps. "Gen'men allays uppy stairs," he said in broken English and pointed toward the ceiling.

In the instant before he melted into the darkness, Allegra saw his almond-shaped eyes, faintly jaundiced skin, and black robe. The next moment he had disappeared.

John brushed past her, not bothering now to order her either to stay or go forward, and she followed him up the narrow stairwell which was illuminated by a single gaslight. As they reached the top, the stench grew much greater. Andrew was here, in this place? It was impossible. "He's not here, not Andrew," she whispered to John.

Even as she spoke, John reached the top and found himself facing the open doorway into a huge gloomy room. In the scant light available he saw row after row of wooden cots, each occupied by a corpse-still body. Through the stench another odor cut a path: the sweet, cloying, sticky smell of opium smoke.

He caught Allegra by the arm. "Don't move!" he whispered urgently. "Don't make a sound, no matter what you see or hear."

Frozen by the horror of what lay before her, she couldn't even nod her agreement. In mute helplessness she watched John move forward between the first row of bunks and bend over the first bed. Slowly, cautiously, he moved from bed to bed, stopping to examine each occupant. Occasionally the gloom was brightened by the red glow of a burning pipe.

She held her breath, her fingernails biting into her palms. Why would anyone think Andrew could come here? What was this place? Who were these people? The touch on her arm sent her whirling about with a muffled cry of fright.

"You looky gen'man?"

Allegra nodded at the Chinese man who had opened the door. He held a bamboo lantern, and as he smiled she was struck by his exotic handsomeness. "Gen'man come two days ago. Pretty like lady. Virgin to den. Not so now. Come."

Uncertain, she looked over her shoulder, but John had worked his way to the far end of the room. She turned back to ask the man to wait, but already he was halfway down the hall. Afraid that he would disappear again, she hurried after him.

At the far end of the hall, the man opened a door. "Gen'man pay for best room. Maybe you stay with him?"

Allegra shook her head firmly.

He shrugged, a slow elegant gesture that was neither an agreement nor an objection, and handed her the lantern.

With a prayer on her lips that Andrew was not inside, she crossed the threshold. The air in the room was no fresher, but the stench was not so strong here. A little mother-of-pearl inlaid table was the first thing she noticed, containing a half-full wine decanter and an empty glass. Then beyond it she saw a low cot on which a figure lay sprawled at an uncomfortable angle. The hair lifted on her neck as she took a step closer, for the man didn't appear to be breathing.

This was not Andrew; it couldn't be Andrew. She repeated the chant over and over as she lifted the lantern. Then the light fell across the man's face and the prayer became a wail of disbelief.

"But who would have done such a thing? And why?"

John looked grimly at her, wishing he could assuage her fears, but the things he had learned about Andrew's disappearance were far from reassuring. "It doesn't matter who took Andrew to the opium den. What does matter is that we were able to locate him quickly and bring him home. I've talked with the nurse and she assures me that he's resting quietly. Still, you can expect him to be ill on and off for the next few days. You say the owner of the establishment told you this was Andrew's first experimentation with the drug?"

"I—I—" Allegra took a deep shuddery breath. "Is that what 'virgin' means? I didn't know."

"It's a good sign that he overindulged. Perhaps he won't be tempted to repeat the exercise."

Allegra checked the watch pinned to her lapel. "It's nearly seven A.M. You must be desperately tired."

John smiled. "Actually, I'm rather invigorated. It isn't every night that I am successful at saving a lost soul."

She tried to smile in answer but could not. "Andy wouldn't speak to me when I went in, but I heard him talking with you. Did he explain any of this?"

John shook his head. "I wouldn't credit anything he might say over the next few days. He's delirious and may speak of things that aren't true or never occurred. Now that the nurse has arrived, I insist that you go to bed."

"I don't think I can sleep. I won't be at ease until I know what drove him to such desperate actions."

John didn't reply immediately. The things Andrew had murmured in his stupor had triggered a half-forgotten memory of a visit by Mrs. Wharton back in the autumn. She had come seeking relief from what she called "the hazards of marital duties." Thinking that she was of delicate disposition and afraid of the rigors of childbirth, he had supplied her with the means to prevent pregnancy. Now he surmised that she was an adultress who sought to prevent the conception of a bastard with her lover: Andrew Grant. The truth would destroy Allegra's admiration of her brother. No, he couldn't do it. Nothing must spoil her perfect innocence. Yet he must supply some story which would prevent her from pressing her brother for the truth.

"Your brother is a personable young man of charming character. Handsome bachelors sometimes find themselves the object of an unstable woman's romantic infatuation."

Allegra stared at him. "What do you mean?"

"Only that your brother may have been a victim of such a woman. You remember the article you showed me?"

"Do you mean—?"

"I don't presume," John answered.

"Desperate creature," Allegra repeated. "Poor Andrew. Poor woman."

"Yes, poor woman. Your brother is to be commended for a sensitivity that allows him to grieve so deeply over her unfortunate illness. Because of this very empathy he must be spared all reference to the incidents of the last days. I must warn you, however, that you may expect rumor to deal less generously with the situation."

"You mean Andrew's name might be linked with the dead woman's?"

"I fear so." He paused. "You, too, must consider the consequences of these rumors upon your own reputation. May I make a suggestion?"

"Yes, of course."

"Andrew needs a change of scenery, now more than ever.

I think he should go ahead with his plans to travel abroad. His absence would do much to remove the incident from people's minds.''

"Should he be alone just now? I mean, if he is suffering so, perhaps he shouldn't be sent on his own to a strange place.''

"Isn't there some friend who could go with him?''

"I don't—'' Allegra paused. She had hated the thought of being parted from Andrew, realizing that she would be forced to return to her parents' home despite her arguments to the contrary. But if a doctor recommended that Andrew not go abroad alone, then why shouldn't she be the one to go with him? She wouldn't reveal her plan to the doctor before she talked with Andy, but it seemed ideal. "Dr. Boyd, your prescription may be the perfect solution for both of us.''

Fifteen

London, August 1892

Allegra laid her pen aside at the sound of a carriage pausing on the street before the town house she and Andrew were renting in Belgravia. For more than a month they had been living on a quiet square where the squeak of nanny-powered perambulators and the occasional carriage wheel composed the major disturbances of the day.

From the moment she suggested it, Andy had agreed that she should accompany him to London. As soon as he recovered his strength, he launched into feverish prepara-tions for their voyage. They never spoke of the incident in Water Street. He never inquired how she happened to discover him in the circumstances too sordid to be discussed in polite society. She, for her part, hoped that by ignoring the event, it would be forgotten.

To all intents and purposes it was. Andrew was suddenly more solicitous and congenial than he had been in months. At dinner he no longer drank more than a single glass of wine. He even set aside his novel, preferring, he said, to keep his muse waiting for *his* attention for a change.

Yet there had been one surprising development. In the short time before they sailed, Andy had furthered his friendship with Lord Drayton. The man's name was frequently on his lips. With each meeting, Andy's admiration for the earl grew.

"A capital fellow," Andy would say, after quoting some bit of advice that the Englishman had offered him about things to see and places to visit in England. "He's a veritable encyclopedia of information."

Allegra always murmured some noncommittal response while waiting for the invitation that would end her suspense: "Why don't you join us?" Yet it never came. Andrew and Drayton met either by chance or at men's clubs.

During the first few days she had kept at the ready a variety of phrases with which to respond should she meet the earl at the opera, theater, or a party, but she hadn't needed them. The earl's interest appeared to be confined to Andrew. Curiosity turned to consternation. After all, in the beginning the earl had seemed to be interested in her. Or was his interest only a ruse to enable him to befriend the famous Writwell?

When they sailed and she found that Lord Drayton's name was not among those on the passenger list, she thought that would end the matter. It hadn't. He was never far from her thoughts.

How could she keep from being curious about a man Andy so openly admired? Then there was the matter of Drayton's kiss. His single kiss had shown her more of life's possibilities than all the hours she had ever spent imagining them. She had finally committed the scene to paper, feeling a kind of exorcism in putting her thoughts and feelings into words. Then she had burned the account.

Two days ago she had read in the paper of Lord Drayton's

return to his homeland. Since then, she had lived in suspense, waiting, waiting, waiting. She knew he would come. Sooner or later.

She rose and went to the window, drawing back just enough of the lace curtain to reveal the tall gentleman who had emerged from a beautiful carriage with a royal crest on the door. He wore a black cutaway tailcoat with gray striped trousers, white waistcoat and spats, and gray top hat. He had come in the most formal of morningwear. Or perhaps he was just dropping by on his way somewhere else. He made a leisurely business of adjusting his coat and gloves, as though he knew she watched. She released the curtain before he turned toward the house.

When she heard the door bell jangle, she hurried over to scoop her pile of papers into a desk drawer. He must never learn of her part in the life of Writwell. She smiled suddenly. The knowledge that she possessed a secret he would never learn gave her a sudden spurt of confidence. Invade her dreams he might. Rattle her composure by intruding upon private moments; yes, he had done that. But he couldn't guess nor even suspect many of the most important things about her.

She sat on a sofa and arranged her skirts as she heard the butler's voice query her guest. She reached for a book and opened it as she heard his reply. She considered telling the butler to say that she was indisposed, but the need to put an end to the waiting overrode her desire to delay their meeting. She was prepared for battle. Let it begin.

Her eyes were on the page before her when she heard him enter the drawing room, and she did not lift them.

Drayton didn't wait to be announced. He had stayed away until he could no longer resist the impulse to see her once more. When he found her lounging among the paisley pillows on the red silk divan, her dark head bent over a book, he knew he had chosen the right moment. She looked at ease in her lace-collared housedress with its white satin sash, but he could feel the tension emanating from her.

"Your servant is a man of limited imagination, Miss Grant. He's of the opinion that my insistence upon seeing you while your brother is away speaks of a desire to seduce you.'' He paused thoughtfully. ''I don't suppose you wish to be ravished?'' It was a query to which she didn't respond. ''I thought not. A pity.''

Allegra carefully closed her book and set it aside. Only then did she look up. ''Do you never tire of casting your bait, my lord? The nibbles will be few in these waters.''

''Good—not exceptional, but quite a good remark,'' Drayton said as he looked about. When he found a chair to his liking he walked over and brought it back, placed it before her, and sat down.

His movement gave her a chance to study him. He seemed both taller and leaner than she remembered, but she reminded herself that she had seldom viewed him except in extreme moments of agitation. Then, once again, those gem-bright eyes were on her.

''Do you play often?'' Allegra frowned. ''The piano, Miss Grant.''

''Oh, that. Yes, I bang away on every occasion. Doesn't every well-brought-up young lady?''

''I wouldn't care to know. I'm glad you didn't play Chopin. Maudlin. Trite. Romantic.''

Each adjective was an invective. ''The Oxford temper,'' she murmured.

He set forward suddenly, his elbows on his knees and a forefinger to his lips. She endured his frank stare as well as she could. ''Are you truly mad, my lord, or is it merely an affectation?''

Over his harsh features a smile came and went. ''Mad as a hatter!''

''Yes, I do feel like Alice.''

''I'd rather be like Alice, dropped down a rabbit hole of my imagination, than like Atlas who bears the world's reality on his back.''

''But, in either case, you'd require a good tailor.''

Again that lightning-quick flash of amusement. ''God! You were wasted in New York!''

She smiled. ''I rather like the city.''

''Galatea knew no better before Aphrodite.''

She lifted her chin. ''Do I remind you of Pygmalion's statue? I must remedy that.'' She had no idea what she should do, but instinct urged her to keep the upper hand. And so she asked the question uppermost in her mind. "Why have you come here?"

"For the same reason that you have awaited my coming. I've come to free you."

"That's a most eccentric notion."

"You wonder at my purpose. Suppose I'm fascinated by the precious loneliness of a lily blooming in the gutter."

"A lily of virtue?"

"Better one of vice," he answered. "Conventionality bores me."

"One may be unconventional without being immoral."

"It isn't nearly so fascinating."

"The fascinator doesn't interest me," she countered. "He has neither a conscience nor a soul."

"Liar."

"*You* have a soul?"

"*You* are fascinated. And I by you. I'm glad you've come. Here in London we can be equals."

"How nice it must be to have all those centuries of overbearing arrogance in your blood."

"You're afraid."

"To know no fear is to mistake the danger."

They were playing a wild, eccentric game of witty phrases and unspoken meanings which left her in doubt of its purpose. A burning hunger lit his eyes and drew the skin tightly across his bones. A hunger for what? She shook her head, throwing off the inclination to be fully fascinated. "You must know that any relationship between us is impossible."

He didn't argue. His expression didn't change. When he rose and turned away, he made no sound at all. At the door he paused and took something from his breast pocket. He touched it briefly to his lips and set it on a nearby table as he passed into the hall.

She waited until the front door closed before rising and going to pick up what he had left. It was a calling card with his London address. Scrawled in the corner was the note: "*Opera. Be ready at seven. Drayton.*"

She pressed it between her palms, as though something of him could be felt in the embossed paper. She wouldn't go, of course. Andrew wouldn't allow it. Andrew! He was out of town for the day, at the races with friends while she put the finishing touches on his Writwell articles. She wouldn't go, in any event. It was too presumptuous of Drayton. "Lily of vice. Rubbish!"

Lord Drayton stood patiently as his valet adjusted his collar. The attention of a good personal servant was one of the few rituals of his position which he allowed himself to enjoy thoroughly. Washed, shaved, and dressed by solicitous hands, he felt at once at peace and competently armed for the battle of surviving yet another night.

He glanced at the decanter of wine which stood at its usual place on the bedside table. No, not tonight. The tranquil oblivion he had sought more and more often this last year didn't appeal to him tonight.

"Nay, let us walk from fire unto fire/ From passionate pain to deadlier delight—/ I am too young to live without desire."

He was young, only thirty on his last birthday, and the desire for passion that ran strongly in him could no longer be denied. If only she did not disappoint him; that was all he asked of the night.

His valet stepped aside and gave his master a measuring look. "You're looking especially fine this evening, if I may say so, m'lord."

"Thank you, Hogan. I feel especially content. I'll wear the diamond pin."

From deep in the corridors of the lower floor he heard the faint jingling of the door bell. "Am I expecting visitors, Hogan?"

"No, m'lord. You gave particular orders that you were not at home."

"Good." He was in fine spirits. A discreet servant was worth more than a thousand acres of barley. His could be counted on at a moment's notice to summon up an appropriate response to any situation.

As Hogan slipped the expertly tailored coat on him, smoothing the cloth over his shoulders with an eye to perfecting the alignment, Drayton heard footsteps on the stairs.

"You've lost a bit of flesh, m'lord," Hogan commented. "A few more potatoes at dinner wouldn't come amiss."

Drayton frowned. "I haven't gained nor lost an ounce since I reached my majority. It's your clumsy handling that's stretched the fabric!"

"Beg pardon, m'lord."

The tap on the door sent Hogan hurrying over to silence it. The earl's moods were never certain these days. The evening's promising beginning hung by the turn of a phrase.

He listened impatiently as the two servants whispered, annoyed that the interruption wasn't dispensed with at once. "Oh, what is it?" he demanded after a moment.

"It's the visitor, m'lord," Hogan said as he turned back from the door. "A young lady who wouldn't give her name says she must speak with you."

Drayton stood impassively, as though the valet had not spoken, but his thoughts were racing. Who could it be? No lady of his acquaintance would dare call upon him without receiving express permission beforehand.

"I'll send her away," Hogan offered uncertainly. "Betsy says she's a foreigner. Expect she's up to no good."

"No!" Drayton smiled. Yes, of course! "Show her into the gold drawing room. I'll be down shortly."

"Very well, m'lord." Hogan's expression did not alter, but his spirits soared. There had been a smile on the earl's face as he spoke; well, as close to a smile as he was likely to express. The lady was someone special. He would avail himself of a peek out of the window when she left, that he would!

A few minutes later, Drayton stood outside the closed doors to his own drawing room, wondering how best to enter. Before he could change his mind, he took both knobs in his hands and thrust the doors open.

Allegra turned at the sound. "Good evening, Lord Drayton. Would you care for a brandy?"

He nodded, amused that she treated him as though this were her drawing room rather than his. As she crossed over to the crystal decanters lined up on a sideboard, he softly closed the doors and then turned back to her.

He noted that she was dressed for an evening out. Her gown was apple-green silk, the exact color of her eyes, he suspected. On one of the empire settees she had laid an evening wrap of gold tissue. When she had poured the brandy and turned back to him, he recognized with a jolt of pleasure that she wore his gift of pearls. He understood now. She had come to surprise and astonish him. She had succeeded.

"Your brandy, my lord," she said softly as she came forward to hand the snifter to him. "Do have a seat. We've matters to discuss."

Feeling slightly dazed, he did as she bid. This was her moment and not for any price would he rob her of it.

Allegra seated herself on a nearby chair, draping her short train in decorative folds before once more raising her eyes to meet his. "You are wondering why I have come. I won't pretend that I didn't dress in expectation of your invitation to the opera. I see that you intend to keep it."

It was a statement, but her pause begged him to confirm it and he did with a nod.

She regarded him frankly. "I hardly know you and what little I do know doesn't engender trust. I'm aware of your reputation as a seducer of women."

Drayton waited out her pause, afraid that the sound of his voice might alter her purpose.

"Thank you for not dissembling. I'll be honest as well. I'm curious to explore the world in a manner unthinkable for a lady in my country. You say it's possible here in London. Will you be my guide?"

He knew she must feel as he did, else she wouldn't have come. Yet she was asking for some assurance from him which he didn't quite understand. "You seek to engage me as your guide? What exactly would this position entail?"

"Honesty," she answered promptly.

"Do you speak of this virtue in the French fashion: no more than one lover at a time?"

She had expected that he would be blunt, yet his wording

startled her. "I don't seek a lover, my lord. Mistresses are easily come by. You don't need me for that purpose."

"Then what purpose?"

"I believe that it's possible for a man and woman to have a relationship without repression, jealousy, or subservience."

"If it's constancy you require, I suggest marriage—to someone else."

She shook her head. "I'm determined to spare myself just yet."

"Yet, unless I am happily mistaken, you reject the possibility of love without matrimonial bonds."

"I expect marriage to be the product of love."

"Among my set, marriage isn't about love, Miss Grant. It's about money."

"A contract, do you mean?"

"Precisely. If that were not so, the horse-faced and cold-hearted would attract fewer suitors. No, the groom buys with his purse, or rather, he opens his purse in hopes of manna in the form of a rich bridal dowry and attached lands." He leaned forward, impatient with this talk of marriage. "American heiresses are all the rage among the peerage at present. You don't need my entrance to accomplish your purpose. All those lovely American dollars in your papa's purse can buy you a dukedom. I am, after all, only an earl."

Allegra stared at him. In his formal attire he was a raring, tearing handsome man—but as unfeeling as a coal bin. "You're too insightful for your own good, my lord. In my need, I was prepared to overlook your glorious ancestry. It's you who cannot forget it."

"Damned Yankee impertinence!" he shouted, coming to his feet.

"Better that than overbearing British snobbery," she rejoined. She stood up. "Which—"

She didn't finish the thought. His embrace was swift. He drew her in so tightly it seemed he would pull her inside his own skin. When the kiss ended they looked at one another in bewilderment, each shocked by the passion that leaped between them.

"You have your brother's blessing in this venture?"

"You know I don't," she answered faintly. "That should make you all the more eager to agree."

He gently touched his lips to her brow. He didn't understand this desperate ache to touch and be touched by her. He'd never welcomed a woman's fondling beyond the most carnal of caresses, but she drew him near with every glance, every gesture. *One pulse of passion—* It soared through him. "I must have a promise from you that you won't turn back once the journey has begun. You'll experience all that I offer you."

Allegra gazed at him. "I must have a promise in return. You mustn't try to seduce me. That's the one thing that will make me desert our bargain."

Drayton released her. What she said made no sense. She knew it. He knew it. Why the pretense? "I agree."

"One thing more, my lord." She saw him tense. "If we're to be equals, shouldn't I know your Christian name?"

"Everett."

"Very well, Everett. If you're ready, I'd be delighted to attend the opera. Then, as she had seen men do all her life, she offered him her arm.

The rare sound of Drayton's laughter startled Hogan, who stood outside the drawing room waiting for a glimpse of the foreign lady. Shortly afterward, the doors opened and he forgot to assess her beauty in his astonishment at the look of relaxed pleasure on Lord Drayton's face.

"A capital idea!" Andrew exclaimed in the faint English accent he had gradually adopted over the last weeks.

"But I know nothing about riding," Allegra protested as their carriage turned into Hyde Park. She turned to her other companion. "Unlike English girls, we Americans aren't taught to ride from the moment we toddle. I've never been on horseback in my life. Besides, you can't expect me to go riding in this outfit." She gestured toward her blazer suit of navy serge.

"It doesn't matter," Drayton assured her. "You've nothing to fear from riding, beyond a few bruises, a scraped knee, a sprained ankle or wrist." As all the color drained from her face, he smiled. "Don't faint, Miss Grant. I promise you, you won't come to harm."

Less than reassured, she sat back in the open phaeton which, despite the sun's warmth, was a rather cool mode of transportation for the day. She scowled at Andrew. "I don't suppose you've considered how you're going to explain to Papa why you stood by and allowed me to break my neck."

"Don't be prissy, sis. Dash it all, you'll jolly well ruin our afternoon."

She leaned toward him, whispering, "I'll jolly well ruin your nose if you don't dispense with that horrid mimicry!"

"Sibling rivalry; I've never experienced it," Drayton observed.

"You're an only child?" Allegra asked. Though he had accompanied her and Andrew to the theater, the opera, and two dinners in the past two weeks, he had never spoken about himself.

"I have a sister, a redhead, I believe. I've never seen much of her."

"Never seen— But how is that possible?"

"She's ten years my elder and was out of the nursery before I entered it. By the time I was allowed at the dinner table, she had had her debut and was seldom at home. I was sent to boarding school at seven. She married the following year, a fellow with a penchant for the Far East. They reside in Bangkok."

"How awful for you."

"Not really. We Draytons find familial attachment unnecessary."

Andrew laid a fraternal arm about Allegra's shoulders. "Don't know what I'd do without a sister. Gives me someone to lord it over. Uh, pardon me. Poor choice of words."

"Not in the least," Drayton returned. "I think your sister would agree."

"I do," Allegra confirmed. "How is it that you have so many hours at your disposal, my lord? You spent months abroad in America. Now you've given over the entire week to entertaining us. What exactly do you do?"

Drayton met her inquiry with a lift of his brows. "I do as

little as possible, Miss Grant. I'm not compelled to do otherwise.''

"He's flush, sis," Andrew explained, lapsing into American slang. "You've heard of Dundare woolen mills. They're his.''

"I see.'' The statement answered the question uppermost in her mind since the night of their agreement, when it had occurred to her to wonder if Lord Drayton's sojourns to the States were fishing expeditions for an American heiress to bail him out of financial difficulty. It would have explained his persistent interest in her.

"Pull up here!'' Drayton stood up in the carriage and pointed with his furled umbrella toward a spot far back from the road. "We'll walk there from here.''

He alit and then offered Allegra his hand.

"The stables aren't nearby. They're farther on," Andrew said as he stepped down behind her.

"Who said anything about stables?''

"What else does one ride but a horse?'' she demanded.

Drayton shrugged. "Come along, children. They're waiting for us.''

The Grants exchanged glances, but there seemed nothing else to do but to follow their host across the grass.

The park was full of nurses and their charges, who steamed about on sturdy, wool-stockinged legs or lolled in their buggies under the shady limbs of trees. The trees themselves seemed to have just caught fire, flaming at their tips in the beginnings of the red-gold conflagration of autumn that would soon consume and then ravage them, leaving behind the gray-black skeletons of branches to pass the winter months.

Conflagration. Allegra repeated the word again and again in her mind as she tried to match her steps to Andy's. She felt the heat of conflagration whenever Everett Drayton was near. The effort not to be consumed took her full attention. She had made a bargain with him to meet him as an equal. The riding was a test which she must attempt—no, pass.

At first she didn't realize why Drayton had paused suddenly on a graveled path. Two young men in caps stood on the path steadying a pair of metal twin-wheeled vehicles.

Only as she and Andrew neared did she hear Drayton's conversation with them.

". . . as fine a pair as ye're likely to see, m'lord. Give ye a ride smooth as silk, they will."

"That remains to be seen," Drayton answered dryly and turned to the Grants. "Your steed awaits, Miss Grant."

"Bicycles!" Allegra said in amused relief. "You never meant that I should climb upon a horse!"

"You can ride a bicycle?" Drayton inquired in disappointment.

"No, I can't," she admitted. "But it's bound to be easier than trying to command an ill-tempered beast who weighs more than I."

With a sweep of his hand, Drayton said, "After you, Miss Grant."

She glanced uncertainly at Andrew.

"Go ahead." As she turned away, he said under his breath to the earl, "This should be more fun than the circus."

"I heard that," she replied as she handed her purse and umbrella to one of the young men.

"We'll steady ye a bit, till ye get the right of it," the older of the two said. "Begging yer pardon, miss, but ye must lift yer leg across this bar. That's right, miss. Ye see them pedals there? Ye're to put one foot on each of them. No, grasp the bars first, miss. There ye go, miss. Now! One foot on this pedal. Aye, that's it. We'll hold the machine till ye're on properly. Don't lean! No, no, no, miss! Ye must keep yer balance!"

Allegra turned at the sound of laughter. "This is impossible! The wheels are too narrow to balance upon. And this seat, it's indecent!"

"Not to worry," Andrew answered between chuckles. "Should you take a spill, there's no one about to recognize you."

She glanced at Drayton, who was leaning casually upon his umbrella, a coolly measured challenge in his gaze. "Oh, very well! Let's try again."

After a repetition of the instructions, Allegra pushed at

the pedals and, to her relief, the machine glided forward, albeit wobbly.

"That's it, miss!" said the man running alongside her as he braced the bicycle. "Keep pushing down on the pedals. Slowly, regularly. Keep pushing! Pushing. Don't lean! That's it! That's it! Ye got it, miss!"

For a moment Allegra experienced the elation of free navigation. Smiling as the breeze rushed past her face, she glanced up from her feet. It was a mistake. The bicycle took a sudden swerve to the right, skidded on the gravel, and came to an abrupt halt that overbalanced her.

She was sprawled full across the machine on the grass when Drayton reached her. With a hand under each armpit, he hauled her unceremoniously to her feet and spun her about. "Are you hurt? Speak to me! Are you hurt?"

"No!" she cried in fury dimmed by a lack of breath. "No, I'm not!"

"Perhaps this wasn't a good idea after all," Andrew said as he bent to pick up her hat.

Allegra snatched it from him. "To the contrary. I think it's a wonderful idea. I'll get the better of it, you just watch me!"

For the next half hour the gentlemen watched as she mastered the intricate techniques of cycling which included starting and stopping, turning a corner, and maneuvering around small children, balls, and dogs.

"Very nice," Drayton commended when she made her first successful trip down the gravel path and back. "Are you ready for a real ride now?"

Too pleased with herself to allow his tone of voice to spoil her mood, Allegra gave him the benefit of her best smile. "I am, indeed. Come on, Andy. Oh, there's only one other machine."

"I'm not particularly fond of eating turf," Andrew said, referring to her two spills. "I'll just go along and see what's being said at the Corner."

"Do you ride, my lord?" she asked with a cocky grin.

"A little," he answered.

He went over and straddled the second bicycle before

setting off in a smooth line down the path. She should have known. She was the pupil and he the tutor.

She followed his lead, often riding by his side though they exchanged few words. Concentration took most of her energy in the beginning, and later there didn't seem to be any need to speak. When at last they dismounted she felt that special satisfaction that comes with the mastery of a new skill. "Thank you for the lesson, Lord Drayton."

He gave her a long look. "What have you learned?"

"That mastery of a machine can be invigorating."

He nodded. "And, perhaps, that the elation of victory over your fear is a satisfaction that bears repeating?"

She frowned, trying to sense what he had said. "It was a very small victory."

"Only in comparison with those you've yet to achieve," he answered. "Come along. Andrew must be as hungry as we. We'll just have time to change before the theater."

She was pleasantly reassured by the touch of his hand at her elbow as he steered her back across the grass toward the waiting carriage. Most often he seemed amazingly detached from the world about him. As Andy often remarked, Lord Drayton was well-informed and well-read, but a very cool customer. He could discuss with equal ease the form of a symphony and the technicalities of the latest reform bill before the House of Lords. Yet, through it all, he maintained a kind of amused disdain for heated debate. It was impossible to rouse him to anger or passionate defense on any topic. In fact, Andy's temperamental displays drew his chiding laughter. It was as if, instead of a heart, he had at the center of his being a gyroscope that kept his emotions level at all times. Yet the passion was there. What else explained the light in his eyes when she sometimes found him silently watching her?

In moments like these, she glimpsed another man, one who was intelligent yet sensitive to the needs of others, and capable of kindness. She had watched him enjoying their ride through the park, as if for a moment he had laid aside his mask of indifference. The duality of his nature intrigued her.

When they reached the carriage she turned to him and held out her hand. "Thank you for the adventure."

Drayton took her hand lightly in his. "We've only begun, Miss Grant."

Sixteen

Andrew stretched his legs out toward the hearth and crossed his ankles. "London may be more civilized than New York, but it's damnably damp and dreary!"

"Your tongue isn't hampered by civilizing influences," Allegra commented as she looked up from the book she was reading.

"Sorry about that," he said absently, his mind drifting on to new thoughts. "I'm thinking we should leave for Paris next week."

The statement brought her head up again. "So soon?"

He sighed. "I'm not prospering in London as I'd hoped. There's not an original thought in my head."

She knew he referred to his new novel. "We've been here only a few months. Perhaps that's not long enough. Dr. Boyd gave strict orders that you were to take a complete rest from your work, which you haven't done. Genius can't be hurried."

He turned his head toward her. "You don't know what it's like to have this intense burning desire inside and be repeatedly frustrated by the whim of the mind."

"The bright lamp of genius can burn itself out," she warned.

"I wouldn't mind being used up in a brilliant flash!" He sat up, drawing his legs in. "Don't you see, it would all make sense then. The sacrifice, the loss, the tragedy would have fed the cause!"

Alarmed by the sudden flush that came to his face, she set her book aside and went to kneel by his chair. "Andy, I don't mind the sacrifices. Truly. Papa's last letter came as a rude shock to us both, but we can survive without his generosity. Writwell's retainer is more than enough if we are careful."

"Writwell! God, how I've grown to hate that name!"

She took his hand and pressed it to her cheek. "We can't spurn all our benefactors. Writwell is the easiest of our problems to solve. I've been making notes for the next series of articles. Would you like to see them?"

He studied her face in the firelight. "So you've been writing again. I should have known."

"Just sketches, Andy. You've always said I had a fair way with vignettes. They just need your polishing touch."

He turned his face away but didn't withdraw his hand from her grasp. Was he reduced to polishing his sister's prose? Was that what fate offered him in punishment for Harriet?

No! No! He mustn't think of that. The pain was still too fresh. It wasn't his fault! He hadn't known, couldn't have suspected what she would do. It was the threat of the madhouse! How could anyone have believed that her husband's vengeful nature would drive him to sign papers committing his wife to a madhouse?

And Harriet—why didn't she believe that he would have saved her? That was what clawed at him in the dark hours, ripping away his peace to expose the deep oozing jelly of his cowardice. She hadn't trusted him. In her last hours she had felt utterly abandoned. *Because I didn't want her!* That was the truth, and his guilty burden.

Allegra watched in sympathetic silence as the myriad emotions of pain, sorrow, anger, regret, and despair played across his face. Dr. Boyd had warned her not to press Andrew on the events surrounding his illness for fear of driving him away. She must say nothing until he did, and he never spoke of what burdened him.

"If you wish, we'll leave for Paris as soon as we've mailed the first batch of Writwell essays," she said softly.

Andrew turned to her. "You're so good to me and I treat

you abominably.'' His hand pressed hers. ''Promise that you'll never leave me. When all the others have deserted me, when society itself would cast my lot in with the fiends of hell, promise you won't desert me!''

The question surprised her as much as the intensity with which he spoke it, but she answered it readily. ''I'll never desert you, Andy. You know that.'' She smoothed back a black curl from his brow, so full of tenderness toward him that her heart felt constricted. ''You're the center of my life. Without you I'd be nothing.''

''Nothing,'' Andrew echoed. She would be nothing. The sentiment refused to clarify in his mind. Instead, the face of Lord Drayton rose to mind. He had seen the look in the Englishman's eyes when Allegra laughed or smiled. She drew him as she drew all men. She attracted people. Her presence gave them pleasure. She gave him joy. Only she dispelled the darkness. He mustn't lose her. To keep her, he must make being with him, her brother, more attractive than the sensual attraction of a man like Drayton.

''Lord Drayton is quite taken with you. I shouldn't be surprised if you married him.''

The bald statement embarrassed Allegra. ''You know my feelings toward the man. I tolerate him because you find his company pleasant.''

''He has a less than sterling reputation with ladies.''

''I'm certain that he contributes regularly to the muddying of his own name in order to appear more alluring,'' she rejoined. ''What little I've seen of him doesn't convince me of his irresistibility.''

''Good girl! Don't be taken in by brooding good looks and a title. A girl can't be too choosy.''

They laughed together at his joke, a thing that she realized they had seldom done since leaving New York. ''What shall we do this evening?''

He sighed. ''Get a cloth and I'll polish Writwell for you.''

She rose with a smile. ''Good! We need the income.''

* * *

"He said it was to be a private party. I didn't think that meant we wouldn't know a soul," Allegra commented from behind her ostrich feather fan as she watched the dozen elegantly dressed couples moving about the earl's drawing room, their voices raised above the music the quartet played in one corner.

Andrew leaned against the wall, his hands jammed in the pockets of his trousers and the pain of boredom on his face. "I might've known that Lord Drayton would invite half the Ton to his 'intimate' affair."

She looked about wide-eyed. "Do you mean to say we're among the Half-Ton?"

Andrew's chuckle drew looks of interest and disapproval their way, but she pretended not to notice. They knew no one, nor did she care to change the arrangement. The majority of the guests were drinking heavily. More than one gentleman had betrayed his condition with immoderate laughter. To her relief, Andrew had refrained from accepting more than a single glass of wine.

As for the ladies, they were all young and beautiful and expensively gowned. She noted in surprise that a few of them wore false complexions of powder, kohl, and lip salve.

"Where is our host?" she murmured. "I hope he's not pulling a Writwell. No, there he is. Who's that with him?"

"A wife?' Andrew suggested slyly, but when he looked toward the drawing room doorway, what he saw levered his shoulders away from the wall. "Why, that's Mrs. Patrick Campbell!"

"Who?" Allegra asked, her eyes never leaving the couple who were making their entrance into the room.

"Stella Campbell. She's found instant success with her part in *The Second Mrs. Tanqueray*, Pinero's new play." He took her arm. "Let's say our hellos to our host so that we may be introduced. Drayton's taste in P.B.s is quite to my liking."

Allegra didn't protest as he led her forth. This was her first sight of a Professional Beauty. Though she hadn't seen the play, the role of the scarlet woman, played by Mrs. Campbell, had been written up repeatedly in the papers. The bolder papers speculated with twittering glee about the extent to which the role of a mysterious and tragic woman was similar to the actress's real life.

The Grants' curiosity was shared by the room at large. Conversation had ceased at sight of the actress. Mrs. Campbell wore an elaborate gown of gypsyish design with exaggerated sleeves banded just above the elbow and trimmed in rows of bright ribbon, beading, and lace. The skirt, tiered below a tightly fitted waist, dripped beadwork, laces, ribbons, and flounces. But the singular point of interest was the bodice, or rather the lack of bodice.

The décolletage plunged to within inches of the waist. From her neck hung pearls, and a gold filigree chain with a single enormous emerald set in diamonds, placed to draw the eye to the inescapable conclusion. She wore no corset.

The actress gave no indication that she was aware of the riveted attention of the earl's guests. Her intense, interestingly featured face was serene as she hung on Drayton's arm, reminding Allegra of an exotic butterfly who'd attached itself to a juicy green leaf. When her great deep eyes turned up toward the earl, who leaned over to hear her whispered remark, she displayed a thick shock of untamed reddish brown hair caught back with a silver Spanish comb.

No woman could have appeared less appropriate in an earl's home, Allegra thought, and yet she clung to Drayton's arm with a familiarity that could only have one meaning.

Drayton stole a glance at Allegra from the corner of his eye. She was radiant in white satin, and flushed as a pink rose by anger. Good. That was the reaction he desired. He directed his attention to Andrew. "Mr. Grant, welcome. Have you made the acquaintance of Mrs. Campbell? Then allow me."

As Andrew made the appropriate responses to the introduction, Drayton turned his gaze to Allegra. "Miss Grant, do allow me to introduce you. Mrs. Campbell, I'd like you to meet a charming young American, Miss Allegra Grant."

Stella Campbell's gaze moved languidly from Andrew's handsome face to Allegra, and her eyes widened slightly. "How . . . do . . . you . . . do?" she said in an astonishingly slow fashion that made one hang on every word. She looked over Allegra's gown. "Yes. You have that . . . American look. As they say of Lady Churchill . . . you . . . have not lost . . . your sincerity . . . to overcivilization.''

"Why, thank you, Mrs. Campbell," Allegra answered in her best-mannered voice. "We Americans strive to maintain a few of the forgotten hallmarks of civilization. Andy, I'm parched. You will excuse us, won't you?"

Given no choice, Andrew bowed his leave and escorted his sister to the punch bowl. "You might have allowed me more time to speak with Mrs. Campbell," he groused.

"Undercivilized, indeed!" she exclaimed under her breath. "Who does she think she is?"

"I thought it was a rather sweet remark. You are wearing white, the color of the virtuous lily."

"Do be quiet!" she answered and deliberately trod on his toe, for Lord Drayton and his partner stood nearby. She couldn't bear the thought of betraying by so much as a flicker of an eyelash her anger, hurt, and humiliation. When Lord Drayton had invited them to dinner, she had assumed that she was his partner for the evening. To have been supplanted by an actress was demeaning.

In spite of her anger, she couldn't keep from glancing at them, and each time she did, jealousy and anger fused a little more. The earl's hand boldly held the Campbell woman's waist, nor did she seem to mind that his gaze frequently dipped below her face to the tantalizing depth of her décolletage.

"She's too thin for fashion," Allegra murmured. "And, really, she's overdramatized herself by wearing kohl about her eyes."

Andrew listened, aware that his sister was reacting very strangely for a girl who claimed to have no interest in the earl. "Do you wish to go home?"

"What, and have Mrs. Campbell think she's driven me off? Never. There's more Yankee stubbornness in me than that. I'd like a glass of champagne."

Andrew paused in mid-sip of the noxious punch. "I could use something more substantial myself. I'm sure I saw champagne on another table."

When the dinner gong sounded, Allegra hoped that her spirits would improve, but once Andrew led her to her place along the silver- and garland-laden table he abandoned her for his place at the far end on the opposite side. The gentleman seated on her left was much older than she and more interested in the lady on his left. The gentleman on her right looked harmless enough, but after a few words, she realized that he was either hard of hearing or grossly rude, for every time she spoke, he leaned indelicately near, as though to peer down the front of her gown. After several minutes, she gave up conversation, preferring to study the other guests. After all, everything was fodder for Writwell's European essays.

She noticed that none of the attractive young ladies wore wedding bands. She noted also the informality with which they treated the gentlemen they sat by. The frequency of the touch of ladies' hands on gentlemen's cuffs increased with the free flow of wine through the first courses.

The first time it occurred, she simply ignored the pressure of a shoe against her slipper, as good manners dictated. The second time, she moved her feet back under her chair. Much later, during the dessert course, as she slipped her spoon into her trifle, she was again touched.

The brush of a hand against her skirt was so light that at first she refused to credit it. But moments later the definite pressure of a hand sliding along the length of her thigh brought her up short. With an indignant gasp she swung her head toward the man on her right. There was a strange laxity about his eyes and mouth now, something that bordered on the indecent, and she realized that he was intoxicated.

"Is there a problem, Miss Grant?"

Drayton's commanding tone turned every eye at the table on her. What could she answer? "Small enough, my lord." She allowed her gaze to slide for an instant to her right. "It seems you've placed temptation before those who cannot resist."

Drayton signaled the servant nearest him with a flick of a finger. He spoke briefly to the man, who then came forward and reached for her dessert plate. As he withdrew it, the plate tipped and the trifle slipped from its bowl and into the lap of the gentleman on her right.

"Sir Hewett, my apology!" Drayton rose at his place,

displeasure clearly marked in his face. "Allow me to escort you out. My valet is a wonder with stains." He rounded the table quickly and brushed aside the servant, who tried unsuccessfully to blot away the red raspberry stain with a napkin.

Caught between suspicion and doubt, Allegra watched the two men leave the room. Surely, Lord Drayton hadn't directed his servant to spill her dessert on her dinner partner, yet she was certain she had seen a gleam of amusement in the earl's glance as he passed her place.

Seeking insight, she looked down the table to where Andrew sat on the opposite corner, but the sight of him was far from reassuring. His face was flushed and his smile was broad. He had been drinking; drinking a great deal.

The next half hour passed with excruciating slowness for her. Yet the company about her grew more animated and boisterous with every minute. The ladies didn't leave while the gentlemen enjoyed their port and cigars. To the contrary, the ladies drank and smoked in equal quantities.

The noise, the smoke, the spirits which she refused to drink, everything made her wish for escape. She tried to catch Andrew's eye, but he was seated at an angle that brought Lord Drayton into view each time. She had never seen the earl so animated, so smiling, so courteous, so engrossed as he was with the actress at his elbow. Finally she saw him lean over to drop a kiss on Mrs. Campbell's naked shoulder.

Mrs. Campbell, she fumed. Where was Mr. Campbell? Suddenly she understood what had been before her ignorant eyes all along. None of the ladies present were married to these gentlemen. They weren't ladies at all. This was that notorious event called a bachelors' party.

Disgusted, she rose and turned to leave. She didn't notice that Lord Drayton rose also and that he followed her when she left the dining room. She was unaware of him until she was brought up short by a hand gripping her elbow as she walked along the hall.

She turned sharply. "You!"

"Were you hoping I was Sir Hewett?"

She pulled her arm free. "I can't believe that you invited me to this, this—"

"Harmless bit of fun?" he suggested.

"Harmless? That man thought I was an actress, or worse."

"Hewett's harmless, I assure you, or I wouldn't have sat him next to you."

"Your idea of gracious company is quite atrocious. I'm not accustomed to being mauled during dinner."

"You were perfectly safe."

"I'm certain to have bruises from the pinching!"

He surveyed her coolly. "Show me evidence of that and I'll horsewhip the man in public."

Fury and embarrassment swept her. "You know very well that— Oh, never mind! I'm leaving." She turned away.

"Breaking our bargain so soon?"

She swung around. "I didn't agree to being molested."

He touched a finger to his lips as though admonishing a small child and then reached to open the door of a nearby room, indicating that she should enter before him.

Reluctantly she stepped into the dimly lit library.

When he had closed the door, he turned to her. "What exactly did we agree I would do?"

"I thought you would show me something of life unbounded by the conventions of polite society."

"You've had a taste of it tonight. You should be elated, yet you stand there with that puritan pinch of disapproval on your face. You're a coward and a hypocrite."

The words stung. "You, you can't condemn me when you've no standards of your own."

"Ah, but I have. I might have surrounded you with ladies of the evening who lure men to their sides in hopes of draining their purses. Instead, I offer you a glimpse of your ideal, the independent woman. A Professional Beauty is a hard-headed businesswoman whose profession is to look stunning and make herself agreeable. Don't you approve?"

"I don't imagine that there's a difference between the poor unfortunates who walk the streets and the women you invited here tonight."

"To the contrary. These ladies may have lovers, but they

aren't 'kept.' They do, however, accept gifts. Tonight Mrs. Campbell wears mine.''

Angry with herself for having worn the pearl necklace he'd given her, Allegra didn't reply. The invitation for comparison was irresistible. "Your friends dress and speak better, perhaps, but they're harlots just the same."

"Is that so? Would you care to compare?"

The challenge opened dangerous possibilities. "No thank you, I've been insulted enough for one evening."

"You wouldn't be expected to participate—unless you desired it."

"Hardly!"

"A pity, but to be expected." He turned away from her. "You aren't as brave as you'd like to think, and I won't continue to have my guests doused with desserts because you've been offended. Go home."

Allegra felt as though she had been struck. Never had she been spoken to in such a tone.

Drayton watched her struggle with the desire to flee and the realization of the ignominy of that flight. Determined not to help her, he reached into his pocket, took out a gold cigarette case, and opened it. After withdrawing a cigarette, he looked up as though surprised that she remained and held out the case. "Do you smoke?"

Miserable yet defiant, she answered, "Not yet."

He took out a second cigarette, saying, "Then the practice will be my final lesson to you." He put them in his mouth and lit the pair.

After the sudden brief flare of his match the room was again in semidarkness, but she had seen his face, and that was enough. Light-headed from the tumultuous emotions assailing her, she watched him approach. Was this infatuation, this thralldom that kept her here when good sense and breeding demanded that she should never have set foot inside the room?

He took one cigarette from his mouth and said, "Part your lips, as if to receive a lover's kiss."

She did as he asked, but the touch of his fingers as he set the cigarette between her lips drew a shiver from her.

"Don't be afraid. It's only a small vice. Let me show you

how small.'' He withdrew the cigarette from her mouth and the other from his before bending slowly toward her.

His kiss was gentle—a cool, tender, delicate kiss whose voluptuous sting devastated her resistance. All reason yielded to the moment, but even as she leaned toward him he backed away.

''Now,'' he said crisply, ''the lesser vice,'' and again he offered the cigarette to her.

Obediently, she took it, vividly aware that the moist tip had once lain between his lips.

''Good. Now watch me. You must inhale slowly, lightly, or the smoke will burn your throat.''

He inhaled deeply, signaled by the sudden bright ember of the tip. Fascinated, she watched him exhale a bluish-white stream of smoke from between his lips and knew the dizziness one experiences before an abyss, the sense of falling, of loss, of annihilation of oneself. Like the smoke, she felt incandescent, weightless, to be drawn in or rejected at his whim.

''Now, you try.''

His quiet voice carried a command, and she complied without resistance. The smoke stung her throat, stopped her breath, sent a tear cascading down her cheek, but she did as he had asked, coughing out the last of the bitter smoke.

''A small vice,'' he repeated as he took the cigarette from her. ''Now it's time for you to go home. I'll ring for a cab.''

''I don't think I can manage Andrew alone,'' she said in a worried tone.

''He can sleep here tonight.'' He reached for the servant's bell, but didn't pull it. ''Would you care to do the same?''

Allegra shook her head and then realized he probably couldn't see the gesture. ''No, I must go home.''

''Yes, you must.'' He sounded amused. ''Don't feel guilty. You don't leave me unconsoled.''

How like a wasp he was, buzzing about and then stinging her when she was most vulnerable. ''We agreed that there would be no constraints. Mrs. Campbell is welcome to you.''

''Liar.'' Definite amusement now. ''Cowardice, envy, and

falsehood: you're collecting vices at an admirable rate. I eagerly await the appearance of lust.''

She was pricked in a dozen delicate places, and most maddening of all, caught in a web of her own making. She had asked for equality without petty ties. Without a word, she turned and walked out.

When she was gone, Drayton took a long drag on her cigarette and stubbed out his. He'd been deliberately cruel, but it hadn't pleased him to be so. He had wanted nothing more than to hold her, to kiss and make love to her. The feelings appalled and frightened him. He didn't approve of weak emotions, certainly not the pretty mask called love in which lust paraded before the world. To realize that he was driven too far from his usual control amazed him.

She was playing at liberation. It was a pose, not a conviction. She was infatuated with whatever romantic notions of decadence she had conjured up, but she didn't yet accept the monstrous beauty and sweet brutality of life—as he did. After her reaction tonight, did he dare to continue to reveal to her those possibilities? And, if he dared, would he lose her?

''Lord Drayton?''

He turned at the sound of a woman's voice. It was Stella Campbell. She stood in the doorway, one leg thrust forward, a hand caressing the door molding in a theatrical manner. ''It's late, my lord. Shall I send my carriage away?''

He shrugged. ''No. You'd better go. I believe I've lost my appetite. Too much dessert, I suspect.''

''I know remedies for delicate dispositions.''

''Nó. Thank you.'' He wasn't accustomed to denying himself. He needed release from the temptation of Allegra Grant. He was free, by Allegra's own admission, to do as he chose. What held him back? He smiled. He didn't know. For the first time in many years he was not entirely in control of his feelings, and the sensation was not wholly unpleasant.

Seventeen

London, November

Allegra folded the last sheet of the correspondence and sealed it in the envelope, but her spirits were far from high. She had spent the better part of the past three days completing work Andrew should have done. "That's it, then. It'll be six weeks before we can expect delivery of the next installment of Writwell's advance. By then we may be in the street with our baggage piled about us."

"It's not my fault that the columns are late," Andrew muttered as he sprawled in his chair. "I can't compose in this bitter cold. It freezes the mind."

She glanced disapprovingly at the glass dangling from his right hand. "You might warm yourself more thoroughly if you chose cocoa over sherry."

He shook his head and winced as pain shot up the back of his neck to throb at his brow. "I ask little enough in my own house. To be left in peace is one thing I demand."

"Your house?" The scornful words were out before she could curtail her annoyance. "Your house! Your columns! Your money! Just exactly where do my contributions lie?"

"Don't press me!" he shot back in injured affront. "You always press me when I'm least able to stand it."

"You've been unable to stand criticism of any kind for weeks. Andy, what are we going to do?" She picked up a stack of letters and waved them in his direction. "Have you looked at these bills? We must do something."

He sat up, anger darkening his cheeks and distorting his face. "Do something? What would you have me do, drain my blood?'' He flung away his glass and it shattered when it struck the grate. Droplets of whiskey flew into the fire and ignited in brilliant bursts of flame. ''I have expenses! Every man of breeding has bills. It's expected!''

Allegra didn't answer. His temper had become more violent of late, but so far the results of it were confined to the occasional broken glass or dish. After a moment, he sank back into his chair with a groan and closed his eyes. She was reluctant to speak again but decided that a better moment was not likely to occur any time soon. ''I've done something,'' she said quietly. ''I've written Mama.''

He didn't indicate that he had heard her.

''I asked for money for new clothes. Mama can't bear the thought of her daughter going about in last year's fashions. I received her answer yesterday.''

His eyes opened but still he didn't speak.

''I'd hoped she would send us the cash, but Papa got wind of it. He's opened a credit line for us at the Bank of England which creditors may draw against.''

Andrew's head swung toward her. ''What good is that?''

''I've been thinking about it. Might we not make a few purchases and then sell what we have?''

He frowned. ''We'd need a market for them.''

''I understand that theaters offer good prices for fashionable clothes to use as costumes.''

''You won't get what they're worth,'' he said, ''and we need to turn a profit in the thousands in order to satisfy old creditors.'' He brightened. ''A line of credit, did you say? Turn the old bills into the bank.''

''Oh, Andrew!'' she said in horror at the thought of her parents learning the extent of their present debt. ''Papa will close it at once. We must find another method to settle those bills.''

Reluctantly, he conceded the point. ''Do what you think best, but get me a few hundred pounds by the end of the week. I've just thought of a way of increasing it.''

''How?''

For the first time that morning he smiled. ''Lord Drayton's always eager to sponsor me in town. There're gaming hells in London where a gentleman may win a thousand pounds on a single gamble.''

"Or lose as much,'' she amended. "No, we must be careful if we're to gain from this bit of luck. The first thing we'll do is find more reasonably priced lodgings.''

"This house was the least expensive in the area.''

"I was thinking of another area. I understand there're some nice flats in Mayfair.''

"You 'understand' a great deal. Whom have you been talking to?''

She blushed. "I read the newspapers, the classified sections, if you must know. Really, Andy, one of us must keep a level head. We aren't entertaining. We've kept apart from the other Americans in London.''

"Damned meddlers!'' he mumbled.

"Other than Lord Drayton, we see no one.''

"*You* see no one,'' he countered. "It's your fault that you don't know more people. I've met dozens. Lord Drayton's offered repeatedly to escort you, but you've had your nose out of joint ever since he played that little joke on you.''

"Lord Drayton may drown himself, and good riddance!''

"Don't be vulgar, sis.''

"I'm still amazed that you weren't insulted that I was exposed to those women of the demimonde. Sir Hewett actually thought I was one of them!''

"He was too staggering drunk to recognize you again.''

Allegra held her tongue, but the same could be said of him. In fact, most nights when he returned in Lord Drayton's carriage, the smell of the tavern accompanied him into the house. Somehow she had to break the earl's hold on her brother. "Andy, I'd like *you* to take me out. There's a concert tonight. As an amusement, we might sit in the cheap seats with the middle classes.''

"Lord Drayton has a box. I'll ask him.''

"No!'' She pounded the desk with a fist. "I don't want to go with Lord Drayton. I detest Lord Drayton. So would you if you could see what he's doing to you.''

Andrew stood up, waving her words away with a sweep of his arm. "Enough. Enough. If you're unhappy, send to Mama for fare back to New York. I'm staying here.'' He turned to her, a puzzled look in his green eyes. "You've changed, Allegra. Once you'd have been the first to indulge in the fun. Now you're as bad as Papa, dragging the unfashionable subject of money into every conversation. Now you want to take away my friend, as you have my columns."

The thrust hurt. Allegra's eyes filled with tears as he turned and walked out. "Andrew, I—!" He kept walking and she didn't try again to stop him.

What was the use? She didn't know how to answer him. He had taught her to debate before she was twelve, but his accusation was too damning to be used simply as fodder for the estrangement between them. She sat back and closed her eyes, too weary from a sleepless night of writing to keep anger simmering.

"Now you want to take away my friend, as you have my columns."

Had she done that, taken away his column? She thought she was helping him, with his blessing. The first series which she waited for him to initiate had been more than a month late, eliciting several publisher's letters threatening to discontinue the project. The second batch had been six weeks late. Attached to the payment were the same threats. The columns in the envelope in front of her would be the first to arrive at the publisher on time—because she had written them without consulting Andrew. Without a check before Christmas, they would be bankrupt.

Andy was neglecting everything, even his novel. While the work waited, he ran about London, eating and drinking, always drinking, with Lord Drayton, and running up enormous bills.

She opened her eyes a slit to stare at the unopened stack of mail that had arrived with the breakfast tray. With reluctance, she reached for them. Perhaps Andy hadn't been completely wrong in his suggestion. A few of the bills might be turned over to the bank for payment, easing the strain on their finances.

The envelopes of thick cream or white contained invitations. She separated them into piles—those names she recognized as American and which Andrew always refused, and two whose seal bore the marks of English peerage. The thin missives were bills, which she placed with the others.

Finally she came to a slim letter addressed to J.A.N.U.S. Writwell. Surprised, she turned it over to discover that the return address was not American. It was in Tite Street, London. An English fan letter, a first. Smiling, she opened it.

For a long moment she stared at it, mouth ajar. She reread it, and then once more. It was short, barely five sentences, but her eyes kept running over it again and again until she was certain she couldn't be wrong.

She rose and hurried toward the door, the letter in hand. "Andrew! Andrew! Come quickly!"

She was halfway up the main stairs when he appeared at the top, struggling into a fresh shirt. "What's wrong?" he demanded impatiently. "Is the house afire?"

She paused, pressing a hand to her mouth to still her inclination to laugh, and waved the letter over her head. "It's a letter! For Writwell!" she gasped out in short bursts. "It's from Oscar Wilde!"

"I should have worn a sack coat," Andrew complained as the carriage rumbled along the street toward Lord Drayton's town address. "This tailcoat is all wrong. Mr. Wilde will think I'm a colonial hick."

"I think you look very handsome," Allegra said soothingly. "Lord Drayton is partial to tailcoats and he's never at fault in his attire. You've said so yourself."

This complimentary reference to Lord Drayton was only one of many that she had contrived to make in recent days, for Andrew's adolescent worship of the earl grew with each day. Besides, she had to admit that it was an act of singular generosity on Lord Drayton's part to offer to host a party for Andrew in Wilde's honor. It had surprised her nearly as much as his continued kindnesses to Andrew.

As if by magic, Andrew brightened. "Mr. Wilde's particularly fond of the peerage. He won't fault the earl's guests. We should count ourselves lucky to know the earl."

"We are," she agreed. What she thought of the earl

didn't matter at all this night. The fame and genius of Oscar Wilde was known worldwide, and tonight she and Andrew would have the privilege of dining with him. She could scarcely contain her excitement. The few words of praise he had written in his letter to Writwell had, even if he didn't know it, been a compliment to *her* talent. The letter had brightened Andrew's spirits as nothing had since the publication of his first work. For his sake and the chance to meet Mr. Wilde, she would make peace with the devil himself.

As they turned into Belgrave Square with its long rows of Regency homes, she saw that the front of Lord Drayton's town house was ablaze with specially erected gas lamps. The fluted white columns of the earl's porch were topped in gilt laurel-leaf wreaths making a vivid display. Despite her dislike of the man, she had to admire the earl's audacity. Mr. Wilde wasn't likely to miss the implication—nor the honor.

As they drew closer she saw that a small crowd had formed in the shadows of the park across the street. "There's a mob out there, Andy. Do you suppose something's happened?"

"Something's going to happen," he replied with his cocky grin of old. "Mr. Wilde is as notorious as he is famous. People watch his every move. Lord Drayton's made certain that everyone knows of this event."

The carriage rolled to a stop before the house, and she heard a murmur from the crowd as she stepped down into the glare of the lights. Disconcerted, she took Andy's arm in a tighter grip than usual.

"Nervous?" he asked.

"Cold," she replied, embarrassed to admit that anxiety had any part in her feelings. "Do hurry. The chill is cutting through my cape."

The door opened on a setting much different from that which she had entered weeks earlier. The foyer was ablaze with the unexpected glow of dozens of tapers, a concession to a more romantic time when all chandeliers were candle-powered. The butler wore livery in the earl's colors of scarlet and gold, as did the footmen carrying trays among the guests. Hothouse flowers graced every niche. Orchid sprays spilled from bay-leaf garlands that draped the doorways and the railing which led to the second floor.

When they had slipped out of their coats, Andrew led her on his arm into the drawing room. Here the glow of gaslight was diffused by rose globes. Fewer than eight guests were present, but Allegra knew at once that they were not the people she had met weeks earlier. This group of animated, eccentric, sparkling young gentlemen and ladies, set apart by their cultured lisps as the flower of English aristocracy, was a welcome contrast to the sumptuously dressed but socially unacceptable actresses and paramours of the last occasion. With a smile and nod of greeting toward those who deigned to look up from their conversations, the Grants settled into an unoccupied corner to await their host.

Allegra knew the instant the Earl of Dundare entered, and turned toward him so as not to be surprised into revealing any feeling. She even managed to maintain that demeanor when she saw that he wore the traditional costume of his heritage: a kilt. Her eyes traveled quickly over the fitted black velvet coat with ruffle jabot to the scarlet-and-gold-plaid pleats of the skirt. In the gap between hem and leggings she glimpsed hairy knees as he approached.

"Mr. and Miss Grant, welcome," Drayton greeted in a tone he might have used when addressing strangers, but he took in with silent approval every detail of Allegra's cream satin evening gown, from its deep crimson velvet sleeves, neck ruffle, and waist trimming to her gloves, fan, and the single lily pinned in her upswept hair.

"Evening, Everett," Andrew greeted with an American enthusiasm he often repressed in London.

Allegra noted the use of Lord Drayton's Christian name, for she had never heard Andrew use it before.

"You've outdone yourself," Andrew continued, feeling pride in the decor which reflected on him as well as his host. After all, his letter from Wilde had made the evening possible. "I don't think I've ever seen a finer setting."

"I don't believe Miss Grant agrees," Drayton answered.

"To the contrary. You're quite impressive in full regalia," she answered, not quite brave enough to glance again at his exposed knees. There was a badge on his chest embroidered with the thistle so well loved by her father. Until this moment she had never given any consideration to the fact that he and she were of the same tenacious Scottish blood.

"Everett, dear man! I've come at last."

At the unprecedented announcement, Allegra turned to look toward the entryway and spied an eccentric-looking lady.

Tall and slender, the woman wore her abundant marmalade-colored hair piled high on her head with an unruly fringe, à la Bernhardt, fluffed across her brow. A diamond-sprinkled net passed beneath her chin and was then pinned atop her hair like a medieval barbette. She had deep tragic eyes of a pale color and the fine bone-china skin of a pre-Raphaelite painting.

By her bearing it was impossible to mistake her for anything other than an aristocrat, yet she wore an old-fashioned, high-waisted pale satin gown whose color appeared to have been deepened by age, and at her wrists, elbows, and waist, strips of aged lace had been tied in bows. The effect was unique, odd, but not without charm.

Drayton took Allegra by the elbow and said, "This is someone you must meet."

Still smarting from the last introduction to one of the earl's lady friends, Allegra approached as an opponent, but the newcomer's face was the kind one couldn't help liking.

"Marchioness, delightful," Drayton exclaimed with more warmth in his tone, Allegra noticed, than he had used in addressing her. "I'm honored that you consented to come."

The marchioness took his hand in hers and looked up at him. "Miss an opportunity to hear Oscar? I . . . think . . . not." She spoke with the same maddening drawl that Mrs. Campbell had used. It must be the fashion, Allegra noted in disapproval, for it gave the speaker the appearance of extreme fatigue or unhealthy shortness of breath.

"I shouldn't have come otherwise," the marchioness continued. "You've not behaved well . . . of late. You were to call me Violet . . . for instance. I exacted that promise from you when you studied with me."

"There are those who're still shocked by such familiarity in public,' Drayton reminded her.

She smiled at him. "So discreet. You must marry, Everett. All the mothers consider you a *parti*. it won't do to fail them. One has so few choices these days."

"The very reason I've never married. There's no one else to match you, Marchioness. Yet I can't fault a flawless artistic sense which prefers the simplicity of four silver balls to the abundance of eight," Drayton answered, referring to the heraldic display on their respective coronets.

"Naughty man! I forgive you too much . . . because you possess an artistic character. What are you doing?"

"Nothing of promise. The muses are not kind to me. They prefer marmalade curls to black ones."

"I've heard the most repellent rumors . . . that you've given up your sculpture altogether . . . and, like Manfred, have taken to brooding about the world . . . only to bring back the most extraordinary specimens. An American heiress, did they say?"

Drayton half turned to draw a reluctant Allegra, who stood a little apart, to his side.

"Marchioness, may I present Miss Allegra Grant of New York City. Miss Grant, the Marchioness of Granby."

"Good evening, Marchioness," Allegra answered, scarcely concealing her indignation at being described as a specimen that the earl had dragged home as if she were an exotic trophy.

"An American?" the marchioness inquired. "Then you must know my dear friend Jeannie Churchill?"

"I'm afraid not," Allegra answered. "America is a very large country, Marchioness. We've many social circles."

"How unfortunately common that makes them all." The marchioness's gaze traveled over Allegra's gown and then came back to her face as if she were memorizing the person before her. "You've a face and figure of exceptional originality. Unlike the majority of your countrywomen, you don't bear a trace of your motherland . . . except for your deplorable accent and your choice in colors. You should never wear bold shades, Miss Grant." She looked up at Drayton. "I'll consider her case during the evening . . . and make suggestions before I leave. Ah, there is that dear man, Welsey. Do excuse me.''

''Well, that's a singular feat. Miss Grant,'' Drayton said in good humor. ''Violet likes few Americans. She feels a resentment toward most because they're making the best matches among our set.''

''In that case, she needn't consider me a threat to her standards,'' Allegra snapped.

Drayton arched a brow in amusement. ''I don't think she does.''

With that enigmatic statement still echoing in her ears, Allegra allowed him to escort her around the room to be introduced to his other guests. They were incurious, distant, but unfailingly polite. Allegra made a mental note to Writwell: *It was like walking among a family of well-fed gibbons. When I neared them they watched, alert to any movement that might betray aggression, but less interested in my purpose than in their own monkey business.*

Andrew, she realized with some envy, was more welcome among the peers. Rumors abounded that he was Writwell, which was enough to interest this literary-minded group. For the next half hour she stood in her brother's shadow, listening as he received the lion's share of attention. Once when she was moved to voice one of her own witticisms, it received such a chilly reception that she didn't repeat the mistake. Andrew was perceived as the Grant wit, she merely a relation. To attempt to be original was bad manners.

She told herself that she didn't mind the anonymity, that these social laurels were just what Andrew needed to recover his confidence so that he could write. Yet, as Lord Drayton repeatedly gazed at her, she suspected that he suspected her jealousy. As a result, by the time he approached her with a glass of champagne, which she very much wanted, she turned him down with a terse shake of her head.

He eyed her in puzzlement but didn't speak. Something bothered her, something that he couldn't put a finger on. For a long time, he had sensed she kept a secret, but never before had it been so obvious. Was it her brother's drinking that disturbed her? She watched him, frowning unconsciously whenever he exchanged an empty glass for a full one, but she never indicated that he should refrain. She spared no one else a look, consumed by her brother.

He frowned. It wasn't the first time that thought had come to mind. She treated her brother like a husband—no, better than that: like a lover. Nothing he did went unnoticed by her, no feat went without the reward of her smile, no transgression was not soon smoothed over. Himself she dismissed as an adversary without feeling or sensibilities. Yet, he wondered, what would she think of her precious brother if she knew how, night after night, he recklessly gamed away his hours in the best brothels in London. Would she condemn her brother? Drayton wondered.

Dinner was set for eight o'clock, but at half-past eight they were still waiting in the drawing room. When the sound of the front door opening was heard, the room became silent, all aware that this must be the man for whom they had assembled.

Drayton reached the entry just as the butler announced the honored guest to the room.

Allegra's first impression of Oscar Wilde was that he was much larger than she imagined. He was well over six feet and huge, so thick about the middle that the buttons of his waistcoat bulged slightly. His long light brown hair was parted in the middle and waved over his ears. He was not handsome or romantic in any manner. His face was long and heavy with pouchy jowls, purplish thick lips, and sad eyes that turned down at the outer edges. His clothing further distracted her, for he was overdressed in an evening coat with velvet collar and a tight cravat that led to the conclusion that everything he wore was a size too small.

Her second reaction came when he threw back his huge head and laughed at the opening remark Lord Drayton made to him and she spied a black front tooth in his mouth. The sight elicited a shiver of revulsion. Was it possible that this grotesquerie was the person hailed by many as Britain's brightest wit and man of impeccable artistic taste? *"I can resist anything but temptation,"* his famous bon mot came to her now as she stared at him, and she believed it. About him was the aura of a man who indulged any and all whims: the decadent emperor of aestheticism.

Many pressed forward ahead of her to be introduced, but to her surprise Andrew was not among them. She turned to him as he came to stand beside her and was stricken by the look in his eyes. "What's wrong, Andy? You look ill."

"I can't face him," he said in a strangled voice. "He will find me out!"

She laid her hand against his cheek, saying in a hushed but stern voice, "Rubbish, Andy! What can he see but what there is, a handsome man with a talent for words. He approached you. He respects you. You won't disappoint him."

Drayton looked up to see the tender scene between brother and sister, and the shock of jealousy quaked through him. She had never touched him like that, not once. He turned to his honored guest, cutting across the remarks being made to him. "Mr. Wilde, I would introduce you to my American friends. I believe you know one of them by reputation."

Allegra snatched her hand from Andrew's cheek when she saw the two men nearing, and took a step back, saying under her breath, "Be your charming self, Andy. I hear he can't resist a handsome face."

Andrew put out his hand before Lord Drayton could speak. "No introductions are necessary. Mr. Wilde, I've known about and revered your work for years. It is my very great honor to be in your presence."

"It was my conclusion a decade ago that the first failing of the American educational system was that they did not teach a proper appreciation for scholarship," Wilde pronounced in his musical tenor as he offered Andrew a limp hand. "You, dear boy, are proof of their rapid elevation in taste."

"Thank you, sir."

Andrew felt a blush creeping up his neck and was mortified to have the poet comment on it as he tapped his cheek. "Quite charming, *c'est exquis*. You must sit next to me at dinner. I am quite curious to know more of your countryman Writwell."

Relieved by the man's warm reception, Andrew stepped back beside Allegra. "Mr. Wilde, I'd like you to meet my sister, Miss Allegra Grant."

The poet's face lit up at the sight of Allegra. He glanced again at Andrew, and the Grants knew he noted their striking similarity. "Her beauty was a beauty molded of many mysteries," he quoted from his own work. "It seems to me to be the face of someone who has a secret."

Surprise rippled through Allegra. It was as though he had read the secret of their duplicity in her face. "Mr. Wilde, this is an honor," she murmured stiffly and knew she, too, blushed.

"Not so deep a blush, Miss Grant. You begin to clash with your gown," he teased lightly. "Take my arm. I begin to smell beef that is within seconds of simmering too long."

From that moment on Allegra remembered nothing of her earlier impressions. There was only the soulful gaze of his gray eyes as she sat on Wilde's left and Andrew across to his right, the gaiety of the great man's expression and the lovely musical timbre of his voice colored by an Irish heritage of charm and the knack for the right word at the right moment.

The dinner table sparkled with Wilde's wit, yet he never dominated the conversation. He left the meat of discourse for others, serving up his words as one adds a dash of salt or a grind of pepper to the dish as spice.

She was astonished to discover the breadth of Wilde's reading habits. From the first issue he had known of Writwell. He read American papers and magazines, devoured French and Italian journals, even the occasional German manifesto, though he detested that country's politics, he said.

To use words as he did, to polish and scatter them in a starry display as he did, to wash the senses in wit and images and provoking challenge, how wonderful that would be, Allegra thought again and again until suddenly an idea to which she had never before given credence came to mind. Why didn't she write for herself? Half of Wilde's praise of Writwell was for phrases she had worked out alone.

"Ah, do not say you agree with me," Wilde declared at one point when she dared to speak up. His gray eyes sparkled with amusement. "When people agree with me I begin to feel I must be mistaken."

Allegra smiled at this extravagant attempt to remain singular in thought and word. "Mr. Wilde, is it true that you believe that art, to be art, must have no useful purpose?"

"I will go further than that," he answered. "It is through art, and through art only, that we can realize our perfection; through art and art only that we can shield ourselves from the sordid perils of actual existence." He leaned forward as if to impart to her a secret, but his voice was theatrically pitched as he said, "We are all in the gutter, but some of us are looking at the stars!"

"If that's true, then what are we to make of ourselves? We're all sinners."

"Spoken like a true child of your land," he answered with a smile of tolerance. "Dear lady, a sense of sin is a symptom of weakness. There is no sin but stupidity. Do not mistake purity for puritanism. Creeds are believed not because they are rational but because they are repeated. Form is everything. It is the secret of life. Find expression for sorrow, and it will be dear to you. Find expression for joy, and intensify its ecstasy. Use Love's litany, and the words will create the yearning from which the world fancies they spring."

"I don't know if what you say is possible," Allegra answered boldly and heard several gasps of disbelief, "but if it is, then it's a selfish form."

"Ah!" he declared enthusiastically, not at all affronted by her doubt. "Selfishness is not living as one wishes to live. It is asking others to live as one wishes to live."

This brought collective laughter from round the table, and the conversation moved on to a new topic as several of the guests spoke up to interrupt her conversation with Wilde.

As he turned to listen to Andrew, Allegra's gaze was drawn inexorably toward Lord Drayton's place at the head of the table. He had said something similar to her earlier about the sweetness of sin and the beauty of vice. He stirred her, and what he stirred she feared, yet she knew that she would never know complete peace until she had learned the reason for his attraction. When he looked up, she glanced away.

At the conclusion of the meal, as the ladies were leaving the table, she heard Wilde say to Andrew in answer to his complaints about his novel, "Mr. Grant, I will caution you in one matter. Do not make the mistake of appealing only to the best heads, for the best heads are never numerous. The hardships of genius move me to tears of blood. Were men as intelligent as bees, all gifted individuals would be supported by the community. We should be the first charge on the state!"

She regretted the necessity of leaving, even considered remaining. She tried to imagine what Lord Drayton would do if she sat down and asked him for a cigarette, but her courage was not great enough to move her to action.

She discovered upon entering the drawing room a little in arrears that "separate" in this case did not imply unequal, for several ladies had lit up cigarettes of their own. One lady, dressed similarly to the Marchioness of Granby, placed her cigarette at the end of a long jewel-encrusted holder, then lounged among the pillows of the sofa as a sweet aromatic odor of smoke filled the air.

Violet Granby neared the young American lady with mixed feelings. Throughout the meal she had watched her and been satisfied that Miss Grant was not too provincial to learn the duties of a countess. Still, she had held her judgment when Everett pressed her on the point. Though he alluded to the fact that he would never marry, she knew too much of the temperament of American ladies to believe that. Miss Grant might succumb before marriage but only to enhance the probability of marriage. The idea did not please her for there were already too many American ladies with English titles. Still, Violet would give the girl the benefit of a few words.

"Miss Grant? Ivory. And gray lace. After the birth of your first child, black."

Allegra smiled. "Thank you, Marchioness. I'll remember."

The marchioness then pulled something from her hair and handed it to Allegra. "This is a bay leaf, symbol of the

Souls. Ask Everett about its meaning, but I beg you, tell no one else. One must be selective.'' She paused thoughtfully. ''Everett has a wonderful talent and a good mind which he wastes on common pleasures. Encourage his work. I do so detest common pursuits.''

Allegra tucked the bay leaf into the bodice of her gown as the marchioness turned away.

More than an hour passed in which Allegra relived in her thoughts again and again the wit and philosophy of her dinner partner. She didn't mind that none of the women spoke more than briefly to her. She had spent the most interesting night of her life thus far in the company of an astonishingly talented man.

When the men finally joined the ladies, she was surprised, as she had first been, by the appearance of Mr. Wilde. As he entered with a paternal arm thrown about Andrew's shoulder, she saw that Wilde was very flushed. The after-dinner port had deepened the color that the wine, which he had consumed in copious amounts at dinner, had produced. Once again she was repelled and at the same time surprised at herself. Was she so shallow, so much a slave to vanity, that when his mouth was not spilling forth gloriously colored phrases, his greatness seemed less to her? She had little time to ponder that thought, for Andrew led him directly over to her.

''Mr. Wilde has asked me to accompany him to the Savoy to meet a few of his friends. I told him I would.''

''Of course,'' Allegra replied, but misgiving touched her as she saw that Andrew, too, was quite drunk. ''You won't be out very late, will you? We have a luncheon engagement.''

''Dear lady,'' Wilde began in an expansive voice, ''I wouldn't for the world allow harm to come to a man of such charm and looks. A veritable Adonis, that's what he is. And his verse is nearly as fine. His work reflects a quality rare in art, the feminine constitution that is too often lacking in our ruffian philosophers. He has a great future, a great future. I'll see to it myself if he consents to remain in London. You must convince him of it. He must have his chance now, for it is well-known that all good Americans go to Paris when they die.''

"I'll just get my wrap," Allegra said to Andrew.

"No need," Andrew answered. "Lord Drayton has consented to see you home. He is thinking of meeting us later." He looked back over his shoulder. "Isn't that right, my lord?"

"Perhaps," Drayton answered with a genial nod which Allegra didn't trust. "London, after the good and guilty are abed, is filled with tantalizing possibilities. In any case, Miss Grant, it would be my great pleasure to see you home."

Allegra nodded. What else could she do? She watched them go, trying to remember what she had heard of Wilde that should fill her with such unease. There were rumors, of course, of his decadent ways, yet she was ignorant of so much of what the word "decadent" described.

"Oscar was a dear at dinner," Violet Granby murmured as she said good night to Allegra. "But you should warn your brother that much of the company that Wilde keeps isn't the sort to leave his reputation unassailed. Good evening, Miss Grant."

With this bit of news to worry over, Allegra failed to notice when the last of the guests had gone. Finally she looked up to see Lord Drayton lounging in the doorway of the drawing room, his kilt exchanged for jacket and trousers. She didn't know how long he had been there, but she had the distinct feeling that he had seen her brooding and guessed the reason. He came forward slowly, opened his cigarette case, and removed one. He lit it, inhaled, and then offered it to her as he sat down on the sofa beside her.

The smoke was more aromatic than that of the first cigarette she had smoked. When she had exhaled she said, "Do cigarettes come in different flavors?"

Drayton smiled. "Oh, yes. For different purposes. Now watch me. You must inhale slowly, hold it a moment, and then exhale. You will come to master the action." He demonstrated, then handed it back to her.

This time she drew the hot smoke into her lungs and released it in a long, slow breath.

They sat in silence, the shared cigarette a silent bridge between them. She had meant to ask him many questions about Wilde, had meant to thank him for the dinner, for the hospitality, for the most wonderful night of her life, but now those words didn't seem important. She felt weightless, as if the act of smoking calmed and yet buoyed her, too.

"No wonder men smoke," she said into the long silence.

"What do you mean?" he asked as he stretched out his legs and leaned his head back against the sofa.

"Why, this wonderful sense of peace. It's miraculous. I think I'll take up the practice."

He smiled and the action of his muscles pleased him. "I wouldn't recommend that you indulge frequently in this particular leaf. It's a special brand."

"Expensive?" she said in slow syllables, intrigued by the feel of her tongue moving over her lips and teeth as she spoke.

"Special," he replied. He turned his head to look at her in the candlelight. "Are you afraid of me now?"

"Afraid?" She tried to hold the question in her thoughts for inspection, but she could only think of the absurdity of it. "Of course I'm afraid of you. But you know that. You've always known that. That's what intrigues you."

"No. That's not what keeps me spellbound by you." He touched a finger to her earlobe, and the skin was soft and lush as velvet. "May I kiss you?"

She shook her head. "No, you mustn't." But when he rose and half leaned over her, she didn't protest.

His lips were warm and clingingly moist, the silk-sheathed sting all the more potent for the intense peace that had settled over her. It magnified every breath, every tremor of pressure of his lips on hers. When his tongue snaked out to caress her bottom lip, she sighed with a shiver that curled her toes inside her slippers.

Drayton smiled. The subtle effects of hashish always pleased him. He wasn't playing fairly, but he didn't want to play fairly. Seduction had never appealed to him. Either the woman was interested or she wasn't. But this time he was determined to win. This would be a cold, calculated seduction that would leave him free of the guilt of pretense and leave her free to hate him without guilt or self-doubt.

Yet, as he felt her softening response to his kiss, a twinge of guilt spoiled that first victory. He could, but he didn't want to take her like this. Perhaps, if she gave herself to him out of weakness, not conscious desire, they would both be cheated. Unless he gave her a chance to express it, how would he know that he experienced her true passion? What was a man to do?

Reluctantly he pulled her arms from about his neck. "Come."

Allegra gazed at him in surprise as he bounded to his feet. "Come where?"

He held out a hand to her. "Before you sink into sin, I think you should see a bit of it."

Eighteen

A light rain had begun to fall, whispering along the lane as Allegra emerged from Lord Drayton's home. She was glad for the anchor of his arm, feeling she might otherwise float away like the mists swirling past the street lamp that stood across the way.

She stepped into the cab he had ordered and moved into one corner to make room for him. She glimpsed his profile as he paused to give an address to the cabby. As before she thought his face contained too many crags and tors for conventional handsomeness, but she now found beauty in that austerity. It seemed the face of a man who had weathered storm and blast, endured long periods of isolation and drought, until every unessential bit of flesh had been worn away to reveal the bare-bone character of the man. And like the bleak moors of Cornwall, of which she had seen pictures, she sensed a pride and disdain for the very elements that had formed him.

She thought, *I am attracted to a man. To Lord Drayton.*

To his kisses. A brief memory surfaced, so paltry by comparison that she was amused to recall it. She had lifted her face for Dr. Boyd's kiss, asking that he repeat it because she couldn't quite accept the disappointment. How droll!

Drayton entered the cab in nearly as good a mood as his partner, who was chuckling to herself. "Happy?" he inquired as he settled himself into the seat.

"Hm, I am." She leaned forward to within inches of his face. "Kiss me again and then let's smoke. Unless, of course, you think it would shock the cabby."

"Which? The kissing or the smoking?" he teased.

She frowned, childlike. "I——I don't know."

"Then I believe you've had enough of both for a while." He gently pushed her back against the seat. "And do keep your sweet mouth shut. There are few enough American ladies in London. You won't want your identity made public where we're going."

"Where are we going?"

"To Sodom and Gomorrah. Are you brave enough for that?"

She didn't reply at once. He was teasing. He must be. "What will we do there?"

"Anything you wish," he answered readily, but his senses were alert now to every nuance of her mood. "You are made for finer things than you imagine," he continued in a slow steady tone. "You can put off the common burden of humanity and walk with the rebellious angels . . . if you dare."

She strained to concentrate on his words, for the hiss of the rain, the jingle of the hansom bells, and the rhythmic clunk of the horse's hooves were each surprisingly distinct in her mind. "You mean Lucifer," she mused aloud.

"I do. As St. Augustine said, 'In more ways than one do men sacrifice to the rebellious angels.' To do so for a higher purpose, to choose to know the evil in beauty and the beauty in evil, is, I believe, worth the gamble of heaven."

"And if one loses?"

Drayton smiled. He had found the answer to that question long ago. "Was not Lucifer once closer to God than any mortal man who crawls on the earth and beats his breast in fear of sins he dares not commit? Like Lucifer, should we not demand to know the price and glory of our desires? If we fail, at least we'll do so with a clear knowledge of what it is to rejoice . . . and repent.''

Allegra stared at him, her concentration narrowed to his choice of words. The ideas were not totally new to her. She had read the works of Poe and Baudelaire. But words on a page, however strong and seductive, had never bid her to come out of herself and declare that she could act on thoughts that the darker side of her nature whispered in seclusion. ''I think I'd rather go home.''

''You lie.''

''Would you force me to accompany you?''

''Force you?'' he echoed in contempt. ''I agreed to be your tutor in the pleasures of the senses. For weeks you've hesitated. Here. Now. Decide.''

Allegra bit her lip, wanting assurances that he would not force her to do things she didn't wish to do, that he would protect her even from herself, but she resented his contempt for her weakness. ''Yes.''

Drayton forced himself to relax his clenched fists, but the raw edge of his nerves was beginning to show through the hashish calm of minutes earlier. He would have dosed himself with laudanum instead, but he didn't trust its effect on his ability to perform. And this night of all nights, he wanted desire to be followed by action.

The wind came up as they continued on their journey past silent rows of heavily draped houses. Allegra pulled up the collar of her cape to keep out the draft. Like those inside the houses, she wished to escape detection, to be sealed and shrouded from view, in fear of—what? Better not to consider it.

She was drowsy yet alert to every sound, every variation in the warm and cold currents circulating about her. It was as though her skin had taken on a life of its own, more sensitive and aware than her drifting consciousness. She burrowed deeper into her fur and closed her eyes.

Drayton waited until she had fallen asleep before gathering her close. She smelled of violets and sherry and the sweet oily spice of hashish. She didn't suspect a thing. Tonight she would discard a lifetime of inhibition. The drug would make it easier.

He slipped a hand inside her fur cloak, into the moist heat trapped there, and found the shape of one breast through her clothing. After a moment he withdrew his hand and opened the window on the frosty night, needing respite from the heat of his own making.

Unaccustomed emotions ran near the surface of his resolute nature, foreign thoughts, thoughts that he wished to evade. It came to him more slowly than usual, but still it came, the trick of disassociating himself from the unbearable. He had a purpose, and like all desires, it could best be achieved if he held it dispassionately at arm's length.

When the cabby suddenly opened the trapdoor of the hansom and stuck his face in, saying, "This here is the place, guvnor!" Allegra started awake.

Drayton quickly climbed down to the pavement and helped her out after him. He led her to the steps of the third residence along a lane of Georgian houses. It was a narrow house of red brick with three floors and a dormered attic. At the edges of each window drapery the faint illumination from a brightly lit room was betrayed.

"Who lives here?" Allegra asked as he urged her up the steps.

"Fallen angels," he answered with a chuckle. He paused before the door and turned to pull the hood of her cloak up over her hair. "Don't speak or reveal your face to anyone. No one will touch you, that I promise . . . unless you change your mind." He paused and said with less carelessness than he had hoped for, "Of course you may make your own choices. I place no claim on you."

His knock was peculiar, a series of short, staccato raps followed by a long pause and then a repetition of the pattern. The door opened a slit, and a pale, featureless face appeared.

"Lord Satan," Drayton murmured, embarrassed for the first time since he'd been given the code name, but, he noted with a sideways glance, she didn't seem to have heard it.

The door swung open at once, the featureless person

hidden behind the door. Once inside, Allegra found herself in a sumptuously decorated hallway. Gilt chairs flanked a table supporting a pair of silver candlesticks and an enormous bouquet of peonies. Pedestaled bronzes and oriental vases lined the hallway. The blue- and silver-flocked walls were filled with paintings. As Drayton led her down the hall, she caught a fleeting glance at one large oil. It was a naval scene by Turner. However odd their entry had been, this was obviously the home of a well-to-do, tasteful person.

At the end of the hall he halted. "Wait here," he said and crossed to an open door and went inside.

From her vantage point, she couldn't see into the room, but the brilliance of the light pouring into the hallway, the warmth of its fire, and the sound of men's and women's voices told her that there was a party going on, a party that he didn't mean for her to join.

When he returned moments later, there was a new look in his eye. He took her shoulders in his hands as though to keep her from bolting. "Once we go upstairs you cannot change your mind. Do you understand?"

"What is this place?"

He stared straight into her eyes. "A place of pleasure for men and women of taste and refinement."

"Like you," she answered.

He smiled. "Precisely. You are here to watch. To learn. To understand."

"And if I don't like what I see and learn?"

His smile was almost sympathetic. "Poor angel, I think you will."

She didn't agree. She simply turned back toward the stairs they had passed and began to climb them.

She gulped down the first sherry, feeling the need of its fire to melt the ice that had invaded her hands and feet and face during their journey. "Another, please."

Drayton reached for the decanter on the table at his elbow but changed his mind. If she didn't relax she would be terrified of what she was to witness.

He opened his cigarette case and extracted another of the hashish variety. "Here, this will calm you. You're completely safe."

Allegra took it from him and when he had lit it, drew the smoke deeply into her lungs. After repeating this twice more, she began to shed a little of her fear. She had been too nervous to give their surroundings much thought when they entered, but now she saw that they sat before a velvet curtain and that the small, well-appointed room was much like a theater box with its rows of chairs replaced by the satin sofa on which they sat. "Are we to see a play?"

"Very nearly," he answered dryly and reached for her cigarette. "The women are usually quite skilled, the gentlemen less so."

She shivered. "Why is it so cold?"

"Is it?" he asked. "I'm quite warm. Come closer to me and I will share my warmth."

She moved into the circle of his arm with misgivings and yet with the realization that misgivings had a curious way of evaporating with the smoke she exhaled.

When he bent his head to her, she was grateful. It ended the suspense. She didn't know or care where they were or why. She just wanted his kisses, those sweet stinging caresses of his lips and tongue that made her soft with pleasure. She didn't hear the draperies move nor notice when the lights were extinguished, but when he finally lifted his head she saw that the room had darkened and that the light came from beyond an oval window now revealed.

Drayton tightened his grip of her waist as she turned to him in question. He put a finger to her lips and said, "Wait. And watch."

She felt a faint start of embarrassment when a man and woman entered the other room, but they seemed oblivious of their watchers. What else explained the fact that they embraced in a long fervent kiss that made the blood creep up the back of her neck?

Out of modesty, she looked away, but Drayton caught her chin and turned her face resolutely back. "You must see everything," he said quietly and held her face toward the window until he felt no more resistance.

The woman being kissed wore a magnificent silk gown. She was obviously a lady. The gentleman was of average height, slimly built, and with a light mustache. The room was hung in wine silk with a half-canopied bed dominating the middle of it. The edges of the room were a little distorted by the dim glass through which Allegra viewed it, and she wondered fleetingly if it was dark because it was not regularly cleaned.

The woman laughed suddenly and pushed the man away, then turned and walked straight toward the mirror.

Afraid they would be seen, Allegra tried to rise but Drayton tightened his grip on her waist. "They can't see us," he said softly. "The glass is silvered on their side. We see through, but we are not seen because we are in a darkened room. You may look your fill with no one to see you."

An old memory, one that she hadn't thought of in years, came stealing back to her. She had spied on lovers in Saratoga. She had never told anyone about that. "It's wrong," she whispered.

"Even if they know and don't care?"

She looked at him and he nodded. "Watch that you may learn."

The woman stood before the mirror, pulling the pins from her upswept hair, which cascaded over her shoulders in thick brunette waves. She reached behind her back a moment, and when she turned back to the room Allegra saw that she had loosened the buttons of her gown. She saw, too, that the gentleman had removed his coat and laid it on a chair. The woman approached him and they embraced again.

Drayton leaned close to nuzzle Allegra's ear and felt her shiver in response. His own passion had ranged far ahead of her embarrassed stirrings, for he knew what they would witness. He nearly reached for her hand to draw it into his lap but decided that it was too soon. Later, he consoled himself. After the first night there would be so many nights, and he would teach her to use her hands, her mouth, all of her body in ways that would give him pleasure and release her from her puritan shame. He picked up their cigarette, took a draw on it, and offered it to her.

As she inhaled, Allegra watched the man pass his hands over the satin curves of the woman's body and then cup her buttocks as he drew her tightly against his legs.

Suddenly she was vividly aware of Drayton's leg pressing tightly against hers from knee to thigh. She drew a little away but his encircling arm limited her progress. He shifted his leg, bringing it again into contact with hers, and when she looked up he was smiling, but his eyes were on the scene before them.

It seemed only a moment since she had glanced away, but that was not possible for the man now stood in his shirt and garters, his trousers mysteriously disposed of, and the woman— Allegra gasped softly. The woman lay perfectly naked on the bed.

The woman raised a hand in invitation and the man began struggling with his shirt. The woman must have made an amusing remark for suddenly he threw back his head in laughter. A moment later he had released the last of the buttons and drew off the shirt.

Allegra shut her eyes at the sight of his nakedness. Expecting her reaction, Drayton bent and whispered, "Are you so much a coward, Miss Grant!"

"It's indecent," she answered.

"It is truth. You wished to know it. Look at it."

She opened her eyes to find that the woman now lay on her back with her legs spread, and a deep burning flush enveloped her. The man stood beside the bed running a hand over the woman's flesh from her shoulder over a breast to her belly and then up again. Finally his hand slipped below her belly into the dark shadow between her legs. The woman dug her heels into the bedding and heaved her hips forward.

Allegra tried to look away but, as the first time, she couldn't. Some shameful curiosity kept her gazing even as the woman began to move rhythmically against the man's hand. Eyes widened by shame, she saw the woman reach out and grasp the tubular appendage of flesh that hung from the front of the man's lower belly. The woman stroked the member until it grew red and stiff in a way Allegra would never have imagined possible.

Uncomfortably aware of Lord Drayton's presence beside her, she tried to draw away, but he wouldn't release her. She was held so tightly that she felt the tension in his body pressed against hers from shoulder to knee, yet he neither spoke nor moved.

Suddenly the man withdrew his hand from between the woman's legs and he threw himself upon her. He positioned himself between the woman's thighs, took his organ in his hand and plunged it with the full force of his body into her. The woman's legs came up about his waist and encircled him as he began to rock back and forth, his narrow white buttocks moving in and out in the same rhythm he had used with his hand.

Allegra's breath caught in her throat. She felt hot and cold and strangely agitated. Her skin seemed too tight for her body. Her breasts hurt and her heart pounded in her chest. She felt distorted, as if her body had changed in proportion and size, and the feeling made her dizzy.

The man suddenly heaved himself forward and held fast, his head thrown back as if in great distress, and then he collapsed across the woman's prone body.

Allegra closed her eyes, certain that she would be sick. When Drayton released her she pulled away from him, deeply ashamed.

Drayton poured another sherry for her and, taking one of her limp hands, wrapped her fingers about the glass. "Drink, Miss Grant. This is only the beginning."

She lifted her head in astonishment. "What more can they do?"

He smiled at her. "One forgets how abysmally ignorant young ladies are." He pointed to the sherry. "Drink it." When she had consumed a little of it he took the glass from her. "Now, watch here."

The woman had already moved from beneath the man, who now lay on his back. She knelt beside the bed and reached out for his soft flesh that had recently been stiff and, bending her head, took it in her mouth.

Allegra shuddered in revulsion and stood up. "I want to leave. Immediately!"

Drayton's face darkened as he remained seated. "There's no need for you to play the scalded maid with me. I applaud your courage in coming here. You asked that I treat you as an equal. I am doing so. I would bring a male friend here for his enjoyment. I do so freely with you."

She turned to him in disbelief. "Do you come here and exhibit yourself like—that?"

The truth was that he didn't and wouldn't, and he nearly conceded it, but he decided that backing off from the point would do neither of them any good. "What if I do? What if I come here twice a week and bring a different woman each time? Is that not my right? My pleasure? What has it to do with you?"

"Nothing," she answered. "And it never will!"

His face lost all hint of magnanimity as he stood up. "Get your cloak. There's no reason for this asinine discussion to take place where we might be identified." He turned to leave.

The threat of discovery was enough to silence Allegra. In fact, her anger was reduced to embarrassment by his tone. She flung her cloak about her shoulders and followed him out of the room, down the darkened hallway where voices echoed eerily from behind closed doors, and down the stairs.

She was surprised to find a hansom waiting on the curb, for the street was empty and silent. She got in, wrapping the sable-lined cloak tightly about herself as she heard Lord Drayton give an unfamiliar address. The cabby answered in startled surprise, and she heard Drayton curse as he pulled out his purse and offered the man several bills. This time she heard the cabby's reply distinctly: "Anywhere ya say, guvnor!"

"Where are we going?" she demanded when he got in beside her.

She saw his mouth tighten in anger and didn't repeat the question, which went unanswered.

The journey took more than an hour. Once they left the narrow cobbled streets of London proper for the countryside, she began to grow alarmed. She recalled lurid details of abduction and rape she occasionally had read in the yellow journals. She considered the scandal and disgrace, of Andrew's worry and her own shame, but none of the thoughts held her attention for long. Despite everything, there was this ridiculous desire inside her to smile.

She felt disconnected, removed even from her own emotions. There was anger, but it was curiously void of resolution. There was shame, but it was muted by the awareness that she had been profoundly stirred by the sex act she had witnessed. The strongest feeling moving through her was curiosity. Seated beside the silent earl, she wondered what thoughts ran through his mind. Did he feel as she did?

Allegra awakened on a bed in one corner of a small, low-raftered room. A small fire had been lit in the grate so recently that the coals were not yet whitened. She sat up, the quilt in which she was wrapped sliding off her. Her cloak had been removed as well as her slippers, but when she swung her legs over the side of the bed, she found the slippers waiting.

She nearly called out but decided that she had displayed enough fears for one night. She glanced at the lace-curtained window for assurance that it was still night and saw only darkness behind the tatwork. She rose and walked toward the open doorway, pausing on the threshold.

The room beyond was lit by candlelight, and she realized that they must be too far from the city gasworks. But that dissolved as she saw the contents of the room. It was not a typical parlor, for there was only a single chair and small table in one corner. What filled the room in eclectic disarray were statues and carvings of every size and shape. Several busts were displayed on the shelves. Other, larger pieces copied from Greek design stood on the floor or occupied columns in the center of the room. It was like a gallery showing, but one without form or focus.

She walked carefully into the room, inexplicably sensitive to the idea that she might in some manner disturb the armless torsos or the bodiless heads. But as she neared the statues, another emotion took the place of awe. Of Greek-like purity in appearance from a distance, they were far from coolly classic up close. The lines were more fluid, as if the marble had been poured over human form. Sensuously and in abandonment the figures entwined about one another, arms lifted, lips offered. One figure, a young girl, stood on tiptoe, her lips parted and her eyes closed, her breasts firm and erect as if waiting to be touched by a man's hand.

Allegra turned away, but a painting in the opposite wall caught her eye. She crossed over to it, astonished by the content. In it, a woman nude except for a blindfold, black laced boots, and elbow-length gloves sat astride a naked man who bore the scarlet marks on his back and hips of the whip which the woman held in her hand. And yet there wasn't pain on his handsome face as much as a tormented ecstasy.

Beside this picture hung another in which a young girl allowed her clothes to be stripped from her by nymphs while she embraced the loins of an aroused godlike man. There were others, all dreamlike, fantastic, their subjects besotted by lustful desire and engaging in acts she had never even imagined.

When she turned back, she saw the statues in a new light. They were creatures in torment or bliss, in attitudes that spoke of unnamable desire, of desperate longing, of abandon.

Uneasy, she moved away to return to the bedroom, but her attention was again snared, this time by a marble high-relief that stood against the far wall.

It was the figure of a nude young man lying prone in the lap of an equally nude nymph in the act of bending to kiss him. It was less sensational than the others, but it intrigued her as they did not. The heavy muscular elegance of the young man's body was the most sensuous thing she had ever seen. With a featherlike touch, she traced the exquisite turn of the hard muscles in his arms. Then taut flesh stretched over his ribs and flat belly drew her hand. She skimmed the satin-smooth bulges of his thighs, daring her fingers for an instant to curl into the depression where his flaccid sex nestled.

"Sweet sin. Does it shock you?"

Allegra withdrew her hand slowly and turned deliberately to Lord Drayton, who now stood in the doorway at the back of the room. "Should it?"

"I hope we are beyond that."

She lifted her chin. "I am."

"Good! Now you begin to understand." He came forward and gestured to encompass the room. "This is where I work when I am so inclined. But I refuse to be shackled even to my passions. I live for my pleasure. You must learn to live for yours."

He took her hand and placed it back on the relief, holding her fingers against the man's groin. "Before you could act, you needed to know what it is you seek. That is why I took you to the bordello. Pleasure, even when taken together, need have nothing to do with a bond between the parties. That is the mistake most women make. They're afraid to accept pleasure without the burden of commitment.

"Passion at its best is the act of an independent soul without the trappings of fear and ignorance. I will teach you the skill of loving without love. There's very little in it, if there is finesse. After tonight, if you should choose to take your pleasure with another man on the same bed as I with a woman of my choice, I won't disdain you for it."

Your pleasure is yours. Mine is mine. Why could she not reconcile those words with reason? Because it repulsed her to think of herself in a stranger's arms. . . . him in another woman's. She withdrew her fingers from under his. "If there's very little in it, why do you bother?"

He smiled. "Because the pleasure is in the sinning. Look about, choose your method of reaching pleasure. There are many shown on these walls." He indicated one she had missed of two women in a lascivious embrace and then chuckled. "My fault. I cannot help you in that."

She stepped back from him. "That's unnatural! Disgusting!"

"No," he said smoothly. "Your squeamishness and middle-class virtue is disgusting and it's hypocritical. What you couldn't conceive of before this night you would grant willingly upon your marriage. A few ancient words with no more power in them than the roaring of the wind, and you'd be willing enough to lie on some man's bed and open your thighs for him.''

"I don't seek a husband," she countered.

"If you understood what it is you do seek, you would lie down for me now. But you're afraid and superstitious. Or are you simply cold?"

She stared at him, her disillusionment in what had always seemed a romantic act starkly etched on her face. "I can't, I won't be your whore."

Drayton stared at her a long moment and then, very slowly, he began to remove his coat. When he had unbuttoned it, he shrugged it away from his shoulders and allowed it to slide down his arms to the floor. Disconnection brought power. With power he was capable of any action. "You will not be my whore? Then let me be yours."

She didn't reply, but she didn't turn away. Satisfied, he continued removing his clothing.

His eyes never left her face as he removed each article. She remained transfixed, the expression on her face unreadable. He was in no hurry, he told himself. She was curious, just as she had been curious about the marble relief. But he was flesh and blood and soon she would see the difference. He opened his trousers without hurrying and then eased them down over his hips. Except for a blink as he exposed himself, she didn't move. He stepped out of them and cast them aside, then stood fully naked before her. "What are you thinking?"

"That you are better made than the thin-shanked gentleman in the bordello," she answered honestly.

The answer pleased him. She wasn't shocked beyond her wits. "You were particularly interested in the marble behind you. Would you not care to examine me as well?"

"The marble does not blush," she answered quickly. "It has no conscience to shame."

"Then I am as marble, for I have no conscience either." She hesitated. "If I am dissatisfied, what then?"

"Marble has no feelings. Use me or leave me. That is up to you."

It was a dangerous gamble to give her the power of

decision, and he knew it. When she finally stepped forward, the relief from the agony of suspense made him shiver.

He is a statue, Allegra told herself as she stepped up to and then around him. She was alone, as she had been before, with no one to see or criticize her conduct. If she wished, she might run a hand over his shoulder. She did this, surprised by the heat on his skin and its dense lush texture. She slid her hand up to his nape where the skin was thinner, more like a girl's, and curled her fingers about the column of his neck where his pulse beat strongly. This reality was too much and she drew away.

Drayton held himself stiffly, but his body responded instantly to her first touch. When she rounded him, she would know the extent to which he desired her. Had it been another woman he would have laughed at his anxiety. He was proud of his virility. But now, with a fully clothed virgin he felt ridiculous, like a well pump with its handle primed. Then he felt her hand again, this time sliding along his spine and down over a buttock, and he silently thanked providence for so stout a handle.

Allegra touched him boldly now, caressing his thigh, marveling at the muscles so like those of the marble. Yet heat and the bristle of fine hair added texture to the pure contours. Trembling began inside her, not of fear but of pleasure. She knew his kiss, welcomed it. She knew now his stature and found it pleasing. An image came of the man she watched make love to the woman. Were all men so made? Clearly, they must be.

She stood behind him, a hand on each shoulder. Slowly she dragged them down to his waist and then carefully threaded them between his arms and sides until her palms lay against his abdomen where she felt the in-and-out movement of his breathing. Her hands moved slowly, caressing as they descended into the nest of hair at the base of his belly and then stroked the turgid flesh.

She heard him sigh like a man in pain and started to release him, but he caught her hands and brought them back, folding her fingers around him and making her press hard. "Yes," he whispered softly as he showed her the motion he desired.

She did as he bid, frowning at her discovery, for unless blind touch lied he was much grander than the man in the bordello.

Suddenly he grabbed her wrists and held her hands away as he gave a little gasp. "I would deny you nothing, but I beg you, wait a little."

She stepped back when he released her. She no longer feared him. She understood what Eugenia had once told her about the glory and shame, the fire and ice of passion. She felt it all in this moment.

Drayton heard the rustle of her skirts and wondered if she were running away, but the sounds never faded. He didn't turn to look for he had promised to be at her disposal. If only she would use him, use him up completely before he burst!

She came up behind him and laid her cheek against his shoulder, cooler now from the chill of the room, and said, "We are equals, now and forever? No matter what transpires between us this night?"

"Equals," he repeated in an unsteady voice, for the impression of her naked breasts was burning his chilled skin.

"Then I ask you to show me your skill at loving."

Slowly, he turned to her. He had never known such a moment, never known such desire to see a woman in her glory, and glory it was.

She stood a few feet away, her shoulders garlanded in her loosened curls. She might have been made of alabaster or marble or even wax, so smoothly and sweetly did the candlelight play over her nakedness.

He didn't spend much time examining her for he was more curious to know what he would see when he raised his eyes to her face. She was pale but resolute, awaiting his verdict. She seemed more vulnerable than he had felt, yet there was a challenge in her eyes, a defiance of her own frailty. He felt again that strange unwanted pity for her, the desire to shelter, to comfort, to draw her into himself, as if by being together they would be stronger than each alone. Foolish thoughts.

He came to her and enfolded her in his arms and she

shivered. What should he say? There was nothing to say. He bent his head and kissed her, and as she sighed and encircled his neck with her arms, he knew that enough had been said.

He picked her up and carried her to the bed, pulling the covers about them as he cradled her in his arms. He lay so for a moment, letting the heat revive him and giving her time to grow accustomed to him.

Allegra lay listening to his heartbeat until she could stand it no longer. She lifted her head to look at him. "What is wrong?"

Smiling, he caught her by the waist and pulled her under him so that his manhood pressed against her. After a careful breath, he reached down and parted her legs so that he lay between them. The feel of her moist heat against his belly made him catch his breath a second time as he bent his head to kiss her. Kiss melted into kiss, honey-sweet kisses that multiplied the pleasure of touching her.

Allegra closed her eyes, not wanting to see his face, only to feel. He stroked her waist, her shoulders, her breasts. He kissed her mouth, her cheeks, her ears. He spread her hair upon the pillow, his movements unhurried. He drew sighs from her, deep voluptuous sighs of yielding to the pleasure of his hands and mouth. She moved under him, seeking the glorious contact of skin upon skin.

When his fingers sought the place between her thighs, shyness made her protest. He watched her shadowed face, quietly urging her to breathe deeply, to open herself, to allow him to stroke her honeyed warmth. When she began to tremble, he smiled. He was a good lover, and because she was not unresponsive to his touch, he was confident that he could please her.

Her arms embraced him and then shyly she reached down between them to caress him as before. He moved to suckle her delicately; then his mouth moved lower to press kisses in the smooth hollow of her belly, and then lower still. Astonishment nearly stopped her heart as he offered her body the most intimate kisses of all.

She kept her eyes shut, remembering his urging that pleasure for the sake of pleasure was all that she should seek. But she couldn't keep the selfish thought before her, not when he caressed her so beautifully with hands that could fashion marble into ecstasy, and when his mouth gave kisses she could not imagine receiving from another. Her pleasure was bound up inexorably with this man. If he didn't wish it to be so, then she wouldn't tell him.

He entered her gently, slowly, with an infinite tenderness which he had not known he possessed. He stopped her protest with his lips, knowing that she would soon understand that this must be even if it seemed difficult. Waiting, he took his cue from the instinctive movement of her hips and suddenly pressed down hard until his full length was buried inside her.

Allegra grasped him tight, wanting to hold him still but unable to keep even herself quiet. She soon urged his rhythm and met it again and again until she felt in amazed confusion the first shuddering flutterings of her body where they were joined, a bright exultation as swift and fleeting as a falling star.

As she shuddered under him, he knew that he had brought her to ecstasy's peak. Immediately, his body found its own.

And then there was stillness.

It came slowly, with the lessening of his heartbeat. But he recognized it as truth. Every moment of the evening till now had been a lie. Every sentiment he had expressed was false, every calculation a mistake. He saw all his frailties; a life of dependencies, fears, and denial of needs. She had exposed them all in the giving of herself.

He felt himself growing smaller inside her and fear trembled through him. This glorious sweet agony of being part of her would come to an end one day. After that, what would he do? For three years he had sought her, though he had been prepared even an hour ago to be disappointed in the act which he so badly desired. What he had dared not hope for was this reality of sweet satisfaction. And yet that didn't explain his feelings entirely. Even now, with his breath scarcely coming back, he wanted her again. She was like a drug, and he was addicted to her.

Very well. He was not an unclever man, and like all users

he knew how to draw out his pleasure, invent new methods of enjoying his intoxication. So it would be with her. He would show her little by little all that he had ever experienced, making a sweet triumph of his addiction to her. And perhaps in time, she would find herself as addicted as he to their mutual pleasure.

Allegra awoke to the sensation of being filled as he raised his head from her shoulder. She smiled up at him. "Everett, are we not finished?"

Drayton smiled at her. It was nearly dawn. He shouldn't keep her here another moment. He didn't know what lie they could fabricate that would satisfy her brother. But in this moment he didn't care. He had to have her once more.

* 1893-94 *

Nineteen

London, May 1893

"Well, what is your opinion, Miss Grant?"

Allegra stood in the foyer of the Haymarket Theatre during intermission, her program gripped in a white-gloved fist. "It is unkind," she said in a low voice. "Unkind and rude and untrue! To think I've had the man to dinner. How could he?"

"You can't think Oscar Wilde meant to portray you in the play?"

Allegra looked up at Lord Drayton. "Who else? A portion of Hester Worsley's speech in Act Two was first spoken at your dining table last November. Don't you remember?"

"I'm afraid not," the earl allowed. "Much of the earlier part of that evening is lost to me, though I can recall in exact and exquisite detail later events. Would you care for me to recite them?"

Allegra turned angrily away from him, her color rising at his reference to the first night they had spent together. "I shouldn't have come. For weeks I've resisted the temptation. Now I'm forced to deal with the truth. Wilde's cast me as a puritanical colonial, self-righteous and mannerless. *A Woman of No Importance* indeed!"

"You're too angry and too severe, Miss Grant. I admire

Miss Worsley very much. Like Lord Illingworth, 'I don't think there is a woman in the world who would not be a little flattered if one made love to her. It is that which makes women so irresistibly adorable.' ''

Far from reassuring her, Allegra was white-faced when she turned back to him. ''Do you think Lord Illingworth is you? Then Oscar suspects us!'' she whispered.

Drayton had been moved to wonder the same thing, but he could see that she didn't share his amusement at the playwright's perception. ''You will give us both away if you continue to stand there in high dudgeon. Rumor can only speculate, but actions give them reality. Or, perhaps you would prefer to publish our liaison to the world? I would be proud to do so.''

She stared at him, unamused. ''What a thoroughly bad man you are.''

He smiled. She wasn't completely undone if she could quote from Oscar's play. ''I am, for I do admire innocence.''

''I should strike you for that remark.''

''Unnecessary,'' he replied softly, continuing the paraphrasing. ''I've already fallen in love with Miss Worsley.''

Defeated, Allegra lowered her gaze. It was a lie. That was why he could tease her with the words she had come to long to hear from him. That he could say them in public, as a jest, hurt her more than not hearing them at all. For six months they had been lovers. Never once had he alluded to the notion that his feelings were more than lustful, while she was constrained from voicing her own by the bargain between them. If things did not change, she would soon go mad!

Drayton watched her struggle with his sentiment, regretting the words the instant they were said. He had promised her that he would never press her for any emotional tie, that she was as free as he, that equality did not imply fidelity or that passion presumed love. How could he have blurted out things that thirty-one years of living had taught him never to express or even consider possible? Love. What did he know of that emotion? Nothing at all. He was far more comfortable with the other emotions plaguing him these last months.

Envy, jealousy, fear, anxiety, ecstasy, desire, and pride: those he knew well.

The bell announcing the beginning of the third act came as a relief to them both.

Allegra turned resolutely toward their theater box, but a familiar face from long ago distracted her brooding thoughts. "Reeba Braumbrucker!"

The young woman in mauve lace paused as she was about to enter the adjoining box and squinted in Allegra's direction. It wasn't until Allegra was within a yard of her that her carroty eyebrows shot up and a smile lifted her features. "Allegra? Is that—it *is* you!"

The two young women embraced in laughter and a variety of inarticulate sounds of delight.

"You look wonderful. I scarcely recognized you, Reeba," Allegra exclaimed as she held her friend by the waist. "What happened to your freckles?"

"Mama and Mingay's Pure Complexion Tonic," Reeba replied in her midwestern twang and blushed a carroty-red shade to match her hair.

"And your glasses?"

Reeba patted her purse. "Mama says men don't care a fig if a lady can't see beyond the end of her nose. Keeps her attention from wandering when he's nearby. I do slip them on now and again, though, 'cause I don't care to speak to horses in the street." She leaned forward to peer closely at Allegra. "You look smart, I must say! Heard you were in London, but Leland didn't take to the English climate so we don't go out much. Says it stodgifies the brain, on account of all the damp."

It was Allegra's turn to raise her brows. "Who's Leland?"

Reeba laughed. "Don't you read your mail? I'm married. Mrs. Leland Wheeler. Six weeks tomorrow." She held out an ungloved left hand which bore a huge ruby and diamond ring.

"But that's wonderful!" Allegra answered as she kissed her friend's cheek. "Tell me everything. You never wrote."

Reeba shrugged, and Allegra had a flash of Mrs. Barrie's face etched in lines of severe disapproval. "There ain—isn't much to tell. Leland works for Daddy in the pork-belly market. That's how we met. Daddy says he's a whiz in the marketplace, but between you and me, he's a slow top when it comes to speaking his piece to a lady. We were courting two years before he came up to scratch. And then another year until the marriage.'' She leaned forward to whisper, ''Of course, I've come to revise my opinion since the wedding. He doesn't look like much, but Leland's a whiz as a husband!'' She blushed furiously again. ''Oh, I guess I shouldn't be making remarks like that to innocent ears.''

''We always shared our secrets,'' Allegra reminded her. ''Now, where is this lucky man?''

''In the saloon next door, I suspect. Leland doesn't much like the theater. Doesn't care much for the English, either. Says they're too full of themselves. I agree they're the most snobbish folk I ever met!''

''Then why, dear friend, are you in London?''

'' 'Cause Leland said he wasn't going to honeymoon in a country where he'd look foolish on account of folks not understanding him. I told him we should've gone to St. Louis in that case.''

Allegra joined Reeba's laughter. ''He's taking me to Paris next week. Like it or not, I told him I didn't come to Europe, sick as a dog all the way, to go home without a few of Mr. Worth's best efforts.''

''Good for you,'' Allegra replied. ''But you will come to dinner tomorrow night? I promise to find Mr. Wheeler the best steak in the city, a real Chicago-style meal.''

''Forgive the intrusion, but we have an engagement for tomorrow night.''

Allegra turned to Drayton with a smile. ''Oh, yes, I'd quite forgotten. But couldn't we excuse ourselves this once?''

''As you wish,'' he answered in a formal voice that betrayed none of his hurt and frustration. It was to have been their first chance to be alone together in more than a fortnight.

Allegra caught him familiarly by the arm. ''Allow me to introduce you. Reeba, I'd like you to meet a good friend of Andrew's and my escort for the evening, Lord Drayton, Earl of Dundare. Lord Drayton, may I present Mrs. Leland

Wheeler of Chicago. Reeba's an old and dear friend. We were in school together and shared mischief."

"Like the time you drank champagne and got so foxed you performed the mad scene from *Macbeth*," Reeba volunteered cheerfully, her full attention on the earl.

"*Hamlet*, Ophelia's mad scene from *Hamlet*," Allegra corrected in amusement.

"That's right. I always did forget which play was which," she said. "Still, I like them all. Whatever that Mr. Shakespeare wrote is scads more fun that this play tonight. Why, I never heard such rubbish in my life! That Miss Hester is in sore need of rescue, wouldn't you agree, Lord?"

"My lord," Allegra murmured under her breath.

"My lord," Reeba corrected in unembarrassed enthusiasm.

Drayton smiled at the homely young woman. "Alas, Mrs. Wheeler, you must make your inquiry of someone less susceptible to feminine charms. For my part, I am in total sympathy with Lord Illingworth. I claim it freely; I'm a thoroughgoing scoundrel." With that, he took her hand and kissed it.

"You devil!" Reeba exclaimed, but between her smiles and blushes Allegra knew that he had completely won her over.

"Won't you join us?" Drayton gestured toward his box.

"I'm not entirely alone," Reeba began but then nodded. "Give me just a moment. I'll tell the others to meet me in the lobby when the play's over." She turned and entered the box where she had been sitting.

"You needn't have done that," Allegra said.

"No?" Drayton smiled ruefully. "But you are so happy and have so much in common; you both detest the play. It seemed the most appropriate thing to do."

"I don't detest the play. I detest being ridiculed in the play. And exposed," she added softly.

As was the case whenever he was near her, he had the most extraordinary desire to touch her, to hold her, but never in public did he display more than the utmost courtesy. "You aren't exposed, Miss Grant, you are speculated upon, and that, in London, is what we all live for."

"It is a decadent pastime," she answered.

"Of course, that's why it's so thoroughly enjoyed by all. Now, about tomorrow night. Invite me to dinner and I'll find an excuse to remain after the Wheelers have gone. Then we'll think of something."

"It's impossible. Reeba is a great talker, as you've seen. When she's exhausted, there'll still be Andy to think of."

"I thought he was in the country with friends."

Allegra evaded his gaze. "He's been ill again. I don't think the English climate agrees with him."

"It's not the climate," Drayton mumbled tersely.

Reeba's return prevented them from continuing, and they went into the box for the completion of the play.

Later in the hansom Drayton picked up the conversation as though there had been no interruption. "I've been thinking. You might as well come up to Scotland and see the family pile. I usually move into the country the first week in June, when fly fishing is at its best."

Allegra tried not to let her spirits soar. Visit his ancestral home? Was that not significant? "How can we manage it?"

"Oh, it's done all the time: country weekends for couples who wish for nothing so much as a chance to exchange partners. Rooms suitably located, a discreet staff, a blind eye, and it's accomplished. Shall I arrange it?"

She didn't think her spirits had risen until they came plummeting to her feet. "I'm not married. That makes it difficult to keep up appearances."

"We'll invite Andrew. One would need a very jaundiced eye to assume the worst in that pairing, though Byron didn't set a precedent in that matter." She was shocked. She didn't say so, but her silence convinced him of it. "Will you never accept what you've done?"

"I accept it," she answered quietly. "It's just that occasionally I see things again from the outside, and they look . . . sordid."

He removed his hand from hers, which she held in her lap, and moved it strongly up her rib cage to just under her breasts. "I've missed you terribly. Sometimes I feel I'll burst with the wanting of you."

She looked at him, not asking the question that had come to mind.

"I'm living like a monk," he volunteered. "It's a new experience for me, I admit. Still, one should occasionally observe the virtues to better appreciate the slide into vice, don't you think?"

"You sound like Oscar," she answered. "Wit spurred by insincerity. Do me the credit of not abusing my intelligence. You're free to seek your pleasure elsewhere, and we both know it."

"So are you," he replied, "and yet you're strangely hesitant to do so."

Insulted, she looked at him. "You may be wrong."

Drayton swallowed on a dry-throated tightness. "Am I?"

"No," she said resentfully, "but that could change. Whom will you invite to Dundare Castle?"

"Shall I name them or merely give physical descriptions?" he asked, jealousy rearing in him at the turn of her thoughts. "I can give you dimensions and suggest their favorite little games. In many cases I will need to demonstrate them for you've not shown much interest in possibilities beyond the ordinary embrace. You'll need a few lessons before the weekend in the country. With attention on your part you'll be up to scratch in no time."

He didn't expect the slap, nor the power displayed with it. The sharp crack against the side of his face took him completely by surprise, and therefore hurt more than he might have imagined.

"You're vile and disgusting!" She thumped the top of the hansom and when the cabby looked in she cried, "Stop immediately!" He obeyed at once and she threw open the door. "Step out, my lord."

"You're jesting?" Drayton answered in amazement, his voice muffled by his hand at his cheek.

"Either you step out, or I will," she answered.

She sounded too angry to cross. "Anything to oblige a lady," he murmured and stepped out onto the pavement. Before he could turn to pay the fare, she called to the driver to move on and he was left in the street.

As the hansom disappeared into the mist, he withdrew his handkerchief and in unhurried fashion applied it to his abused face, only to discover that her slap had caused his lip to bleed. He smiled. The impression of her hand was too sweet to sting him to anger. She was as proud as a duchess, and still innocent enough to be shocked by the very thought of misconduct with a man other than himself. He'd been stupid to suggest the idea. Jealousy had made him reckless. He resented it when she even spoke to another man, her damned brother included. If she ever crossed that barrier, as she had crossed the first with him, was she not too passionate natured not to seek ever more adventure? If that occurred, would she leave him for other men?

He had only one hope, and that was so to enthrall her that she would never believe that another man could equal his ability to please her.

When an empty hansom picked him up a few minutes later, he directed it to an elegant address in Belgravia where a certain titled gentleman kept an opium salon. Almost at once he countermanded the order and gave the cabby his own address. His thinking was being muddled by the rude shocks of emotions newborn, emotions that threatened his sanity. Love. That's what this gathering threadwork of feelings was. Mastery of Allegra Grant was what he once desired. Now he knew that what he wanted, and needed, was the return of her love. Was it too late for her ever to love him?

He had seen that look of wishful envy when Mrs. Wheeler showed off her wedding band. Gaudy and crass as it was, he knew Allegra had seen in the ring a reflection of what her future could be if she chose it. Not every lady was a virgin in these times. When the time came, she would marry someone else . . . unless he offered for her first.

The idea still rankled. He didn't want her bound to him by law and convention. He wanted her to be with him freely. If he declared himself, he would never be certain that she had married him for love alone, not just for appearances. Yet, if she did abandon convention for the sake of love, he would see that she never suffered for it. Perhaps they would go to live in the South of France, or even Greece, somewhere where people did not care that they were not wed.

* * *

Andrew grinned as he read the latest edition of *Lippincott's* magazine. "Here's another letter praising Andrew Grant's publishing debut in Britain. 'The Twain of London, the Wilde of New York!' How about that?"

"Did you write that one, too?" Allegra questioned in exasperation.

"No, I didn't. Oh, all right, Ernest Dowson did. Oscar asked him to, as a favor to me. Nearly every member of the Rhymers' Club was kind enough to lend his support."

"It's false support," Allegra answered as she finished her tea. It was five o'clock in the afternoon and a rare treat that Andrew was home.

"Not at all! Oscar says that the way to become famous is to proclaim one's own celebrity. If one does so often and loudly enough, the general public begins to believe it."

"Which isn't the same as its being so," she countered.

"It sells the work and makes money, which is the only criterion of public appeal in any case."

"There's good judgment. Many of our most famous poets and authors were not well received in their time. Only time and distance showed who possessed that eternal spark."

"To hell with eternity. I want my fame while I can still use its power and feel its adoration. What good are laurels heaped on ashes?"

"I see. Then you should make the most of the next weeks. I think it's time we went back to New York."

"Go back to America? You're joking. I'd as soon be shipped to Borneo. I'm staying where I'm appreciated."

"You're staying where your whims are indulged," she returned. "Andy, after that hateful play by Mr. Wilde, can't you see that he's merely amusing himself at our expense? He'll drop your acquaintance as soon as he's finished his next play, in which, no doubt, you'll figure prominently."

"God, I hope so! My future would be made. You're only jealous that most people remain in ignorance of your relationship to *A Woman of No Importance*. If Oscar chooses to pattern a character after me, I'll throw him the biggest party this city's ever seen.''

"On what income?'' she asked bitingly.

"You're in a damnably bad mood. Is it Drayton? Has he dropped you?''

Allegra gave her brother a scalding look. "Since I was never 'picked up,' I cannot have been 'dropped.' If you're asking if Lord Drayton has ceased calling on me, the answer is no, which fact you might be aware of if you ever came home at a reasonable hour.''

Andrew shrugged. "The Rhymers keep late hours. You know where I am. A message sent round to Ye Olde Cheshire Cheese would fetch me in a trice.''

Allegra tried not to be affected by his adopted accent, though it grated on her nerves more and more. "That isn't the point. People must be talking about the fact that I receive a gentleman caller alone after teatime.''

"Let them talk. Unless they can prove misconduct——'' He sat upright. "Say, Drayton hasn't done anything, well, out of the ordinary?''

"Just what would you consider out of the ordinary?''

"He hasn't, uh, tried to make love to you?''

"But of course he has!'' she answered boldly, knowing that he would never suspect what had actually occurred. "Did you think he wouldn't? You don't know him very well, in that case.''

Andrew's eyes narrowed as he whistled through his teeth. "I should have guessed as much, but as you never say anything, well, what was I to do?''

"Lend your presence,'' she suggested, "however dubious it might be.''

"What do you mean by that?''

"I mean, Andy, that you've not been completely sober in a month. Look at you. Your tie's crooked, your shirt's spoilt, your trousers need a crease, and you need a haircut.''

He touched his flowing locks defensively. "Oscar says a head of hair like mine should be worn with dramatic abandon. He says the ladies love it.''

"Ladies? Are there ladies in the Rhymers' Club?''

"No, and don't be smart.''

She wet her lips, bracing for the discussion that she had been waiting to introduce for weeks. "Doesn't that group hold a rather unsavory reputation?"

"Who told you that? Drayton? He should talk. What I could tell you— Well, never mind."

"That's right, don't change the subject. There's talk of a nature I must address with you. You are aware of what rumor says of Mr. Wilde and his reputation in certain circles? The term is 'vicious appetites,' I believe."

"That's a lie! You've no idea what you're talking about. My God! What does that make me, I'd like to know?"

"Gullible," she answered. "Oh, Andy, I'm not accusing you of unspeakable conduct, but you can't be ignorant of the rumors any more than I am. Associating with Mr. Wilde is dangerous."

Andrew ran his hands through his hair. "Even if what you say had foundation in truth, and I say *if*, then I don't see what it has to do with me. Oscar's been a friend, no more than a friend, a helpful admirer of my work. Don't you understand, I need someone of imagination and true genius capable of appreciating my abilities. Oscar does that as no one else can."

He darted a glance at her and saw with a certain unconsidered satisfaction that his remark had wounded her. "You've been good to me, too, in your own way."

Allegra looked at him. "I don't care that you think I'm not your equal. I have never tried to be. But I will say to you what you once said to me: you can't touch scandal's tar brush without it's rubbing off on you."

"It's different for a man. A lady can't recoup a lost reputation, whereas many men thrive on scandal. It adds a certain dash."

"Can you survive Mr. Wilde's reputation when it remains to be seen whether or not he can?"

"You're jealous! You're jealous!" Andrew cried in amusement. "Why didn't I see it before? All the praise being heaped on me, the attention Oscar's crowd gives me, the letters and published articles; you're jealous of my success!"

Allegra looked away, too wounded this time to answer what was so patently a lie. *He's drunk,* she thought. *He doesn't know what he's saying or else he wouldn't have the nerve to say it to my face.* The recent articles were hers and they both knew it. It was an open secret between them, yet, because he never voiced the truth, neither did she.

Her silence seemed to confirm to Andrew's befuddled mind the truth of his accusation, though somewhere in the dim recesses a nagging doubt remained. Feeling vindicated and therefore able to be generous in his victory, he came and put an arm about her shoulder. "Come, sis, don't be angry with me. You've every right to scold me, but don't. I'll even speak with Drayton if you like."

"I'd rather you didn't," she answered in a tight voice. "As a matter of fact, he's invited us up to Scotland for a few days. There're others going. I'd like to go, too."

Andrew frowned. "How soon?"

"Next weekend."

"I can't. Oscar's asked me to participate in a series of readings he's giving. You know what that could do for my public standing. I can't very well turn down the chance."

"No, I can see that you can't. I'll send our regrets."

"Why do that? Go yourself."

"Alone?"

"You'll know one or two of the ladies. I daresay Drayton's not the type to force himself on a guest, for all his reputation as a ladies' man."

"I rather thought that I might force myself on him."

Andrew laughed in full belief that what she said was impossible. As Allegra watched, she wondered how they could have drifted so far apart in so brief a time. Was it because she had secrets that he must never learn, just as he kept secrets from her? It was strange, this unseen rift between them that could only grow wider unless bridged soon. "Andy, why did you run away from New York?"

Andrew sobered instantly. "I don't know what you're talking about."

"You ran mad a few weeks before we left New York. I'll never forget the night Dr. Boyd and I found you on the riverfront. What drove you there, Andy? I won't condemn you for it, no matter what it was."

Andrew felt shaken to the soles of his feet. "I—I don't

know what you're talking about. A man's entitled to a few vices. Women! You'd make monks of us all!" He swung away from her in dramatic fashion. "God! I need a drink!"

It was useless to pursue the subject. Everything she said eventually provoked him to drink. She rose from her chair as he searched among the decanters. "I will go to Scotland, I think. When do you need the final drafts of Writwell?"

"Tomorrow, if you can. I want to show them to Oscar," Andrew replied as though none of their conversation had taken place. "And see if he can put a bit more wit in that last paragraph. Oscar says it doesn't ring."

Scotland, June

Allegra lay beside Drayton as he set adrift lazy blue-white smoke rings into the air above them. "Well?" he asked after a long silence.

"Oysters, the taste reminds me of raw oysters," she answered thoughtfully.

"And the texture?" he questioned in amusement.

"Sausage, my lord, a large salty sausage."

"Is it a meal you would again tuck into with relish?"

"Why, yes, my lord, if it were fed to me a little more slowly. By the end I was near choking."

"I very much beg your pardon. It is sometimes with men a matter of some difficulty to remember civilities when in full expression, as it were."

"I see."

"And how are you?"

Allegra half shrugged, looking for precisely the right word. "Adrift, my lord, in a fog with the lighthouse quite gone out."

He handed his cigarette to her. "One doesn't always need a lighthouse to find one's direction into port." He raised himself on an elbow. "Shall I demonstrate?"

"By all means," she answered with a smile and inhaled.

He didn't move quickly. There wasn't any need for furtive action, and the impetus of his own desire was countered by the voluptuous languor of the hashish. He stroked her, first one breast and then the other, enjoying the feel of fine smooth skin and the puckered crown of each peak. His hand moved to her ribs and into the valley where he bent his head and teased her navel with his tongue. Never before in his life had he felt as he did with her. This desire to touch and be touched, to join and hold as one for as long as was possible. It was like discovering a new and wonderful part of himself. Yet, because she was different from him, the discovery was better and more fulfilling.

She liked the sustaining power of hashish, and had not been overly shocked when he explained what it was and how it acted. If she had since felt he had tricked her the night they first made love, she must have remembered that when she gave herself to him the effects had worn off, for she never spoke of it.

Lazily, meanderingly, his tongue and lips traced a glistening trail down her belly until the spicy perfume with which he earlier anointed her skin began to be mingled with the seashell odors of her sex. She had enjoyed her new knowledge of a man. A woman's body did not lie if the man was skilled enough to recognize the signs. She sighed a little when he bent her knee at a right angle, exposing her to his exploring tongue.

The shock of this most intimate kiss surprised her into drawing her legs together, but, without a word, he merely rearranged her to his satisfaction and then returned to the hot, moist cavern of her flesh. She gasped again and again until her lungs were parched for breath. She felt a swelling burst of pleasure, deep-burning and yet different from the filling thrust of his member.

The rapture was not independent of him, even so. Behind lids closed in order to sustain and better absorb the sharp joy, she pictured Drayton's face, its tight concentrated expression of passion in the moments when he first entered her. She loved to give him pleasure and in that giving received much of her own. But even in this independent servicing of one another, there was no loss of her need for and her overflowing sensation of love for him. For no one else could she imagine this trust and joy.

Then she couldn't hold back broken cries of ecstasy as a

keen, fierce pleasure shook her from head to toe. She had no sense of time or place or even herself. When he rose slowly over her and entered her with strength and warmth, it might have been her own voice that whispered, "Yes, take all the pleasure you can from me" and his that whispered in reply, "And you me, for I love you!"

Or perhaps it was the other way round.

Drayton looked up with an unexpressed smile that stayed in his eyes as he saw her coming across the grounds toward him. She carried a basket on one arm and wore the scarlet and gold tartan of his house. With her hair caught back by a barrette that left blue-black curls trailing across her shoulder, she seemed a true Scottish lass come to feed her laird and husband. Had he been alone he might have run to meet her and tumbled her in the grass under the clear light of day. God! Was there no end to wanting her?

"She makes a fine-looking woman, my lord," one of Drayton's gamekeepers said, for he, too, had caught sight of the young American lady whom the villagers could not talk about enough. "Is it true she's got Scots blood in her?"

"Aye," Drayton answered and turned away. He didn't want to talk about Allegra to anyone. In the daylight hours they kept a polite distance to keep his other houseguests guessing about their relationship. But at night, in his bed, she was his alone. More and more he wished he had brought her down immediately, in the dead of winter, when the nights were twice as long as the days.

He made a secret lair for them and filled it with the exotic and the erotic. They didn't sleep on a bed but upon a pile of furs which they moved about at will, now before the fire, now in the light of the moon streaming through the window, again on the balcony under the stars, where they lay in naked abandon until exhausted by their own efforts. The air was perfumed by pomades and burning incense. With fine oils of sandalwood or flowers he scented her body with his own hands, finding indescribable delight in the act. Sometimes at breakfast with the others he would catch a faint whiff of the lingering scent that soap hadn't washed from her body, and his flesh would bloom in his trousers, high and stiff as if it had been six months since he had touched a woman.

He had managed to extend her visit into three weeks. Just the night before he had extracted from her the promise to remain another. If not for her brother, he believed she would spend the summer with him. Damn Andrew Grant anyway! He was a sot and a poseur, and worst of all, a coward. He was going to hell in his own time. If Grant didn't do it soon enough, he might have to find a way to help him, for as God was his witness, he wasn't about to let Grant take his sister with him to ruination.

That was the only reason he had begun those loans to Grant in the first place. Allegra loved her brother and couldn't acknowledge what was happening to him. Neither would she accept money from her lover, so he'd given the money to Grant with the promise that she never learn its source. The most amazing thing was that Grant continued to produce good work, better work in fact than he had in New York. But it was just a matter of time before he failed, and then their need for money could grow acute. Drayton didn't like to think of binding her to him by the sordid business of money, but he had no pride left. He would keep her however he could.

"Hello!" Allegra waved a hand and called out when close. In disappointment she saw him turn and walk away in the opposite direction. She told herself that he must not have heard her, but later that night, the thought remained that he had simply snubbed her.

"Why didn't you greet me today on the hillside?" she asked when they were alone.

He finished stripping off his trousers and then joined her under the furs, saying, "Because I would have embarrassed you and the gamekeeper and the wildlife."

"How so?"

He swung himself aggressively upon her and entered her without so much as a kiss. "Like this!"

Allegra winced. "You hurt me!"

"A little pain is a good thing. Do you understand?"

She shook her head, but despite the initial pain he was throbbing inside her, an intense pulse like a heartbeat that her own body answered before he began to move.

"Are you afraid?"

"No."

She spoke softly, calmly, but he saw in her widened eyes that he had frightened her. He rolled over and pulled her into his arms. "Don't cry, darling. I wouldn't do anything to hurt you. Remember our bargain? Only your pleasure, as much or little as you desire."

She rested her head against his chest. The tears weren't from fear. With Everett she had shared not only her body but her dreams and desires. Sometimes at night she read to him from her favorite books and poems, all of which she found in his private library. To her amazement, he knew many of the passages by heart. She didn't mind the pretense of polite distance with which they greeted one another during the day, for he was not the cold and contemptuous man he once seemed but someone she could love. Yet it was too soon to speak of love, too soon and too late. Andy had cabled that he needed her back in London. Immediately.

She fingered the crisp curly black hair on Everett's chest, absorbed his odor, tasted the heated texture of his skin with her tongue, heard his quickened breathing, felt the insistent throb still buried in her. "I trust you."

He knew what that cost her and in the knowing he took her with more care and tenderness than usual. But in the final moments, with her nails dug hard in his back, it was she who begged him to move harder and deeper and met every thrust by lifting her body to him. He didn't think of gentleness anymore. He rode her as though she were a woman of great experience, whose all-consuming need was the sating of sexual appetite.

Drayton lay a long time listening to her even breaths of sleep. How much longer could they have existed in this idyll? Life was suspended here, not lived. Every hour together was stolen, every kiss a sequestering of moments from reality. His guests would be leaving soon, but Allegra wouldn't be going with them. She would join him in a new life.

He touched her cheek tenderly, searching out her features with his fingertips as he did so often when she slept beside him. With a sculptor's sure perception, he memorized her against the time when he would lose her. No, he mustn't lose her. Tomorrow, in the full light of day, he would ask her to go away with him. The arrangements were made. He had taken a villa on the Italian Riviera where they could spend the rest of the summer. After that? He turned his head and kissed her brow. After that, somewhere else. They'd become vagabonds of joy, together, forever.

The decision made him feel lighter, more at ease than he could ever remember. He had always been afraid to lose himself in the life of another. How selfish and childish that fear had been. Tonight was a night of joy, of anticipation of a perfect future. They should celebrate.

Allegra awakened with a start, surprised to find Drayton gone from her side. There was something she hadn't yet told him. She turned to find him standing naked by a Turkish table inlaid with semiprecious stones. He opened a small jeweled box and took out what appeared to be a ball. When he saw her looking at him, he closed it.

"What is that?"

"Nothing of which you shouldn't remain in ignorance."

"Don't be mysterious," she answered and rose from the bed, dragging the bedding with her. "Let me see."

Shrugging, he lifted the lid from the box and took out a ball which he pulled in half to expose a green waxy opaline substance with a heavy sweet fragrance like that of incense. He held it out. "Do you know what that is?"

She shook her head.

"It's opium. Quite pure and quite deadly."

"Then why do you keep it?"

He closed the ball and returned it to the box, saying, "As a reminder of a time when I didn't believe that there were some temptations which aren't meant to be indulged."

"Have you changed your mind? Do you now believe that they're things you wouldn't do?"

He cocked his head to one side as he looked at her. "Does that surprise you?"

She shook her head. She had learned too many contradictory things about him in the last weeks to feel that she could accurately predict his behavior.

He picked up a pipe. It had a long narrow curved stem with a tiny bowl at the end. With this he scooped a bit of another substance. When the pipe was lit, he handed it to her. "I offer you a taste of voluptuous dreams and sinful ecstasy."

She drew on the pipe and a sudden wave of dizziness swept her. "What is it?" she remarked.

He took another draw himself and then turned it back to her. "A new variety of hashish. In celebration."

"Of what?"

He smiled. "Of us."

The second inhalation made her return his smile, and as he helped her back upon their fur bed she watched his smile as it seemed to grow ever wider, as if it would split his face.

Thoughts came more slowly, in jewel tones of ruby and sapphire and emerald. Opal transparencies distorted by time and every sense floated in her mind. Then, after a time, she stopped wondering about anything at all.

Drayton was there with her, caressing her legs for what seemed hours on end, until she cried out for release.

Her skin grew so sensitive that a mere breath sent ripples along her body down to her toes.

Kisses swelled her lips like bee stings.

He pressed love bites into her neck until the sharp little nips made her writhe.

Again he stroked her until she was like a wild thing under his touch.

When he entered her, he lay perfectly still for what seemed hours, enjoying her quivering need for fulfillment.

When he moved she couldn't stand the friction upon her skin. She fought him, with words and hands and feet.

He bound her with silk scarves, adding cotton padding to prevent burns, but even the cotton was an unmerciful burden on her tender skin.

He fondled her with his tongue until tears drenched her face and matted her hair and the delicious torture became some absolutely new pleasure.

When he released her, she fell on him, avid to have her revenge. He gave of himself freely, not defending himself against her teeth and nails, or her mouth and hands when desire outgrew rage.

She rode him to exhaustion in unflagging need until, slaked with his sweat and hers and permeated with the commingled odors of their spent passion, she fell into deep dreaming sleep.

Opaline dragons with ruby-throated fire snaked through the verdant jungle, their gold-scaled underbodies undulating in the sunlight. Giant butterflies with multicolor wings more brilliant than peacock feathers flitted past. Flowers, succulent and heavy-stemmed, dripped with honeyed dew.

Drayton bathed her, slowly, soothingly. Every inch of her he soaped and rinsed, pausing to press a kiss here, offer a lick there. When he was done he massaged her into acquiescence. In peace they again shared his pipe.

The bonds were again applied, but this time he didn't torment her so much as himself. He held himself inside her until he groaned with the need of a release that he would not permit. Finally he fell asleep, tumescent and throbbing, aware of her beneath him.

He shivered in his sleep, cried out for help, like a man consigned to hell. She could not hold him, could not soothe him with her embrace. And so she brushed her cheek against his, called his name softly, and licked away his tears until he was quiet again.

Somewhere in the deep dark of the endless night, when even the moon and stars had ceased to lend their ephemeral light to their ecstasy, hands turned her onto her stomach and tucked cushions under her belly. He anointed her with oil, speaking words she could not comprehend. "I won't hurt you," he said again and again as his hands caressed her buttocks and thighs.

The luxuriant feeling drawn forth by his hands seemed to go on forever, and she surrendered to the pleasure. Even when his fingers invaded her in a way she'd never consid-

ered, she didn't draw away. There was such pleasure in his touch, his soothing voice which spoke of promises to bind them together forever in a way that neither of them would ever share with another.

She was afire when he began his slow entry. By his slowness he seemed to erase from her mind all thought of what he intended to accomplish. But suddenly, sharply, pain reared its head and she cried out. He fell still, so still she thought he had withdrawn, but he had not. Slowly, so slowly it often seemed that she slept between the agonizingly sweet moments when he moved until finally she felt him quietly, impossibly, enclosed inside her.

Fire, branding heat, and shameful, deep-riding pleasure, derived from the erotic dance as old as time itself. In the end she joined his cries, her desire for him returned in fierce, demanding force.

"I must go home tomorrow."

Drayton didn't look up as he donned his robe. "Why?"

"Andrew telegraphed me yesterday. He needs me. He has work that must be made into final copy."

He glanced at her. "Tell him to hire a secretary."

"He won't. He doesn't allow anyone to see his work until it's finished."

"But it is finished. You say he wants you to copy it."

"It isn't the same. I act as his editor," she replied. Andrew's cable had been full of accusation because she hadn't sent him work after the first week of her vacation in Scotland. Drayton gave her so little time to herself, and even when he was not with her, all she would think about was being with him again. "I've stayed too long as it is."

"Ah, I see now. You grow bored." He turned slowly toward the bed.

"I'm not bored, Everett, surely you know that!"

He smiled ironically. "What am I to think when you prefer your brother's company over mine? Tell me."

"That we have had three glorious, improbably beautiful weeks together and that now it's time to return to life."

He gripped her wrist and pulled her up from the bed. "And if I don't want it to end?"

She touched his face, which was granitelike again. All the time they had been in Scotland it had been softer, full of human feeling. "There'll be other times for us."

He let her go. "I've made arrangements to see that that's so. I've rented a villa in Italy. We can leave in the morning, if you'd like."

Embarrassed by her nudity, Allegra reached for her Japanese dressing gown. "Oh, Everett, I wish you'd consulted me first. I must go back to London. Perhaps in the fall I can come back to Scotland for a few days."

Drayton tried to contain his anger. "Does that mean you won't even consider my invitation?"

"I'd love to, truly, but it's impossible. How would I explain it to Andy?"

Andrew Grant. Always her damnable brother! Drayton felt a slipping away of control. "You've a curious, one might almost be tempted to say, unnatural, fealty towards your brother. More than once I've considered him to be my greatest rival for your affections."

"That's childish! I expected better of you."

He looked down at her with the beginning of an untender smile. "You should always expect the worst. For instance, I am more curious than ever to know of your devotion to Andrew. Does it extend beyond sisterly bounds? Often in the last weeks, I've listened to you make comparisons between us, how much alike we are in intellect and interests. Tell me, are you curious to return to London to discover if we share the same proclivities in bed?"

Allegra shrank back from his wintery gaze even as she refused to believe that he'd accused her of such sick and twisted desires. "You don't know what you're saying."

"Don't I?" he answered. "Then prove it. Choose to remain with me and your brother be damned!"

"I—I can't."

Drayton stiffened as the bitter winds of disappointment swamped him. "Then I suggest that you dress immediately. There's a late train for London which you can just make."

Allegra shivered at his curt dismissal. "I must pack."

"Not at all. The maid will send your things later. Well?"

The ignobility of her situation wouldn't allow her to ask him for a night's grace. She gathered her gown tightly about her. "I'll be gone within the hour."

"Good."

It wasn't until she had fled the room that Drayton trusted himself to move. He had said stupid, unpardonable things. He would go after her. Apologize.

But on the way to the door, he spied from the corner of his eye the sandalwood box containing opium, and it drew him as unerringly as flame does a moth.

Twenty

London, August 1893

Paddington Station was a thunderous confusion of engines, voices, tramping feet, smoke, dust, and heat. The thought of travel had always invigorated Allegra, but as she stood waiting for the arrival of the train from Liverpool, she felt only anxiety mixed with an accompanying deterioration of her nerves which the last month and a half of seclusion had done nothing to heal.

When the train at last rolled into view with a great letting off of steam and screeching of wheels on the track, she hung back from the crowd that surged forth, adjusting her veil so that no one would glimpse her strained expression.

She knew him at once, but she did not approach him immediately. Lean and slightly loose-jointed, he strode the platform with a typical American self-assuredness. He wore a summer suit of natural linen, his light brown hair cropped short over a complexion less fair and ruddy than the many Englishmen about him. His mustache was brushed straight over his lip and clipped, being at once more prominent and less formalized than continental tastes demanded. Something deep inside her stirred, a pang of nostalgia for the aggressive self-confidence of American men she had not realized she missed until this moment.

She stepped forward, as he would have passed her, and laid a gloved hand on his arm. "Welcome to London, Dr. Boyd."

Startled, John Boyd stared down through the wispy veiling into the face of the young lady accosting him. Then recognition as stunning as it was pleasant came to him.

"Miss Grant! I can't believe it!" He covered the hand still resting on his arm. "This is a pleasant surprise. Is Andrew with you?"

"No, he isn't." She smiled. "It's so good to see you. When we received your cable last week it seemed sent from heaven itself. You couldn't have chosen a more perfect time to come to London, John."

He didn't mistake her use of his Christian name nor the tremor of the hand under his. Something was wrong. Most likely its cause was Andrew Grant, but this was not the place to discuss it. "Seeing you here, I'm more glad than ever to be in London."

"And of course it isn't every day an American doctor is invited to England to give a paper," she added.

"Ah, yes, the paper," John murmured unenthusiastically.

Allegra produced a card from her purse. "This is our new address. May we expect you this evening? The hour is unimportant. We'll wait for you."

"I can come with you now," John offered.

"No, you mustn't disappoint your hosts." She looked about for a likely individual. "Weren't you to be met?"

"Well, yes, I suppose," he answered vaguely. "Perhaps it would be best if I settled in at my hotel first."

"Until tonight?" she repeated.

"As you wish, Miss Grant—Allegra."

"It's wonderful to see you again, John." She turned and walked in a fast but ladylike manner toward the exit.

John watched her until she was out of sight. The long train ride had wearied him, but the sight of Allegra had revived him. He had been appalled when she announced that she was accompanying her brother to England, but there was nothing he could do to prevent it. He had hoped she would return in a month, then two. Finally he had realized that he must forget her. He had tried but the image of her as his ideal of womanhood would not fade.

He glanced at the gold-embossed lettering on the card. The original address had been struck through and a new one inked in. It was quite like the Grants. Etiquette demanded that one keep one's calling cards current. Yes, something was afoot. He should have insisted on going with her then and there. The lie about an invitation to read a medical paper was only an excuse to explain his appearance in London to the Grants.

He had always known it was just a matter of time before fate would catch up with him. The abortion on a minister's daughter had been a foolish risk. The scandal had been hushed up only when he agreed to leave New York forever. That was when he realized that he was free to go anywhere, even to London. He was wealthy, independent, and still young enough to begin again . . . and marry.

Never in his most fervent imaginings did he expect to be met by Allegra. For an instant he wondered if rumor had ranged on ahead of him, but her warm welcome belied that fear. Perhaps it wasn't bad luck but fate that had brought him to London.

"You had no right to invite him!"

"I have every right," Allegra replied. "He's our friend, Andy. We've not many of those in London. Besides, he can tell us what we've missed in New York. Our friends must think we're never going home."

Andrew paused in his pacing and turned. "I'm not."

"Not now, of course," Allegra temporized. "You're doing so well with the English publishers that you can't think of returning home just yet. But later, perhaps next spring, we might go home for a while. I miss Mama."

He mumbled a curse and began pacing again.

She thought better of continuing their conversation. At least he hadn't refused to see Dr. Boyd nor had he bolted at the news that Boyd was coming to see them. As far as she could tell, he hadn't even had a drink so far this evening.

She smoothed down the skirt of her yellow gown. It was last season's dress, but she knew Dr. Boyd wouldn't notice such details. What she was certain he had noticed was the struck-through address on her card. She must remember to remark casually sometime during the evening how they had changed locations so recently that the printer had not yet delivered their new stationery. If only Andy weren't so unpredictable. He might blurt out that they had moved weeks ago, the day after her return from Scotland.

She winced, forcing the thought of Scotland from her mind. She had moved without Andy's knowledge or consent. Afterwards she had sent word around to the Cheshire Cheese to inform him of the new location. What resulted was the worst fight they had ever had but not the last. She had invented a story about a break with Lord Drayton and extracted a promise from Andy not to reveal their new location to anyone. Of course, Mr. Wilde had turned up a few days later, and then at rare intervals other writers dropped by— but not the man she feared and hated.

When the door bell jangled, both Grants drew in sharp breaths. Andy turned to her, his handsome face showing the strain of sobriety. "Do I look all right? Mustn't have Boyd thinking I'm still in need of his services."

"You look fine," she answered confidently as she rose to straighten his tie and smooth back a lock of hair. "We'll convince him that the poetic look is all the rage."

He smiled ruefully, and the boyish charm that had been long absent rose to the fore. "Perhaps I should offer to show him a bit of the city, act the expert and all that."

Allegra nodded and turned at the sound of footsteps.

"Dr. Boyd has arrived," the maid announced at the door and then stepped aside to allow the guest to enter.

"John, how wonderful of you to come so early," she exclaimed as she held out both hands in welcome.

"Yes, nice of you to drop by," Andrew added in an overly hearty tone.

John took Allegra's hands and gripped them firmly. "I don't believe I've ever seen you look lovelier. You're positively radiant." He glanced at Andrew as a deliberate afterthought. "And you too, Grant. You're looking well."

"I look like purgatory and I know it," Andrew answered with a grin. "It's this blasted damp. Keeps me with a stuffed head. It's nothing that a dose of medicinal spirits won't set right."

"Oh?" John said with a curious glance at Andrew. "I was of the impression that you'd forsworn the indulgence."

Andrew flushed. "Only now and again. Isn't that right, sis?"

"I couldn't swear to your forebearance since I see you so little," she qualified, then hurried on. "Come and sit, John. We saved dessert in hopes that you'd be in time to join us. Let me ring— Oh, thank you, Agnes. You may set the tray on that table. Coffee, John?"

"Wonderful." He sat down opposite Andrew, aware that despite the smiles tension underlay the congenial setting. "Shall I tell you what you've missed by being in London, or will you tell me what I've missed by remaining in New York?"

"Oh, you go first," Allegra answered quickly. "I've thought so much about home in the last weeks. Mama and Papa are much on my mind. If you're sufficiently persuasive, I may return with you. That is, along with you."

"I prefer your first phrasing," John replied with a special smile for her. "You know you're the only lady in New York I've ever looked at twice."

Allegra missed the cup in her pouring and coffee splashed into the saucer. "Oh, John, don't tease me or I'll be forced to return to calling you Dr. Boyd."

John held up his hands. "I yield. So, about New York. Where shall I begin? Ah, yes. Did you know about . . . ?"

To Allegra's relief, the next hour passed in peace while they exchanged stories about mutual acquaintances and consumed plum tarts and slices of mince pie. She saw Andrew gaze lingeringly at the brandy decanter on the tray, but as she didn't offer Dr. Boyd a glass, Andy didn't ask for any.

"You're bigger literary news than ever," John said when Andrew had told him at length of his publications abroad.

"Yes, but as usual there's never enough money in it," Andrew answered.

Allegra glanced at him in surprise, for Andy always went out of his way in public to display a careless disregard for the price of things. Only with her did he quibble about the last penny. "I doubt the royal treasury could fulfill your accounting of the worth of your golden words," she quipped.

Andrew turned to her, the lines of strain reforming into combative dishumor. "You've never appreciated my talent. If not for my good sense in coming to London, where I've been surrounded by men of discernment, you'd have convinced me to abandon my genius for common toil!"

The unexpected and undeserved attack left Allegra speechless and acutely embarrassed.

"Isn't that doing it a little brown, Grant?" John asked at once, seeing her distress. "Every other word your sister's ever spoken to me has been in praise of you. She's been quite your best and most loyal admirer."

Andrew stood up and shoved his hands into his pockets. "You defend her because you admire her. If you truly admired me you'd never have taken her to the riverfront that night." His expression became ugly. "We've yet to settle that score, you know. I've not forgotten it, nor the method by which I can exact my revenge. You wouldn't want me to return to New York. Think of that the next time you're tempted to do me a favor."

"Andrew Grant!" Allegra rose to her feet. "You're insulting a guest. I won't have it."

A blush crept up Andrew's neck but his expression remained belligerent. "If you're so ready to be a good hostess, then pour the man some brandy, and I'll have one as well."

"No, thank you," John answered quickly. "I've a speech to give in the morning and I need a clear head."

Andrew's flush deepened. "Meaning, I suppose, that I don't need a clear head because I'm not doing a thing tomorrow. Glad of it, I say!"

Allegra reached for the decanter as his hand shot out for it. "Andy, don't." She formed the words inaudibly.

Andrew stared at her for a long moment, aware that he was behaving unforgivably to both his sister and a man whom he'd hoped to impress with his stability and new-found successes. He looked way and spied the frayed hem of one of the drawing room curtains. It was this place, that's what had him on edge. How could Boyd believe his stories of success when they were forced to hole up in a cheap house in Mayfair? What he needed was a fresh start on the evening or, better yet, a drink.

He pulled his watch from his pocket and studied it. "Good lord! I'd clean forgot. I'm expected at the Cheshire Cheese at this very moment." He looked sheepishly at John. "Would you care to come along? I'll introduce you to Oscar and a few other fellows whom I predict will one day have the reputations they deserve."

"I think not this evening," John answered politely. "As I've said, I must be fresh and alert in the morning."

Andrew shrugged. "Suit yourself. We keep late hours, as a rule. Let me know when you're not so particular about the morning after." He glanced at Allegra but he didn't meet her eyes. "Don't wait up. I'll be in late, as usual."

"You are coming home? At a reasonable hour," she added belatedly for John's benefit, for Andy's "as usuals" had come to mean that he wouldn't return.

"As usual," he repeated and reached out to shake John's hand. "Another time?"

"I'd be delighted," John answered. "You two are the only people I know in London. Perhaps you'd join me for dinner tomorrow night as my guests?"

"Perhaps," he hedged. "Allegra keeps the calendar."

"We'll make a date then," she offered cautiously.

Andrew nodded and took his leave.

"How long has he been like that?" John questioned peremptorily when he was gone.

Allegra grew a deep breath and made her decision. "It was never really much better. Oh, the first weeks he was so relieved to be out of New York that I think anyplace would have seemed like heaven. He actually began to write again."

''Write again? He never missed a beat, to judge from the amount of work you two tell me he's produced this last year. I've seen the New York editions and I'd say he's never been in better form.'

''You're right,'' Allegra added hastily. ''I meant his novel. That's why he came abroad, to work on his novel. But he's neglected it for months because of his friends . . . and his drinking.''

''Ah,'' John said in his most professional voice. ''You're worried, I can see that much. Is he very difficult when he's imbibing?''

''Not so very, most times.'' Allegra smiled weakly, wishing now that she hadn't been so precipitate as to go to the train station to meet him. It made her seem so needy. ''Perhaps I'm overly concerned, but it's been a difficult year, alone in London and all.''

''Have you no friends? No suitors?''

He looked so astounded that Allegra's smile became genuine. ''Oh, yes, lots. Most particularly suitors.''

John stared at her, permitting himself to remember that little more than a year ago he had held her in his arms and kissed her pretty face. ''You look beautiful but worried. I intend that before I leave London you will look both beautiful and rested. How may I best achieve that?''

''I must have frightened you indeed for you to make such an offer, John. I apologize for meeting your train. It was only eagerness to see a friend that drove me to it. Andrew was quite furious about it and I don't blame him. It must have been an embarrassing thing to explain. Please forget the episode.''

''I'd as soon forget to breathe,'' John answered, and then because he had gone that far, he said, ''I haven't been able to forget you. After you sailed I couldn't stop regretting that I hadn't tried to prevent you from going.''

''John, don't—''

''No, let me say what I should have said then.''

Allegra said quietly, ''You were right to say nothing. Your heart was wise then. Listen to it now and don't rescind your resolution.''

''I meant to say noting at all if I found you married or at

least happily courted by a man. But, to my great joy, I don't see any indication that this is so.''

She rose quickly and turned away. "Oh, John, don't be melodramatic. I'm quite unfit for parlor games this night."

He rose, too, staring at the graceful lines of her back and shoulders. He had thought he had lost her, but here she was, needing him and wanting him. He had felt it in the hand she placed so confidently on his arm in the station. Yet she was in genuine need, not a simpering coquette full of tricks and strategies. He must handle her more carefully this time, for he meant to win her.

"I won't press you, Allegra. This is new for both of us, but, you'll see, it will come right this time."

Allegra turned, a distracted look on her face. "No, you're wrong."

A tremor of apprehension ran through John. "Then I'm wrong. There is someone."

"Was someone," she answered with dignity.

"May I ask who?"

"You may recall him. Lord Drayton."

"A friend of Andrew's, was he not?"

"Yes. He was most helpful in helping Andrew prepare for the trip. Since we've been in London, they furthered their acquaintance."

"And you furthered yours with him."

"I suppose that's as good a way of expressing it as any." She didn't want to discuss Everett Drayton, certainly not their relationship, which was still too painful for her to consider. "We soon discovered that we don't suit. It does happen."

"Yes. It happens."

She looked at him in sudden appeal. "I need a friend, John, and I would like it to be you, but I won't use your generosity. I tell you plainly and honestly, I won't allow you to court me or even entertain hopes in that direction. I shan't marry—ever. That must be said between us."

"Every young lady of feeling believes that of herself," he answered gently.

"I'm not every young lady," she said with a ghostly echo of her sense of humor.

"I couldn't agree with you more."

"Then you'll accept my friendship on this basis?"

John saw no point in belaboring the issue at this juncture. "I agree. It's a bargain between us."

"No!"

The horrified tone of her voice surprised him into withdrawing the gentlemanly hand he offered her.

"No," she said more quietly. "There'll be no bargains. A simple understanding." She put a hand to her flushed cheek, struggling internally for control of her emotions. "I must be more tired than I thought," she said lightly. "You'll think the Grants have both run mad."

"I think you've been under a great strain that in no little part is due to your brother's neglect and intemperate ways. You no longer carry that burden alone." He smiled. "I've not come all this way to turn quickly around. I may stay a month."

Allegra's face lit up. "A month? That's wonderful."

"I'll renew my acquaintance with Andrew, see if I can steer him a straighter course. Who knows? I may be able to persuade him to return to New York."

Allegra looked at him with all the gratitude she dared not express for fear of dissolving into tears. "Thank you, John. I'm so glad you've come."

He squeezed her hand. "So am I."

Their address was known to too many for him to long remain in ignorance of it, but she wasn't prepared at all for the sight of Lord Everett Drayton standing over her as she awakened from a nap at her desk.

The sight of him was so sudden, so unexpected that she first confused it with one of the nightmarish torments that dogged many of her sleeping hours. Despite her feelings, in spite of her anger and hurt and humiliation, overriding all considerations was a sudden brief soaring of her spirit, an intense joy that even in her dreams he still sought her out.

Instantly the dream shifted into the solidity of reality.

Everett. In an instant she saw him clearly and it made her gasp. Where once he had been lean he was now gaunt, as though he had suffered a long sickness. "You've been ill!"

A grimace that might have been the beginnings of a smile ended in a spasm of a muscle in his right cheek. "I've been without you, which is worse."

Allegra rose shakily to her feet, all too aware that this was not the way the conversation between them should continue. Why had she fallen asleep in the middle of the afternoon? To be left so defenseless was unforgivable. She straightened up and crossed her arms across her bosom. "Who let you in?"

"The ineffective maid whom you've set like a shepherd to guard the door."

He seemed to take great pleasure in saying the words, though no emotion animated his too-pale face. The weight of his direct gaze had once been daunting; now it was a thing from which to seek refuge. She looked away.

"Have you become a coward once again?"

She didn't answer. A thousand things ran through her mind as she continued to stare into space: that she was poorly dressed, that her hair was caught back by a ribbon for comfort, that behind the desk she had slipped off her shoes, that every inch of her body was alert and trembling, in need of his touch.

She turned her head sharply toward him, her gaze her only defense. "I don't see why you've come here. If it's to enact some melodramatic scene, you may save us both the distress for I won't believe it. Two months is a long time to hold unbearable yearning at bay."

"There are methods," he answered darkly. He had tried the most dangerous and failed. "Why did you run away?"

"I didn't run. I left."

"Why?"

"Need you ask? How could you—?" She caught herself on the hysterical rise and inhaled a breath. "You put me out, as I recall."

He leaned forward, bracing himself by his hands on the desk top. He looked haggard, his light eyes shining out from beneath the cavernous overhang of black brows. "You might have stayed and fought me."

She took a frightened step back. "Fought? For what?"

"For us," he said softly and levered away from the desk.

"I offered you—" He broke off as he saw her glance fearfully at the open door. He strode over and slammed it shut, then came back, his anger now released. "Shall we be delicate or shall we be honest? I did nothing but give you the excuse you wanted to run home to your brother. I begged you to stay. If you'll remember, it was you who wanted to leave."

She shook her head wildly. "Not for the reasons you suggested!"

His smile came now, full of mockery and pity and tinged with what seemed to her contempt. "I remember you in the throes of hashish's delirium begging me never to cease. When I thought I was beyond rekindling you took me in your—"

"Stop!" She pressed her hands over her ears and turned away from him. "You make it all so sordid and disgusting!"

"Missish airs! I expected better of you. Am I so frightening, so much a temptation that you can't look at me without fear that you'll again succumb to desire?"

She turned to him, her eyes wintery with despair. "You made that impossible with your horrid accusations. How else shall I look at you but as the instrument of my damnation?"

"The instrument of your deliverance?" he responded.

"What we did, what we shared, I see now it was vile, demeaning, and disgraceful. How else could you think me capable of—?" She turned away, unable to say the words.

Drayton felt a rip begin deep inside him, a painful searing slash caused by her words. No, he wouldn't accept her assignment of guilt or allow her to shame him into disavowing the only true happiness he had ever known.

He came slowly around the desk. "Listen to yourself. Where is your courage, your contempt for the ordinary, for the quiet desperation of being no more than the least of us?

"You cry because you've bruised your toe on one of pleasure's more rude courses. Well, listen, my girl, there's no such thing as delicate bliss. Pleasure's not found in dignified intercourse with dry genitals and elegant movements. Pleasure demands that we fuck with grinding and oozing, our asses jiggling in ridiculous fashion. We are base, so let us glory in it. We are animals. Then let us rut in bestial delight. Don't turn in false shame from what you desire.''

"What I desire?" she echoed in disbelief. "To think, oh God, that I thought I—! No!" Appalled that he had reached for her, she grabbed the letter opener on the desk and held it menacingly. "Stay away from me. I swear I'll do you harm if you don't keep away!"

A sudden blush replaced her pinched white-faced misery, and he knew he had succeeded at last in rousing her emotions, and in that lay possible victory. He folded his arms, his head cocked in inquiry. "Would you kill me? I'd wait a bit before I plunged into that sin—do excuse the pun. You don't mind if I await your decision seated, do you? I'm rather fatigued."

He took a seat behind the desk and picked up one of the papers. " 'Reflections on a London Evening.' How quaint. Does your brother give you a list of the brothels and gaming hells he frequents?"

"Don't speak of Andrew to me! You're despicable!" she whispered and reached for the paper, but he held it away.

"Why this antagonism? It's only a piece of paper. Your brother generates them by the dozens." He looked down at it. "Ah, I see. It's your copy. You've a nice hand." He glanced at the other papers on the desk, a frown coming to his face as he did so. "You take his dictation?"

"No. Yes!"

He didn't know where the notion came from. Certainly when he recalled his thinking later, he could never resolve logic and the sudden leap of intuition that allowed him to make the connection. But, as he looked down again, things were immediately, stunningly clear. He looked up in wonder. "*You* wrote this!"

Allegra froze, unable to speak or even act. In one blinding flash she knew that he knew the truth and would never be turned back from it. He wanted control of her and now he had found it. Even if he couldn't prove it, the scandal of rumor would wreck Andy's tenuous faith in himself. "He's ill," she said, pleading what might be a fruitless case to this heartless man. "I've been helping these last weeks because the strain is too much for him."

"Liar." He said it softly but with finality, and she gave no further defense against his accusation.

He stared at the page, trying to assimilate this new knowledge of her. He recognized the style. It was Writwell's style, and that meant . . . Andrew Grant's work was good. Wilde praised it as well as the more staid reviewers in *Punch* and the *Times*. Yet, in reality, they praised . . . Allegra Grant. "Why do you allow this?"

"I don't know what you mean."

He held out the paper to her. "You're the author of Writwell and God only knows how much else, yet no one knows that you compose a word. Why?"

She shrugged. "It was our agreement."

"Was it?" he murmured softly, but his eyes narrowed. "I see the benefit to your brother. What has been your gain?"

"By living with Andy I am free to go about in society and meet interesting people."

"You might have done that by marrying."

"Oh, no, it wouldn't be the same. I'd be at the beck and call of a husband."

"Andrew offered you freedom, is that it?"

"It's not what it seems. I only helped a little, in the beginning."

"Yet you now write every word. It's better than his efforts ever were, and you know it. Why don't you demand your right to the praise?"

She shook her head. "The praise means nothing. I've been free to do as I please. Until now."

Drayton frowned. "What the devil are you talking about?"

She worried the collar of her blouse with a nervous hand. "What is the price of your silence in this matter?"

"Blackmail?" He was incredulous. "You think I'd blackmail you?"

"I'd believe anything of you."

"Anything evil or despicable or vile," he countered, hurt more deeply than he showed. "You think you're different from me, but I know you better than you know yourself. You shy from a truth that I realized a long time ago. You are like me! You're exactly like me!"

"I pray to God you're wrong," she whispered.

"Why, because you're willing to debase your worth for your brother's gain? That's not virtue, that's cowardice. You display a remarkable tendency to martyrdom, yet you deny me the pleasure of pleasing you. Better you look to the greater rape by your brother!"

The sound of a stumble outside the door gave them both pause.

"Your servants are less discreet than one should hope," Drayton observed drily. "Sack her immediately. It's the only thing that will counter the gossip."

"How can I?" Allegra asked in horror that they had been overheard. "She may repeat what she's heard for revenge."

"She may do that in any case," he replied dismissively. "But let's not digress at this point." He rose from the chair. "You've a talent and you're squandering it on a lost cause."

"How dare you accuse me of squandering talent? At least I use mine to good purpose. But what about you? I've seen your sculptures. They're good. Yet you prefer to waste your life dallying in scandal and vice rather than put your creativity to the test. I rather think it's you and Andy who are most alike!"

He reached for her, drawing her in as she twisted violently to escape, but once their lips met she gave up. The kiss went on and on, and when it ended they stood in mute wonder at the passion that flared with such intensity between them.

"If you cannot free yourself from your brother's tyranny, I'll do it for you," he said quietly.

"Don't bother, my lord. I'm going back to New York."

"I can follow you."

"You can go to hell!"

"If you're there, it will be worth the voyage."

* * *

The sound of moaning, of someone in pain, slowly seeped into Allegra's troubled dreams. When it came again, louder and more intense, she sat upright in bed. She knew at once that it was Andy. He must have come in after she went to bed. She dressed quickly in robe and slippers, but by the time she entered the hall, someone else was there before his door with a candle.

"It's your brother, miss!" the new maid exclaimed. "He must be ailing something fierce."

"Send someone to Claridge's. Tell him to ask for an American guest by the name of Dr. Boyd. He's to bring Dr. Boyd back here at once! Hurry!"

"Yes, miss." The maid gave one frightened glance at the closed door as a cry pierced the night, and scurried down the hall.

Allegra opened the door in trepidation. The room was dark save for the light from one small lamp above the hearth. In its glow she saw Andy. He was thrashing about in the bed like a man in agony. She hurried over and touched his brow, which was slick with sweat. "Andy, what's wrong?"

He fell still at the sound of her voice, and she repeatedly smoothed his brow. There was no fever. In fact, he was inordinately chilled. Suddenly he jerked upright in the bed, his mouth opening to release a howl that raised the tiny hairs on her arms.

"Andy! What is it!" she cried, throwing her arms about him, but he began to shake so violently that she bumped her chin against his shoulder and bit her tongue. The pain made her release him and he fell back among the covers, arching his back and jerking spasmodically like a man in a fit. It *was* a fit, she realized in acute alarm.

She threw herself across him to keep him from falling off the bed. He bucked under her, alternately swearing in bluest profanity and whimpering in pain. She was no match for his strength, but she had fear to match his senseless rage, and when he began clawing at his face, as if to tear his skin, she pulled his hands away and slapped him as hard as she could. When he reached for his face a second time she struck him again and he gave up and fell quiet. Appalled at herself and at him, she shimmied off the bed. She turned and saw for the first time the bottle of wine by the bed and a vial of brownish-red liquid. She picked it up and opened it. The smell was unmistakable. She picked up the empty glass, fear shrinking her flesh against her bones. There was a wine-mixed sludge in the bottom. Andrew was an opium eater.

She pounced on him in anger and fear and frustration and desperation, and shook him with all her might. "Who's done this to you? Where did you get it! Speak to me, Andy! Who gave it to you?"

For a moment Andrew thought that Harriet stood above him. Her wheat-blond hair slid along his cheek. Her soft delicate fingers urged him to awaken to passion. He caught her by the waist. "How beautiful you are," he said softly. "I thought you'd left me forever!"

"Oh, Andy," she cried in relief at the sound of his voice.

"What's this? Tears? No tears, my love. We're together now. Come to me."

Allegra entered his embrace willingly until he suddenly lifted his head and put his mouth to hers. Shock registered as an icy chill of revulsion as she twisted away.

"No, Andy! Please!"

It wasn't Harriet's voice, Andrew mused. Another woman? There had been so many these last months, each an attempt to erase the memory of Harriet. He released her.

Allegra sprang away from him. He was ill, she told herself. He was too delirious to know what he was doing. Why, then, did Drayton's mocking words come to mind? *I consider your brother my greatest rival for your affection.*

"No!" She forced the thought away. That was evil, unspeakably vile. She mustn't allow his poisonous venom to ruin her life. Only then did she see the maid standing openmouthed in the doorway.

"Did you send for Dr. Boyd?" she demanded in embarrassed anger as she climbed off the bed.

"Yes, miss. The cook's boy went."

"Then why do you stand there gaping? Go stand by the door to admit the doctor at once!"

The girl bobbed a curtsy and left, but not before Allegra

saw the look of scandalous disbelief that was mirrored in her own heart. She had witnessed the kiss!

She took a tentative step toward the bed. "Andy? Andy, can you hear me?"

His eyes opened at once. "Allegra? Is that you?"

"Yes, Andy. You've been calling out in your sleep."

"Dreams," he amended in a wistful voice.

"Where did you get the laudanum?"

He was silent a long time.

"Andy?"

He smiled. "His lordship's a true friend."

She didn't question it. She thought she must have known the answer all along. *If you cannot free yourself from your brother's tyranny, I'll do it for you.*

She stood there for what seemed like hours before she heard John's voice and then his hurried footsteps on the stairs. When he entered the room, she merely pointed at the vial on the bedside and said, "He's been violent, had a fit. Please help him. I must go out."

John looked from Andrew to her. "Out? It's nearly three o'clock in the morning!"

"Yes. Even so."

"I can't permit—" John's voice was drowned out by a cry of agony erupting from Andrew's throat. As he turned toward the bed, Allegra slipped out of the room.

"But, miss, you can't come in here! It's three o'clock in the morning!" the butler protested.

"If you don't open that door this instant, I shall begin screaming as loudly and as long as I can. See if his lordship prefers that!"

He had seen dunners on their way, and tarts and belligerent drunken nobles, but the Earl of Dundare's butler gave ground before the determined American young lady. "You must wait in the hall, for there's no fire in the drawing room," he directed as he shut the door behind her.

"That won't be necessary." She started for the stairs.

"You can't do that!" the butler cried in horrified amazement.

She didn't pause. "I'll tell his lordship I overpowered you."

She didn't know exactly where she was going, but she discovered that it was remarkably easy to find one's way to the master's chamber. It lay beyond the door with light streaming from beneath it. She didn't think of knocking. The latch gave way under her hand without protest.

The scene before her shouldn't have shocked her. How could anything about him shock her at this juncture? It was simply the eeriness of the moment. It was like looking into a mirror. The young woman's hair was the same midnight shade as her own and she wore the silk kimono Lord Drayton had given Allegra in Scotland, the one he'd not included in her baggage. Where it fell open the woman seemed remarkably similar to her own size and shape. Even their embrace was achingly, hauntingly familiar.

Though as drunk as he had ever been in his life, Drayton knew at once who had entered his bedroom at three o'clock in the morning. He had wished her here. After weeks of failure, he was at last drunk enough to make flesh of his most fervent desire. He lifted the prostitute off him, vaguely embarrassed by the raging evidence of his preoccupation of a moment earlier. Even so, he slid from the bed without embarrassment for his nudity. "Miss Grant!" he greeted with a crooked smile. "Welcome. Welcome!"

Drunk and without shame. Allegra fought the impulse to be ill. She held out the vial she had concealed in the folds of her cloak. "Does this belong to you?"

Drayton squinted at the object she held and then shrugged with a deprecating air. "As I cannot see it, I cannot answer."

"It's a vial, my lord. A vial of laudanum which you gave my brother."

"Did I?" Drayton frowned. Why had Allegra brought that with her? And why did she think he would give anything to the man he hated most in the world? This was his dream; she should act as he desired. "Leave that to Andrew. If it's pleasant dreams you seek, I don't recommend the method. It's entirely too unpredictable and ultimately deadly."

An icy stream seemed to replace the blood in her veins. "Thank you for confirming my suspicions." She turned to leave.

"Wait!" He caught her by the arm, surprised at the power of desire to give substance to shadow. "Don't go. You've just come."

"You don't need me, my lord. You have company."

He made a deprecating gesture. "She's nothing. Come, and let's show her what it is to love truly!"

"What? Perform for your whore?"

The horror in the green eyes staring into his penetrated his stupor slowly, and he shuddered as his own words resonated in his head. Then he understood what he had not known before. Until this instant, no matter what she had said, how much she had nursed her resentments toward him, there had been an emotional intensity in that animosity that bound them as surely as love. Now it was gone, severed by his words as carelessly as one would cut twine that bound a package. He grasped at words, trying to put his chaotic thoughts in order. "I didn't mean that! I don't mean to hurt you."

"Yet you always do," she answered and pulled free of his grip. She moved backward toward the entry, her nerveless fingers reaching for the door. "Good-bye, Lord Drayton."

"Wait!" He reached out but she was gone, pulling the door shut after her. "Allegra? Allegra! *Allegra!*"

Twenty-one

"Well, what do you think?" John Boyd asked anxiously. "Won't it serve all our needs?"

Allegra looked about the furnished drawing room of the Mayfair town house. "It's very nice, John. Very nice."

"But?"

"But I think it's too much for you to take us on. There must be two dozen things you should be doing at this very minute. It isn't every day that an American doctor decides to open a brand-new practice in London. Your time won't be your own. We'd only be a disturbance."

"To the contrary," he countered. "You've graciously offered to act as my hostess. And, though I regret the need to point it out, Andrew needs constant medical supervision."

"Which he and I can't, at present, afford."

"We've talked about this before," he said patiently. "If you and Andrew move in with me, the second floor shall be entirely yours. When I'm out, you'll be here. When I'm home, you'll be free to come and go as you please. Andrew will never be left alone."

"I still think we should return to New York."

He gave her a paternal pat. "You know that's not possible. How would you care for him on the voyage? A missed dosage, too little or too much, and what would be the result?"

"You say that Andy must be weaned from his addiction slowly, that his body can't withstand the shock of sudden withdrawal, yet I say again that we aren't your responsibility."

"I make you my responsibility. I'm a family friend. I know Andrew's case better than any doctor you could call in at this point. It goes without saying that discretion is absolutely critical to his reputation." He smiled and took her hand. "Think of my fortune as tied to your own. I couldn't have guessed that I'd decide to remain in London and set up my practice when I came a month ago. Yet it's happened. Fate smiles on us. Don't disdain it."

She smiled at him but disengaged her hand. "You must allow me time to think."

"I've paid the first month's rent and I certainly wouldn't have chosen anything this grand if not in expectation that you two would join me."

Guilt pricked her. "Then you must allow us to pay a part of the rent."

"Does that mean you agree?"

Allegra shook her head and swayed.

John put out a hand to steady her. "What's wrong?"

"It's just a continuing light-headedness," she answered. "It's bothered me for weeks."

John pulled out the chair for her. "It's only to be expected. You've been greatly upset by Andrew's illness. You should've kept the nurse I hired."

Allegra didn't look at him as she sat down. "It was an unsupportable expense."

"Have Andrew's habits run you into debt?"

She nodded. "I didn't realize to what extent until a few days ago." She looked up, her complexion a little pale. "Dunners came to our door. It was awful. Andrew owes money to the most peculiar people."

"My poor dear. Then it's settled. You'll move in here until Andrew's on his feet again."

"That might be some while." Her expression hardened into resolve. "I must be honest with you. Andrew has borrowed heavily from his publishers against future work. He must complete those assignments before he can hope to have further income."

"Your parents?" he suggested gently.

She looked up at him frankly. "Papa cut us off when we didn't return to New York last Christmas. Don't look so horrified, John. We've done well enough until now. Papa did extend bank credit to keep us in vegetables and linens." She smiled saucily. "We've paid for the meat and silks ourselves."

"How brave you are."

"It takes no bravery to go on as though nothing has occurred," she answered dryly. "Bravery is in facing reality, which neither Andy nor I have been very good at."

"Then face it now with me." He grew serious. "I know that I've no right to press you, that I agreed not to court you in any manner, but you must see that this is a practical solution in every sense of the word."

She rose and held out her hand. "You are a true and loyal friend. I hope you'll never regret your generosity."

"How could I when it places you at my dining table both morning and night?"

"It's unorthodox," she persisted. "There'll be talk."

He smiled. "Andrew and I were in college together. What's more natural than that we should decide to reside *en famille* when in a foreign land?"

"How clever of you to phrase it like that. I'll use it myself."

He pressed her hand warmly. "Welcome to your new home, Miss Grant."

She smiled but without a full return of his warmth. "Welcome to London, Dr. Boyd."

Allegra sat and stared at the small space that was her new bedroom. The green chintz curtains with their cheerful ruffles matched the half-canopy of her narrow wrought-iron bed. Green wallpaper patterned with white daisy bouquets complimented the dull green carpet and the green-and-white Roman stripe of the upholstered chair on which she sat. Every surface displayed a doily or dust ruffle. Even the narrow mantle was draped in a green shawl. The ceiling had been papier-mâchéd to simulate Jacobean plasterwork. The room was perfectly sweet, perfectly proper, and perfectly awful.

She gently stroked the tiger rug thrown across her lap, the only item in the room with which she was at ease. "I can't complain," she said to the rug. "John's been absolutely wonderful. But I do wish he'd given me the bachelor room down the hall."

She had one glimpse of it; moroccan leather chairs and loden green wallpaper with golden fleurs-de-lis. There had even been a tartan plaid rug on the floor which reminded her of— No, mustn't think of that.

Allegra let out a long, slow breath as another of the nagging pains zagged through her lower abdomen. She mustn't be ill now, not when it seemed that Andy was going to get the help that he so desperately needed. She glanced toward the open door. Across the hall his bedroom door was shut. He had refused to speak to her since entering Dr. Boyd's home that morning. It was a miracle that Andrew had agreed to come at all. It must be, she thought, a measure of how ill he was.

The next pang made her catch her breath. It's just anxiety, she thought. An hour earlier she'd been too cold. Now she felt near suffocating. A drop of sweat trickled down the side of her face. She had never suffered incapacitation during her monthly cycle, as many women did. At school she had often scoffed at Reeba, who took to her bed for three days. Never again.

She rose and went to poke her fire, for now she was trembling with a new chill. A little chamomile tea and rest, that's what she needed. As she bent to pick up the poker, a sharp searing pain knifed through her middle. Groaning in agony, she grabbed the mantle edge and gritted her teeth. The spread of wet warmth down her legs accompanied another intense pain. She needed help but couldn't gather the breath to call for it. Nauseating pain rose like a red tide before her eyes. The shawl she clutched slid from the mantle and then she herself was falling.

Andrew opened his door, crying angrily, "What the devil's going on? Allegra? Allegra!"

When she didn't answer he cursed and crossed the hall, all too ready to find any excuse for a fight.

She lay spread upon the carpet, surrounded by broken bric-a-brac, the shawl still clutched in her hand

"Allegra!" he cried, rushing over to kneel beside her. She moaned when he touched her. He sprang up and jerked the servant's bell before turning back to her. Only then did he see the blood that streaked the toes of her shoes and carpet. He fell back, aghast, and bellowed, "Help! Help! Someone help!"

Allegra awakened with reluctance. Unconsciousness was preferable to the pain. But with the opening of her eyes the pain did not return. Where there had been knife blades, there was now only a dull empty ache.

The first thing she saw was white daisy bouquets on a green background. The next thing she saw was John Boyd's face, and his horrified expression struck fear in her heart. "Am I dying?" she whispered huskily.

"No." His voice was dull and cool like metal. "I daresay you'll live a good while yet, though you've lost the child."

Allegra didn't think she moved or spoke again, but suddenly he was bending over her, holding her arms tightly as she screamed and screamed at him for lying to her.

"A female disorder," John said coolly as he met Andrew's haggard expression. "Not uncommon, I assure you."

"If it's not uncommon, then why can't I at least see her?" Andrew demanded furiously.

"She has a fever. She's delirious and saying things she'd be embarrassed for you to hear."

"What kinds of things?"

John couldn't focus on the young man before him. His head pounded with pain and shock. The only woman he had ever loved had given herself licentiously to another man, and suffered a miscarriage as a result! He had seen it with his own eyes. He looked down at his hands, expecting to see that her blood still befouled them though he had washed repeatedly. She was his perfect flower, risen from the muck of the world. Now the muck had sucked her back. The thought of another man touching her sent blinding fury trembling through him. "What do you know of Lord Drayton?"

"Drayton?" Andrew frowned. "Why? What's he to do with Allegra?"

"I don't know," John said, smoothing a crease in his trouser leg to keep his hands busy. "It's a name your sister has repeated in her delirium."

"Oh." Andrew shot the doctor an appraising look. "You may as well have it straight. Allegra isn't the kind to say a word, not even to me, but I think she fell in love with the earl. They've parted. She's better off without him."

"I see."

"I hope you do. I'm not blind. You're helping us because

of her." He jerked his head toward Allegra's door. "If you want my opinion, I think you're the better man."

"Thank you for the rare compliment," John returned formally.

Andrew's eyes narrowed in calculation. Lord Drayton had cut him off without a penny once Allegra returned from Scotland. There were past debts and those he proposed to make in future. He needed an ally, and in this case, one was as good as another. Allegra would ultimately make her choice, just as he was about to make his.

"I could help you in the matter of Allegra."

"Why would you do that?"

Andrew shrugged, embarrassed by his ungenerous feelings toward his sister. Still, the earl's attention wasn't serious. He hadn't come by in weeks. There hadn't even been a calling card from the noble bastard. He didn't like the doctor, but beggars couldn't be choosers; yet he wasn't without leverage. He smiled. "You're one of us, an American. That counts for something, I say. For instance, I don't take every rumor as truth. I say a man should be able to leave his country without scandal following ever after."

"How gentlemanly of you," John continued in a neutral tone, but he understood the implied threat. Andrew had heard rumors concerning Boyd's hasty departure from New York. He withdrew his wallet. "As we are to be partners, surely there's something I can do in return for your, ah, support?"

The phrase "Thirty pieces of silver" came to mind as Andrew reached for the money, but he shoved the thought aside. He wasn't a traitor to Allegra. He was trying desperately to shore up their unraveling lives. They needed a benefactor. If encouraging this fool was the price, he wasn't too proud to do it. "I'll repay every penny."

When Andrew was gone, John's passive expression altered to one of malevolent intensity. Damn the Grants! If it were in his power, he'd destroy them both. But perhaps they would take care of that in their own way. Suddenly the humor of the situation came to him. Grant was a drunkard and his sister a fallen woman. It remained to be seen who had more to lose in the game of spider and fly.

* * *

Allegra drank the broth set before her. It was the first time in more than three weeks that she had been allowed out of bed. Sitting in the chair by the window made her feel human again. Well, more alive than dead. The numbing effect of shock was a therapy all its own, but now that it had worn off, she was left with a sense of being nothing more than a walking, talking shadow.

A child. She couldn't conceive of it! A pun. A Writwell pun. Once it might have seemed funny. Now laughter only mocked her pain. Everett's child. She had never even suspected.

She didn't look up when the door opened and John entered. She hadn't been able to look him in the face since the night he told her what had happened. She would leave his house as soon as she was strong enough. She and Andrew both would go home, back to New York; no, Philadelphia. She needed motherly arms about her, even if her mother must never know the reason for the comfort she gave.

"How are you this morning?" John inquired formally.

"Better." It was all she ever said. It was true enough, for each day she felt a lessening of the anguish, the sorrow. Slipping into shadow; it was really quite easy.

"If you're feeling up to it, I've a matter to discuss with you that's quite urgent."

Her head snapped up. "Is it Andy? Is he ill again?"

"No," John replied, annoyed that she roused herself for a brother who cared very little about her while she hid from him even when he was in the room with her. "It's about this." He held out several letters. "Andrew gave them to me to give to you. They came shortly after your illness but I've held them till now."

She took the proffered letters and with nerveless fingers fumbled the first one open. She was prepared for a dunner's note or even the threat of legal action. What she read in the first letter drained her face of color. The second and third were nearly identically worded. She looked up in wordless misery.

"There was an altercation at the Cheshire Cheese, Andrew

tells me," John began in explanation. "It seems one of his editors lodged a complaint about the extent of Andrew's indebtedness and the laxity with which he appeared to treat his deadlines. They'd all drunk a great deal. Words became accusations, accusations became insults, and so forth. I'm told Andrew won the fight. But not, unfortunately, the war."

"They can't cancel all his assignments," she protested. "He's been paid for them."

"Allow me to point out the obvious. They have." He took a turn about the room, gauging closely the effect the letters had on her as she reread them. There was no reason to shield her now that she was healing. After all, he jeered inwardly, she was a woman of the world. "Andrew disappeared the day after the letters came. He was gone three days."

"Opium?" she whispered, as if invoking a curse.

"Regrettably, yes."

"Where is he now?"

"In his room. You must face facts. Your brother was in no condition to meet his deadlines even before the struggle. Now, well, it'll be days, perhaps weeks before his mind clears completely. Perhaps this is for the best."

"The best?" she repeated. "How can it be for the best? Writing is his livelihood. No, it's more than that; it's his life's blood."

"You seem to care a great deal more than he does. He says he's glad it's over."

"He can't simply allow this to happen. We must eat!"

The frantic edge of her voice surprised John, and out of habit he nearly reached out to pat her hand, but he refrained. No, no more of that, not ever again! Her lovely face hid a netherworld of lies and deceit. "I'm still at your disposal in that matter."

Allegra shook her head. "I can't expect it. It was a mistake from the beginning. Had I only known—" She broke off, for the shadow was threatening to become all-too-real pain. "In any case, we must leave here. At once."

"To go where?"

She pressed a thin hand to her brow. Thinking was becoming impossible. She was ill. Andrew was ill. They were destitute, without any means of employment. "Andrew will write a letter of apology."

"He's not up to it," John reminded her.

"Then I will write it!" she cried impatiently. "With the apology I'll enclose the first of the work that's due each publisher."

"I suggested that, but Andrew says he doesn't have them."

"Of course not," she rejoined scornfully. "I've not yet written them!"

Her words hung in the air like the sound of pistol shots. She was quite amazed to see their effect on John. He stared at her as though she had stood up and blasphemed in church. It struck her as funny. He hadn't looked nearly so undone when he told her the cause of her illness. It was amusing, wasn't it? She gave a sad-funny little smile. "I write Andrew's columns. I was writing them before we left New York. You never guessed. No one did. It was quite clever of us, wasn't it, John?"

"Quite clever." His voice sounded oddly strangled in his ears. More duplicity! How could he have ever thought her an innocent?

"You don't believe me!" she said in frank amusement. "Shame on you, John, for your sense of masculine superiority that denies a woman may achieve equally with a man."

John stared at her anew. There was so much he never suspected about her. Each revelation made more shamingly obvious his own gullibility. He looked at the other item in his hand. "It's a morning for rude shocks all around, I fear." He laid the paper beside her bowl and left.

Allegra quietly finished her soup before touching the newspaper. It was bad news. Things always came in threes, her mother often said. Good news. Bad news. Luck and disaster. Always in threes.

It was a good likeness of him. The cameraman had caught his characteristic scowl. The woman was less flatteringly portrayed, a pity when one considered the fact that she made her living by her face and figure. Still, they stood closely together, arm in arm, and her bon voyage bouquet was quite an impressive size. Bound for the Continent, the caption said. Lord Drayton, Earl of Dundare, and Miss Olivia Sutton, the darling of the West End theater district. An extended tour was expected for both.

She hadn't wanted to think about him or even hear his name spoken. From the moment she left Scotland she knew that she carried with her a love for him, but the secret she carried had been greater than she knew. It seemed extraordinary that her love had been evoked by a man who neither liked nor respected her. But her love for him abided, waiting for her at all hours of the day and night. She had suppressed the feeling, believing it to be an aberration brought on by her highly emotional experience with him. It wasn't until she had walked in on him in bed with a whore who wore her clothing that she realized that nothing would change her feelings—nothing. Yet all hope of reconciliation had now vanished.

She didn't think there were any tears left, but seeing his picture reminded her that her child might have looked much the same as he. For that loss there didn't seem to be enough tears in the world.

Violet Granby was only fifteen minutes late. It was the exact degree of lateness adhered to by those fashionable persons who never arrived on time but were sufficiently eager to reach their destination. Allegra had been stunned by a note from the marchioness, inquiring if she might come for a visit.

Dressed in the palest mauve shade, from her veiled hat to the lavender-scented gloves, Violet Granby spent exactly a quarter of an hour on the social amenities of a formal visit before broaching the purpose for which she'd come.

She had thought at first she wouldn't come at all. She'd never thought to embroil herself, however slightly, in matters between a man and his mistress. Not even her personal liking for Allegra Grant would have moved her to speak if she had not received the note from the Earl of Dundare. The intensity of feeling contained in the brief letter had quite shocked her. He said nothing, of course, about an affair with Miss Grant, or the fact that he had left her. He urged only that she warn Miss Grant of certain rumors. He didn't elaborate. He didn't need to. She had heard them herself within a fortnight of the earl's departure for France.

The rumors were so outrageous that she had laughed the gossiper into embarrassed silence. Unfortunately, others were willing to lend more credence to the matter, once word of Andrew Grant's blackballing by his publishers became common knowledge. The young man was a wild American, of whom anything might be believed, and was. It was really all too much, but at least it wasn't common.

Allegra watched her guest with guarded interest. Even when she had been frequently in the company of Lord Drayton, the marchioness had never been more than pleasant to her. This unprecedented visit had made her quite nervous. She had changed her dress three times before settling on a cream gauze morning dress. The moment the marchioness set eyes on her, Allegra had sensed an approval of the choice. Only then did she remember the lady's advice about pale colors.

"We haven't seen . . . much of you . . . or your brother," the marchioness began. "Of course . . . one's been in the country. Would be still . . . except that I can't abide the cold . . . and damp . . . and the country all at once. It isn't fashionable . . . to return to town . . . until November. That's another week off."

"You're fortunate to have so understanding a husband, Marchioness."

"Indeed. One's choice of company . . . is quite the most important choice . . . a lady may make. So few suitable matches. So few gentlemen of title. The Earl of Dundare, for instance."

Allegra allowed the shock of the name to roll over her like thunder, for she knew at once that this was the opening blast of the storm to come. "I wouldn't count him out yet, Marchioness. He has, after all, yet to make his choice."

"Do you think so? There was a time . . . not so long ago . . . when I thought he had."

So this was the manner of Drayton's farewell. The coup

de grace, delivered by the wife of a future duke. She must certainly be honored—and feared. "I'm surprised to hear your ladyship say so. I, for one, was never in doubt that his emotions were as unencumbered as ever."

Violet smiled, relieved that she was not stepping into one of those untidy situations so common among the bourgeoisie. "Your brother?"

"He's been ill," Allegra answered, alert for another blow.

"How unfortunate. He seems to be a most . . . exceptional example of your countrymen. Illness can be so taxing . . . on one's health and abilities. Unreliable tempers often develop."

Allegra smiled. This she was not afraid to discuss. "Then you've heard that my brother has been abominably abused by his publishers. He's been refused, in short, denied a livelihood for a moment of intemperate anger."

"Intemperance, indeed, though not all of anger, yes?"

"Perhaps, Marchioness, you'll speak more plainly that I may do so in turn."

The marchioness dropped her eyes. "How very very vexing this all is. There are rumors . . . my dear. Dreadful, unspeakable rumors."

"About Andrew?" Allegra demanded in a protective spirit.

The marchioness lifted her eyes. "And you."

"Andrew . . . and me?"

"You sacked a young servant girl for listening at keyholes last month? Rumors are circulating."

Rumors. Andrew . . . and she. It was like being caught in a snake pit with no possible hope of escape. Once inclined toward hell, there was no evil of which one was not thought capable. "You seem amazingly well-informed, Marchioness. Who was your source? Lord Drayton?"

The marchioness blushed and rose. "I see now that I've made a mistake in coming. Do forgive my intrusion."

Allegra rose, too, and laid a restraining hand on the marchioness's arm. "Don't leave without telling me, I beg you. I don't deny the rumors. Who can speak of them at all without in some way validating the reason for their existence? Yet I must know if they are believed by . . . certain parties."

The marchioness searched the drawn face of the young woman before her and was moved to rare pity for a fellow creature not of her class. "I would believe nothing that does not speak well of a friend. As for my friends, they do me the honor of behaving remarkably as I do."

Allegra nodded, too full of emotion to speak.

"But I should warn you that my friendships are few, and limited to the most high-minded. Vermin thrive on offal. Look to your back, Miss Grant. I should go home, if I were you. England can be the most chilling, dismal, and murky of worlds in the wintertime."

When she was gone, Allegra climbed the stairs to her floor, pausing outside Andrew's door. Was he aware of the rumors that circulated about them? Did he care? She had protected him so long she couldn't remember when she had not thought first of him and second of herself—except during the weeks she'd spent in Scotland. Better, then, that she be publicly branded a slut than the debauched sister in an incestuous affair.

She removed her hand from the knob. She couldn't say the words. She couldn't, not even to him.

"It would solve everything."

Allegra stared at John. "It solves nothing. Marriage is out of the question, as you well know."

"It would quell rumor, allow you to move again in society." His manner was polite but unemotional. "Your parents should be delighted. Or is that it? Are you afraid Angus Grant won't think I'm enough of a catch for his daughter?"

"Don't be foolish, John. It is *I* who am not worthy of your name and we both know it."

"And if I don't care about your past?"

"How can you not?"

"Then, if I'm prepared to put it behind us?"

"It won't ever be completely behind me," she replied. "As for my standing in society, the best way to handle that is to ignore it. As soon as Andrew's able to travel we'll leave England."

John had expected her reaction to his proposal, yet the rejection, given so out of hand, smarted. She was as arrogant as ever, despite her tumble, but he was not so easily defeated. "You'd best put ideas about returning to New York out of your head. Rumors of a very awkward nature have preceded you there. Besides, Andrew is convinced that he must avenge himself before he can leave London."

She looked up at him and wondered why she saw so little when she did. Once he had seemed a savior, and, if truth be told, he was still. Yet he became somehow smaller and less significant each time she looked at him. Perhaps it was only pride born of shame that forced her to reject him as a suitor. Or perhaps it was something more, some sense that he knew absolutely nothing about her, saw less of her desires and faults than Andrew, or even Lord Drayton had. "I'll go and talk to Andrew myself."

She was glad that John didn't try to prevent her from seeing Andrew, as he so often did. When she reached the second floor and knocked, Andrew opened the door so quickly that she knew he had been waiting for her. She realized then that John must have told Andrew what he intended to do.

"I won't marry him, and that's final," she said at once.

"Bully for you!" Andrew answered and motioned her inside.

He was smiling as he had in days of old, his eyes crinkling in the corners, his face, though thinner than she'd ever seen it, radiant with some inner light, some inner secret. She smiled back in spite of herself. "What are you up to, Andrew Grant?"

He laid a finger against his lips as he closed his door. Then, catching her by the hand, he pulled her over to his fireplace and pressed her into the single chair. He then slid gracefully into a cross-legged position beside her. "I've discovered a way out of this wretched mess, Allegra. Would you like to hear it?"

"Very much, Andy."

"We're going to write a book. Yes, a book. It will be a satire, a complete and scathing attack on the hypocrisy of

English society, especially its literary circles. When the public reads it, I won't be surprised if it doesn't pull down the government.''

Allegra's smile saddened. "Andy, English society is something we know very little about. Secondly, if we were able to accomplish the feat, who would publish it?" she questioned, exasperated with his daydreams. She had hoped for a moment that he had found an answer to their predicament.

Andrew mumbled under his breath. He had come out of the other side of his last opium journey feeling more alert and eager for life than he had in months. Just two drops in his dinner wine had elevated those feelings. Now Allegra sat before him telling him his ideas were impossible. "You've changed," he said defensively

"So have you, Andy. So have you."

He cocked his head to one side. "You don't look very well."

"I'm perfectly fine." She stood up. "I'll think about what you've said. Perhaps there's something to be written in our defense. I've been thinking lately that I'd like to try my hand at a novel."

"Novel?" he scoffed. "Don't flatter yourself a novelist because you can turn out a passable column."

She didn't answer.

Two weeks before Christmas. Two weeks. Was that not astonishing? Allegra put the calendar down and picked up her pen, ignoring the twinge of pain in her fingers as she gripped the pen. Pennies a word. It wasn't much but the few pounds she had collected for writing advertisements for magazines and newspapers made her feel useful, important, able, and confident. "Two pounds and you're proud as a lord!"

Her own laughter always surprised her these days. There was so little to be amused about. Shut up in a few rooms, day in and day out, no wonder her own amusement entertained her more than the cause of it. She glanced at the fireplace and resisted the impulse to relight her fire. Coal cost money.

A shovel of coal was worth several words. She would write them, write a whole bucketful of words, and then keep her fire lit tomorrow night.

But her fingers refused to hold the pen properly. She laid it aside and began to massage her hands. She'd cut the fingers from an old pair of woolen mittens, hoping to keep her hands warm while she worked, but tonight the wool and the coaxing were not working very well. John had warned her that the spasms might be the beginning of rheumatism, but she refused to believe it. Her hands were just tired and cold.

After a few minutes of rubbing each joint separately and then trying and failing to maintain the proper grip because of continued pain, she glanced at the vial of medication John had given her. A few drops in warm milk. It had worked, until he admitted that it was an opium derivative. Since then she'd refused to touch it. Opium had become the bane of her life.

But tonight her gaze lingered on the bottle. She was afraid of it, yet John had assured her that taken in moderation and with the knowledge of its power, she could not possibly become addicted. She had work to finish before morning. She couldn't afford to lose the only job she could obtain.

"Just a drop or two," she said to no one in particular.

Half an hour later, smiling dreamily, she pulled her pen across the sheet. Pennies a word. So many fine words. Pennies became pounds so quickly!

Twenty-two

London, Spring 1894

Allegra's head nodded forward onto the desk top. She had been working for nearly forty-eight hours without pause.

Now it was complete: her novel. All the months of self-denial, all the suffering, all the pain and anguish, bled out like leechings of old. There was only peace left, and the vague distortion of time and place that had accompanied her for months. And the nightmares.

They were the reason she didn't sleep until exhaustion claimed her, often in the middle of a word. Some were worse than others. One in particular had returned with more frequency of late. Even as she fought the stupor of encroaching senselessness, she heard the beginning of that dream take place in her flagging consciousness: the scrape of a key in the lock on her door.

She lifted her head and saw him standing there. She didn't cringe or moan as she had when the dream first thrust itself upon her months earlier. There was only resignation in her expression, the resignation over having to do battle.

He was freshly dressed and shaved. Was he going out or coming in? Was it day or night? Ultimately, it didn't matter. He stood in a roseate halo of light, no more real or less fearful than a nightmare should be.

He didn't speak. It seemed he found nothing to say in moments like this. And, of course, he was right. It wasn't a battle to be won by wits or reason. It was a game of shadow and light. But she had a secret weapon, something he didn't suspect, even though he often succeeded in stealing her work.

She smiled as he approached. The finished copy of her novel was secreted away from him. She'd caught on early to that part of it. Essays, she had given him only essays while the pages of her novel lay in her mattress, a bulky secret that turned her smile into a grin. And so to the game, and the battle with the devil himself.

When he reached out for the papers on the desk, she snatched them up. It was part of the game. She had learned to play her part well. When he smiled she knew that this was what he wanted. He would touch her now. The struggle was only an excuse to touch her.

Strangely, she didn't feel the fingers of his hands gripping her arms, only a vague pressure. In these minutes, she was as insubstantial as he. He shook her and she raged at him using epithets she didn't know she knew. But it felt good to spew violent, filthy words. They dimmed his aura, blending the rose into a violet ether. She struck her hip against the desk in her struggle, but there was no pain.

As he drew her in against his chest, she felt the first inkling of panic. She wouldn't, must not, kiss him. All was lost in a kiss. She'd learned that lesson. No kisses, no sweet words, no lingering, languishing nodding toward passion. His mouth slid past hers, falling on her neck like an icy sting.

Rage swelled up in her as his hands moved from her arms to her waist. She screamed like a madwoman, clawing, shrieking, ripping, shredding, tearing at the phantom demon embracing her. She felt the wet slick of blood under her nails and heard his cry of pain. The howl only served to redouble her efforts. Once and for all she would rid herself of the nightmare.

She scarcely felt the slap though the blow snapped her head back. She did feel his clothing give way under her hands, and then the heat of his flesh as she sank her nails into his chest, curling and tearing a path down his ribs.

A kick sent her sprawling, but she didn't mind for she saw him stagger toward her door, cursing as roundly as she had been. This time he didn't bother to close the door.

For what seemed like hours, she lay listening to her heart gallop like hell's own fury. When she finally lifted a hand to brush back the hair from her eyes, she was astonished by the sight of blood on her fingertips. Her nails were broken and bleeding but she felt no pain, no pain at all. She had defeated the demon. Strange that he should have come in the disguise of her savior this night. In her own way, she'd always been fond of John Boyd.

Allegra dressed very carefully. Her hip still ached, though she couldn't recall the fall which John said she had suffered a week earlier in an attack.

An intruder in the house. It was remarkable! She felt quite foolish when she was told, and much too embarrassed to confide that she had thought the attack had been part of a nighmarish dream.

Poor John, he had struggled with the ruffian and been mauled himself. There were still ugly red nail marks on his face. If only he hadn't struck his head, he vowed, he would have beaten the prowler senseless.

She gazed at her image in the mirror. She looked older than her twenty-two years, thinner and more pale than she would have liked. Her skin was like fine candle wax, smooth and semitransparent. Often in the past months she had willed herself simply to disappear, and it was as if the effect of that wishing had manifested itself in the new translucence of her skin.

She picked up a pink silk rose nosegay and pinned it at the neck of the white blouse. She wore the new blazer suit that her parents had sent her for her birthday. She had been quite astonished to receive it, for in one short year fashion had changed dramatically. The sleeves of the jacket were puffed up like balloons above the elbow and the blouse had a mannish styling, both serviceable and yet elegant.

It was the first communication she had had from her parents in nearly a year, and the sentimental gesture at once deepened her sense of isolation and strengthened her resolve to face the world again. Her mother had mentioned that her father was thinking that a trip abroad might be in order in late summer. The fact that her father was considering the trip told her that she and Andrew were missed as much by their parents as they missed them. All the more reason for her to go ahead with her plan. By late summer their troubles should be resolved.

She ignored the pang in her stomach. Indigestion had plagued her since the attack, but her hands were completely well. The pain had disappeared magically when the last chapter of her book was finished. She had been able to complete the rewrite without a single dose for rheumatism. If not for the ache in her hip, she would have suspended all use of John's prescribed medicines. Even so, the painkiller dulled her senses and she refused to be dulled or lulled this morning.

The noise and sunlight of the street at first surprised, then frightened her. She paused at the top of the steps even as the butler hurried down them to open the door of the hansom that stood waiting for her. Six months. It had been six long exhausting months since she had been out of John Boyd's residence. She clutched the package in her arm. No one knew what she was about to do. She could change her mind and not have to explain to anyone. New pangs began in her middle. She was going to be sick.

"Ain't yer going then, miss?" the driver called.

"Yes. Yes!"

She fought the nausea to a standstill in the cab. By the time she reached the Savoy in the Strand she felt well enough to go ahead with her plans. By reading the papers this last week, something she hadn't done in months, she discovered that Mr. Wilde could almost always be found lunching at the Savoy. When she had paid her fare, she lifted her head and entered the imposing facade. She didn't know where to look for him and so chose the boldest of strategies.

She approached the maître d'hôtel and said, "Would you kindly direct me to Mr. Wilde's table?"

The man's eyes widened as he looked the American lady over, but he could find no fault in either her appearance or her bearing. "Mr. Wilde is not at present in the dining room, miss."

"Ah, then I must be early. I shall be happy to wait at his usual table."

Again the maître d'hôtel hesitated. Individuals were always hoping to crash the dining room without a reservation, but it didn't seem likely that a young lady of obvious breeding would do such an outrageous thing. He raised his hand in signal and drew to his side the head waiter. "Cesare, the young lady is dining with Mr. Wilde. Show her to his table, please."

The slim dark Italian gave her the same frank, if more fleeting, appraisal, before saying in a chilly voice, "If the lady would follow me, please."

Allegra slid into her seat, feeling tremulous once again. She hadn't eaten breakfast, not trusting her delicate stomach. "Coffee, please, with cream and sugar."

For the next half hour she sat and pretended to read her manuscript while hope dwindled. If Mr. Wilde did not make his appearance soon, she knew she would be asked either to order or vacate the table, for she could feel Cesare's eyes on her each time he passed by. Because of this, she had stopped glancing up every time someone approached the table.

"Why, Miss Grant? This is a pleasure!"

Allegra looked up, relief adding extra warmth to her greeting. "Mr. Wilde! I'm so very glad to see you."

He smiled down at her over the considerable bulk of his floral-waistcoated middle. "Your smile reminds me of moments when 'all existences seemed narrowed to one single ecstasy.'"

"Grant?" murmured a sulky, Oxfordian voice. "Is *she* the one?"

Allegra looked at the speaker and was astonished by the golden handsomeness of the young man standing a little behind Mr. Wilde. From his violet eyes to the gleam of his gilt head, he was perfection. Then she noticed the look of distaste on his pouting mouth and remembered his disdainful question.

"Be kind, Bosie," Wilde said with tolerant affection. "This is Miss Allegra Grant, a dear American friend. Miss Grant, may I present Lord Alfred Douglas."

"She's the look of her brother," the young lord remarked. "Same features. Same vices?"

Allegra rose, feeling light-headed and nauseated all over again. "Excuse me, perhaps another time."

Wilde caught her arm as she half swooned, saying softly, "Do sit down, Miss Grant. The entire room's watching. I do so hate dramatics outside the theater. Common rooms are hardly ever lit sufficiently to give proper advantage to the spectacle."

Caught between amusement and weakness, she did as he suggested. "Sherry!" she heard him order as he sat down heavily.

"What do you think of Bosie's translation of *Salomé*?" he asked conversationally and then went on as though she had answered. "I agree. *Salomé* is the best thing I've ever done. Bosie says it will make me immortal. I told him that I reached immortality at an early age. There's nothing left me but deification. Of course, I shall refuse. I can't imagine anything more revolting than to be held up to one's fellow creatures as a model for goodness and virtue!"

Allegra drank a little of the sherry placed before her, grateful for his kindness which did not pry or make observations. When a little of her color had returned, she saw that he was eyeing the manuscript. She put a possessive hand on top of it.

"Grant's new work?" he inquired.

"Yes," she answered.

"Is it good?"

"It's the best yet," she replied, though her hand trembled when she picked up the first few pages to hand him.

He didn't accept them. "I don't combine reading with lunching. It too often causes one to curdle the other."

"Then I suggest that you read first. If you lose your appetite it will be a blessing," Lord Douglas said in a waspish voice.

Startled, Allegra looked at the young man, but Wilde either didn't hear him or chose to accept the insult as the merest tease for he patted the young man's hand. "For you, Miss Grant, I will jeopardize my digestion."

From nowhere a plate appeared before her, filled with thin slices of veal, potatoes, and green beans, but she could not touch it. Nor could she bring herself to look at Wilde as he read, and most certainly she had no desire to speak with the young English lord who watched her with an intensity of dislike she had never before experienced. He might be as lovely as Oscar was grotesque, but she much preferred obese kindness to beauty's contempt. She sensed a kind of malignancy in the young man, a vile poison of the senses, as though he might taint by a look, maim by a touch.

He read far longer than she expected and when he finished the first chapter, he began thumbing through the next. Finally a smile as beatific as a babe's blossomed on his round face. "Your brother's absences from the club have been noted with regret. When this is published, regrets will become howls."

"You think it has merit?" she ventured.

"Merit, what is merit? Merit is what a schoolboy earns for conjugating his Latin. This has the spark of genius! But why didn't Andrew come himself?"

"Pride," Allegra answered, allowing her chance to proclaim the work as her own to pass. If Wilde thought it was publishable it really didn't matter whose name went on the jacket. "There've been certain rumors, Mr. Wilde, of which you cannot be in ignorance."

She heard his companion's snigger but Wilde spoke. "Scandals and slanders that have no relation to truth."

"That may be true," she replied, "but most people believe that slander has its basis in some crumb of fact."

He smiled encouragingly. "Slander and scandals are related more closely to the hatreds of the people who invent them than to the images or effigies of the person attacked. For myself, I contrive always to be of interest. The public grows indifferent to goodness."

"I will try to adopt your philosophy, Mr. Wilde. Yet the ugly realities remain. Andrew's been unfairly banned by London publishers, yet this book must be published, and quickly." She gave Lord Douglas a sidelong glance. "There are extenuating circumstances."

"Money?" Wilde suggested.

"Pride," she answered quickly. "It's a matter of pride that he succeed on the very field where he was brought low so unfairly."

"Would it not be easier to call the publisher out and shoot him in a duel?" Lord Douglas offered in a bored voice.

"You wish me to help your brother," Wilde said, ignoring his friend.

"I beg you to intervene on Andrew's behalf. If you think the work is good, that will go a long way toward persuading others at least to look at it."

Wilde seemed to ponder her statement, but his next words surprised her. "I shall soon begin work on a new play, or did I say so? I'm calling it *An Ideal Husband.* Do you believe there is such a thing?''

"I couldn't say, not having had one of my own."

"A good answer. So I will give you good advice. Like the Old Testament, marriage begins in the Garden of Eden and ends in Revelation. Is the veal not to your satisfaction? They serve a delicious lamb chop."

"No, thank you. I did not come to intrude upon your meal." She opened her purse. "Allow me to pay for my—"

"Miss Grant. You are a diverting luncheon companion, but if you lay so much as a ha'penny on the table the patrons may assume that you're purchasing service of the kind which they do not allow in this fine establishment!"

Embarrassed once again, she closed her purse. "Thank you."

"Don't despair. Andrew owes me a meal and I shall remind him of it when I bring him news of the sale."

She looked at him in noncomprehension, for he scattered her thoughts with his sudden changes of topic. Then her heart began to pound. "You will help us? Thank you, thank—" She paused, arrested by the sardonic lift of his brows. "Andrew will host a dinner for you with his first royalties." She turned and left before she further embarrassed both him and herself.

"Not bad looking, for a woman," Bosie said and reached for the first page of the manuscript. "Is it swill?"

Wilde caught his wrist in his large fist. "Don't be naughty, Bosie. I rather admire a woman with the courage and determination to live her life as she sees fit. Lord Drayton lost someone rare when scandal drove him off. But, really, it takes a saint to suffer fools gladly!"

Sweat poured from her until she and the sheets were drenched. Gritting her teeth she sat up and reached for the vial by her bedside and quickly tipped a little of it into the milk the maid had brought up earlier. She drank it in huge gulps that allowed it to trickle from the corners of her mouth. When she was done, she fell back against the pillow, exhausted by the effort.

She was all alone. John was up at Cambridge to give a lecture while Andy was soaking up the country air down in Suffolk. He'd been gone for nearly three weeks, without writing once. A tear slid out of her eye. Andy hadn't even taken the time to say good-bye. They were very nearly strangers. After the night he had embraced her, she couldn't at first bear to look him in the eye. Rumors had planted a vile seed of doubt, and opium had taken away his control. Later, locked in her own pain and months of work, she had nearly forgotten Andy while John supported him through his ordeal to overcome addiction. Perhaps now she no longer existed for Andy. He was well and whole, John assured her. It was she who lay prostrate with pains which might kill her.

Was it appendicitis or a pinched bowel? She knew both were deadly. Where was John? Why didn't he come when she had sent a telegram to fetch him? No, she hadn't done that. She had only thought to do that. She would send for Andy, instead. She needed to tell him that she was sorry she had neglected him and of the good fortune which was about to befall them.

She sat up. The medicine worked quickly; it always did. Even as she slid from bed, she felt her feet touch the floor with a cushioned sensation that was the trademark of the drug. Soon she would be cocooned in the dreamy slumber of peace. But tonight she would lie in Andy's bed, for it was as close to him as she could get.

She crossed the hall without seeming to move. Thought became reality without action. That was the power of the drug. She turned the key that had been left in the lock and entered the room, startled by the faint glow of a candle. "Andy? Andy, are you home?"

The stench did not at first register with her. There were sights to consume her gaze long before the smell of sickness penetrated the cocoon of laudanum's embrace. She couldn't comprehend what she saw. Where once his bed had been, there was now an iron cot. Hanging loose from the corners were leather straps. An old-fashioned slop bucket stood nearby. Littering the floor were empty bottles of wine, dozens of bottles, enough for weeks of drunkenness. Small vials lay mingled with them, few in number but ultimately more horrifying.

She approached the bed because a shape lay there and she couldn't leave without knowing the truth. She was audibly praying by the time she reached it and stood looking down. He must have heard her, though she could not hear herself, for he turned slowly from his side onto his back and opened his eyes.

Once she had thought him the smartest, strongest, most handsome man in the world. Now a wraith lay staring up at her, all stained teeth and sunken cheeks, cavernous eyes in purple sockets, and wild black hair thickly mixed with gray.

"You came." It was not his voice, so dry and weak and shrunken like his body—but it was he.

"Andy?" She dropped to her knees, not daring to touch the creature before her. Perhaps it was only a nightmare.

He smiled, a hideous parody of Andy's beautiful smile. "You came." How long had he waited? Weeks? Months? Each time it took longer before he could again reach this blessed awakening, this soft coming to his sense of himself. And yet she never came. John Boyd was always there instead. But this time Allegra had come! Everything was going to be all right this time. He moved his hand slowly from the bed to touch her hair.

Allegra flinched as the skeletal hand with yellowed nails long as talons touched her. It was a nightmare. It must be!

"Help me!"

Allegra looked up. Had she spoken? No, the man on the bed was speaking. He was saying things to her. She must listen but it was so hard.

"Where's Boyd?" he asked, his eyes darting continually toward the open doorway.

"In Cambridge," she answered

Andrew closed his eyes in relief. So, Boyd had made a mistake at last. His eyes flew open. "Are you sick? Has he hurt you? How has he kept you away from me?"

"Who?" she queried in confusion.

"Boyd."

The contempt with which he spat the name made her

shiver. "John's in Cambridge," she repeated. "Do you need him?"

"No!" He grabbed her wrist, pressing as hard as he could. "You mustn't tell John we've spoken. We must get away, Allegra! We must get away from him. Tonight! Do you understand? You must help me get away!"

Frightened and confused, she pulled against his restraint. "You're hurting me!"

He folded himself carefully, pulling his legs up almost to his chin before rolling onto his side and levering himself into a sitting position. He ached in every part of his body. All his flesh seemed to have disappeared, leaving only bones to grind against one another when he moved.

Repelled yet fascinated by this unreal thing that moved like an elderly man and spoke with the ghost of Andrew's voice, Allegra watched him. "Who are you?"

Andrew leveled his most lucid gaze yet on her and reached for the candle that burned on the bedside table. He held it close and grabbed her chin to turn her face to the light. She stared at him, the green of her eyes almost blotted out by black pupils. "Damnation! He's drugged you, too!" He set the candle back and took her by the shoulders, shaking her slightly. "How much have you had today? How often does he give it to you? Answer me!"

With a cry of alarm, Allegra broke free of his grasp and scuttled crablike among the bottles to get away from him. "Who *are* you!"

Andrew dropped his head in his hands and began to sob softly until tears ran between his fingers and down the backs of his hands. The sound of his anguish convinced her as her sight could not that this was her beloved Andrew.

She crawled closer and reached out to stroke his hair. "Don't cry, Andy. You never cried before. You're the stronger of us, you always were."

He lifted his head, the grime on his face partially washed away. "Do you know me now?" he asked softly.

"Of course I do. You're my Andy." Her face lit up. "I've the most wonderful news. I've been to see Mr. Wilde and he's going to get your new novel published!"

Andrew shook his head, thinking that she was delirious.

He knew only too well the power of opium dreams. They were sometimes preferable to life itself. "What have you been drinking, Allegra? What sort of dose do you take?"

She smiled at him. Andy was here when she had thought he was not. How perfectly wonderful. But what had he asked? "I get the most awful pains, Andy, here in my stomach. John gave me medicine for them and it works, but I don't like it. I only take it when the pains are very bad."

"And were they very bad tonight?" he asked gently.

She nodded.

"How much did you take?"

"A few drops."

He looked at her skeptically. "Only a few drops?"

Again she nodded like a small child.

He grinned. "Good girl!"

She came into his arms then, not minding his unwashed body and scraggly beard. "You're not the same. You're too thin."

"And you," he answered as new tears threatened him. "Now," he said after a moment, "you must go and dress. Do you have any money?"

"I have money. I've earned it," she said proudly.

"Boyd allows that?"

She nodded. "John's been very good to me."

He couldn't ask her what she was required to do in exchange for those kindnesses. Whatever had happened, it was his full responsibility. He had come to that realization while in the throes of his most recent annihilation of the spirit. Harriet's death, his failure as a writer, Allegra's unhappiness; all his fault. "Allegra, I must tell you something. John Boyd means to kill us."

She listened, certain she had heard him wrong. "Why, Andy, what a silly thing to say. He's our friend."

"He's a deadly enemy," Andrew countered, feeling the gnawing ache begin. "I couldn't understand it at first. It wasn't until you were ill and he wouldn't let me see you that he showed his hand. He wants you, Allegra."

She smiled for she was feeling quite wonderful now. "He can't have me."

Andrew smiled. Perhaps he had jumped to too many

conclusions. "I said the same, threatened to expose him if he laid a hand on you. That was my mistake. One should never cross an enemy in his own lair." He took a breath. Speaking was more difficult with the cramping, but he fought it. "He put it in the food. I would have noticed it in the wine. Then when I was addicted, he kept supplying the vials until I no longer cared what happened."

He looked at her. She was thin but still healthy. Perhaps, for her, it wasn't too late. "He's always hated me. Never knew it. Now he hates you as well. Stand up and give me your arm. I must dress."

Allegra did as he asked. "Where are we going?"

"Away. Far, far away."

The sound of a door opening below brought Andrew's head up sharply and then Allegra, too, heard John's voice. "Go away!" Andrew hissed. "Go and take the key. Hurry! Don't say you were here! Please!"

He gave her a shove and fell heavily back into his cot, breathing like a man who had run miles.

"Take the key!" His voice was fainter. "Come back! Later!"

She left only because his imperative tone overrode her concern for him. She even took the key, though she couldn't imagine why she should need such a thing. She had just closed her door when she heard footsteps on the stairs. Like a child awake after bedtime, she turned off her light and crawled into bed to fake sleep. Moments later she heard the faint scrape as her door was opened. She lay perfectly still, amused that the childish game had lost none of its anxious fun. When the door closed, she smiled.

It was three o'clock in the morning when Allegra came to consciousness. She'd had a horrible dream: Andrew like a ghoul; herself caught in a gigantic spiderweb; filth and debris everywhere. Then she felt the impression of a key in her hand and knew the truth.

She dressed quickly, packing no more than a change of

clothing, and got out her sable-lined cloak though it was June. She had twenty pounds in notes.

She opened the door. When she found no one in the hallway, she picked up her small case and went to try Andrew's door. It was locked. She put her case back in her room, then put the key in the lock in Andrew's door, turning it slowly.

The room was as she remembered; only this time Andrew was tethered by the ankles and wrists to the bed. She wondered why she had never heard him, why he didn't cry out in protest, and then she saw that he was gagged. His eyes were open but they didn't seem to see her. She unbound him quickly. He didn't move.

"Andy," she whispered sharply as she bent over him, trying not to inhale the stench.

He moved, the slightest gesture of life. She shook him and when he groaned she shook him harder.

His eyes opened slowly and she knew what had happened. "How much, Andy? How much did he give you?"

His head rolled on his pillow. "Too much," he murmured. "Let me die in peace."

She looked about for his clothing. She found fresh things in his cupboard and began stripping him. She didn't think about what she saw or the extent of the personal duties she had to perform for him. She went back across the hall and fetched water to wash him. She trimmed his nails, hacked at his hair with scissors until he was close-cropped. She trimmed the beard back, hoping that in the dark of night he would pass for normal company.

He didn't help her but he didn't resist and she sensed about halfway through her ministrations that he was rousing himself to consciousness but holding action in abeyance until it was needed most. She didn't think of the time passing; she told herself that there was plenty of it. He was ill, but she thought perhaps he had lost some of the poison in being sick. It was four-thirty when she finally looked at her watch. Dawn was beginning to pink the sky.

She helped him to his feet and into the hallway without a word passing between them. He was so weak she could hardly hold him upright. He leaned heavily against the wall, and when they reached the stairs, she despaired of descending. "You're too weak," she whispered.

Andrew gritted his teeth and sagged against the wall. The hall was swirling about his head. He wasn't certain he could move his feet another step, but he had to, to save Allegra from Boyd.

She pushed her case forward with her foot to the edge of the landing. Once she got him down she would have to come back for it. She placed her sable-lined cape about Andrew's shoulders and pulled the hood up over his head. He looked ridiculous but warm.

The maid's appearance in the front hall was the last thing she expected. The house was brightening with every moment, but she didn't expect anyone to be about in the front hall yet. The shock froze her as the maid looked up, straight into her face.

"Oh, good!" she heard herself say as she began descending the steps. "Kate, you're the person I need. Go out and hail a cab for me, please."

"A cab?" the girl said in surprise. "This time of day?"

"Yes. My brother and I have to go to the hospital. He's not feeling well."

"Shall I get the doctor then?"

"Oh, no," Allegra said as she neared the girl. "Dr. Boyd is with Andrew now. He asked me to dress and go for a cab. Now that you're here, you can do it."

"I suppose," the girl answered, reluctant to brave the morning chill before a cup of tea. "If he's sick, you'll be needing it right away," she said mostly for her own motivation. "Shall I look for one to carry three?"

"That won't be necessary," Allegra answered, every nerve in her body aware that voices might rouse John, who made his bedroom in the former library. "Do hurry!"

When the girl went out the door, Allegra hurried back up the steps. To her amazement, Andrew was smiling at her. "You always knew how to take care of things."

She didn't bother to answer. The steps were a greater obstacle than the maid had been, and they both knew it. Allegra went first, his arm thrown about her shoulder, his free hand gripping the banister which he leaned against.

More than once she thought they would topple over. Each step was a giant effort. They had just cleared the final one when the maid burst in, saying, ''I got it!''

Allegra thought her heart would stop as the cheerful refrain echoed up the hall.

''Oh, he doesn't look good at all,'' the maid said as she peered up into Andrew's face.

''He's very ill. Nothing catching,'' Allegra added hastily. ''Take his other arm. We must hurry.''

The maid was small but sturdy and her added efforts got them out of the house and down the steps in a surprisingly short amount of time.

''Thank you, Kate. You can go back in now,'' Allegra said when they reached the cab.

The maid turned back as Andrew climbed laboriously into the cab and fell heavily half in, half off the seat. Allegra was too uncertain of his strength to press him, but the yellowing of the sky left him exposed to anyone who might pass on the street.

Finally he got a leg up under himself and with a heave deposited himself on the seat. She climbed in quickly after him.

''Miss Grant! Miss Grant!''

Allegra's head swiveled around in panic at the sound of her name, expecting John Boyd to be in full pursuit. But it was Kate who came flying up to the cab. ''You forgot your case, Miss Grant!''

''Thank you,'' Allegra said in a strangled voice and took the case which contained all the worldly belongings they would own for some time. ''Now hurry in and have a cup of tea. Drive on!'' she called quickly to the driver.

''Where to, miss?'' the cabby asked.

''Victoria Station,'' Andrew replied before nodding forward in a swoon.

The worst was far from over. Later Allegra wondered how either of them had had the strength to survive the journey they undertook. She was again experiencing stomach pangs, and he was trembling like a man with the ague when they reached Victoria Station. She had to pay the cabby to help Andrew aboard the train for Dover. It didn't occur to her that she hadn't brought along a single vial until they were pulling away from London. Andrew said nothing when she told him, only turned his face toward the window and stared out. She didn't know whether he was grateful or angry. She didn't know what she felt herself.

They both roused themselves to go to the dining car, where she pretended that she had enough money for them to eat a dozen meals. They even talked a little, trying to piece together the lost months of their lives. Later, back in their compartment, each sank into a kind of stupor overladen with a gnawing craving for the milk of the poppy.

Allegra stared unseeingly, the glory of the English countryside reduced to the dirty edges of countless villages, the occasional scruffy mongrel, an abandoned hovel, a crying child, a burned-out cottage. Everything she saw was tinged with disgust, despair, and ruination. It was as if the hand of perdition had smote all within view, just as she was being smitten inside. If not for Andrew she would have gotten off at the next station and gone—gone where?

She thought first of Lord Drayton. She was accustomed to the thought. Once she stopped fighting it, it became a most pleasant diversion. His town house in Belgravia came to mind, then his "pile of stones" in Scotland. She had thought herself a prisoner there. How wrong she had been. She had been a wanted and willing participant in passion. Perhaps it was the wanting too much that had destroyed the possibility of having it forever. Was he well? Was he safe? Had he been stronger than Andrew and resisted despair? No, Andrew had been imprisoned, just as she had been, made a slave to the most destructive of addictions. Now they were free, or were they?

Andrew began to moan about midday. She moved from her seat to sit beside him. Even clothed in fur he shivered. When he reached out to draw her close, she went gratefully. It had been so long since she had been held. They fell asleep in one another's arms, in a safe peace which neither had known in more than a year.

The change from the train to a packet for Calais was a nightmare. It was raining, a slow, cold, insistent rain that ran down the backs of collars and seeped up through the stitching in the soles of their shoes. She didn't have enough money to purchase two first-class tickets and have anything left over for a room once they reached France. She bought deck space, thinking, how long could the rain last? It lasted the entire voyage. Andrew became very ill within yards of the shore. She became ill later. In the midst of the voyage it was all she could do to keep from jumping overboard and drowning. At least her torment would be over, she told herself.

She thought of her mother and father. She would cable them once she and Andrew were safely in France, and then they would be home before the races began in Saratoga.

The quaint shipping village on the French coast looked like paradise. One of the sailors, who appreciated her fluent French, helped her get Andrew on shore. He was prostrate now, hardly conscious at all. The sailor took them to a small inn; neat and clean and inexpensive. She tried to pay him but he wouldn't accept a penny. He did accept a kiss on the cheek and promised to look her up on his return voyage.

At first she was grateful that Andy hadn't suffered a fit until they were alone, and then she wasn't grateful at all. His horrible pains made him cry out in a voice that woke the residents of the inn.

The other guests complained irritably. She fought with the owner, who threatened to put them in the street. Her brother was ill. *"Mon frère, il est gravement mal! Gravement mal!"* She said it every time they came to the door, then quickly shut it. Her head ached. She made restraints out of her petticoat to keep him from tearing at his face, but she couldn't bring herself to gag him. She sat by him all that first night, whispering to him, stroking his face, begging him to be brave a little longer. When the delirium subsided, fever took its place.

She knew it was serious when she awakened in the chair and heard his breathing. He sounded as though he were drowning. At least now he was quiet. The innkeeper's wife, taking pity on her, sent up hot broths and fresh sheets, pleased that Allegra thanked her in Parisian French. It was then that Allegra realized Andy had taught her yet another thing for which she was truly grateful. Even he, in lucid moments, resorted to French when the woman came in.

The days settled in softly while she slept. The nights swept in on fever and chills and long vigils. The evenings became their refuge when the warmth and peace of early summer lulled the world with sweet sights and sounds.

He told her about Harriet one evening when the sky was exchanging light for darkness. She wasn't shocked, only a little sad for them both, and she told him so.

She told him about Everett as one evening wore through to purple dusk. Not everything, not the child or the decadent passions of some nights, but enough so that he knew that they had been lovers.

She never knew what determinations he made about their severed relationship. When she told him about accusing Everett of supplying Andy with opium to maintain his addiction, Andy laughed at her and called her a beautiful fool for not recognizing their real enemy.

It was his last laughter.

He died before dawn.

She buried him in a little churchyard above the sea. She lied to the priest and said that Andy was Catholic because the cemetery had the best view. Andy would have liked her reasoning, she decided. There were flowers and candles, and even the sailor friend made a week earlier and the innkeepers were there to weep for him.

With the last of her money she bought a marker for his grave, a solemn sweet-faced angel with stone wings and a boyish curve of cheek that reminded her of the brother she loved best in the world.

* **1895-96** *

Twenty-three

Paris, August 1895

Allegra sat on a stone bench along the Quai de Montebello at sunset and ate the Spanish *sanguine*, blood orange, that she had purchased in the market. The sky above her head was a pure rare rose-gold, throwing into ink-black silhouette the surrounding trees and rooftops. Behind her, across the Seine, the famous outline of Notre Dame seemed to float like a medieval fantasy on the Île de la Cité. The heat of the day lingered, as did the sights and sounds and smells of this ancient, vitally alive city.

Simple pleasures. The sweet tangy juice ran into her mouth and down her chin. Her feet inside her shoes ached slightly from her walk from the Rue St. Louis on the Île St. Louis. Her cheeks stung from a slight windburn. She had spent the day in the parks with the children. One pocket bulged with her monthly wage. The other contained a check for her latest contribution to the *Paris Herald*.

She could afford now to buy a new dress. But she might not. Her dress was threadbare in places but more comfortable than anything she had ever worn. The choice was a simple one, but important. Just as everything she had done since leaving Calais fourteen months earlier had been a matter of simple but important choices, everything she did in the future would be weighted against necessity.

When she finished her orange, she licked her fingers, pretending not to notice the young man in a bowler who paused in his stroll to watch her. He tipped his hat, murmuring some objectionable appreciation of her activity, and then, when she did not respond, he moved on, murmuring in melancholic French phrases about the vagaries of life.

She didn't rise from her seat right away. She wanted to savor this particularly sweet evening, so rare, so precious, so simple.

She had been wrong. Andrew had been wrong. Lord Drayton had been wrong. As all the last century of poets had been, they who had whispered seductively about the lost mystical joys of past worlds and self-experience. The secret of joyous living was not to be found in ever more sensation, ever more variety, ever more stimulation. She had come to believe, as did the city's Impressionist artists, that the secret lay in the world as it existed around them, in light and color and simplicity. True beauty was transitory, unpreservable, inarticulate, and, like this sunset, too easily passed over if one were preoccupied with oneself.

She had never wanted more to live than she had in the days following Andrew's death when she thought she, too, would die. Parched throat, terrible pains, muscle spasms—

Allegra shook her head, stood up, and began a purposeful stride along the quay. In the first few weeks walking had been all that had kept her sane. When finally her body had cast off addiction's torture, she set out on the road for Paris. She had chosen Paris rather than returning home because she needed a goal. She had never seen Paris. Andy had wanted to see it once more. Paris had been their goal. For his sake, she felt the need to succeed.

How strange she must have appeared to those on the road. She might have been set upon by thieves, raped by farmers' sons, and beaten by bullies. But no one, in all the weeks of her journey by foot, ever sought to harm her. Was it the madness of determination in her green gaze or the incongruity of a lady in tattered finery strolling along the highway that gave people pause? At the time it didn't occur to her to wonder. Now she knew she would never know the answer.

She had arrived in Paris without a cent, had left Calais the same. Yet she had eaten nearly every day. There were methods of earning money—or one's livelihood—if one's needs were simple. Hers had been the simplest. A place to sleep. A meal. Water was free. The air was free. The beautiful days were free. Summer's warmth was free.

She paused to watch the fishermen who'd come in to tie up along the quay. Lighted barges sailed on the Seine, music and laughter floating up from them.

She had written her parents about Andrew's death and entrusted the letter to American tourists she met on the road who promised to deliver it. It was nearly a month later before she had the wherewithal to write them again. She told them only that pneumonia had claimed him and that she would not be coming home. Since then, she had written home once a fortnight, never giving a return address. It was difficult for them, she knew, but it was also difficult for her.

When she reached Paris she begged work in a *boucherie*, sweeping up the butchers' scraps and wrapping up packages for customers. The wrapping was old newspaper which she read after hours before she slept in the back of the shop. Butcher boys were more persistent than their rural cousins. Sleeping with a meat cleaver soon dampened their actions if not their interest. She had found her present employment while wrapping lamb chops. There, on a newspaper page, was an ad for an English-speaking nanny.

Allegra smiled in remembrance of the interview. She had worn her one change of clothing and taken special pains with her hair. It didn't occur to her until she was walking along the tree-lined avenues of the Île St. Louis that she knew nothing about children. By then she was too desperate to think of turning back.

She had been asked by a footman to wait in the vestibule. Fifteen minutes passed, then thirty while she sat in complete isolation. At the end of an hour, just when she had risen to her feet to leave, a door at the head of the magnificent staircase opened and a couple emerged, the lady screeching at the man at the top of her lungs. Allegra's French was greatly improved by her weeks in the butcher shop, and the lady's invectives quite shocked her, as did the fact that she wore, in disregard for fashion, a bustled gown in the style of a decade earlier. Suddenly the couple paused, realizing that a stranger was privy to their exchange. "Who are you?" the lady demanded hotly.

"I've come about the position as governess," Allegra replied in French.

The woman smiled. "*Tiens!* Why do you not announce yourself? So foolish, this English custom of forebearance," she pronounced in Parisian English. "Come, come up quickly, *petite!*"

Allegra soon found herself seated in a salon which had last been furnished during the reign of Napoleon Bonaparte. Between sips of champagne and bites of caviar on toast, served by the butler, she lied about her present place of employment, her reason for coming to Paris, gave references with noble English titles which she guessed correctly they wouldn't bother to check, and at the end of the hour became an English nanny of two girls: Hermine, four, and Bini, seven.

She soon learned that her employers, like most of the inhabitants of the island who were old Bourbons or Bonapartists, possessed the same arrogance and freewheeling natures that for centuries had allowed abysmal poverty to coexist with gilt and splendor as the natural order of things. *La madame* wore bustled gowns because she thought them the most elegant style of dress of the century. *Le monsieur* dipped snuff from a box given his grandfather by Louis XVI. They were an eccentric couple but a happy one. Because of this, they allowed her a great deal of freedom.

That Allegra often had opinions and dared express them, they found delightfully refreshing. Women with minds were appreciated in Paris, even foreigners. When she chose to rent a third-floor room in the Impasse Maubert where she could write in peace, though she had the use of a suite of rooms in their seventeenth-century mansion, they didn't protest. "But that is charming, charming!" *la madame* had proclaimed.

When Allegra's first article appeared in the *Paris Herald,* her employers gleefully boasted to their friends of the *petite* journaliste who was their nanny. She was even invited to accompany them on rare occasions to visit their artistic friends, among whom were painters, poets, intellectuals, scientists, and musicians. But now they watched her with the eyes of aristocrats who had experienced too often the ingratitude of the lower classes. With independence, they thought, would inevitably come revolt.

No matter what the temptation, she adhered to her full day and night of freedom each week. Sometimes she rode a used bicycle around the city. On rainy days it made travel between the Left Bank and the Île St. Louis easier and quicker. On other days, like today, she simply walked and watched and listened and smelled and tasted all that life had to offer. Then, after dark, she went to her rented room on the Left Bank and wrote until near dawn when she returned to the Île St. Louis.

She turned into a street cafe, choosing a table where the evening paper had been left on an empty chair. One's needs were easily met, if one didn't mind used news. She had eaten half of the cream and potato omelet that was her usual fare when she saw the notice.

She left the omelet unfinished, but she didn't leave the paper behind.

Allegra entered L'ecole des Beaux Arts from the Rue Bonaparte, wearing a new black dress and veiled hat. She had waited three days before coming and she knew that in doing so, she ran the risk of finding her review of the exhibit unsalable due to its tardiness. The other press critics had been invited the first day, but she hadn't been able to bring herself to come then. She told herself it was because her day off wasn't until two days later, but the real reason was that she was afraid to see him again.

She crossed the open courtyard of the school and entered one of the sculpture studios. Several students looked up from their work, but she didn't acknowledge them. The showing was small, confined to a narrow space in one corner, but from the moment she saw the first of the graceful torsos she knew it was Lord Everett Drayton's work.

For the next quarter hour, she wandered among the busts and nudes and reliefs, stopping to gaze at each one as if she knew its history. She did know it, at least the moving passion behind the hard-won fight to derive beauty, grace, sensuality, and elegance from one of nature's hardest stones. There was triumph in the execution of the works, a feeling of pride and joy that she had never known in the man. She was glad for the veil which hid her smiles, then her gnawed lip, and finally when she saw the last piece, her tears.

He had never asked her to sit for him. She had never suspected that he studied her well enough to carry in his memory the smallest details about her. Yet there the work stood, proudly, the lift of the chin a challenge to those who would dare to make sport of her nudity. Surely she had never exposed her natural glory in such cool disdain for convention. Despite its cool look, the statue was not that of an immortal. A multitude of small details made her all-too-human a creature. The scar on one knee, the slightly crooked tilt of the nose, the slant of one brow slightly higher than the other, even the imperfect small toe on the left foot; they all had their reality in her flesh.

As she walked around the sculpture, noting in fleeting amusement that in these past months she had lost that lush fullness of hip which beckoned to be touched, she looked up into the long tangle of free curls cascading down the figure's back and gasped.

Was it real or her imagination?

At the back of the statue's head, tangled in the marble curls, was a face, a man's face. Andrew's face!

Allegra blinked. The image was false, the play of light and shadow in the deeply curlicued stone. Yet when she opened her eyes the image remained. So subtle was its power to attract and then fade, she wondered if it were not simply a monstrous irony, a mistake that only she saw. Greatly shaken, she moved back before the statue and then her gaze fell on the title etched in the base: *Janus.*

And then she knew the answer to the question that had haunted her from the day Violet Granby mentioned the vicious rumors circulating about an unnatural relationship between brother and sister. Like the two-faced Greek god Janus, she and Andrew had completed each other. Beginnings and endings. Everett had given her dominance. He had suspected that she would survive while Andy would not. But the courageous face on the statue was not yet hers. She didn't know if it ever would be.

Paris, November

Allegra sat by her open window composing a piece for *The Yellow Journal*. The fragrance of dried wisteria blossoms saved from the vine that climbed the apartment building to her level filled the room. Below, the streets of the Left Bank were thronged with people, the bump of wagon wheels on cobblestone, and the clatter of horses' hooves. It was a bright, crisp morning. The heat of the sun had already lifted the pearly mist spread by the Seine.

She had been due back on the Île St. Louis at six o'clock, but she had not gone. Now it was nine o'clock. Hermine and Bini would be asking for her, for their cocoa and toast which came before the English lesson.

Her employers had not understood her need for the extra day but had concluded that her newfound fame had gone to her head. Frank Harris's inclusion of her critique on the École des Beaux Arts exhibit in his popular but controversial *The Yellow Journal* had been seen as the cause of her rebelliousness.

"Now," *la madame* had said to her husband, "you see what comes of our generosity? She thinks to become an American bohemian! What will it cost us?"

But they were wrong. She was waiting for someone. She didn't know for whom or why, but the imperative in the letter had been so strong that she had put on her black dress, her journalist's dress as she thought of it, and even styled her hair with the pair of jet-beaded combs that had been her employers' gift from last Christmas.

When she heard footsteps on the rickety stairway that led

to the apartments in her building, she raised her head and laid her pen aside. A man's footsteps. He took his time in climbing. Was it the heavy tread of an elderly man or simply one reluctant to climb past the *rez-de-chaussée*, past the *premier étage*, past the *bourgeois étage*, to the cheapest rentals, the servants' floor? When he paused outside her door, she had the sudden wild hope that he would knock instead at the door across the hall. A door was between them, their meeting a knock apart. She rose slowly and went to open her door.

He stood with the brim of his top hat clutched in both hands, his shoulders rounded because of the low-beamed ceiling. He didn't smile. He didn't frown. "Good morning, Miss Grant."

She was stunned to find him there. In all the world she had not expected it to be he, and yet who else? "Lord Drayton."

He smiled at her, a slight wistful smile without any of the arrogance and mockery he had once displayed. "Will you see me?"

Unable to speak, she backed away from the door and allowed him to enter. She noticed several things at once. He was as well-dressed as ever in a heavy topcoat of the finest gabardine, yet he didn't seem well cared for. His hair was a little too long and threaded with silver which demanded its own form. The hands clutching his hat were covered with fine scars. Some had healed while others were new and pink. A sculptor's hands. He was heavier than she remembered, lean when last he had been gaunt. She looked into his face last, fearful and curious and strangely shy.

What she saw surprised her anew. Heavy lines spanned his brow in permanent waves. The square chin had granite in its angles, but the mouth had surrendered its thin uncompromising line to the slight curve of human frailty. It was the face of a wiser man, a sadder man. Yet his light eyes shone with a new gentleness, a new knowledge of the endless possibilities of life. He had found solace in his art. She understood that.

He seemed in no hurry to speak. He walked about the narrow confines of her room slowly, examining without touching all that he saw. She didn't resent his exploration. She would have liked to have done the same to the rooms that he inhabited. They knew so much and yet so little about each other. Yet when he found the clippings from the many papers which reviewed his exhibit, she felt very much embarrassed. He picked up one and glanced back at her. "Your countryman Whistler was less than kind in his remarks."

She smiled in disavowal, still silent, still waiting.

He put the article down and picked up *The Yellow Journal*, which was open to her review. He smiled as he began to read. He nodded when he was done and laid it back exactly where it had been. Now he turned to her. "I hoped you'd hear of the exhibit. That was the only reason I agreed to it." His smile grew rueful. "I find I'm a modest man, as an artist. The paper gave me your address. I recognized the work as yours even before I saw that you'd signed it A. A. Janus. I didn't expect that you were so close, that you'd go to the exhibit, or that you'd be so generous in your judgment of it."

"I wrote the truth as I saw it. I always have." It was a defensive, ungracious statement and she regretted it. "Would you care for tea? I brewed it a few minutes ago."

He nodded and took a chair.

Drinking tea; how ordinary the exercise was. Hospitality at its simplest. The conversation that accompanied it was simple but not commonplace.

"Your bicycle on the landing?" he questioned as she poured.

"Yes. Some of what you taught me has been helpful."

"I'm glad. Have you been in Paris long?"

"More than a year. Since Andy's death."

"I heard. It must have been terrible for you. Pneumonia, the papers said."

She handed him the cup. "Opium," she said softly. "His body couldn't withstand the shock of illness."

The horror in his face was more eloquent than any words of sympathy. "I didn't—" he began, then fell silent.

"I know," she answered. "Andy and I talked."

"Why did you come to Paris?"

"I ran away." She smiled thinking of the first time she had run away.

He looked about again, this time in full comprehension of her surroundings. And suddenly she knew that he was the one person in the world she had longed to see again, to whom she wanted to talk of herself.

She began with the present, explaining what she did for a living and how and why. By the second cup of tea, she had worked herself backward to the weeks she had spent on the road from Calais. He listened to her in silence, his expressions feeding and encouraging her to double back in explanation or rush ahead to string dissimilar events together by her own peculiar logic.

Her time in Calais was much more difficult to explain. Several times she found herself silenced by sorrow, yet he never moved or spoke. Little by little she told him everything, the details she remembered more clearly than last night's meal, of the conversations with Andrew, her confession, his confession.

Her account of her last year in London was muddled. He swore suddenly when she told him of her own addiction, and she thought he would leave. He stood up, staring straight ahead with the old, dangerous burning gaze. She waited, not daring to ask him to remain. Then he looked down at her, returned from a long journey of the mind, and sat down again. "Why did you do it?"

She hesitated. The truth. What was the truth? At the time she left London she had thought John had tricked her into the addiction, using the pains in her hands as the excuse. But now, looking back, she wondered if she had not been punishing herself for the loss of Everett's child. She knew the risk, had seen the effects of the drug firsthand, and yet she allowed herself to seek comfort from her pain with opium.

In precise detail she told him of Andrew's troubles with publishers, of the scandalous rumor that cost them their income, of John's machinations, her own illness. She skirted the truth of her miscarriage, but he must have seen more in her face than her words revealed, for when she fell into one of her many long silences he said, "Were you pregnant?"

She looked up in anguish. "I didn't know! I didn't know until it was too late. I would have taken care of it, of your child. I swear I would have loved it! But it was too late!"

Somehow she was in his arms sobbing, and through the bitterness of her own grief she heard his husky weeping.

It was dark when they descended into the street. They ate in a sidewalk cafe and then walked for hours, scarcely speaking at times, then suddenly overflowing with words. Two years lay between then and now, and neither knew if it could or should be bridged.

Yet, by evening's end the first filaments of the span had been established. The next morning she gave notice, feeling a little guilt at abandoning the two children who had been her students for more than a year. Still, she knew that she was again fighting for her own survival and that this would be the toughest battle of all.

As fall slid into winter she began a new novel, the first since abandoning her work to Wilde in London. During the days, she wrote furiously, consumingly, exultantly. In the evenings, when like the rest of the city their daily labor was done, Everett came round to see her. They always went out. He bought her meals in inexpensive bistros. She refused his offer to take her to fine restaurants, and if he grew tired of student fare he never complained.

Little by little Everett told her of the past two years of his life. He, too, had suffered. He, too, had fought himself and won. In the winning something was lost, but something more precious was gained. He seemed at peace, or at least had managed an abiding truce with his darker side.

On the weekends when it was not too cold, they went to the parks. When it rained, they went to museums where they walked hand in hand, pretending that they had just met. Before the first snow he took her to the Marché aux Fleurs, where he filled her arms with the last of the season's flowers until they trailed from her embrace like a huge bridal bouquet. It was a chaste and deep friendship without a single kiss to adulterate the joy of being together.

One night when he arrived, she didn't meet him in hat, coat, and gloves. The smells of cooking filled her apartment. With the help of the concierge, she had made her very first meal. He professed delight in her accomplishment, but she wasn't certain he even knew what he ate. As always, he watched her, as though by look alone he could absorb her into him. She blushed often in his presence. She felt awkward, shy, schoolgirl-like. He laughed, touched her hand with a finger, and moved away.

At the end of the evening he turned when he reached the door and stood looking mutely at her. She came to him and standing on tiptoe, placed a kiss on his cheek. She saw a spasm of emotion cross his face, but he didn't touch her.

A week later, on Christmas Eve, he arrived with a huge box with a red velvet ribbon. She had bought him a gift, too. When he opened the box and read the contents, she saw his face pale. It was advertisement space in the *London Times* to announce a showing of his work to be held in London in the spring. He had resisted the idea but now merely shook his head and smiled and acceded to her wish.

His gift overwhelmed her. It was a long plush coat with Russian sable collar and cuffs, and matching fur hat. He demanded she wear it though she protested that it was much too nice for her present station. When she was bundled up, he led her down into the street where a small crowd had gathered. The cause of the curiosity was his Christmas present to himself. It was a Peugeot Petroleum Phaeton. He boasted of its twelve miles an hour as he helped her climb in. He took her for a ride to the Bois de Boulogne. At the Horseshoe Pond they rented ice skates and skated under the stark limbs of the age-old trees, which two hundred years earlier had sheltered Charles X.

Allegra laughed and smiled, happier than she had thought possible. Then she caught sight of Everett's laughing face and she knew that she might be happier.

When they stopped to drink tea at one of the cafes that had set tables out on the ice, she caught his face in her mittened hands and kissed him. His lips were cold to the touch but they warmed quickly. Too quickly. She pulled away and playfully slapped his cheek. "You're too wicked, my lord, yet I—'' She clapped a mitten over her mouth. She'd nearly said, *Yet I love you!*

He took the hand from her mouth and held it between his own. ''I love you. Marry me.''

A group of children swarmed by on skates, squealing and screeching in delight at their speed.

''Did you hear me?'' he asked, impatience showing through for the first time since he had found her.

She nodded with the beginning of a smile. ''I heard you.''

''Well, then!'' he demanded, the strain showing on his face.

''Is it a demand, my lord?''

He blushed despite the cold, but he squeezed her hand harder. ''No.''

''There'll be a scandal. My reputation's ruined. I won't be received by your peers or their wives. We'll be snubbed in all the best places and—''

''Gossiped about in all the tabloids,'' he agreed, grinning at her now.

''I'll be called a brash American woman—''

''And a title-seeker,'' he added. ''At least I'll be spared the accusation of marrying you for your money. I'm really quite rich.''

''I will continue to write, perhaps terrible novels, and demand that they be published—''

''While I litter our home with marble shards,'' he countered.

''I've very strong opinions about the rearing of children.''

He looked at her and she wondered if it were possible to be loved as much as his gaze seemed to convey. ''We will have them,'' he said quietly. ''Lots of them because no child should grow up alone. We'll name the eldest son Andrew.''

February 1896

Allegra stared at the headline in the *London Times*, anger and disgust making her tremble. When she looked up at her husband, she saw sympathy in his face.

"I would have shielded you if I could have."

"But how is this possible? It's a lie! Andy never committed a crime in his life."

"You'd better read the column for yourself," Everett said.

She looked down but her head came up at once. "It says the American writer Writwell was arrested this week for murder!"

"Please try and keep calm until you've finished it," he suggested.

She looked down again, but the words swam before her eyes in amazing phrases. J.A.N.U.S. WRITWELL ARRESTED FOR MURDER, the headline read. *"Bogus English lord and popular New York columnist of the early '90s, Writwell was arrested for the murder of Miss Gracie Stanhope."* She shivered. *"In a startling declaration to the press, American physician John Boyd admitted his guilt and at the same time revealed his pseudonymous life as the writer Writwell."*

"John!" she whispered incredulously. "But why would he do this? How can he hope to be believed?"

"It seems he's produced work which adds credence to his claim," Everett replied as he took the paper from her.

"Produced work? What work has he produced?"

"I cabled friends in London. I'm told Boyd claims that he and your brother were collaborators, first in New York and then later in London. He says that he came to England in order to save Andrew from opium addiction and when that failed he turned to writing for himself. He's produced original columns which have never appeared in print. He even has a novel which several former Writwell publishers have identified as being Writwell's work."

"But Andy never finished his. It must be my novel!" she exclaimed. "God in heaven, how did he get it?"

"From Wilde? Perhaps Wilde returned your work to Boyd's address after you'd left the country."

Allegra's expression saddened. "Poor Oscar. Two years in Reading Gaol, how awful for him." She looked up. "But that's it! That's the proof we need! Oscar read the work which I gave him myself. He knows that Boyd isn't Writwell."

Everett smiled sadly. "My dear, that may be so, but

Oscar's voice is not likely to be heard publicly again for some time. As for giving evidence, I suggest you think twice about attaching his name to your brother's. London has buried Oscar as good and truly as if he were dead. His books have disappeared from the shelves, his plays have been closed. His name is never mentioned. He's become a plague and all who knew him still fear contamination."

"It's all fallen, hasn't it?" she said, thinking of the spellbinding life of London she had left behind.

"It deserved to," he answered. "It ruined many. It would have ruined more. It nearly ruined us."

She reached out and caressed his cheek. "That was my fault. I wanted to know everything without paying the price for any of it."

"Then perhaps we're both guilty, for once I'd have sold you to hell to possess you."

She looked toward the window, but her thoughts ranged across the channel. "I must do something. Andrew's reputation deserves better than—" She turned back to Drayton. "Andy said Dr. Boyd always hated him. This must be his final revenge."

"Admitting guilt to murder in order to sully Writwell's name? He'd have to be mad!" he answered.

She stood up. "I'm going back to London. I must clear Writwell's name for Andrew's sake, and my own."

London, April 1896

"So you would have the court believe, Miss Grant, that *not* John Boyd, *not* your brother the deceased Andrew Grant, but *you* are the real J.A.N.U.S. Writwell?"

"I don't claim to be the sole creator of Writwell," Allegra answered as she stood in the docket of the Old Bailey to give testimony on her own behalf. After Boyd's conviction for murder made him a celebrity, she had no recourse but to sue for the right to claim Writwell's work as her own. "I have explained that it began as a joint venture with my brother in which I took a limited part. Only later did my efforts overshadow his because of his illness. What I claim is that the work misrepresented by Dr. Boyd as his and Andrew's is in fact mine and my brother's.''

The advocate for the state picked up the exhibit manuscript. ''You would have the court believe that you, a young lady of charming but average ability, and no formal training, are capable of sustaining the mental strain of producing a work of this magnitude?''

''It has been known to occur,'' she answered curtly. ''You've only your own countrywomen to look to. The Brontes, Miss Austen, to name but a few.''

''Yes, well, the court finds no contradiction in the admission that such rare women have and do exist, but, in your case, I see no evidence of exceptional ability.''

Allegra willed herself to keep her temper. In the last few days she had had ample opportunities to discover how quickly the accuser could become the accused. ''If it were the requirement of exceptional ability that it be clearly marked on the faces of its possessors, we might save the government a great deal of money by simply reading faces at birth to determine which men and women, regardless of birth and breeding, should or shouldn't be given an education or, perhaps, even a seat in the House of Lords.''

Everett clenched his teeth as her words caused a roar among the gallery. Tweaking the nose of the aristocracy was a dangerous pastime which might go against her.

The barrister smiled as he looked at her. ''Are you telling the court that you despise people who have gained, shall we say, advantages from the circumstances of their birth?''

''Indeed not!'' she countered. ''What I said was genius is not determined by a set of bone and flesh. Man is more than the sum of his parts or else he's nothing but a beast, however pleasant to gaze upon.''

Another murmur, clearly of approval, circled the gallery this time.

The barrister adjusted his collar as if to assert his complete disregard for the popular opinion. ''Is it your testimony that you wrote a novel which contains in it references to certain unsavory practices?''

"Perhaps you would be good enough to specify which practices you consider unsavory," Allegra replied.

He gave her a sharp look, uncertain whether he had heard mockery in her tone. "Very well. One character is referred to as 'a man who loves beauty and, because of this love, becomes obsessed with beauty's degradation.' Would you please explain to the court what is meant by 'beauty's degradation'?"

"Yes. Is that all?" she asked. When he inclined his head, she turned with a smile to the gallery. "Who among us cannot be so described? Surely some of you are gardeners and are quite proud of your efforts. But, think a moment. In the pursuit of that perfect rose or tulip or pink, do you not get down on your hands and knees in the muck to weed so that your flowers may thrive? Do you not dig in dirt, rake manure, discuss with your fellow gardeners the feeding habits of slugs and worms and the breeding times of beetles, all in the attempt to preserve the beauty of your gardens? Is it possible to love the beauty without becoming conversant with the reverse? Oh, one may admire a flower, but only the man or woman who knows the cost of bringing that beauty to fruition can stand in full appreciation of it!"

The barrister gave her a strange glance. "Well said, Miss Grant. But there are other, less easily explained examples which I should like to offer."

"Offer them as you will, sir, for I have answers." Allegra smiled. "And if I don't, surely you realize that I'm quick-witted enough to construct them."

The laughter in the gallery was echoed in the amused gazes of the court, and for the first time Everett felt himself relax. He had married a wonder, a stunner, and quite simply a brilliant lady!

The barrister looked at his colleagues. He had been assured by his solicitor that this case would be quickly and summarily dismissed. Now he stood the chance of being thoroughly embarrassed by a young woman who might well have written the work in question. He turned to Allegra. "It has long been held as truth that the artist, the writer and poet in particular, draws from life experiences. From what source would you have learned of the 'certain peculiar practices' of the 'lotus eaters,' for example?''

The audience was electric with interest, the silence strained by eagerness. ''Where every literate person in your nation and mine may learn of it,'' she answered. ''In the newspapers.''

''Are you saying that you have no firsthand acquaintance with such vile practices?''

Allegra nearly answered and then she saw the path he had opened up. ''Thank you for the compliment. That you perceive my writing to be so compelling that it should seem written from firsthand experience is far more reassuring than any critic's praise.''

Laughter again shook the courtroom while the chief justice gaveled the group to order with the threat of dismissal.

''I didn't suggest that you wrote the work, Miss Grant. To the contrary, I say you couldn't have written it for the very reason you appear to maintain, which is that you know nothing of such practices.''

''Forgive me, sir, but I would imagine that you have never committed a crime and yet I accept that you are fully capable, as an officer of the court, of judging the guilt or innocence of those who may have. No doubt you sometimes stand where you are now and describe in accurate detail the motivation of a man you don't know as he plotted a most heinous crime. No one here would suppose you guilty of the crime you describe. Likewise, I can suppose what might run through the mind of a man driven to opium addiction without the necessity of proving that I had not myself endured such addiction.''

In a last-ditch effort to save his case, the barrister opened the manuscript. ''I will choose at random a few lines. If you are, indeed, the author, you should be able to finish the paragraph for me.''

Allegra's solicitor came to his feet in objection, but she turned to the lord chief justice herself and said, ''I will agree to the test.''

''It's most unusual,'' the lord chief justice said, but he was disposed to like the young American lady, and it was nearly lunchtime. ''If the defense is in agreement?''

''We are, your lordship,'' the barrister answered.

"Agreed," said the lord chief justice.

The barrister took his time choosing the page. He wanted nothing memorable. No dialogue that would spur recall. No flowery passage that, like poetry, might find a rhythm in her ear. "Here we are. It begins, 'She made her home the center for all those of any interest—' You may continue."

Allegra shut her eyes. He had chosen poorly, for in this particular passage she had written about Andy and herself. " 'She made her home the center for all those of any interest—especially those in the height of fashion. She entertained in a manner appropriate to society for the suppression of virtue.' " She opened her eyes triumphantly and held out her hand. "My manuscript, thank you."

She forced herself to enter the cell while Everett stood outside in testy unhappiness. She had to see the prisoner. No one understood that, but she had to see him one last time.

He sat on a cot at the far end of the narrow cell, his left ankle and wrist chained to the wall. He wore an ill-fitting suit stamped with a broad arrow. His hair was cropped, his mustache gone. He stared unseeingly ahead though the warden had entered with her.

Allegra took a few steps closer until the jailer stopped her. "John. Dr. John Boyd?"

When he looked at her, she thought he didn't recognize her, and then he smiled and the hair lifted on her neck.

"You've come back at last. I thought you were dead."

"I came back to clear my brother's name," she said.

"Too late," he answered. "I killed him and now I've ruined his reputation."

"No, you didn't kill him nor have you ruined him. I've been to court and reclaimed what is rightfully Andrew's and mine."

He seemed not to hear her at first. "It's your fault Andrew's dead," he said finally. "You were the one who really killed him. You were the better writer and he couldn't stand it." He smiled at her. "He told me so, over and over on those nights when you were writing and he was drifting in a drugged bliss. You didn't come to see him and he wondered why you had abandoned him."

"You know I didn't abandon him! I didn't know you had drugged me as well until it was almost too late."

John sighed. "I loved you. I would have married you, ~~made you happy. Andrew was soft,~~ a coward, and a leech. He would have sucked you dry while I would have worshiped you. But you didn't think I was good enough."

"I never loved you, John."

"Oh, you might have, if you hadn't gotten those notions in your head about marrying above yourself. An English lord for the daughter of a Scots tinker? That was a laugh. Couldn't bring himself to do it, could he? Bedded you and then left you. I know that tale well enough.

"But I'd have married you even then," he continued. "I looked after Andrew for you, as I promised. He was in bliss as much as any man can manage." He looked at her sharply. "But you cheated! You hid yourself from me, writing that damned novel. But I got even."

"It was you who stole my work night after night," Allegra said as memory stirred anew.

"You never suspected, did you?" he said in mild surprise. "I was terrified that you'd remember the fight we had; only you believed the lie I made up about the intruder who had stolen your manuscripts."

Allegra shook her head, more afraid of the memory than of the actual event. It hadn't been a nightmare. She held herself stiffly. "Why, why did you kill the woman?"

John looked at her in amusement. "Because she looked like you. I wouldn't have thought so at first, but then she told me about a lord who'd once bedded her because she reminded him of someone else. He dressed her up, a whore, in the lady's clothes and even called her by the other woman's name when he rode her. She reminded me of you. I wanted to ride you and so I rode her." He smiled. "I wanted to kill you, too. You'd gotten away from me once. I couldn't resist breaking her neck!"

"You're mad," she said softly.

He smiled at her so sweetly. " 'These deeds must not be thought . . . so it will make us mad!' "

Allegra was shaking badly by the time that Everett led her out of the prison and into the cab. "You shouldn't have gone there! I said it! I warned you! God in heaven! You're a stubborn one!"

She huddled in his arms. "I had to, for Andy's sake. John couldn't hang thinking he'd won."

Everett held her so tightly he knew he must hurt her, but she didn't complain. "So then, it's over."

"Not yet," she murmured. "I must set it all down. I never liked the ending of that first book. It didn't have a conclusion. This one will."

"Put it out of your mind."

"Oh, no! It's the story of a time that's passing. Even now we're becoming history. It must be set down as it happened."

"And what will you call this masterpiece?"

She raised her head and smiled at him. "You gave me the title years ago. Don't you remember?"

* **1900** *

Twenty-four

New York City, January 1900

The harbor was filled with people who had come to greet the passengers disembarking from Liverpool. Frosty breath misted the air, and the press of bodies was a comfort against the stinging January wind.

Mufflered and gloved, Tom Pachard jostled his way through the crowd, feeling equal amounts of curiosity mixed with anticipation. He had been sent eight hundred miles to cover this particular story for his Chicago paper and he wasn't about to miss the moment.

"Tom!"

Tom swung a hand up in greeting as he recognized the fellow journalist who called to him. Pushing more eagerly now, he made his way to the press area where dozens of reporters and photographers had been herded together behind a rope.

"Jack! Never thought to see you here," Tom said. "San Francisco's a bit far away for this kind of thing. Think your readers will be interested?"

"If it's news in Chicago, it's news in San Francisco," Jack answered. "Have you seen her before?"

"Never. She's been out of the country ever since she became famous."

"True, but there're advantages in seniority, son. I was sent to London to interview her just last year."

"Is she as pretty as they say?"

"Pretty? That's not the word for a countess, son. She's royalty now, remember? Wouldn't matter if she were three feet wide and plain as Jake's cow, you'd be expected to describe her as 'regal' and 'stately' and 'proud.'"

"Yeah, but is she, well, you know? Is she a ravisher?"

Jack's expansive grin widened. "Son, fortune don't make them any finer than the Countess of Dundare. Of course she's had it all from the very first. It's easier to be beautiful when life doesn't hand you any hard knocks. Now her father's another story. He's what I call a fine example of the American success story."

Jack pointed to a small group standing beside the gangway. "That's him there in the brown tweed. Next to him in the black, that's Mrs. Grant. Angus Grant's done it all. Immigrant. Poverty. Hardships. Came to America and made himself a tidy little fortune and produced a duchess for a daughter into the bargain. Son, that's the stuff of which dreams are made. That's how I'm slanting my story. Calling it, 'The Rise of the Common Touch.' That'll sell my newspapers. Look about you. Maybe there's a new Angus Grant treading past you this very moment."

Tom shrugged. He'd seen Ellis Island, watched the crowds of immigrants, their gazes wide and startled, as though what they saw and felt might not be real. They didn't seem to him to be the material for front-page stories. But then, who knew?

"That's what makes this such a great country," Jack said. "Uh, son, here they come!"

Tom didn't see her at first in the press at the top of the gangway. And then he wondered how he could ever have doubted that he would recognize her. Her pictures had been in all the major papers and magazines for months. THE ORIGINAL REBELLIOUS ANGEL one odious headline had read, referring to her successful first novel. It was impossible to believe the rumors that had circulated about her upon the book's publication. Some said it was autobiographical, that she was the woman portrayed in the book as the wicked and morally loose socialite who had repented and found happiness.

As he looked up at her he couldn't credit the rebellious part, but angellike she did appear. He jotted down every impression, ready to spin columns not only for the front page, but the society and the fashion pages as well.

She wore a dark green cape trimmed in sealskin and carried a matching muff. A white fur hat with ribbons partially covered her nimbus of blue-black hair. A gold promenade dress with pleated skirt flared out about her fanlike as she descended the gangplank. She was beautiful, regal, every inch a duchess. Where was the betraying hint of the repentant sinner? He didn't see it.

He glanced past her to the man who followed and found himself equally impressed. The earl wore a topcoat over his formal dress, a silk top hat, and a neat mustache. He appeared aloof yet he carried a sleeping baby in one arm and held the hand of a small boy who walked beside him. The child, no more than three, was dressed in a white wool coat with squirrel trimming and leather leggings: the picture of pink-cheeked health that every mother desired as her own.

Tom smiled in recognition. This was Master Andrew. Already the arrogance of his father was stamped on his solemn little face, but when the child looked up at his sire, a joyous smile brightened his face and was returned. Decadence, hah! They were the picture of familial wholesomeness.

Allegra smiled and nodded at the clutch of reporters waiting for her as dozens of flash bars exploded in her direction. But when her eyes fell on her parents, she forgot that she was a world-famous—and somewhat infamous—writer, a countess and the mother of two young aristocrats. She ran the last steps of the gangway and threw herself into the waiting embraces.

"Well, well, well! If you don't look every inch—every inch—a duchess," Angus Grant declared, clearing the emotion from his throat between phrases. "Grand you look, daughter. Just grand!"

"Mama! Papa!" There was too much and nothing to be

said, and so she kissed and hugged them both again and again.

Angus pulled back first, a matter of pride that he not shed too many tears in public. Then he spied his son-in-law and his grandchildren. He put out a hand. "Your lordship. Welcome to America and to my family."

Everett nodded at his father-in-law. "Thank you, sir, for your daughter and your greeting. I'd like you to meet your granddaughter, Marabelle. And this is—"

"I know," Angus said quickly and bent a stiff knee to lower himself to his grandson's level. "You're Andrew. I'd know you anywhere."

Andrew smiled shyly, and Angus's heart contracted with emotion. He had his father's gray-blue eyes but the smile was all Andrew Grant. "You'll like me, I think," Angus said.

Andrew nodded and said in a very formal voice, "Oh, I shall. Mummy says I shall . . . Grandpapa."

When the family had entered the waiting cars and driven away, Tom Pachard flipped his note pad shut, a little surprised that there were tears in his eyes. Why shouldn't they be happy together? After all, they were the lucky ones, the ones who had always had everything they desired. They had never known grief or loneliness or despair. They were the American dream. Sentimental. He was growing sentimental.